Leviathan Rising

A USS Bull Shark Naval Thriller
Book Two

Scott W. Cook

Leviathan Rising
A USS Bull Shark Naval Thriller - Book Two

© 2021 by Scott W Cook and Spindrift Press.

PREFACE

Welcome to the next installment of the adventures of the USS *Bull Shark* and her crew. Before we, if you'll forgive a rather obvious pun, dive in... there are a few things I feel are necessary to address. Necessary so that you go into this story with an understanding of what you will and what you will *not* find.

To begin, this novel, as with the first, is dedicated to that greatest generation of Americans who sacrificed so much to win a titanic struggle that engulfed the world. Most especially, those men and women, most long gone and those few who are still with us, of the branches of the United States military. To them, the entire world owes a debt.

With special attention and with very sincere gratitude, I'd like to acknowledge the men of the silent service during WW2, and those 52 submarines and their brave crews who never returned. Those more than 3,500 courageous men who are still on eternal patrol today. It is in memory of them that these books are written. To try and bring them to life in a way that removes this intriguing period of our shared heritage from simply a list of names, facts, and dates to a collection of very human and very relatable people.

Now, let me address a few points that cropped up from responses to book one in this series. I feel it necessary to point out that what you are about to read is a work of *fiction*. Although real names and places are used, they are used fictitiously. This is not a documentary, a revisionist's ideal history, nor is it meant to be a textbook into military protocol, submarine operations, or any other manual thereby related to the subject matter presented in this book. I'm not trying to educate nor train you... although if you do learn something new or interesting, I'm glad... my only goal here is to entertain you.

To that end, let me say now that I endeavor to be somewhere between 85 and 90 percent accurate. However, in that 10 or 15 percent lies fantasy. In the last book, for example, our hero submarine is of a class that didn't officially launch until much later in 1942. Why did I do this? Because these books stem from a portion of a story from book #6 of another series I write, Scott Jarvis Private Investigator. In that story, which takes place in 1945, *Bull Shark* is a *Balao*-class boat. So, either I began this series nearly a year into the war, or I fudged things a little. I chose that option because 1942 is just too important to skip.

I also gave her a snorkel, which, although invented years earlier, wasn't officially employed in World War Two until 1944 by the Norwegians and then captured and put into wide use by Germany. This was done for the same reason – *Bull Shark* had one in 1945... so she has one now... now being the timeframe of this book.

As if these alterations weren't enough, I created a command-and-control ship that oversaw... until our heroes dealt with them... Operation Drumbeat. I even suggested that a German floatplane could fly right into our country and kidnap a woman! Preposterous and untrue, you might say.

Perhaps... but while not historically accurate... it is historically *plausible*. That could've easily happened at that time. Why do I mention this? Because this story, too, features some flights of fancy. Some scenarios I invented in those gaps in historical fact to liven up the plot and make you want to turn the page. To present you with something new and not just another rehashing of what hundreds of other writers, most more talented than I, have already done. Please keep that in mind, and you may find even more enjoyment from my occasional leaps beyond truth.

Finally, this novel is not primarily about the Battle of Midway. However, as it takes place around those events, it is impossible not to include many of the crucial moments in that epic and history-altering conflict. It is here that I try to stay very close to historical truth, because the truth of Midway is so incredible and dramatic that it needs no embellishment by an over-imaginative writer to make it one of the most compelling few days in human history.

Thank you for purchasing this book, and I hope you have even half as much fun reading it as I did in writing it.

Scott W. Cook
Semi-historian, storyteller and crackpot

Prologue

Hitokappu Bay, Island of Iturup, Southern Kuril Archipelago

44°54' N, 147°35' E – Between the Western Pacific and the Sea of Okhotsk

Even in late spring, the remote and only semi-protected anchorage was bitingly cold. It could've been worse... although, to those unfortunate enough to be posted there, that would be a hard thing to imagine indeed. Yet even over a thousand kilometers from the Kamchatka peninsula, it seemed as if the terrible fury of Siberia couldn't be sated until it froze every Japanese in the island chain to death.

This island, and this bay, had gained a nearly mythic status among the Japanese people over the past six months. Because it was from here, in this frigid, storm-tossed anchorage, which Admiral Isoroku Yamamoto had sent the mighty Kido Butai on its historic mission to smash the American naval base at Pearl Harbor. That massive fleet, the most powerful ever assembled in terms of firepower at least, had sailed from this very bay on November 26 of the previous year. They'd sailed into history... that was never in doubt. As to how that history would play out... that was still a matter of opinion.

The war with the United States was only six months old. Thus far, the mighty Kido Butai, the combination of the various Koku Sentai that Yamamoto had assembled into the First Air Fleet, had done well. Not as well as he'd have liked, thanks to the timidity of Nagumo... yet it had done well, in spite of a hard and very recent loss.

In war, sacrifices must be made; Yamamoto was the first to agree with that sentiment. However, what he had difficulty accepting was when such sacrifices came not from boldness but from folly. Chuichi Nagumo was no fool. He knew his business and understood the value of the big picture. Yet, he was a worrier and tended to fret over insignificant details to the point where he might hesitate to act. Yamamoto knew of quite a number of occasions where Admiral Nagumo would actually call his inferiors to him and ask for their reassurances that his ideas and decisions were the right ones.

This brand of hesitancy was alien to the dynamic Yamamoto. It was he who pressed for Operation AI, the attack on Pearl Harbor. Even then, Yamamoto knew that this surprise attack on the bulk of America's Pacific fleet wouldn't ensure Japan's victory... it was meant only to slow down the United States while Japan secured its hold on the much-needed resources in the Western Pacific. And although partially successful, Yamamoto still fumed over Nagumo's decision not to send in a third attack wave. He had also been displeased that not a single American carrier had been taken out on that fateful day.

And now, early in the month of May, a somewhat indecisive battle had been fought in the Coral Sea. It had not yet been a week since the engagement, and both sides were still assessing the tactical significance of the three-day conflict. Yes, Japanese forces had taken Tulagi, but no, they hadn't taken Port Moresby on New Guinea. Yes, they had sunk the USS *Lexington* and the USS *Yorktown*... or so they thought... but they'd lost their own carrier *Shoho* and nearly lost *Shokaku*, which had to return to Japan for repairs.

Yamamoto was further irked by the lack of zeal from the naval commanders in that conflict as well. Hara had not pressed his advantage and pursued the American fleet. Inoue, who was in overall command, did not press either. As a result, they did not take Port Moresby and thus lost a potential base that would've secured the far eastern front of Japan's expansion and allowed for a greater coverage and observation of U.S. activity in the Coral Sea.

As Yamamoto stood on the high precipice that overlooked the wind-blown bay below him, he pondered the situation and his next move. The Battle of the Coral Sea *had* demonstrated to both sides a great many things, not the least of which was the power of aircraft carriers at sea. It had shown the Japanese, for example, that American fighting ability needed improvement. It had shown the Americans that the Japanese were far better equipped and far better fighters than they'd suspected. And the battle had set the stage, at least in Yamamoto's opinion, for a more decisive conflict that would pit IJN carriers against USN carriers in a battle over a barren speck of nowhere that would determine the course of the rest of the war. However, Yamamoto was no fool. Like many officers in his military, as in Germany, he'd been to the U.S. He'd seen first-hand their enormous industrial might. Hell, it was the United States who'd been supplying most of Japan's oil before the attack on Pearl. Even if Yamamoto could wipe all of America's remaining carriers off the sea in one fell swoop, he knew that they could, and were no doubt already building more. It was as if someone had removed a cork from a bottle and allowed a very powerful... and very *angry* genie to escape.

So, no matter what the outcome of the next major offensive at the beginning of June, the brilliant Japanese admiral knew that something else was called for. A way to re-cork the bottle and slow down the United States enough for Japan to bolster itself, its possessions, and its strength so that she could withstand anything the enemy far across the Pacific could throw at them.

Thus, only days after the lukewarm victory in the Coral Sea, and only weeks before the Kido Butai would crush Midway, Yamamoto stood on the balcony of a lonely outpost on a lonely island awaiting a monster. Something right out of Japanese legend. A Leviathan that would rise from the sea and strike terror in the hearts of her enemies. A monster that Yamamoto himself had helped bring to life.

"She is late," Lieutenant Ryu Osaka stated quietly from the admiral's side.

Yamamoto half-turned to his personal aide, "Is she, Osaka? Is she? I think not... watch."

The two men looked out over the bay. Today at least, the sun was rising into a clear day. No fog to obscure the bay, and although the wind was biting, it was from the north and left the bay relatively placid. An odd place to stage a raid in any case, as it was so far north of the equator and any viable targets. Yet this made it an unlikely place to be scouted as well. The odds of an American submarine coming this far north of the Japanese homeland, or a Soviet submarine coming this far south of Kamchatka, was slim. It's why Yamamoto had assembled the Kido Butai and the support vessels for the Pearl Harbor attack there the previous November. It was why he'd lured the monster here now.

From out in the bay, perhaps a kilometer from where the two men stood apart from the other observers, something began to happen. Yamamoto raised his field glasses and took a closer look. The sea in his view frothed and foamed, and then a monstrous black shape rose, snorting seawater as her great back broke into the sunlight. The thing was huge, so huge that the men who watched it breach couldn't believe that such a thing could have ever stayed below the surface in the first place. That, and it was the oddest-looking thing any of them had ever seen. A long shape made slender by its proportions and yet looking clumsy and unwieldy due to the long, rounded humps along its dorsal surface. Yet it did move. It turned toward the men, gliding slowly through the water and giving them all an opportunity to examine its odd shape and yet ominous hidden power.

"What... what *is* that thing?" Osaka asked in bewilderment.

Yamamoto smiled thinly, "It is Leviathan, young man. It is a monster that rises from the deep and delivers a terrible vengeance. A creature whose only purpose is to defend our sacred homeland."

"Is it... *Kaiju?*" Osaka asked in awe.

"In a sense, yes. A monster whose insatiable hunger will consume our enemies," Yamamoto said, gazing at the thing in the bay. "But all metaphor aside, Lieutenant, she is an experiment. A prototype for a new class of submarine. Something I call a submarine carrier. Although this one is far greater than what will be produced in the mainstream program."

Osaka gazed at his superior with a mixture of awe and disbelief, "A... submarine carrier? How is that possible?"

Yamamoto laughed, "It's something I've been working on for years. As you know, Lieutenant, I believe in a strong naval air division. It's already been proven, over and over, that the days of big ships with big guns winning wars are over. Battleships and cruisers are still useful... but air power is far more so. Remember the *Bismarck,* the *Prince of Wales*... mighty capital ships sent to the bottom by a handful of tiny, fragile aircraft."

Osaka nodded, "Yes, sir. It is undeniable."

"Well, youngster," Yama moto continued, "we're already designing a new class of submarine, the I-400 Sentoku. It will carry three seaplanes and be the largest submarine in the world. It will have a range long enough to encircle the globe and then some."

"Is this the prototype then?"

"Not exactly... this is something special I've had custom-built for a very special set of missions. In truth, this is a secret weapon that puts even the as-yet built I-400 to shame."

Osaka looked on raptly. In the year or so that he'd served as the great admiral's personal yeoman, Osaka had found Yamamoto to be an extraordinary, if a bit eccentric man. Brilliant, charismatic, and forceful, the admiral also seemed to see things others did not. To conceive of things others couldn't even dream of. The monstrosity below them, now coming closer at a leisurely three knots, was just another example. A thing that couldn't possibly be... a thing that most would say was impossible... and yet because of one man's vision and tenacity, it lived.

"Tell me more, sir."

Yamamoto chuckled softly, "She's a hundred and forty meters long, with a sixteen-meter beam and a draft of eight meters. She displaces over four-thousand kilograms, has a test depth of a hundred meters, and a range of fifty thousand kilometers."

Osaka drew in a sharp breath and only stared at the odd-looking submarine below.

"She has six diesels and six electric motors," Yamamoto went on, "giving her a surface speed of fourteen knots. Not particularly fast, even for a submarine, but with very long legs. Beneath the water, she can travel as fast as seven knots. She has *three* batteries giving her a lengthened submerge time in spite of her bulk and unwieldiness."

"What are those... tubes to either side and behind the conning tower?" Osaka asked.

"Those are the aircraft hangars for the eight Aichi floatplanes," The Admiral went on. "And you can see the two forty-meter catapults on her bow. The planes are stored folded. Each carries an eight hundred kilo bomb and has a range of over a thousand kilometers at a top speed of three hundred and sixty knots."

"Impressive," Osaka breathed.

Yamamoto nodded, "She is what the Americans would call my... ace in the hole. One of them, perhaps I should say."

"Sir?" Osaka asked as the huge ungainly submarine, which looked to him as if someone had strapped two giant logs to its broad back, turned in profile once again.

"You have served as both pilot and as a gunnery officer in submarines, have you not, Ryu?" Yamamoto asked, his tone sounding almost distracted as he studied his creation.

"I... yes, sir," Osaka replied after a moment's pause. "I flew a Zero off *Kaga* during the Chinese conflict a few years ago. After, I decided I wanted a change and transferred to the submarine service. I did three war patrols aboard I-15. One as torpedo officer and two as communications and electrical officer. This was just before I was given the honor to work for you, sir."

Yamamoto ignored the praise. It wasn't that he didn't appreciate sincere admiration. In Osaka's case, he believed it to be just that.

However, it was simply that so much had been heaped upon him over the past year that he had simply grown tired of it. Instead, he turned to face the younger man full on and even deigned to sketch a modest bow.

"It is I who has been honored, Ryu," the venerable admiral said. "You have proven loyal, reliable, intelligent, and honest. More than that, you have proven yourself worthy of my trust and of a special assignment. An assignment that requires a special sort of man with a special sort of background. Would something like that interest you, Osaka san?"

Osaka felt his face flush. Yamamoto was doing him an enormous honor. Although the lieutenant didn't yet know what it was, he knew that there was but one answer he could give his mentor.

"Of course, Admiral San. I will serve in whatever way you desire."

"I'm glad to hear that, Ryu Sama," Yamamoto said in a fatherly tone. "For you see... there is much happening in this war. We fight more than our adversaries... we must fight amongst ourselves as well."

Osaka nodded, "There are factions that would enjoy seeing you fail, sir."

Yamamoto nodded, "Exactly. Those who claim that my... experiment out there is an eccentricity. A waste of precious resources. Tojo has authorized it... but only if the ship's captain can be one of his choosing."

"I see..." Osaka commiserated. He really didn't see, at least not entirely, yet he had the general picture.

"A favored son of one official or another," Yamamoto said wearily. "A typical story. However, I insisted that the executive officer at least be a man of *my* choosing. A man I can trust. A man who will be my eyes and ears and... and who will make *certain* that it is *my* plan that is carried out. And I want you to be that man, Ryu Sama."

"I can never be anything else, Yamamoto San."

The admiral patted the young man on his firm shoulder and smiled, "I never thought you could. Come, it grows bitter up here. Let us go inside and discuss things over a hot cup of tea... Lieutenant Commander Osaka."

CHAPTER 1

STATION HYPO – PEARL HARBOR, HAWAII

CRYPTOGRAPHIC DIVISION, RECENTLY CODE-NAMED ULTRA

MAY 11, 1942 – 2340 HOURS, LOCAL TIME

"I'm telling you, Ed, you bonehead... the Japs are gunning for Midway."

Commander Edwin Layton, intelligence officer and assistant to Admiral Chester Nimitz, narrowed his eyes at the man who met him at the heavy doors that opened into the secure basement where the Navy's cryptanalysts worked tirelessly to crack the Japanese code. Or, more accurately, to *continue* to crack it. They'd already made considerable headway on JN-25, but their crack was hardly complete, and many of the IJN's movements and plans were still mired in heavy fog.

As if to underscore Layton's doubts, this latest declaration was being made by a man wearing a bathrobe over his khaki uniform shirt and who'd replaced his black shoes with an old pair of bedroom slippers. A man who looked like he either needed a fresh cup of coffee or who'd passed his caffeine limit three cups back. Layton could've wished that he'd at least dragged a comb through his bird's nest of a haircut.

"And what do you base that on, Joe?" Layton asked, moving over to the coffee maker and pouring himself a cup. If he was going to have a serious conversation with the head of Pearl's Ultra division, then he'd need to take the edge off of what the three martinis he'd had at dinner that evening were doing to his cognitive skills.

"What, are you kidding me, Ed?" Commander Joseph Rochefort asked indignantly. "It hasn't been me and my staff that's been locked up in this bank vault for twelve, fourteen hours a day since the first damned Zeke flew over Ford Island? For Chrissakes... look at this latest decoded transmission. Yamamoto *himself* references an imminent attack on a mid-Pacific American base!"

Layton sighed. It seemed like he was always having one argument or another with the eccentric cryptanalyst. For all his brilliance and skill, and there was no doubt of them, Rochefort could be a bit on the fanatical side at times.

"Op-20-G, and even Station Cast, believes it's more likely the Aleutians or Port Moresby," Layton finally said patiently. "After all, Joe... the IJN just made a play for Port Moresby a week ago."

Rochefort bit back a scathing retort about what he thought of either of those sources. Instead, he drew in a deep breath and let it out slowly. He held up the message so Layton could read it, "Look, Ed... this is a direct message from Yamamoto himself. He's organizing another big fleet. Almost the entire first air fleet, what the Japs call the *Kido Butai*. He's sending those carriers, along with battleships, cruisers, destroyers, and even subs, to a crucial spot in the mid-Pacific he calls AF. By seizing this asset, the admiral hopes to secure a far eastern stronghold, and not only that... he wants to smash what's left of our Pacific Fleet!"

"Oh, come on, Joe!" Layton said. "It didn't work at Pearl... not really. Yes, we lost ships and a lot of good men, but it hardly drew our teeth."

"Exactly, dammit," Rochefort insisted. "He's moving in to finish the job. Yamamoto knows even if he succeeds, he won't stop us forever... but long enough for Japan to dig in and possibly maintain a permanent hold on all the territories they've seized. AF has to be Midway. It's the *only* logical choice. The Aleutians are too far north. Port Moresby is too far west... won't you at least consider it and take it to the admiral?"

Layton bit his lip, "Okay, Joe. I'll let the Old Man know... but what he does with the info is up to him. For one thing, this decode doesn't specify dates. That would help."

Rochefort sighed and rubbed his eyes, "I know... and I've got some ideas on that. We're going to make some comparisons of all the JN-25 messages we've decoded and find numeric patterns for all the date and time stamps. I think we can figure out the date... but based on this text, I think it's going to be within the next thirty days. So, it's *vital* that Admiral Nimitz has time to plan, Ed."

"All right, Joe," Layton admitted. "In the meantime, what do you need to crack the date and time key?"

Rochefort frowned, "It's really a matter of time... no pun intended... and manpower. Or womanpower... I could use more computers. The more good eyes we have on this, the faster the patterns will surface."

"Okay... do any of your staff know anyone we can recruit?" Layton asked. "I'll look into it as well, but we obviously need trustworthy people. And we're short of them, men or women."

Rochefort shrugged, "I'll ask. Thanks, Ed."

Layton finally smiled and clapped his friend on the shoulder. Joe was a bit odd, but he was a good egg and dedicated. And his powers of language and mathematics were impressive.

After Layton stepped out and headed for the stairs, Rochefort poured himself another cup of coffee and moved to the far end of the room where Lieutenant Commander Joe Finnegan was sorting through a pile of punch cards and sheaves of paper, "Catch any of that, Joe?"

Finnegan glanced up at his boss and grinned, "Now, you know I'm deep into this data, Commander. I don't have time to eavesdrop on private conversations with an admiral's aide."

Rochefort chuffed, "Uh-huh."

Finnegan chuckled, "I might know at least one person who can help me in this, though, Joe. The wife of a submariner I know. He used to be based out of Pearl until the Japs attacked. Last I heard, he was shipped off to New London and given command of a new boat. Something about hunting down Nazis."

Rochefort tapped his chin thoughtfully, "Yeah... name's Turner, right? I met him one time at a staff dinner. Pretty wife. Both a few years younger than you, if I'm not mistaken. I believe, although I'd have to check on this, that Turner and his boat are headed here right now."

Finnegan grinned, "That means Mrs. Turner... Joan is her name... is on her way with the kids, too. If she hasn't already arrived."

"Is she in cryptology?" Rochefort asked.

Finnegan shook his head, "No... but she's sharp as a tack. Went to Duke and got a degree in mathematics. Was gonna be a math teacher at the high school and even college level. Calculus. But then she met Art Turner, they got hitched, started a family... you know the drill."

Rochefort smiled, "She's a civvy, though."

Finnegan scoffed, "It's not like they're letting WAVEs out here to work with us. Other than military nurses, women aren't allowed to serve overseas. So, we've got to rely on civilians. Just like the Brits at Bletchley Park."

"Yeah, the computers," Rochefort said. "You think Joan Turner could be our first one?"

"I do," Finnegan said. "I've heard a rumor about that mission of her husband's... something about Joan being aboard a ship or a submarine or something."

Rochefort smiled. He'd heard that too. Although much of that mission was classified, he was in a unique position to hear things, obviously. When a new boat goes up against a couple of Nazi ships, and her captain earns a Navy cross, the word spreads. He didn't know all the details, except there *was* something about the skipper's wife being kidnapped...

"Okay, Joe," Rochefort finally said. "Set it up. You know the Turners?"

"Fairly well," Finnegan said. "I've met Art, and my wife and I have had dinner with them a couple of times. Joan and Gladys are closer friends, though."

"Great," Rochefort said. "You meet with her, both of them if possible, and see if we can put her to work. The more, the merrier. We've got to crack that date cypher, Joe. I have a feeling I'm going to need more to convince Chester Nimitz I'm on the right path here."

"Oh, hey..." Finnegan said, rifling through his papers and pulling out a hand-written sheet. "George decrypted this about an hour ago. It's incomplete but references two locations... HW and AW."

Rochefort examined the hand-written note, "Hmm... let's see... we know already that HW is Hitacappu Bay... several officers to rendezvous there... pretty lean... then something about strategic importance of AW and decisive attack to take place on... well, we don't know when, do we? Hmmm... well, we'll keep at it. I'll file this. For now, we need to focus on AF."

"Will do," Finnegan said.

Rochefort sighed and took the new message and his coffee back to his own desk. It would be another late night. He wasn't sure what bothered him more sometimes... that there were far more late nights than not... or that he was coming to think of that as normal.

CHAPTER 2

USS Bull Shark - Eastern Pacific ocean

1 day out of the Gulf of Panama

"Only five thousand miles to go, Skipper," Ralph "Hotrod" Hernandez stated from his place on the bridge beside Lt. Commander Arthur Turner.

"Be there in no time, Hotrod," Turner said, sipping his morning coffee and gazing out over an unusually placid Pacific seascape. "After all, we're not running submerged for a while, so our batteries are nice and stuffed. Running on all four rock-crushers, we're doing a nice twenty knots, making five hundred miles a day... be at Pearl in less than ten days."

"We're only at about ninety percent, though," Hotrod observed. "In the village of my youth, it was considered *disrespectful* not to give one-hundred *por ciento*."

Turner paused in the process of lighting a cigarette to turn and cock an eyebrow at Hernandez, "Is that right, quartermaster?"

"*Si*," Hotrod deadpanned.

A low laugh from behind caused both men to turn just as Lieutenant J.G. Frank Nichols hoisted himself out of the bridge tower hatch. He moved forward to stand near the other two men, "In your village, huh, Ralph? Aren't you from Long Beach, California or something?"

"*Si,*" Hernandez replied with a lopsided grin playing on his handsome, swarthy features. "I am but a simple peasant, *señor.*"

Turner guffawed, "I'm fairly certain that joking around with officers is grounds for a general court, Hotrod."

"*No habla inglés.*"

"Oh, for God's sake!" Nichols laughed.

Turner drew on his Lucky Strike and sighed, "Beautiful day. Our poor immigrant here has a point, though, Frank. What do you say about running at max since we don't have to submerge for a long while yet?"

Nichols shrugged, "We could, Skipper... but I'd rather not run up to or over the MEPs. We've still got to top the batteries off now and then, which we can do with the aux gennie, of course. But it's better to run for a long time just a hair under full-throttle on the diesels. Not to mention the oil we burn."

Turner nodded. He knew that, of course, but it never hurt to get an expert opinion. Especially if it meant adding another forty or fifty miles to their daily progress.

"I've already discussed it with Joe," Frank said. "He's of the same mind... although we can certainly give you overdrive when you need it."

"How's that working out, anyway?" Turner asked. "I mean all the officer changes. It's only been a week, but a lot has changed since we got back to New London after the battle with the Nazis."

Nichols shrugged again, "Having a full-time electrical officer has been nice. I know that Joe's a little disappointed he's not comm officer, but that's really a junior officer's billet."

Turner nodded. He knew that, too. Yet that wasn't really what he was asking, and Nichols knew it.

After a moment's reflection, Nichols drew in a breath. He seemed hesitant, "Burt Pendergast knows engines and generators. Has quite a bit of experience as trim officer, too."

Turner waited. When Nichols had nothing else to say, the captain decided to press. He didn't usually like to do that, preferring to let men express their thoughts freely and without coercion. Yet when it came to the overall morale and working situation aboard a submarine, he had to keep his finger on the pulse. A submarine was too small and too tightly knit a community of men for personality conflicts or other issues to be allowed to fester and grow.

"How about as a shipmate?" Turner asked. He decided to express a bit of his own feelings, hoping that would make Nichols feel comfortable talking about something he might not wish to discuss. "For my part, losing Elmer and getting a brand-new XO has been... odd. Tom Begley knows his job, but he seems a bit reserved. Taking a while to really get comfortable in the wardroom, at least when I'm there. And there seems to be... some kind of tension between him and Pat."

Nichols chuckled softly, "I think I can explain that. I guess... well, I guess Pendergast is an all-right sort of gent. I get the same impression from him as you get from the XO. I get that, too. They both seem kind of awkward... or maybe not quite fitting in yet... but it's early days."

Turner flicked an ash out over the deep blue sea around them, "That's probably it. Just some wearing in that needs to be done. But you say you know why our two new officers and Pat Jarvis seem at odds?"

Nichols drew in a breath and frowned, "Sir... I'd rather not discuss that. It's none of my business. I think if you ask Pat, he'll tell you. You know he's not the kind of man to keep things bottled up or who's too shy about talking."

"Okay, Enj," Turner relented. "I understand. Just keep me apprised if we have any issues, though, huh? We've got ten more days to get to know our new men before we get new orders from Pearl. Probably not much more after that and we'll be in combat again, if Admiral Edwards's information about a big Jap offensive is right."

Nichols went below and left Turner and Hotrod alone. The quartermaster got the sense that Turner had fallen into contemplation and moved just a little away to give him some space. The captain made a mental note of that. Hernandez made a good QM and would probably move up to chief fairly soon. If so, *Bull Shark* would likely lose him.

They already had four chiefs aboard. Although the ship had been slightly undermanned during their special mission to find and sink the German C and C ship, she still didn't technically have room for a fifth

CPO. For one thing, there were only four bunks in the chief's quarters. For another, it was felt that as men advanced and gained experience, the Navy liked to spread that experience around the fleet.

Turner had already lost his XO after only a few months with him. While it was true that Elmer Williams was attending and finishing his PXO School, Turner had doubts as to whether or not he'd get him back. Elmer had come a long way in those few months. He'd always been smart, yet he had also been somewhat indecisive. But Turner had seen him begin to blossom into a man who'd soon be a topnotch executive officer and then onto a top shelf sub skipper.

That was hardly the last change. His sonar officer, Joe Dutch, had been moved to electrical officer, which they hadn't had on their first patrol. The communications officer, who was responsible for overseeing sound, radar, and radio, was also in charge of the commissary department. This was, as Dutch had known, the most junior officer's billet most of the time. It only made sense that a man with Dutch's rank and experience be moved to a more advanced position. Both because he deserved it and because he needed to fulfill his own department heads tour before qualifying for XO or CO.

And besides, Turner had told himself, Chet Rivers had proven to be a first-rate sonar tech. Also, Dutch could be put on the gear whenever Turner needed.

The biggest changes, however, were the addition of two new officers that had been hastily assigned the day before the boat left New London for her long transit to Pearl. Tom Begley, who'd just completed his PXO School and his friend with whom he'd served in S-boats, Burt Pendergast. Pendergast got Post's old billet as second engineer, and Andy Post was given the comm officer's slot, which, while not a demotion, was at best a side-step. The young man hadn't complained, though. He seemed eager to learn new things and take on new responsibilities.

Begley and Pendergast were qualified, at least. On their very brief pre-patrol training, they'd both done well with a torpedo test fire and indoctrinal depth charge exercise. Of course, that was far different than actual experience, and Turner knew that neither man had seen combat in the nearly six months of the war. Not that this was damning by any means... many currently serving officers and men hadn't... yet Turner and his crew had, and in a big way. They now knew each other and their boat. They'd known what they could expect from their officers. And now, after only a few months in commission, that had changed.

The *Bull Shark's* captain couldn't help but feel as if he were starting all over again. Taking an untried crew to sea into unknown dangers. Well, he'd just have to deal with it, as he had the last time.

––––––––––

Down in the wardroom, Pat Jarvis was thinking very similar thoughts. He missed Elmer Williams and had been none-too-pleased when he'd heard who was taking his place and who was coming along for the ride. He'd only had one very brief encounter with both of the new officers, and it had not been a pleasant one. A confrontation and a fight were no way to make the acquaintance of men with whom you'd be locked up inside a cigar tube for months at a time.

Although Jarvis, Begley, and Pendergast hadn't spoken of the night, Jarvis couldn't believe they'd forgotten. No matter how drunk they'd been. He also had to admit to some curiosity about why they both had such a low opinion of Elmer. To Jarvis, who'd served with Williams, the man was not only capable but likable as well. They'd become fast friends.

So far, only a week out of Connecticut, Jarvis and the two new officers had hardly said a dozen words to each other that didn't relate to duty. He knew that must be because of the fact that they'd both been drunk when he'd met them. Also, that Begley had been dating Elmer's ex-fiancé. Finally, there was something of a potential ill-feeling in that Jarvis hadn't been made XO. He'd certainly earned it, and it did irk him slightly that some new man was simply shoved into Elmer's slot.

Yet Pat Jarvis wasn't a vindictive man. He truly enjoyed being the gunnery officer, and he *hadn't* done PXO School yet... another war patrol or two and he'd probably be *forced* upstairs, so to his mind, he'd enjoy being the ship's fish pusher as much as he could.

The watch bill had thus far saved the three men from coming to grips with each other, if that were to happen. As XO, Begley stood a watch, as did the captain and Jarvis. Each one had an assistant officer of the deck, Jarvis's being Pendergast and Begley's being Dutch. That usually meant that Jarvis and Begley weren't on standard watch at the same time. As for Pendergast, the man Jarvis had actually punched, he had his own duties as AOOD or JOOD, depending on who was describing it. The two men's duties kept them busy and limited their communication to official ship's business.

And Pat Jarvis was introspective enough to give them the benefit of the doubt. Begley and Pendergast *had* been pretty loaded that night at the bar. The situation *had* gotten out of hand... but that was more than two months ago. Maybe time would tell, and without Williams's presence, it might go smoother, and things would work out.

"Penny for your thoughts, Mr. Jarvis."

Pat looked up from one of the General Electric motor manuals he'd been studying and grinned at Eddie Carlson, the officer's steward, "A penny, Eddie? Seems kinda cheap. My thoughts are worth a good dime."

"Hell, sir," Carlson drawled as he topped up Pat's coffee and added some fresh cream that he'd managed to finagle during *Bull Shark's* twelve-hour layover before the canal passage. "I's just a poor sailor man. What would I be doin' with a dime?"

Pat chuckled, "Is it just me, Eddie, or is every enlisted man on this boat a wise ass?"

"Only the good ones, sir," Carlson said as he set out a plate of freshly baked sweet rolls and donuts. "Least until they crack wise once too often around Mr. Begley or Pendergast."

Jarvis cocked an eyebrow at him, "Somethin' on your mind, Eddie?"

Carlson made a dismissive gesture and smiled thinly.

"Maybe I should ask Buck to come in here?" Pat pressed.

"Aw, hell, Mr. Jarvis... just me jaw-jackin'," Carlson said cheerfully. "You know how it is with new officers. Gotta make their mark, make sure everybody knows who they are and all that. Nothin' new under the sea, sir."

Pat frowned but didn't push it any further, "Okay, Eddie... you brought it up. Good coffee, by the way. No way this is Nescafe."

Carlson beamed, "No, sir! Along with about a gallon of this here good dairy, I got some fine Costa Rican as well. Only about two pounds, but it ought to make the trip to Pearl a little nicer."

Jarvis chuckled, "It will at that! Do I want to ask exactly *how* you managed to snitch this stuff, Eddie?"

Carlson just waved it away, "Good old Yankee tradin', sir."

"Uh-huh," Jarvis said and only shook his head. "Well, you just be careful and make sure Mr. Begley doesn't get a whiff of your wheelin' and dealin', Eddie."

"Who's wheeling and dealing?" came the bemused voice of Joe Dutch as he slid the green curtain to the wardroom aside.

"Have a cup of coffee and find out, Joey," Pat said with a crooked grin. "Eddie here wrangled us up some real cream and some fine Costa Rican."

"Reefers?" Dutch asked with a twinkle in his eye.

That got a laugh from the other two men. Carlson only shook his head, "My mama told me never to fool around with that mess. Says it turns your brain into tapioca and it'll make your torpedo limper'n old Sparky's."

"I heard that, you som bitch!" came a gruff Alabama drawl from the vicinity of the hatch to the forward torpedo room. The three men were still laughing when Walter "Sparky" Sparks, torpedoman's mate first class stepped into the wardroom with a notebook in his hand and a scowl on his broad features. Sparks was an imposing man, an inch or so under six feet and built like a line-backer. Although he scowled at Carlson, there was a merry twinkle in his brown eyes. There usually was, even when he was balling his torpedo gang out.

"Welcome to the party, Sparky," Jarvis said. "Pop a squat here, and Eddie will get you a cup of joe."

"Shit," Sparks pretended to grump as he slid in next to Dutch. "Least he can do, spreadin' rumors like that."

"So, what've you got there, Sparky?" Dutch asked.

"Routine report on our forward fish," Sparks commented.

Jarvis raised his eyebrows, "Again? You guys just inspected those fish day before we put into Coco Solo."

Sparks grumbled something unintelligible and sipped his coffee. He smiled briefly and sighed, "Yes, sir... Mr. Begley's orders. Said he wanted to see what we done to them fish to make 'em work so good... and figured since we was pullin' one of them fish apart anyway... we might as well check all fuckin' *sixteen*, sir... pardon me."

Jarvis shook his head and frowned slightly, "Officers, huh? Well, long as you've done the job, I might as well take a look."

"Jesus Christ..." Dutch muttered but refrained from commenting further.

While the comradery aboard a submarine, and *Bull Shark* in particular, was high even between the officers and the enlisted men, there were certain things that shouldn't be done. Not without good cause. It was important that the officers maintained a respect and respectability. It didn't do to badmouth anyone in front of the men, even a leading Petty like Sparky.

At least not without a damned good cause.

"Well, looks like every fish is 4-O," Jarvis said, sliding the notebook back. "Good work, Sparky."

"Course it is," Sparks mumbled.

Jarvis could see the man was perturbed. He tried to lighten the mood by asking, "Got my personal message still painted on number three, right?"

Sparks grinned genuinely then, "Yes, sir... the old one-finger salute!"

Dutch and Eddie chuckled.

———

It was a few minutes before 1600, ship's time, when Begley stuck his head up through the bridge hatch and requested permission to mount to the bridge. Jarvis granted it naturally, and the XO stepped up and joined Jarvis and the quartermaster of the watch, Richard "Mug" Vigliano on the cramped bridge.

Although the ship observed dog watches for the men, the officers didn't. Each of the watchstanders and their junior OODs stood more or less the same watches. The XO had the four to eights, the captain the eight to twelves, and Jarvis the twelve to fours. It was an arrangement that had been worked out during the *Bull Shark's* first patrol and had suited everyone on board just fine.

It meant a regular schedule for the officers, and it also meant that the enlisted men would rotate through watches with all of them, getting to know the officers and working different stations to keep up their skill sets and to practice for their submarine quals. Everyone on a submarine, regardless of rating, got a chance to work every station... including the less desirable details. It made for a highly-skilled, highly-trained and very close-knit community of professionals.

"Afternoon, Lieutenant," Begley said formally to Jarvis. "I come to relieve you. How are things up here?"

Jarvis definitely felt the tension between himself and Begley. He knew that sooner rather than later, he was going to have to do something about it. He briefly met Mug's eyes before turning to the XO.

"You're a good relief, sir," Jarvis said casually. "We're on course two-eight-zero, speed is twenty knots. All four engines on propulsion alone. Auxiliary generator standing by to top up charge on both batteries, but they're currently at ninety-seven percent. We're still running with fuel ballast one-able and one-baker online. Ship is at surface condition and trimmed slightly by the stern. Lookouts report no sightings. No night book alterations... all's well. A smooth cruise, XO."

Begley smirked, "Yeah, real exciting. Bet we won't be on FBT one-A and B long, not at this speed. We gotta be burning through a hell of a lot of fuel."

"Yeah," Jarvis remarked. "With five thousand miles to go, the skipper is anxious to cover the distance. Could never get away with this in peacetime... Final watch radar sweeps in five, by the way."

"Good," Begley said. "Mr. Jarvis—"

"Sir!" one of the lookouts called. "Something on the horizon, two points off the starboard bow... possible aircraft, sir!"

Jarvis saw Begley tense up, but there was a smile on his square features. The odds were that it wasn't an enemy, not this close to Panama, but you never knew...

Jarvis hit the bridge transmitter button, "Conning tower, bridge. Periscope, give me a high look, bearing about zero-three-zero horizon. Lookouts report possible aircraft."

"*Bridge, conning,*" came the periscope watchstander, torpedoman second-class Peter Griggs. "*Starboard bow high observation, aye.*"

"Let's check with the Sugar Dog," Begley said.

Jarvis was mildly irked by this, but he was the XO after all, "Conning, bridge. Initiate next radar sweep, both units in succession. Start with the SD."

The order was acknowledged just as Griggs came back on, "*Bridge, conning... positive contact! Looks like two aircraft bearing zero-two-niner... low down and headed our way!*"

Above them, and above the lookouts, the SD air search powerhead hummed and then the SJ surface search radar head hummed and spun. Jarvis frowned, "Any contact on the radars?"

A pause and then Ted Balkley, radarman first class, reported, "*Negative, bridge.*"

"I see them, sir!" the same lookout cried.

Jarvis put a pair of 7x50 binoculars to his eyes and scanned the horizon off the starboard bow. Sure enough, two dark shapes seemed to be headed their way. They were very distant but certainly had the shape of aircraft. Strange that they didn't show up on radar though... He had to make a decision.

"Clear the bridge!" he shouted and thumbed the dive alarm twice.

CHAPTER 3

As the diving alarm emitted its unique *ah-ooga, ah-ooga,* the lookouts scrambled down from the periscope sheers and dropped through the bridge hatch. Next went Begley with a grin playing on his lips and then Mug and finally Jarvis. As he slid down the bridge ladder, Mug reached up and yanked the lanyard and dogged the hatch.

"Emergency dive!" Jarvis ordered. "Helm, all stop and standby to answer bells on batteries. Close main induction, rig out bow planes, open the snorkel. Diving officer, take us down to periscope depth when you've got a green board! Flood safety, flood negative and flood bow buoyancy! Stand by to go deep."

A moment or two of confusion, orders acknowledged and then Burt Pendergast, the assistant officer of the watch and diving officer of the watch's voice floated up through the conning tower hatch, "Making my depth six-five feet, sir! Christmas tree is green. Good pressure in the boat."

"Very well," Jarvis said just as Turner's head appeared as he mounted the ladder from the control room.

Jarvis was just about to report when Begley beat him to it, "Two possible aircraft approaching from the starboard bow, sir. We thought it prudent to dive..."

"Understood," Turner said, exchanging a quick glance with Jarvis. It was the torpedo officer's responsibility, as officer of the watch, to report. Turner didn't make an issue of it, though.

"Periscope depth!" the helmsman reported.

"Close all vents," Jarvis said. "All ahead two-thirds. Blow bow buoyancy tank. Blow negative to the mark... Grigsy, what've you got in the scope."

The young man was standing with his face pressed to the search periscope's rubberized eyepiece and turning the device left and right slightly as he adjusted the lookup angle, "I don't... wait, got 'em, sir! It's... uhm..."

"What is it, man?" Begley snapped.

"I'm no expert on this, sir... but I think it's a pair of frigate birds," Griggs reported a bit sheepishly.

"What?" Begley snapped and pushed the young man aside to look for himself. "God *dammit!* It's just a pair of friggin' birds!"

"Frigate," Jarvis said.

"This isn't a damned joke, *Lieutenant!*" Begley said. "Who was on the forward starboard lookout sector?"

The three lookouts were still in the conning tower, making the compartment seem cramped with so many extra men. One of them, a medium-height and muscular young man with a handsome square face and hair the color of midnight, stepped forward and cleared his throat.

"Uhm... fireman second class Fred Swooping Hawk, sir," the young Navajo man who wasn't yet twenty-one said.

"Do you realize what you've done, fireman?" Begley snapped.

Turner wanted to intervene. The kid hadn't done anything wrong. In fact, he'd reacted quickly and properly. However, he held his tongue for the moment, curious to see how Begley would handle this.

"Sir... I..." the fireman didn't quite know what to say.

"XO," Jarvis cut in, "the kid was doing his job. You can't harangue him in hindsight. Suppose that *had* been a couple of planes and he'd waited too long?"

"Personally, I'd rather dive well under a couple of birds early than wait and be bombed out of the water by a Val," Joe Dutch stated.

"I didn't invite a debate," Begley said and levelled his gaze at Swooping Hawk. "You're dismissed, fireman. Expect a visit from the COB."

"Oh, come on, Begley!" Jarvis blurted. He caught Turner's eye and clamped his jaw shut, but it took an effort.

"All right," the captain finally said. "Excitement is over and there's no harm done. Let's dismiss the watch below and get the ship back on top and running for Pearl. We'll consider this an unscheduled trim dive. That is all."

———

Chief of the Boat Paul "Buck" Rogers was an imposing man. Standing at six feet and just over two hundred pounds, he was taller than but not quite as broad as Walter Sparks. However, his position and his lantern jaw lent him tremendous authority.

Part of this he'd earned with the men who'd been aboard *Bull Shark* during their last, and first, patrol. Part of it was because he was a personal friend of the Captain and Mr. Dutch. Mostly, though, Rogers led by example and with a firm but reasonable hand. He wasn't afraid to be the first to get his hands dirty or stick his neck out for a man facing a disciplinary action.

On the other hand, the COB was often the man who'd be the one doling out the discipline. More than one veteran sailor aboard the boat had served with other COBs who thought that a swift kick in the ass or a middle-watch blanket party was in keeping with the best naval tradition.

Buck was not that kind of COB, however.

As he led Fred Swooping Hawk through the control room and the after hatch into the crew's mess, he could clearly see the unease resting on the young Native American's brow. Once clear of the control room and at the coffee urn, Rogers turned to the young man, pouring him a cup of java.

"Take it easy, Freddy," Rogers said kindly, "you didn't do anything wrong."

"That ain't what Mr. Begley says," Freddy said in his western accent. "And he's the one who's gonna write me up... or send me to a captain's mast over it."

"Look, kid," Rogers continued, "he's a new officer. New XO. He's just... well, it's what my old man used to call smellin' his piss. He thinks he's got to prove himself, especially on this boat. Hell, you know our skipper is already getting a name for himself. They're calling him Anvil Art Turner. For a guy like Begley—"

"And his pal," Fred muttered bitterly.

Rogers drew in a breath, "You having trouble with Mr. Pendergast, too?"

The man's ruddy complexion blushed a bit, "Nothin' big yet, Chief... but you seen it. Whatever his buddy the XO says and thinks, old Pendergast falls right into line."

Rogers wanted to disagree. He wanted to tell Swooping Hawk that he was just making a mountain out of a molehill... but he couldn't bring himself to say so. The kid was right, and it was becoming a concern for the COB.

"Okay, so we're off to a rough start," Rogers allowed. "Give it time. And you know our skipper. He's pretty easy-going."

"Yeah... unless you fuck up," Fred mumbled.

"Unless you fuck up *repeatedly*," Rogers corrected. "Captain Turner allows for guys to slip up now and then. He gets that we've all got to learn. Even us old-timers, Fred. This is *real* war now. None of us has seen it before, 'cept maybe a handful of guys like Murph in the after room who crewed in British boats last year. The Old Man has given a lot of us a break... and that included Mr. Williams and Mr. Post. So, don't think he'll go hard on you for doing your fuckin' job. It'll all blow over by tomorrow, you'll see."

"You really think so, Chief?"

Rogers grinned, "I do. Now, why don't you go back and hop into your bunk and do a little studying, huh? Them silver dolphins ain't just handed out... like that sub combat pin you got on."

Rogers grabbed an hour old sweet roll and donut and sat down at the unofficial chief's table with his coffee. He was thinking about the situation on board when chief electrician's mate Harry Brannigan, chief machinist's mate Mike Duncan, torpedoman mates first-class Walter Sparks and Walter Murphy, who was in charge of the after room, came and crowded around him.

"You guys come to kick my ass or what?" Buck jibed.

"Naw, Buck," Sparky said. "We come to see if you can *stop* any ass-kickin's."

"What's going on, guys?" Buck asked, although he had a feeling he knew.

"It's the new XO and his flunky," Brannigan said in his relatively quiet but firm voice.

Duncan, who was a tall, lanky man whose arms seemed unusually long and had the strength to go with it, chimed in with a bit less aplomb, "Been breakin' our asses in both engine rooms ever since they come aboard, Chief."

"Not to mention that poor Indian kid just now," Sparky said. "I was in the control room when the XO chewed him out, for fuck's sake! Kid were only doin' his fuckin' job, Chief! Now what's gonna happen? Nobody on the perch is ever gonna take a chance again, and then what?"

Murph chuckled, "When we start gettin' slammed with twenty mike-mike the damned XO will know it's a Jap plane."

"I know," Buck lamented. "I know. I'm hoping the XO is just asserting himself right now. Lettin' everybody know he's the top dog. I'm hoping he'll settle down by the time we get to Pearl."

"It ain't just Begley," Sparks put in. "It's his lapdog, Pendergast, too. The two of them are bosom buddies, so the prick thinks he can say and do whatever he wants! Comes into my room and tells me how *he* wants my fish routined... how *he* wants them stowed! What the fuck, COB? He ain't even in the fuckin' department."

"Did the same to me," Murph said. Like Sparky, he ran a tight room. Unlike Sparky, he wasn't quite as volatile unless heavily provoked. "But shit, we only got eight fish back there, and four are in the tubes... so I just smiled and said yessir and ignored the bastard."

"Well, he sure is in *my* department," Duncan offered. "Every damned time he's on duty prowls the two engine spaces like he's just *waiting* for one of my Black gang to screw up."

"Right on," Brannigan submitted. "Same deal. My juice jerkers are starting to get a complex."

Rogers sighed, "Yeah... I'm aware of all this. Christ, we've only been at sea a week, and already it feels like the boat is... well, I'm not saying falling apart but..."

"But it ain't the same," Sparky stated. "Last patrol we all worked like a well-lubed diesel. Now there's all this... tension, and everybody seems edgy."

"It ain't healthy," Murph added. "And it don't seem to fit the skipper's way of doing things, either. Nobody knew what to expect a few months back, what with all the changes and us being rushed to sea... but Captain Turner more than proved himself and gave all of us a chance, too. Same goes for Mr. Post and Mr. Nichols, who are new to the service, too."

"It's up to you, Buck," Sparky stated. "You're the COB. It's your job to straighten out a man who's gold brickin' or put a damned sea lawyer in his place... well, it's your job to straighten out an officer with a goddamned boat hook up his ass, too."

Buck chuckled and shook his head, "Yeah, no pressure, though, huh?"

"Hey, this is a fuckin' submarine, Buck," Duncan said with a wry grin. "There's *always* pressure."

———

The sun was nearly touching the horizon only a few points off the *Bull Shark's* port bow as she plowed through the calm seas at twenty knots. Tom Begley stood on the bridge, gazing out at the seemingly endless expanse of ocean and smiled to himself. He'd finally made it, or almost.

No, he wasn't in command of his own boat, but he was the executive officer and on a boat that had already made a name for herself. He was just a few patrols away from prospective command and being sent back to New London to new construction to get a boat of his own. He could *feel* it... all he needed to do was to prove just how capable he really was.

There were several things that truly pleased Begley. First was that he'd slid right into that asshole Williams's slot. Not for the first time, either. First, it had been his ex-fiancé, Maggie. Now Tom had taken his billet as XO, too. That thought made him grin broadly.

Sure, it hadn't worked out with Madge. After that scuffle at the bar between him, Burt, Elmer, and that big nosey bruiser Jarvis, she'd cooled down quite a bit. No big loss. Plenty of skirts in the world.

What was even better was that his long-time buddy and confidant Burt Pendergast had been assigned to the ship with him. It helped. It helped Begley not to feel sort of alone... like the new kid in a new school. Burt would back him, and his presence gave Tom the needed support to assert himself and make his mark on the new crew.

It wasn't all a bed of roses, though. For one thing, that fucking Jarvis was still here. They were the same rank and pretty much had identical seniority, but whether he liked it or not, Jarvis had to call him sir on account of his position. Still... he was a tough guy. Big, strong, and mentally tough. He might be a problem.

Begley had to remind himself to be careful of Jarvis. Not because he wanted to avoid a fight; that didn't bother him. Jarvis was a few inches taller and built like a football player, but Begley was no stranger to scrapping and he'd always have Burt, who was closer to Jarvis's size.

No, it was more that Jarvis was well-liked among the crew, by the officers, and by the skipper. Then there was the skipper himself.

Turner was capable, that couldn't be denied. But Begley thought he was too soft on the crew. Sailors were what they were and would always be sailors. Any chance to screw off, shirk their duty, sneak hooch when they weren't supposed to... get in trouble on the beach... you had to ride herd on them. Your average sailor was like a kid. Give them an inch and they'll snatch a mile. Yet Turner didn't seem to agree. It could be a source of tension... but it could also be an opportunity.

An opportunity to show the Navy just what Tom Begley was made of. What a real submarine captain could and should be. Not only that, but because of Turner's tendency to allow his officers and men to do *his* job... periscope watches, approaches, and even firing fish... Begley would be able to show them all what he could do. Who knew? Maybe Art Turner would, in his own thoughtless way, undermine himself. Maybe, just maybe... a few good kills would show that Anvil Art Turner had only been lucky and Tom "The Torpedo" Begley ought to be *Bull Shark's* captain.

When he saw the engineering access hatch open aft and three men ascend to the after deck, Begley couldn't help but frown. It was none other than Pat Jarvis, Joe Dutch, and the COB. No doubt having themselves a little bull session about their asshole new XO. Begley wondered if it could be a problem, but he really didn't have any grounds to stop it. Even going aft to the other end of the cigarette deck would be a pretty obvious attempt to eavesdrop. He wanted to, but he had to be cautious. Maybe there *was* something he could do, though...

"Nothing like it, huh, sir?" steersman and quartermaster in training Wendell Freeman said from beside Begley. He indicated the sunset with his angled chin.

Begley's first instinct was to remind the E3 of his rank and the divide between them. Yet, he held back. There were times when shooting the shit with the crew could come in handy. He'd need their support, of course, and a handful of guys who thought he was all right might come in handy.

So, Begley pulled his pack of Newports from his duty blouse... even now he didn't stand a watch in a T-shirt like some of the others did...

and held it toward Freeman, "Sure is, Wendell. Kind of a nice perk, huh? Smoke?"

Wendell was a bit taken aback. Although he'd so far had no issue with Begley, he'd always felt the man was aloof and sort of a hard ass. He smiled at the kindly gesture and took a cigarette, "Thanks, sir. Appreciate that."

"Nothing like a good smoke and a sunset," Begley commented. "Well... a good lookin' broad wouldn't hurt, huh?"

The two men shared a laugh and a smoke as Sol slid silently below the rim of the world.

———

"It ain't right, sir," Buck was saying to Jarvis a hundred feet astern of the bridge. "That kid has sharp eyes and is a good seaman."

"I know, Buck," Jarvis said, drawing on his newly lit cigar. "He's in my watch section. There's no reason to kick him in the balls like Begley did. It's a bunch of shit! And on my goddamned watch, too. Fucker just swaggers in and pushes everybody aside? Bullshit. What I wouldn't give to have old Elm Tree back."

Dutch sighed, "It's gonna be a problem. I work pretty close with his pal, Pendergast, and he's just as much a prick."

"Yeah... they sort of brace each other up," Buck said. "Give each other confidence. I'd like to believe it's just a breakin' in phase... but I don't know."

Jarvis sighed, "I don't either, Buck. I'm glad you brought all this shit to me, although Joe and I already have sniffed most of it out. We officers aren't as oblivious as you working Navy guys might think, y'know."

Rogers chuckled, "No, sir... nobody could be."

The laughter they shared helped to lighten the mood a bit. They watched the sun set for a few minutes before anyone spoke again.

"What about the skipper?" Dutch asked. "He's got to know what's up."

The COB shrugged, "I can't imagine he doesn't. Not much gets by

Art Turner. I think he's trying to give the new officers some rope, though. What we need, what we all need, is a good solid fight. Nothing pulls a boat together like combat."

"Or splits it down the middle," Jarvis grumbled. "Literally and figuratively."

"It could get the dynamic duo in line," Dutch offered.

"Yeah, or it could create more strife," Jarvis sighed.

"I'm willing to try it," Rogers said. "It's the true test. You guys know that."

They all did. Jarvis nodded, "You're right, Buck... but I think you need to speak to the skipper. And now. He needs to hear it from you. To get your impression of the crew's state of mind. We'll talk to him as well, but you're in a unique position. Is he coming to the movie tonight?"

Rogers shrugged, "Don't know. It's supposed to be a surprise... but Eddie let me in on it. We got a pretty good collection this cruise. Supposed to be the Maltese Falcon, though."

"Bogart!" Jarvis smiled in spite of himself. Then in a flawless impression said, "Nobody should miss Sam Spade, sweetheart."

"Convince the skipper to go," Dutch told Buck. "Then maybe we can have a word during the picture, or you can."

Rogers nodded and sighed, "But I want to see Sam Spade, too..."

The three men laughed, and Dutch clapped him on the shoulder, "Don't worry Buck, it'll probably show a dozen times over the next couple of months. Let's break this up. I can see old Begley on the bridge scoping us... oh, and look who's come on deck. Pendergast, inspecting the snorkel."

"For Chrissakes..." Jarvis cranked. "We're trying to fight a friggin' war out here. The last thing we need is this junior high nonsense."

It was true. Burt Pendergast was near the after end of the cigarette deck making a big show of closely examining the highly useful and unique piece of equipment that only *Bull Shark,* in all of the U.S. Navy sub fleet, carried. It was entirely possible that she was the only boat on Earth that officially carried it. The three men had heard bits and pieces from the captain and the OSS man, Webster Clayton, that an American spy had sniped the idea from the Norwegians late the previous year and that it had been specially built for *Bull Shark* years before anybody was supposed to fit their boats with it.

Although it was certainly proper and reasonable for the assistant engineer to study the unique device that allowed the diesels to run as far down as periscope depth, it was painfully obvious that the inspection was just a cover to try and overhear what Jarvis, Dutch, and Rogers were talking about. It was no good, though. Pendergast was too far forward, and the apparent wind of a ship running at twenty knots drowned out anything the three men said. It was a useless endeavor but one that only engendered more suspicion and distrust.

CHAPTER 4

MAY 10, 1942 – 1925 SHIP'S TIME

1°45' N, 90°15' W – NORTHERN BOUNDARY OF THE GALAPAGOS ARCHIPELAGO

Art Turner had been looking forward to the movie the previous evening. He didn't always attend, but once or twice a week, he'd join the crew in the forward torpedo room and get into the spirit of a little taste of home. He was a fan of the private detective genre, and Bogart in particular, so seeing Bogie's interpretation of Dashel Hammet's famous book was something to miss a cribbage game for.

He'd just finished creating his sundae... strawberry iced cream thanks to the boat's luxury of having an ice cream machine in the crew's mess, frozen strawberries, caramel syrup, and fresh whipped cream made up by the galley cooks. They didn't have popcorn, an oversight that Turner would see to, but a nice strawberry sundae would really hit the spot.

Chief yeoman Clancy Weiss had come through the hatch from the control room with a decoded message flimsy in his hands and a slight frown on his face. Turner half-hid a sigh. He had enough to think about, what with the apparent tension between the hands and the new officers. Now, from the look on the yeoman's face, he had something unpleasant to share.

"Evening fox and follow-up, sir," Weiss said, almost sounding apologetic. "You're gonna want to take a look at this."

Several times during the day, the Navy would send out a Fleet Broadcast. This was often shortened to the phonetic alphabet Fox Baker or just Fox. It did sometimes contain specific information aimed at a specific vessel. In that case, either the general Fox would indicate such or would simply be followed up by an encoded message.

"Is this going to ruin my appetite, Yo?" Turner asked with a raised eyebrow and a nod toward his delicious creation.

Weiss shrugged, "It's nothing bad, sir... just unusual. And not all bad news, either."

In fact, it was half good news. Part of the brief message said that Joan Turner and family had arrived that afternoon in Honolulu and when they'd checked in at Pearl, had been informed that their old house, the one they gave up when Turner was transferred to new construction, had become available. Turner was glad of that. It was a good neighborhood that adjoined the base, and the kids liked their school.

The second part of the message was odd and a little disappointing, as it would delay their arrival at Pearl a few days. The official part of the message read:

```
SS-333 to proceed max speed to northern
Galapagos islands.X
Naval construction team and radar station
report possible enemy activity.X
Suspect Japanese submarine and/or merchant
convoy.X
Suspect associated escorts. Reasons unknown
but assume interference with Baltra station
setup.X
Might also be trade convoy to Chile.X
Intercept, reconnoiter and interdict if
feasible.XX
```

From their current position at the time of receipt, the destination was only about a day's travel. Turner had ordered Begley to plot a course and proceed at four engine speed, maintaining their twenty knots. They'd arrive in Galapagos waters near sunset of the next evening. With that done, Turner went forward and did, in fact, enjoy the movie... mostly.

During an intermission for head breaks and coffee and ice cream seconds, Pat Jarvis and Joe Dutch, along with Buck Rogers, waylaid Turner, and the four men had crammed into the captain's tiny stateroom. Turner knew full well what the confab was about.

"Sir, I think it's more than just a breaking in phase," Jarvis stated. "And in our opinion... they're eroding the morale of the boat, sir."

"Concur," Dutch stated. "We've all seen the results."

Turner looked to the Chief of the Boat, "Buck?"

Rogers drew in a breath and let it out slowly, "Sir... it's not my place to criticize the officers... but..."

"But it's your place to watch out for the men," Turner said gently. "Come on, Buck, give me the straight dope."

"The guys are already starting to call Mr. Begley Breadfruit Begley," Rogers admitted. "And Mr. Pendergast Pain in the Ass Pendergast."

Jarvis snorted but said nothing. Dutch frowned, "Breadfruit?"

Turner had to school his face so as not to grin, "Breadfruit Bly. What they used to call William Bly after his men mutinied on the *Bounty's* expedition to Tahiti. And that isn't good, although it's not the end of the world. I'm sure they've got nicknames for all of us."

"Sure they do," Dutch said with a grin. "They call me Volts, Pat here is Angler because he's a fisherman and he's in charge of the fish... Frank is Gears, and Andy is Tunes."

"Pretty normal and not unflattering," Jarvis pointed out.

"And what about me?" Turner asked bemusedly. "Probably old hardass."

Rogers grinned, "Nope. They're already calling you "Anvil" Art Turner. These are good guys. Professional, smart, and dedicated. Not to mention loyal. Every officer on this boat... and no longer on it... proved themselves in that last patrol. Christ, our skipper has a Navy Cross, our officers bronze stars, and the boat a unit citation. Every guy aboard who was with us has a sub combat pin. That's impressive for one short patrol... but now..."

Turner drew in a breath, "I appreciate you men bringing me this info. I'm not unaware. I can tell you now that we're diverting to the Galapagos for a day or two to check on some suspected Jap activity down there. I'll have a talk with our new officers. I also think that a little real submarining might get their heads in the game and let them see just how a well-oiled boat works."

"And Freddy Swooping Hawk, sir?" Buck asked. Turner noted Jarvis give him an appreciative nod. "Mr. Begley wants to send him to a mast."

"I'll squash that," Turner assured him. "I don't want that kid punished for doing what he was supposed to do. I'll have a talk with Begley and Pendergast, and then I'll meet with you and Swooping Hawk, Chief."

"The last thing we need are lookouts afraid to report," Jarvis said.

Turner nodded, "True. Like I said when we first shoved off, Buck... on this ship, the shit flows uphill. I'll see to it that the two new officers get with the program. I don't mind them wanting to make their mark, but there's a right and a wrong way. Okay, that it? Then let's go watch some more Bogie, huh?"

The plan of the day didn't allow for much free time, as the ship was being readied for a possible battle and every department was drilling. Turner would speak with the two officers, but he also hoped that seeing *Bull Shark* in action, or at battle stations at the very least, would soften Begley's and Pendergast's attitudes. They'd see what a well-run ship could do. Neither of them had seen actual combat yet during the war, and their only real experience was training operations in Panama a few years back.

Turner didn't know the details, but he did know a little about the situation between his former XO and Begley and his friend Pendergast. He knew that Williams and Jarvis had gotten into a minor scuffle in

New London and that Begley had been *dating* Elmer's ex. Further, having served at Coco Solo himself a few years ago, Turner knew the CO there personally and had gotten the cliff notes on the other side of the coin.

Apparently, Begley, Pendergast, and Williams had all been on the same S-boat during a war game. Elmer had been in charge of the approach and setup. He'd taken a bit too long in firing on the target ship, and another boat in the group had scored the first hit. Turner's friend said that Begley had blamed his not being sent to PXO School sooner on account of Elmer's hesitation. In truth, though, it had been a bad situation. Williams might have delayed, but he was working his boat around a shoal and had he tried to take a shortcut, might have run the boat aground.

Well, now it was going to be Begley's turn. Turner was going to give him operational control over the Galapagos mission. Should they encounter any Japanese submarine, tin can, freighter, or other vessel, Turner would con the approach and allow Begley the setup to fire. If they encountered something while Jarvis had the watch, then Turner would instruct Pat to handle the approach and let his assistant officer of the deck, which would be Pendergast, handle the setup.

It was a style of command that Turner had used many times in the past. It had been done for him, and in his opinion, made him a better officer and a better leader. Men learned by doing. Sure, it was expected that the captain would do it all. The crew expected that their skipper could set up and shoot fish and kill ships. But what was needed, both for the men's morale and the potency and safety of the boat was for all the watch leading officers to be able to do the captain's job, too. Even the junior officers should be given a shot as well. In Turner's view, every officer aboard was a prospective captain. And what a captain needed in addition to technical skill was confidence. And confidence only came from *doing*.

So it was then, that near sunset, *Bull Shark* was following a course that would take her within sight of Darwin Island and then encircle the western perimeter of the chain in a rough half-circle to the southern end and then reverse the course in a wider arc that would cover the offshore region before heading back to Pearl. Turner considered plotting a course that would wind the submarine through the center of the islands, even stopping at the Baltra base construction site, but he assumed that this area would be covered by the Navy's aircraft or support vessels.

Begley had been working on their track for most of the afternoon and now had the deck, conning the ship from the bridge at three engine speed. Joe Dutch as JOOD, stationed in the control room, updating the course on the chart, and his maneuvering board using the dead reckoning indicator. He was also waiting for a return call from the Baltra base commander on Turner's orders.

Turner had long ago decided that he preferred his plotting party to work at the master gyro table in the control room. There was more room there, and it gave more men an opportunity to work on tracking and plotting. There was usually somebody in the conning tower at the chart desk as well, both to backstop the tracking party and to take advantage of the dead reckoning tracer and provide another point of view for the officer of the deck.

Arnie Brasher, radioman first-class, stepped out of the small radio shack and up to Post, "I've got Captain Gignac on the horn for the skipper, sir."

"Very well," Dutch said. "Call it up to the OOD. I'll go inform the captain."

Turner accompanied Dutch back to the radio room and sat down at the set, picking up the handset so that he could have at least a semi-private conversation with the base commander.

"*Captain Turner, this is Captain Morten Gignac,*" a man's gravelly voice said. "*I'm in charge of the Baltra project, and I command the USS* Topeka, *CL-44. I've got a support freighter and a DE, the* Jackson Elliott *with me as well.*"

"Pleasure to make your acquaintance, sir," Turner replied. "Any air cover?"

A harrumph, "*We carry a floater for recon. Part of the airfield is already finished and there's a squadron of Buffalos... the older ones, a squad of Dauntlesses, and a couple of Devastators for now."*

"Any sign of the Japs?" Turner asked.

"Nothing as yet," Gignac replied. *"But yesterday afternoon, our long-range cap thought they spotted smoke on the horizon. About..."*—there was the sound of rustling paper—*"four-hundred nautical west, southwest. Couldn't tell a heading, as that was extreme visual range and the Buffalos had to turn back. Been thinking about sending the DE out there, but once Pearl contacted me and said you were right around the corner... I thought I'd wait. Or we could do a joint effort. I don't have many assets out here, but being so far from the front and so forth..."*

"You're the senior officer, sir," Turner said graciously. "I'll abide by whatever decision you think is best."

"Well, I've got a new O4 commanding the destroyer escort," Gignac stated. *"He's junior to you, I believe. So, if you don't mind, I'll assign him to you, and you can act as a task force. What was your thought on your patrol here?"*

Turner explained his half-moon around the western side of the islands and then back again at a greater distance. Gignac thought that was a fine idea but suggested that since the DE could cruise at twenty-five knots and make thirty-two at flank, that she take that side and that *Bull Shark* do an end-around to the east. If a Jap task force or a German task force were trying to sneak up to the Galapagos from the southern Pacific... or if they were trying to get to Chile unnoticed, then Turner might be in a position to head them off with the *Jackson Elliott* creeping up on their sterns.

Turner acknowledged, made radio contact with the destroyer and the two captains, and worked out a quick plan. Then he called up to the bridge.

"XO, we've been assigned a DE and have a slight change of plans. Come down into control with me for a quick briefing."

"Aye-aye, sir," came Begley's response over the open bridge circuit. *"Mr. Dutch, come up and take the deck."*

Dutch frowned at the lack of courtesy. Not that it was required, but it had always been something done on *Bull Shark* and on his previous assignment, the *Tautog*. He and Turner had carried that mentality with them when they transferred to *Bull Shark*.

"Sir?" Begley said after sliding down the ladder from the conning tower.

"Change of plans," Turner stated, pointing to the chart laid out on the gyro-compass table. "Instead of doing a long curving course on the western side of the islands, I want to cut straight through and come out on the southeastern side. Baltra reports seeing something, a possible smoke trail, on the horizon bearing about two-four-five from the base. Maybe four hundred miles out. They couldn't get a heading for it, or if it was even a ship or convoy. What do you think?"

Begley opened his mouth, closed it and then shrugged, "I've never heard of Japs operating this far to the east, sir. Could it have just been an inversion or a cloud or something?"

Turner met his gaze, "You tell me, XO. You were stationed at Coco Solo recently. I assume you know the situation in South America and the Galapagos better than me. What would the Japs gain by coming here?"

"Hit the base construction," Begley said. "Baltra is supposed to secure the refueling stop after ships leave the canal. But Chile isn't that much further, and they're not in our camp... they export nitrates and copper. It's a long way to run for the Japs, sir. What... eight thousand miles or so just to get to Taroa?"

Turner agreed, "Yeah... but they're after new territory. Suppose they could start hitting island chains in between. Tahiti, Fiji... set up a supply chain and run goods back and forth? Might even let them snag this group of islands before it's heavily fortified. Imagine what the Japs could do with the Galapagos in their hands?"

Begley was dubious; Turner could see that. Yet orders were orders, and even the slim chance of meeting a small Japanese fleet ten thousand miles from home would be a great opportunity to put a medal on his chest.

"I'll get right on that course, sir," Begley said. "Since we've got the snorkel, should we run at periscope depth?"

Turner frowned, "Not yet. Let's get across the islands and link up with the DE. Then we can run at radio depth during the day and keep in touch with them. I'm going to work up a code sheet with Mr. Post and Chief Weiss. Let's see it done, XO."

"Yes, sir," Begley said enthusiastically and then snapped his fingers. "Permission for Mr. Pendergast to join you, sir? He was comm on the S-60 when me and Elmer Williams served together. He's a cracker-jack code man."

Turner shrugged, "I don't see why not. I'll be in the wardroom. Send him forward if he's not in his rack. If so, it can wait, and he can review Andy's and Clancy's and my work later on. Oh, Tom..."

Turner turned back and put a hand on the man's shoulder. He leaned in and down to address the shorter, stocky lieutenant.

"Sir?"

"I know it's tough, coming into a new boat and replacing somebody the crew has gotten used to," Turner said quietly so that only Begley could hear. "I know it's been a little tough on you and Burt. But give these guys a chance, Tom. You do right by them, and they'll support you. Trust me. I couldn't have gotten through our last patrol without these boys."

Begley stiffened at what he thought was a veiled rebuke. Turner noticed and squeezed his shoulder, "No criticism intended, Tom. Just a little advice from a guy who was an XO himself not long ago. As soon as you've got that course, let's proceed on three engine speed."

Begley relaxed, but internally he wasn't quite sure he trusted what the skipper had said. Turner had already torpedoed his punishment of the Injun kid. Was this a subtle warning? He decided to wait and see.

"In that case, sir," Begley said, testing the waters a little. "Since we've got full batteries... and the trip across will take a good ten, twelve hours at fifteen knots... can I have permission to take each growler offline in turn and have the motor macs and the machinists give them a good going over?"

"You know Brannigan and Duncan ride those engines and generators like mother hens," Turner said casually. "And now with *three* engineers, even more so... but if you think it's a good idea to double-check and do a little tuning on each one... I'm not opposed. Would you rather have Pendergast on that or on the coding?"

"I think he can do both, sir," Begley said. "As you say, we've got Mr. Nichols and Mr. Dutch."

"Very well," Turner said and headed forward.

Begley looked after him for a moment before bending to his plot. He wasn't sure what to think. Either Turner was playing a game, or he was simply slow on the uptake. It didn't matter, though. With Burt in on the coding team and overseeing the overhauls on the four General Motors engines and their attached Allis Chalmers dynamo generators, it gave Begley a pipeline into everything that went on aboard the ship.

He couldn't help but smile to himself as he began to work out the navigation.

CHAPTER 5

"What's taking you so long, Daddy?"

Art Turner stared at his little girl, her blonde curls framing her angel face. She sat on her favorite toy; an old antique rocking horse Art's mother had given her when she'd turned three. Dotty's dress was bunched up around her legs and spotted with grass stains. Her bare feet were coated in grass clippings, too. Turner thought she was just about the cutest thing he'd ever seen.

"Taking so long, honey?" he asked, unsure of what she meant.

"Yeah," Dorothy Turner said impatiently. "We're s'posed to play Go Fish."

"Dad's busy, sis," Arty Junior said as he walked up in his little league uniform.

"Nah-ah, Arty!" Dotty insisted. "He's just lying there."

"Okay, everybody!" came the voice of Joan, who was stepping out through the back door of their little house. "It's time to get ready for church!"

"Church?" Art asked from his hammock. "There's no church today, Joanie."

His wife treated him to a raised eyebrow and a wry smile, "Then what's with the bells?"

In an instant, the comforting domestic scene vanished, and Art Turner found himself staring toward the end of a narrow bunk. The gyro-compass repeater read two-one-zero, and the depth gauge read forty feet.

Then he understood. The general alarm was gonging. Now that his dream mind had put it into words, the alarm did sound a bit like church bells. Turner sat bolt upright, yanked on his shorts and a T-shirt, slipped into his sub sandals, and bolted out into the passageway. He slammed chest-first into Walter Sparks as he was headed forward.

"We gotta stop meeting like this, Sparky," Turner said with a brief smile. "People are gonna start to talk."

Sparks laughed, "And you a married man, sir."

"What's up?" Turner asked as the two men turned sideways to get past one another.

"Dunno, sir," Sparks said. "Was just grabbin' a cup of coffee when the bells sounded. Mr. Jarvis is callin' for battle stations torpedo, though."

Turner patted the man on his heavy shoulder and moved aft into the control room. Burt Pendergast stood at the gyro table, updating the plot. Beside him stood Dick "Mug" Vigliano making notations and starting a target track. Harry Brannigan stood beside the duty chief's desk with a maneuvering board in hand. On the desk, somebody had placed a tray of coffee mugs and sweet rolls. The ship's clock read 0300.

"Morning, sir," Pendergast said. "We just got a radio transmission, and Mr. Jarvis wants to speak to you. Think we've got a target, sir!"

Turner nodded, "Very well. You fellas starting a plot, I see?"

"Yessir," Pendergast said, evident excitement in his voice. "Me and Vigliano are on it. The chief of the watch, too."

Turner made quick eye contact with Mug and Brannigan. The two veteran *Bull Sharks* nodded slightly, and the captain scrambled up the ladder into the control room. Every station was manned, and Pat Jarvis was standing by the lowered periscope with the sound-powered battle telephone around his neck.

"What's the story, Pat?" Turner asked.

"*Elliott* made contact a few minutes ago," Jarvis said. "They're about fifty miles to our southwest. Good moon. They say they've sighted smoke on the horizon and suspect at least two ships. Apparent heading seems to be just south of east. Maybe a hundred, hundred and ten. By the look of it, the contacts are moving at twelve knots."

"Meaning at least one merchantman," Turner speculated. He did some rough calculations in his head. "So, you've figured a two-one-oh ought to bring us to the party."

Jarvis grinned, "Exactly, sir. Figure at three engine speed... number four is still being gone over until the end of the watch... we'll intercept them by dawn."

"So, why are we at battle stations now, Gunner?" came the sleepy voice of Begley. "Could've let us all get a few hours more of shut-eye."

Turner wondered that himself and was going to ask the same question, although not in nearly as piqued a manner. He waited to see what Jarvis would do.

The big man's jaw flexed, but that was the only indication of how he felt. He drew in a deep breath, "The DE reports two aircraft headed in our direction. They suspect armed floatplanes. I figured better safe than sorry."

"Japs flying at night?" Begley scoffed. "Everybody knows the Nip can't see for shit in the dark. Not so great in daylight either with them slanted eyes."

"Well, *somebody* is flying those birds," Jarvis said and then wished he hadn't used that term. It only reminded Begley of the previous day's debacle. "If we spot them, my thinking is we go up top and man the AA guns. Give them what for."

"Very well," Turner said. "In the meantime, let's have all hands stand easy at battle stations. Inform the galley to start on the morning meal and see if we can get everybody fed before the action starts. Pat, I'd like to put our new XO in the hot seat. Would it hurt your feelings too badly if I let him con the attack?"

Jarvis shrugged and managed a half-hearted smile, "Aah, sir... I don't really have many feelings anyway. Rage... greed... and lust. Especially lust."

That got a round of chuckles from the men in the conning tower. All but Begley, who frowned slightly and said, "This isn't a joking matter, mister."

Jarvis locked eyes with the man and, still maintaining his strained smile, replied, "Well, I'm not feeling lust or greed right now, XO. With your permission, Captain, I'd like to take a quick turn through the torpedo rooms."

"Granted," Turner said, taking Jarvis's place by the scopes. "And when you see Buck, have him let the men slated as gunners for the next watch know their services might be needed."

"Aye-aye, sir," Jarvis said and disappeared down the control room hatch.

Begley made a dismissive sound and leaned against the chart desk, "Guy's a hot-head, sir."

"He's a good man, XO," Turner said in a way that was conversational, but that clearly held an undertone. One that stated that no further opinions on the subject would be allowed at that time.

"If you say so, sir," Begley said.

It was about an hour later when Turner's nose caught the scent of something savory wafting up from the control room. He grinned and turned to Begley and Jarvis, who was by then back at the torpedo data computer, "Something smells *good* below, gents... think I'll go down and have a look-see. Keep her off the bottom for a few minutes, Tom."

"Would you like me to go, sir?" Begley asked.

Turner chuckled, "And get first dibs? Nothin' doin', XO. Captain's privilege."

In the control room, the ship's cook first-class, Henrie Martin, and his assistant, Bill Borshowski, had just come through the watertight door from after battery, each carrying the end of a rather large tray. On it was a stack of plates and silverware arranged at either end of a half-sheet cake pan filled with something that was still steaming from the oven.

"Damn!" Buck Rogers said from where he stood near the high-pressure manifold. "What in the world is *that?*"

Borshowski laughed and, in his heavy Chicago accent, said, "Another one of Henrie's Cajun concoctions. Personally, I prefer Polish sausage and eggs."

Borshowski, and by then everyone on board, pronounced Henrie Martin's name in the French, or more accurately, Cajun way as "Onree Mar-ten." The dark-skinned Cajun cook in question only grinned broadly.

"You Chicago boys don't know nuttin' 'bout dem breafas," Martin suggested. "Dis here my mama's own Cajun egg bake! Whooo! Got dem un-ion and dem peppuh... got dem good Lousiana so-sees... got my secret blend of spices and keep you boys going four or tree hour, I gar-run-tee!"

Everyone in control laughed and shook their heads. Rogers rolled his eyes.

"Don't worry, there ain't no *ham* in it," Borshowski said as the two men found sufficient room on the gyro table to set the tray down temporarily and started to dole out the meal. "Got all the ham we need right here."

Martin grinned and began passing out the plates. Pendergast took a bite of his and made a face.

"No good, sir?" Martin asked.

"Spicy," Pendergast said with a frown. "How about some regular food once in a while, huh? Not this... this *farm* cooking."

"Like what, sir?" Martin asked cheerfully, ignoring the subtle hint that most of the other men picked up on. Pendergast hadn't said anything outright, but stress on the word farm in relation to Martin's skin color was suspect.

"I don't know... some good southern food," Pendergast stated, sounding reasonable enough. "Grits... biscuits and gravy... chicken fried steak. Maybe?"

"How 'bout dem chicken and waffle?" Martin asked.

"There you go," Pendergast said.

"Well, I think it's outstanding, Henrie," Joe Dutch said.

"Yeah, you can hardly tell they're powdered eggs with all the cayenne and whatnot," motor machinist Mike Watley said from his seat at the bow planes station.

"Delicious, cookie," Turner said. "Thank you."

Martin looked pleased, and he and Borshowski finished doling out the food for the control room. They then took turns sending plates up to the conning tower. Afterward, Martin approached Pendergast on his way out.

"Don't you fret some, none atall, any, Mr. Pendergast," Martin said. "Tomorrow you gonna have the best Georgia breffas you never had, and that's for true!"

Pendergast looked up from his plot and nodded, "Sounds good, Martin."

"Sir! Sir!" Arnie Brasher suddenly burst from the radio shack, a bit of egg still clinging to his upper lip. He was headed for Andy Post, who was just about to go up the conning tower ladder. However, when he saw Turner, he hesitated, unsure of whether to report through the proper chain of command or simply to the captain directly.

"Go ahead, Arnie," Turner said. "What's up?"

"Radio message from *Jackson Elliott,* sir! They say they're under attack!" Brasher exclaimed. "I've got Lt. Commander Walcott on the line for you, sir."

"Very well," Turner said calmly, hoping his tone would settle the young man down. Inwardly, though, he thought it might be bad. He strode into the radio shack and picked up the handset.

"Commander Walcott, this is Turner; what's your situation?"

A crackle of static, "*Those damned scouts must've spotted us, Commander. We've got two Fubuki destroyer-leaders bracing us, and they've opened fire!*"

Christ, Turner thought, "Two of them? What about the rest of the fleet?"

"*Haven't seen them, but lookouts report more smoke to the south,*" Howard Walcott reported. "*We're holding our own now, but the two aircraft have just popped up on our radar scope and headed back. How fast can you get here?*"

"Andy!" Turner called for his new communications officer. "We need to RDF this transmission and get an exact course. What's *Elliott's* last known position on our chart?"

"They're about twenty-five miles to the south, southwest," Pendergast called.

Turner bit his lip, "Howard, I want you to head zero-three-zero at flank speed. We'll head two-one-oh at flank. We should meet up in less than half an hour. Can you hold out until then?"

A long and worrisome pause, "*I think so. They're eight thousand yards astern of us... but they're faster. Radar says thirty-eight knots to our thirty-two.*"

Turner did more rough math, "Okay, so they'll take three miles off before we get there. That's okay; you should be able to hit them with your stern guns more effectively than their forward ones. Have your plotting party keep track of everything, Howard. Because once we sink these bastards, I want to know what's so important that the Japs sent two Fubukis across the ocean for."

A short, tense laugh, "*Roger that, Art. Gotta be something vital and probably an oiler, too. No destroyer has* this *much range.*"

"I'll keep my comm officer in touch with you," Turner said and signed off.

He walked out into the control room, "Sound battle stations torpedo! Buck, get on the 1MC and let Martin and the crew know they've got fifteen minutes to eat."

He flew up the ladder as the alarm gonged once again, "XO, the DE is under attack, and we need to get there. Is that number four ready for action yet? I want flank speed."

Begley flushed and turned to Jarvis, who still had the battle telephone around his neck, "Gunner?"

Jarvis spoke into the sound-powered telephone, "After engine room, conning tower. Report status on number four engine."

A moment went by, and Frank Nichols replied, "*Conning, after engine. Number four ready to go.*"

"Tell him to fire it up," Turner said. "Helm, ring up flank speed on both screws. XO, rig ship for surface. We're faster on top. Captain has the con. Burt, you stand by on periscope. I'll handle the approach; you handle the fish."

Bull Shark breached the surface of the ocean, her superstructure spitting water from the limber holes and her main exhaust belching smoke as they took over from the snorkel. Turner shoved the hatch open and went up on deck with Hotrod Hernandez, the senior quartermaster after Buck Rogers, hot on his heels. It was still dark at 0500, but Turner knew that by the time they met up with their destroyer, dawn would be lightening the sky. A perfect time for his submarine to make an attack on two destroyers he hoped didn't know he was coming.

Turner thumbed the bridge transmitter button, "Conning tower, bridge, get me lookouts up here, crews for all three guns and the Ma Deuces, pronto!"

"*We're gonna attack on the surface?*" Begley's astonished voice asked from the tinny speaker.

Had that been a rebuke in his tone... or fear, Turner wondered, "Possibly, XO. I want to be prepared. If so, I'll handle the deck, and I'm still going to have you handle the torpedo attack."

From beside him, Hernandez grumbled something deep in his throat. Turner eyed him with a slight frown. Hernandez pretended not to notice. From the bridge hatch, lookouts came up and began to climb the periscope sheers. Turner was glad to see that one of them was Fred Swooping Hawk.

Soon thereafter, the gun access hatch opened as more men popped up on deck through the mess hatch and the bridge hatch. Turner was glad to see Paul Rogers sliding the butt strap of the Pom-Pom over his backside as his assistant began digging ammo from the ready locker on the fairwater. Buck was the best Pom-Pom shot on the boat. He watched as Eddie Carlson slid into the left seat of the five-inch, with Sherman "Tank" Broderick's beefy form in the right seat. Behind them, a line formed to serve the five-inch shells to the gun. Martin and Borshowski appeared as well. Borshowski stepping behind the 20mm Oerlikon with Martin acting as ammo server. Even more men, those not assigned to the reload gangs in both torpedo rooms and those not directly responsible for ship handling came up the hatches with the ship's two Browning M2 .50 caliber machine guns. One man mounted a "Ma Deuce" into its special stud on the cigarette deck railing, and the other carried up several belts of ammunition. A damned fine set of teeth for a submarine.

"Five-inch ready!" Carlson shouted.

"Anti-aircraft weapons ready!" Buck Rogers added.

"*Bridge, control,*" Begley's voice filtered over the speaker, "*we've got targets on the SD and SJ radars, sir!*"

"What!? I didn't order a damned radar sweep!" Turner snapped, real anger rising inside him.

Although he would have eventually, keeping the sweep short and fast, he had no idea how long the two radars had been active. The truth was that any emission of radiation was a two-edged sword. Radio transmissions could be overheard and homed in on. Sonar beams had the same problem. Radar transmissions could also be traced, although as yet no one knew if the Japanese could trace radar... but as Tsun Tzu once said, you prepared for what the enemy was capable of doing, not what they planned to do.

"*Well, sir, I...*" the XO prevaricated, realizing his error. "*I thought since we were so... I only just ordered it, sir... sorry, sir.*"

Turner bit back his anger and the dressing down that was itching to come spilling out. Instead, he drew in a breath and replied, "What's done is done. What've you got, then, XO?"

A pause, "*Distant surface contact bearing zero-one-five. Range sixteen-thousand yards, closing fast. Two more contacts further off, almost the same bearing, but they appear split. Ranges are twenty-one thousand yards. Two air contacts as well, range near the first target. Assess Commander Walcott's floatplanes."*

"Very well," Turner said. "Conning tower, I'm going to slow down so you can order the rooms to open their doors. I want a plot on both the more distant surface contacts. The nearer one will be our DE."

"*Concur,*" Begley said. "*Already have Burt and the plotting party on them, sir.*"

"Okay, Hotrod, put the brakes on," Turner announced.

Hernandez grinned and rubbed his hands together, "Helm, bridge, reduce speed to all ahead one-third."

The order was acknowledged, and the sound of the four diesels temporarily flattened as the ship lost almost two-thirds of her way. The frothing bow wave she was throwing eased to a modest wash as the boat shed speed.

"Radio, bridge," Turner suddenly decided. "Put me in touch with the *Elliott* up here."

A moment went by, and then Howard Walcott's voice crackled over the speaker, "Jackson Elliott, Elliott *one speaking, commander.*"

"Howard, we're less than eight miles from you," Turner stated. "Slowed down to open our doors. After that, we'll ramp back up to about fifteen knots. I want you to keep your pedal to the metal, keeping your ship between us and the Japs until we're about a thousand yards apart. Then you drop back to one-third and spin around. We'll get right in behind you. Then when I give the word, you go to flank and charge the left Fubuki with guns and torpedoes. We'll break off and go after the starboard DD. Once the Japs see us, they're gonna shit a gold brick, so be ready. We'll probably have to dive, but I've got every surface weapon on board locked and loaded for now."

"*Roger that, Art... but they probably know you're here, thanks to those planes.*"

"Maybe. Not much we can do about that now... but I bet once you turn to fight, they'll come down for a strafing run. If so, I'll open up with all I've got."

An irreverent chuckle over the radio, "*You always been nuts, Commander?*"

Turner laughed, "Only since December 7th... though my wife might disagree. Standby, *Elliott.*"

"*Bridge, conning tower!*" Jarvis reported. "*Forward and after room report all torpedo outer doors open.*"

"Very well," Turner said, trying not to acknowledge the butterflies in his belly. Once again, he was taking his ship into combat. Once again, he was charging an enemy on the surface. "You ready for this, XO?"

A pause that seemed overly pregnant and then, "*Yes, sir. Standing by to fire.*"

Turner drew in a breath as he saw the American destroyer escort barreling toward him at a combined forty knots. Straight for his ship, and the speed was about to increase.

"Okay... here we go," Turner muttered to himself and then to Hernandez, "Hotrod, open her up!"

CHAPTER 6

"Lookouts below!" Turner ordered as the ship accelerated, and once again, a luminous phosphorescent bow wave began to grow and cream down her sides.

If the ship had to dive quickly... or perhaps it might be better to say *when* the ship had to dive quickly, the fewer men that had to scramble down the hatches, the better. Even with the lookouts gone, there were already eleven men on deck, including himself and Hotrod.

Ahead of them, the looming black shape of the *Jackson Elliott* was growing rapidly larger by the second. With the two ships closing on each other at a combined rate of forty-seven knots, the gap between them, now only two thousand yards, was closing by twenty-four yards per second. Already, even with the wind of the submarine's passage whipping by their ears, everyone on deck could hear the boom of multiple five-inch guns. Strangely, at least from the Japanese ships, there seemed to be no muzzle flashes. Yet, there had to be. Each of them had four deck guns that could bear on the American. And every few seconds, a rolling rumble that reminded Turner of what the broadsides of old might have sounded like filled the air. Yet, there were no flashes, except from the stern of the American destroyer. That was odd... he knew the Japs were firing... so where were the muzzle flashes?

He knew it was pointless, but Turner called down anyway, "Conning tower, bridge... anything on sound?"

"*El* conditions *es no bueno, señor!*" Hernandez cackled.

Turner guffawed and elbowed the quartermaster lightly in the ribs, "You better watch that smart mouth, Hotrod! You'll be on report!"

"*No comprende.*"

Both men had to stifle their nervous laughter as the bridge speaker crackled with Chet Rivers's report, "*Bridge, sonar... sound conditions poor. I think I've got our destroyer's fast screws, but the acoustic profile is terrible with all this high-speed running, sir.*"

"Very well," Turner said and fit his binoculars into the V of the TBT.

The special glasses had been outfitted with a thin vertical line in the center of their lenses. This was used as a targeting reticule so that the observer could line up his bearing and then press the transmit button on the target bearing transmitter housing. This would send an exact bearing to the TDC down in the conning tower. There was a duplicate device mounted to the after end of the cigarette deck for generating bearings for the after torpedoes as well.

"She's making her turn, sir!" Hotrod called, pointing at the *Elliot*, now towering high over the low submarine.

Ahead of them, the destroyer slowed and heeled to starboard as she whipped around to face her pursuers. Even as her side was exposed to the enemy, all six of her deck guns boomed out, roaring and flashing and temporarily lighting up the ship. Yet even as she did so, a shell from one of the Fubukis struck her forward well deck, creating a blossom of angry red flame.

"She's hit!" Tank Broderick screamed in rage.

"And she hit the one to starboard!" Hotrod shouted and pointed.

Sure enough, the Fubuki to the right, now no more than four thousand yards off, was sporting an angry red rose of her own. It was hard to tell in the dark, but it appeared to be near the bridge.

"Conning, bridge!" Turner shouted into the speaker. "Torpedo target is the starboard Fubuki! Order of tubes is one through four! Standby for bearings and range. Pat, feel free to get Chet on the sugar jig; it's not like the Japs don't know somebody's out here now. We'll be behind the DE for a minute or so, and when I con her around, you should have good bearings and a radar lock. XO, backstop me on the scope as well."

"Helm, reduce to all ahead one-third!" Hotrod called down. "Our DE is slowing!"

Once again, the roar of *Bull Shark's* diesels quieted some and the frothing bone she held in her teeth diminished to a gentler ring of foam. Ahead of them, no more than three hundred yards, the squat fantail of the destroyer escort was lined up perfectly with the submarine's bull-nose. Forward, Tank Broderick cranked the azimuth wheel and trained the muzzle of the stainless-steel deck gun on the still visible bow of the starboard Japanese destroyer. He and Eddie were shouting at each other, and the officer's steward was himself adjusting his elevation wheel. The eleven-foot gun, including its barrel and circular two-seat control mount, rotated easily, and soon its deadly muzzle was aimed right for the Japanese.

"Open fire when ready, gents!" Turner told them. "And when you've got her homed in, fire for effect!"

"Yessir!" Carlson and Broderick shouted in unison just as Eddie pushed down on the firing pedal and the gun boomed into deadly life.

Fred Swooping Hawk stood behind the gun mount, wearing heavy gloves. After the gun discharged, the empty shell casing was ejected from the breech and into his waiting hands. Swooping Hawk set it on deck and received a new fifty-two-pound shell from the ammo server through the open gun hatch. This he quickly fed into the breech of the gun.

"Ready!" Swooping Hawk announced, and the gun roared again.

Although there was a ghostly bit of light off to the east now, it was still nearly impossible to see the fall of the shot. With the gun's muzzle velocity of over two thousand feet per second, the shell reached the onrushing Japanese ship in less than two seconds. So far, there was no explosion, but Turner knew there would be soon.

In the conning tower, Pat Jarvis waited at the TDC, watching Tom Begley's back as he peered through the attack periscope. He wished the captain would call the shots himself. Turner had proven to be a crack torpedo shot, and this situation wasn't the time to let a novice test his skills. Not with two tin cans out there who'd shortly be very pissed off about the arrogant Yankee submarine daring to challenge them.

"Okay, Jarvis..." Begley was saying. "I've got the Fubuki in my sights... order forward torpedo to set depths on tubes one, two, three, and four to ten feet."

Jarvis cleared his throat, "That's too deep, XO."

Begley glared back at him, "Are you questioning me, mister? I'm familiar with the ONI-208J. I know the draft of a damned Fubuki!"

Jarvis bit back the snide retort he wanted to make. He wanted to tell the shit for brains that it didn't matter what the ship recognition manual said about draft. That the Mark 14s Mark 6 magnetic exploder mechanism didn't work. Further, that the torpedoes tended to run eight feet or more too deep. He drew in a calming breath.

"Mr. Begley," he said evenly, "the Mark 14 runs eight to ten feet deeper than set. Further... we've deactivated the magnetic feature and are only using contact exploders."

"In contradiction of BeauOrd regs?" Begley asked incredulously.

"On orders of ComSubLant," Jarvis said tightly.

Begley scoffed, "Fine, have it your own way. We'll talk about this later, gunner... order forward torpedo to set depth on all weapons to four feet... that satisfy you?"

Jarvis didn't respond, only spoke into the sound-powered telephone around his neck, "Forward torpedo, conning tower. Set depth on tubes one through four at four feet. Speed is high."

"*Conning tower, forward torpedo. Set depth on tubes one through four to four feet. Set speed to high,*" the forward torpedo room phone talker replied.

The TDC lit up with a bearing from the bridge's TBT. Jarvis noted that it read zero-one-niner. A second later, Begley spoke.

"Constant bearing... mark!"

Chet Rivers, who was acting as periscope assistant while his sound gear was more or less useless, read the numbers off the bearing ring around the scope, "Zero-two-two!"

Jarvis was faced with a conundrum. By Turner's own orders, Begley was in charge of fire control. The captain was only backstopping him. Yet Jarvis trusted Turner's judgement far better than Begley's. In a situation where the stakes were as high as they could get, should he override the XO?

It was only three degrees... the torpedo officer cursed silently and cranked Begley's bearings into his machine. They'd change anyway, but this initial data was enough to start the solution.

"Range to target is..." Begley fiddled with the stadimeter knob on the periscope for what seemed a long time. "Mark!"

"Three-four-five-zero... repeat, thirty-four hundred and fifty yards," Rivers reported.

"Angle on the bow is port three-five-oh!" Begley exclaimed.

The ship repeatedly shuddered as the deck gun boomed out. Everyone in the conning tower and in the control room below... hell, everyone in the ship was tense, waiting for the range to close and the real shooting to begin.

"Ted Balkley, seated at his radar station, watched the SJ surface radar scope carefully. The scope was a small, cathode-ray tube screen with a horizontal green line that stretched across the center. As the powerhead spun on the radar mast, its return signal would alter the line if it should hit a contact. The line would display a spike upward. Another indicator told the operator in what relative direction the head was pointing. Balkley could stop the head and aim it at a specific bearing or, using a series of adjuster knobs, set a limited sweep between two bearings.

He did this now, allowing the radar to swing only between three-three-zero and zero-three-zero. This gave him a fairly accurate picture of what was ahead of the submarine. There were three spikes. Strong, sharp upward peaks indicating the three destroyers, with the American ship being the largest.

"Range to target confirmed, sir!" Balkley said.

Next to the surface scope was the scope for the SD air search unit. This one was represented by a fuzzy thin triangle that rotated around a central pivot point. Unlike the SJ radar, however, the SD simply sent out a pulse in all directions and returned ranges but no specific bearings or heights. When it hit a contact, a small blurp would appear on the scope's round screen. Two did so now.

"Sir! Sir!" Balkley almost bleated. "Incoming aircraft! Range six thousand yards and closing fast!"

"Report to the bridge, mister!" Begley said, gritting his teeth. "They'll be the captain's problem."

———

High above the surface of the sea, the two Aichi E16A floatplanes circled around and headed toward the now oncoming American ship. Both planes carried a two-hundred-and-fifty-kilogram bomb as well as twin 20mm machine guns in their wings.

"*Dragon Flight, Dragon's Wing,*" came the voice of the senior commander aboard the lead destroyer. "*Begin attack run on American destroyer. Dragon's Wing Two has taken a hit.*"

The pilot of Dragon's Flight One acknowledged and began a high-speed dive toward the bow of the American ship from two thousand meters. He lined the bridge of the ship up with the crosshairs painted on his forward windscreen and pushed his throttle to the stops. The E16A wasn't a true dive bomber. It was intended to be an armed reconnaissance aircraft. Its dive, therefore, wasn't as steep as a standard carrier-borne D3A, what the round-eyes called a "Val."

"*Banzai!*" came the battle cry from the observer behind the pilot and from the two men in the other aircraft.

He grinned and was just about to second the sentiment when he caught sight of something else. Glancing upward from his steep sixty-degree dive, the pilot saw a long slim dark shape surrounded by a halo of glowing foam perhaps two ship lengths behind the American destroyer...

"Submarine!" he shouted. "American submarine directly behind the target!"

He yanked back on his stick, reducing his angle of attack so that he could drop his bomb on the submarine. No doubt the boat was going to fire on one of the Fubukis.

The pilot laughed out loud, and then hollered loud enough to be heard over the whine of his screaming engine, "Banzai! Banzai, Ame-kohs!"

A flash of light behind him and a thunderous roar that rocked and shook his plane. The altimeter read five hundred meters. Anti-aircraft tracers began lancing toward his aircraft, their deadly firefly lights drawing ever closer...

The plane was hammered over and over as fifty caliber, 20mm, and even big 40mm rounds smashed into the fragile airframe, shredding the aluminum skin, igniting fuel, smashing glass, and ripping through soft flesh. In his last impulse, the pilot smashed his thumb down on the bomb release button even as he, his observer and his plane were consumed in an aviation gas fueled fireball.

———

"Here they come!" Hotrod shouted as the two float planes dove out of the lightening morning sky toward the *Jackson Elliott*.

Even as he shouted, the AA guns on the destroyer began to bark out in protest. Rogers, Borshowski, and the men on the Ma Deuce fifties began firing as well, sending tracer rounds into the sky amid a cacophony of thundering deck guns and the throaty rattle of machine gun and AA cannon fire.

"Break off!" Turner ordered Hotrod. "Head for the damaged

Fubuki but head us a little starboard of their course so we're not shooting directly down their throats!"

Even as Hotrod was giving the helmsman these orders, Turner noticed that one of the floatplanes had altered its descent angle. It was now homing in on the submarine. There was enough light now to see the five-hundred-pound bomb slung between its pontoons.

"Jesus!" Turner gasped. "He's headed for us, Hotrod! Hard right rudder, all ahead full!"

"Helm, bridge, belay my last!" Hernandez shouted into the bridge transmitter. "Right full rudder! All ahead full!"

Again, the *Bull Shark's* mighty diesels roared as they cycled up to nearly their maximum output, their attached generators sending almost five million watts of power into the four General Electric motors that drove the propeller shafts. The ship heeled to port as she came out from behind the DE and headed to the right of her true target.

"Everybody down!" Turner roared over the din of weapons, wind, and engines. "*Down! DOWN!*"

As he dropped below the bridge fairing, dragging Hernandez with him, Turner's eyes were turned skyward, and he saw the Japanese airplane, now hardly more than a thousand feet overhead blossom into a white-orange ball of incandescent death... and backlit by the explosion, the unmistakable shape of a bomb hurtling toward the sea.

"Sound collision!" he shouted. "Everybody hang on!"

Wah-*BOOOOOSH!*

The bomb plunged into the sea where *Bull Shark* had been only a few seconds before. The sea a hundred feet off the ship's portside bulged upward as a concussion wave lit internally by the detonation rose and rolled toward the ship. The ten-foot-high wave slammed into the submarine, heeling her over thirty degrees to starboard.

Men slid; tons of water rolled across the decks and hundreds of gallons poured down the hatches. Down below, loose articles flew from tables and shelves. Men were knocked off their feet to tumble unceremoniously into bulkheads, valve stems, and to the decks.

As the ship righted herself, Turner struggled to his feet, dragging

Hernandez up beside him. A quick glance around showed him that the gun crews were still at their posts. Some of them had wrapped themselves around railings and stanchions, and others, those strapped in or seated, had fared better.

"Jesus Christ, that was close!" Buck Rogers howled from his position at the Pom-Pom. "Got the bastard, though, sir!"

"Good work!" Turner shouted. "Now, let's get that fucking tin can! Weapons free! Everybody all right below?"

This last he shouted over the bridge transmitter. A few seconds went by before Begley responded.

"*We're all right, sir! How's everyone up top?*"

"Intact, XO," Turner said. "We're gonna go right for that Jap tin can! Stand by for another bearing! Keep her at that, Hotrod!"

"Helm, meet her!" Hernandez said into the bridge transmitter. "Maintain course and speed."

The boat's turn had put the onrushing Japanese destroyer a couple of points off their port bow now. Amazingly, she was still headed for the *Jackson Elliott*. Somehow the Japanese hadn't seen them!

It was a commonly held belief in the service that the Japanese had poor vision. It was thought that because of the slant of their eyes that this somehow impaired their sight. However, the epicanthic fold that created this effect didn't impair vision at all. In fact, as the Americans would soon learn and Art Turner was already beginning to suspect, the Japanese not only had sight as good as anyone but were also *very* skilled night fighters. Another misconception held by the Americans... that the Japs weren't good night fighters. The truth was, at least this early in the war, that it was the Japanese who were better night fighters, as the nearly successful attack by the Aichi floatplane clearly demonstrated.

Down in the conning tower, Tom Begley was clutching the periscope handles for dear life. His heart raced, and his muscles bunched and unbunched. He told himself it was excitement and not fear, but he was only fooling himself. It was natural to be afraid during a battle, especially when a bomb went off just outside your walls. Yet to deny the fear was to ignore it. Ignoring one's fears and not controlling them could be dangerous.

"What've you got, XO?" Jarvis asked impatiently.

Begley had to white-knuckle the handles to keep his hands from shaking. He rotated the scope to starboard at first, astonishing Jarvis.

"To port, Begley!" Jarvis snapped.

"Give me a radar range!" Begley called out.

"Can't, sir!" Balkley stated. "That blast of seawater caused a short in the SJ... have to replace a couple of fuses first..."

"Goddammit!" Begley exclaimed as he turned the scope. "Okay, got her! Uhm... constant bearing... mark!"

"Three-three-five!" Rivers announced.

"Angle on the bow is port three-one-zero," Begley said. "Range... Jesus Christ! She's close! Mark!"

Rivers read the stadimeter scale, "Range is one-two-zero-zero yards!"

Jarvis worked his machine, "Set! Shoot anytime, XO!"

"Fire one!" Begley shouted, and Pat depressed the firing plunger.

The ship juddered as the thirty-three-hundred-pound torpedo was blasted from its tube by a giant's hand of compressed air. There was a slight pressure change even as far back as the conning tower as the impulse air that had shoved the torpedo out into the sea was sucked back into the boat by the Poppet valve.

"Fire two!" Begley announced. He counted backward from seven and then, "Fire three... fire four!"

"All tubes fired electrically," Jarvis reported.

"Fish running hot, straight, and normal!" Rivers announced from his sound gear.

"Jarvis, report to the bridge!" Begley said, still clinging to the scope.

"I think they've started to get the hint!" Turner said.

The light had grown brighter now, and it was easy to see the three destroyers. The American ship was headed almost due east, cutting hard to come to grips with the further Japanese vessel. *Bull Shark's* target had spotted them, and several five-inch shells, one hundred twenty-seven millimeter to the Japanese, whooshed over their heads.

At the same time, Carlson stomped down on the firing pedal, and his and Tank's shell blasted out of the gun's barrel and, in less than a second, struck the Fubuki amidships right at the level of her main deck.

Right where her side-mounted torpedo tubes were affixed.

A tremendous *ka-boom* and one of the torpedo racks erupted into fury and light. This set off the one astern, and soon the entire side of the ship was obscured by brilliant white light and red flame.

"Ha!" Eddie whooped.

"That'll learn dem rice-gobbluhs better than to brought demself roun' here!" Henrie Martin hollered triumphantly.

And then, in perfect unison, every man on the *Bull Shark's* upper deck, including their captain, shouted, "I gar-run-tee!"

The whoops of laughter that followed were mostly born of released tension and fear and were short-lived. Although the hit had been hard, it hadn't put the Fubuki out of commission. In spite of a respectable armament, the submarine was outmatched on the surface by the big tin can.

"*Eighty-five seconds to go on torpedo run!*" Jarvis's voice filtered through the bridge speaker.

"Clear topsides!" Turner shouted. "Everybody below, now!"

He smacked the diving alarm and two loud throaty *ah-ooga, ah-oogas* filled the ship. Men quickly unshipped machine guns, slammed lockers shut and vanished through the deck and bridge hatches. Turner and Hotrod were the last to descend. Turner last with Hotrod hanging onto the ladder to secure the hatch.

"Green board!" came Frank Nichols's voice from the control room. "Good pressure in the boat!"

"Rig out dive planes... full down on the bow planes," Begley was ordering. "Flood safety, flood negative, flood bow buoyancy..."

"Periscope depth!" Turner ordered. "Captain has the con! How long for our—"

A thunderous rumble filled the ship. Begley, who was still looking through the periscope, shouted in triumphant glee.

"A hit! A hit!" he announced. "Sir, Fubuki is going down by the head!"

Turner stepped over and took a look. Sure enough, one of the *Bull Shark's* torpedoes... only one... had struck the ship dead center and must have set off her boilers. A watery ball of flame and displaced sea was still settling. Even among the chaos, Turner could see that the ship had broken in two and that her two halves were already angling skyward as hundreds of tons of seawater hammered into her spaces.

"Good shot!" Turner complimented. "Anybody got a camera?"

"Yes, sir!" Rivers announced. "Always keep my Kodak up here just in case."

"Get a shot of this," Turner said. "Frank, belay periscope depth. Keep us at radio depth. Helm, come left full rudder. Get your course from Mr. Rivers when he's done playing tourist. We've got to assist our DE."

Everyone chuckled. Rivers placed the lens of his camera against the periscope's eyepiece and snapped off three shots. He then went back to his sound gear, slid the bulky headphones on, and began adjusting knobs.

"I've got two sets of fast screws," he announced. "Bearing... three-zero-five... one-one-five true... range three thousand yards."

"You heard him, helm," Turner ordered. "Steady up on course one-one-five. Increase to all ahead full. Pat, tell Sparky to set his depth on tubes five and six to four feet. Andy, you down there?"

"Yes, sir," Post called from the control room. "On plot with Mr. Pendergast."

"Get me in touch with Walcott again," Turner said. "XO, please go down and assist with the plot."

Begley looked a little hurt but slid down the ladder. After a moment, Post called up.

"I've got Commander Walcott, sir!"

"Put it on the telephone up here," Turner said and grabbed the handset.

"*Nice shooting,* Bull Shark," Walcott said cheerfully.

"Thanks, Howard... how are you guys doing over there?"

"A little banged up, Art, but still in fighting trim. Got a plan?"

"I do... I want you to fire off your starboard fish, then turn tail and run. We're headed your way at one-one-five. You scream by us headed three hundred, and we'll arrange a little welcome for our Japanese visitors."

"Assuming we don't sink them first," Walcott said.

Turner laughed, "Roger that, Howard. Let's get these bastards!"

In the scope, the captain could see the two ships almost a mile and a half ahead. Because of the snorkel, someone at Gratan had thought to reinforce both scopes. It would hardly do to be able to run at high speed at periscope depth with no periscopes, after all. However, this did mean that both his scopes were considerably thicker than the standard models. Turner wondered which trade-off was worth it. Go faster with bigger scopes but be spotted easier...

Turner saw the flashes on the *Elliott's* starboard side as her two turrets, each containing three torpedoes, launched their fish in the direction of the Fubuki destroyer, which was currently making a hard port turn to no doubt do the same thing.

Although destroyers and even cruisers carried side-launched torpedoes, and quite a few of them, the odds of scoring a hit, at least on a maneuverable destroyer, were slight at best. There was no delicate mathematics for solving angles and leading the fish like aboard a submarine. It was simply point and shoot and send as many weapons at the enemy as possible. The trouble was that the enemy could do the same as well, and they had a better torpedo.

The Japanese used what they called a Type-95 Long Lance torpedo. These fish, larger, faster, and more heavily armed than the American Mark 14, were quite accurate and devastating.

"Helm, reduce speed to all ahead one-third," Turner ordered. "Take us to periscope depth, Frank. I don't want to be seen too early."

"Good sound profile now, sir," Rivers said quietly from his station.

"Can you tell the two ships apart, Chet?" Turner asked.

The young man nodded, "Yes, sir... two sets of fast screws. One is clearly to port. The other is a bit further and a bit to starboard. He must have a nicked or bent propeller blade, sir. Getting a slight vibration or something... makes it easy to tell them apart."

"Good ear, Sonar, I'll hold you to that," Turner said. "Once *Elliott* passes, I may ask you to go active. I want to be sure of a good angle on this bastard. I'm going to send our last two forward fish, and then if we need to, swing around, and give him our after tubes... standby."

For the next two minutes, as the submarine moved forward at a leisurely three knots, Rivers continually updated them on the positions of the two vessels. Turner ordered all stop when the American ship was five hundred yards abeam and the Japanese ship a thousand yards off their port bow.

"Up scope," Turner said.

He turned the scope to the left and saw the Japanese vessel. There were clearly burn marks on her hull and superstructure. He quickly spun to the left and noticed that the American light destroyer looked to be in the same shape. Both vessels were a bit battered but still functional. None of either of their torpedoes had hit.

"Okay, here we go..." Turner said. "Constant bearing... mark."

"Three-four-five," Balkley, now acting as periscope assistant, said.

Out of the corner of his eye, Turner could see Hotrod Hernandez at the chart desk rapidly scribbling on a maneuvering board. He looked at Turner and nodded.

"Angle on the bow is three-four-zero port... range to target... mark," Turner announced.

"One-four-zero-zero yards," Balkley reported.

A moment passed, and Jarvis said, "Set. Shoot anytime, sir."

"Fire five... fire six!" Turner ordered.

On the bridge of the Dragon's Wing One, or what was left of it, the captain smiled grimly. The slightly smaller American ship had put up a valiant fight. Several of their 127mm shells had struck the Fubuki along with a fusillade of anti-aircraft rounds. These had smashed the forward viewports of the navigation bridge, killing several men and even penetrating to the combat information center just aft.

However, it was all for naught. The gunners in the two forward twin 127mm gun emplacements had the American ship bore-sighted. In the next few seconds, their stern would be smashed by four shells and the depth charges on their stern would go up like their Fourth of July.

The captain knew there was an American submarine out there somewhere. Yet, he didn't concern himself with this. Both destroyers were running at thirty knots, and any torpedoes launched from the submarine, wherever she might be, could be evaded. Also, the last known sighting was miles away.

"Torpedoes in the water!" the port lookout suddenly shrieked in terror, almost gibbering incoherently with fright.

The captain moved to the port bridge wing and saw. Two bubbling fingers of doom headed not for him but for a point off his bow. For where the mighty Fubuki would be in another thirty seconds or so.

"Full left rudder!" he shouted to the helmsman. "Reduce to ahead one-third! Begin active echo ranging! Find me that boat!"

A good trick. The American DE had turned about and led Dragon's Wing right past the waiting submarine. However, this captain would not be fooled. He would not turn *away* from the incoming torpedoes but into them, allowing them to pass harmlessly off his starboard side. Then he'd relentlessly hunt down the submarine and punish her for daring to fire at him and to avenge Dragon's Wing Two.

Perhaps because of the excitement of battle or his desire to punish the submarine, the captain had momentarily forgotten something. He'd forgotten that the American's guns had also been sighted in on him. So, while it was true that his quick thinking had caused the two American torpedoes to pass harmlessly less than a hundred meters from his starboard bow... it was also true that the American destroyer had fired on him. Those two shells were aimed true and, in a twist of irony, struck Dragon's Wing Two in *her* depth charge racks.

The entire ship rose, stern first, into the air. It was as if one of the Kaiju, the gargantuan monster-gods of legend, had smacked the stern of the Fubuki. Even as her depth charges exploded in a devastating chain reaction that disintegrated the entire after quarter of the vessel and ignited her boilers, which cracked her in two like an egg, the captain could only scream in defiance.

His last thoughts before a wall of flame and flying debris consumed him was of mindless rage and abject despair at his failure.

CHAPTER 7

PEARL HARBOR

MAY 17, 1942

Paula Poana's had been a staple of Waikiki Beach since the Great War. It had started as a local watering hole, but when Paula married a tourist who'd come to Hawaii after the end of the war, the two of them had expanded her little bar and added the grill portion.

Now, twenty years later, the couple still owned and operated the restaurant. The spot was popular for the delicious blend of authentic Hawaiian cuisine and international flavors from the U.S. to French to Italian. The spot was also quite popular for the fact that the outdoor dining sections commanded a spectacular view of the beach as far as Diamond Head.

On that early Sunday afternoon, the skies were clear, and the beaches were quite packed. There were plenty of locals, of course, along with hundreds of military personnel. The Royal Hawaiian, used by the Navy primarily as an R and R spot for incoming submariners, was nearly packed. In a few days, a large number of rooms would empty, only to be turned around again when USS *Bull Shark* put in.

Joan Turner sat beneath the umbrella at a table overlooking the beach. With her were Joe and Gladys Finnegan. He was in the Navy, and they had two kids about Arty's and Dotty's age. Gladys had been one of Joan's closest friends before they'd moved out to Connecticut at the beginning of the year.

"It's so nice to have you back, Joanie," Gladys was saying.

"It's nice to be back," Joan said. "I liked New England, and we got to visit my mom for a bit... but who can beat paradise? Well almost... I wish Art was in port. I can't seem to get a straight answer as to when *Bull Shark* is supposed to arrive."

Finnegan smiled, "I have it on good authority he should be in by next weekend, Joan. *Bull Shark* got side-tracked for a couple of days near the Galapagos. The boat's fine, as I heard it. So, how are you doing getting settled in?"

Joan sipped her cocktail and shrugged, "Oh, just fine. We got our old house back, as you know, Gladys. That was nice. Being near you guys and the kids near their friends and all. Just a short drive to the base, too. It hasn't even been a week yet, but it feels like we've come home."

Gladys beamed. Her husband smiled as well.

"Any plans now that you're back and Art is going to be operating out of Pearl?" Finnegan asked.

"Not really... I was thinking that now that both kids are in school, at least until summer break starts in a few weeks... that I might try to find a teaching position," Joan offered. "Put my education to some good use."

Gladys chuckled, "A woman who works! What's the world coming to?"

Finnegan laughed as well, "Hell, it's the *norm* these days. And I'm not just talking about the usual stuff, either. A lot of women are working factory jobs, electrical, you name it."

"Rosy the Riveter," Joan said with a grin. "Wendy the Welder. You men are going to be in for a shock when this war is over. A lot of women aren't going to want to go back to the status quo. You know... the little woman who keeps house while the man goes off to work."

"There's nothing wrong with that, though," Gladys said. "Being a housewife, I mean."

"Of course not," Joan said. "It does have its advantages, especially with kids. But women are just as smart, just as capable as men. And while our men ride into battle, the ships, planes, tanks, Jeeps, and weapons they're taking into battle are being built by women. Often better than the men used to, as I hear it."

"You're absolutely right, Joan," Joe remarked. "Not only that, but women are proving to have a head for code-breaking, too... which is one reason we asked you to lunch today."

Joan grinned, "Got a heavy math problem for me, Joe?"

He smiled, "As a matter of fact... I do. Ever hear of Bletchley Park?"

Joan frowned, "I think so... isn't that a town in England or a section of London or something? Anyway, they're the folks working on the German Enigma code, right?"

Joe nodded, "Exactly. It's a big job. A *lot* of deciphering. They're using computers to help with the bulk work, and it's going pretty well."

"Computers?" Joan asked. "Like the TDC aboard a submarine?"

Joe almost forgot that Joan had more than a passing familiarity with submarines. She'd been aboard her husband's boat during her final battle with a couple of German ships. After looking into the matter, Finnegan had been floored to find out she'd actually been at the wheel for most of it. The woman not only knew Navy technology... she had combat experience and a citation from President Roosevelt, no less.

"No, not mechanical devices," Joe replied. "Although I hear they're working on something like that... no, the computers I'm talking about are people. Whole banks of them who sit and hand-decode the ciphers. And almost every one of them are women. Women, or at least some of them, seem to have a knack for the work. Well, Joe Rochefort and I thought that you might be interested in being *our* first computer, Joanie. We've got a particularly troublesome and time-sensitive code we could use a mathematical mind on."

"Rochefort... isn't he that weird guy who works in the basement and hangs around in a bathrobe and slippers?" Joan asked. "I think Art and I met him one time."

Joe and Gladys laughed, and Joe said, "Yeah, he's a bit eccentric. But sharp as a whip. Knows Japanese and has a real talent for the work."

"I'm flattered, Joe," Joan said, "but I'm no cryptographer... I'm not sure I'd be any real help."

"You'd be surprised, Joan," Joe said. "Believe it or not, we've got quite an odd mix in our team. Navy officers that aren't quite fit for line assignments but better than desk jockey material... we've got enlisted too. Believe it or not, we've got the entire ship's band from the *Arizona* working for us."

"What?" Joan and Gladys asked in unison.

Joe laughed, "Well, they weren't aboard during the attack, but their instruments were. So, the Navy, in its bizarre and infinite wisdom, said they were unemployable and gave them to us. Turns out musicians make great code breakers. You play the piano, right?"

Joan shrugged, "Yeah, I fool around a bit... you really think I could do this, Joe?"

"Oh, I bet you could, Joan, honey!" Gladys emoted. "You're the sharpest lady I know. And tough as old boots, no offense."

Joan chuckled, "Well, it does sound interesting... and besides, with summer coming, there really aren't any teaching jobs open... what would I be working on?"

"Well..." Joe said with a crooked smile. "That's classified. We'd have to get you a security clearance, sworn in, etc. Depending on how staff sees things, we might even give you a naval rank. Like a lot of officers and men now in the reserves. They step up to serve on active duty for the duration of the war plus six months. Not sure about that part, but I'm sure we can get you started ASAP. *Need* you to, in fact. So, what do you say?"

Joan was taken aback, "Well, I... it sounds great, Joe... but I really should talk it over with Art."

"I'm sure he wouldn't object, Joanie," Gladys stated.

"No... but there are the kids to consider," Joan said. "I can't be gone twelve hours a day like you, Joe."

Joe waved that away, "Joe Rochefort is flexible. We can work around whatever schedule you've got. And Gladys has already agreed to have Arty and Dotty stay at our house while you're working."

"Oh, I'd love it," Gladys said. "The kids would, too."

"Well, I'll say a qualified yes," Joan said. "So long as Arty agrees. I wouldn't feel right without talking with him first."

"Okay," Joe said. "And if you need me to, I can have a talk with him. *Bull Shark* ought to be in port for at least two weeks. There's some dockyard work that's scheduled for her."

Joan smiled, "I can't imagine that Arty would mind... when do I report, Mr. Finnegan?"

Finnegan laughed, "Tomorrow morning if you can swing it. If you need a day or two more, I understand..."

Joan shook her head and snapped him a quick salute, "No, sir! I'll be there, *sir!*"

CHAPTER 8

PEARL HARBOR

MAY 20, 1942

L t. Commander Art Turner stood on his bridge beside Tom Begley, who was conning the ship into the submarine base. They'd just passed the 10-10 dock and were approaching the southeast lock at one-third ahead. The special sea detail was set, and men stood at the ready positions to receive mooring lines under the sharp eye of the COB. All other men who weren't needed to run the boat while she pulled in were lined up on the after deck in shined shoes, clean dungarees, and brilliant white dixie cup hats.

All of them had been lined up in perfect order since the ship moved past battleship row. All of them to a man respectfully quiet and overcome by a sense of sadness at the sight of the wrecked battleship fleet. Some ships were in the process of being raised, while others, such as the *Arizona*, would never be moved. It was a sobering sight, to be sure, and its effect lasted until the ship neared her dock.

"All set, XO?" Turner asked.

"Yes, sir," Begley said. "All the chiefs have their material condition reports ready. I've gotten with Nichols, Pendergast, and Dutch, and have a complete E and R sheet ready."

"And our guys have already come at and re-stowed the refrigeration room, cold room, and pantry," Andy Post said from behind them.

Turner turned and winked at him. This was a common practice in the silent service. When a submarine arrived at a base for her two-week R and R and overhaul, just about everything was pulled and replaced by the base. This included torpedoes as well as foodstuffs. The tendency was for the base to remove the best food and re-provision the boat with what was readily available. This could often mean whatever was handy, not what was desired. So, the commissary department aboard a boat would put all the best foods in the back of the various storage facilities and leave what they didn't want out front. The "easy to come at" mentality was the order of the day for the removal of provisions as well.

"Sir..." Begley began slowly. "What about our fish?"

Turner nodded, "I know what you're asking, XO. Admiral Edwards provided for that. I've got an order from him stating that we're to keep all of our remaining fish. The base torpedo shop is not to remove any of our fish, only provide reloads from their stores."

"Which means duds," Post grumbled.

"Probably," Turner said. "But we know how to handle those."

They were approaching the dock now. Begley gripped the teak bridge railing harder, "Standby to mark the turn, quartermaster."

"Standing by," Hotrod Hernandez stated soberly.

He didn't joke around with the XO the way he did with the other officers. No one did. The mood aboard the ship hadn't improved much since the excitement at the Galapagos ten days earlier. Begley and Pendergast were still riding the crew hard and micro-managing. If anything, the situation had degraded, although for the first day or so Turner had thought there was an improvement.

Morale was riding high after the sinking of the two Fubukis, as one might expect. There were no injuries aboard and no damage other than a few minor issues when that five-hundred-pound bomb rocked them. A handful of burst light bulbs, some spills, and a few shorts, but nothing that a couple of hours of work couldn't put right.

The *Jackson Elliott* hadn't faired quite as well, but even her damage was relatively light. They did have a few deaths and about two dozen wounded. The ship, though, was still fully functional. They'd taken it upon themselves to search for the ship or ships that the two Jap destroyers had been protecting. That had been the first thing that put Begley and his pal back on the warpath.

They'd taken it personally that *Bull Shark* hadn't gone after the theoretical fleet. However, as the DE was much faster, she could cover the ever-growing sphere of ocean that the Japs could be in more effectively. Further, she had a recon floatplane that she could deploy as well. Finally, the *Bull Shark* had an appointment to keep at Pearl.

As it turned out, nothing was found. Whatever the Japanese had been doing, or whatever ships had been south of the Galapagos had escaped detection. That had soured Begley's mood, and soon after, the same rigid discipline and the same fault-finding had begun. By the time the boat passed the five-hundred-mile circle for Pearl, she was no longer the happy submarine she'd been when she'd left New London two weeks earlier.

"Mark!" Begley announced. "Port back one-third, hard left rudder. Standby to take mooring lines."

Turner felt the turn was a little early for the slip assigned to *Bull Shark*. However, he caught Hernandez's eye, and the experienced quartermaster took his time relaying the order. It was only a couple of seconds, but it made all the difference. The boat spun to port, coming in just a few yards away from the concrete dock. When she was lined up, Begley ordered all stop and then all back full, the two screws churning the oily water at the boat's stern and taking the way off her.

"Now remember what I told you!" Buck Rogers snapped to his line handlers. "Don't try and catch them monkey's fists. It's full of lead, and it'll break your hands. Let it come aboard, then haul in on the heaving line and then put the bite of the mooring line over the cleat. Then coil them heaving lines down nice and neat, you hear me, there?"

The ship was nearly still now. The men waited tensely.

"Pass the mooring lines!" Begley shouted.

The shore party along the pier tossed their monkey's fists, and they hit the boat's wooden deck with substantial thumps. The line handlers snatched them up, hauled in, and secured the heavy dock lines to the cleats along the boat's port side.

"Double up mooring lines," Begley announced. "Secure the diesels."

The growl of the four sixteen hundred horsepower engines suddenly died, leaving in their place the sound of cheering, applause and the band playing *Stars and Stripes Forever*.

"Ship secure, sir," Begley said to Turner.

"Very well," the captain said with outward calm as he scanned the crowd of onlookers. When he spotted his wife and two children, though, his heart began to thump excitedly in his chest.

"Permission to take the gangway, sir?" Rogers asked, turning to look up at the bridge.

"Granted," Turner said.

Two heavy-duty metal brows were snaked over to the *Bull Shark's* main deck and secured. Men also began connecting the water, power, and telephone lines that would support the ship while she was docked. Two officers crossed the forward gangway and stopped just before stepping onto the deck. One was a captain that Turner didn't know, and the other everyone knew. A burly man with admiral's stars on his working khakis.

"Permission to come aboard, Captain?" Admiral Chester W. Nimitz asked.

Turner smiled, "Welcome aboard, sirs."

The two officers stepped onto the deck and saluted the flag before shaking Turner's hand in succession. Turner introduced Tom Begley, and they shook hands with him as well.

"I'm *damned* impressed, Captain," Nimitz boomed. "You're hardly in commission more than three months, and you've already got three Swastikas and a rising sun on your battle flag and painted on the conning tower! *That's* what I'm talking about, Bob. That's the kind of aggressive heller we *need* out there. Excuse me, gentleman... this is Rear-admiral Robert English, submarine base commander. I don't believe you've ever met?"

"No, sir," Turner said. "An honor, sir. Admiral Edwards did ask me to send along his compliments, though, sir."

English grinned, "All mine, Commander. Welcome back to Pearl. Got yourself a fine boat and a fine crew here. The relief crew is standing by, as are the appropriate base shops. The buses to take your men to the Royal Hawaiian will be here shortly. Uniform of the day is dress whites, covers, and shined shoes. Please have your material condition reports ready."

"All done, sir," Begley said.

"Excellent," Nimitz said. "Excuse me, gents. There's somebody I'd like to say hello to."

The fleet admiral walked forward to where Buck Rogers stood and shook his hand. Turner's eyebrow rose.

"Didn't know they knew each other, eh, Captain?" English asked casually. "They served together several times as I understand it."

Begley said nothing but Turner thought that he caught just a hint of a scowl cross his features. He cleared his throat, "It was kind of the Admiral to greet us, sir."

"Nonsense," English said. "We've both been hearing about you, Captain. And about this new boat... I'm only sorry we're going to have to cut your leave short."

"Sir?" Begley asked with just a hint of pique.

"Dick Edwards laid the situation out for you before you left New London, if I'm not mistaken," English stated.

Turner nodded, "The Japs are mounting for a hard hit after the Coral Sea engagement. Have you figured out where and when yet, sir?"

"Not exactly," English stated with a frown. "We're working on it. We suspect early June, though. So that's just enough time to get you refitted, re-supplied, and out of the gate to be there. You saw the empty dry dock when you came in??"

"Yes, sir," Begley said. "Looks like a lot of work about to be done."

English chuffed, "That's putting it lightly. *Yorktown* was heavily damaged in the Coral Sea. She's due in in a couple of days for major repairs so Admiral Nimitz can get her back out there with *Enterprise* and *Hornet*. We're not sure she'll make it... and unless she does, that leaves only *Enterprise* and *Hornet* to face the entire Kido Butai... what the Japs call their first air fleet. At least four flat tops. We got one in the Coral Sea and damaged two more... but they still outgun us. We'll talk more about it in the morning, Mr. Turner. Tonight, you fellas get to rest and visit with your families."

"Did you say refitted, sir?" Begley asked.

"Oh, yeah," English said. "You're light a deck gun. We've got a nice shiny five inch at the weapons shop just itching to go to sea. We're going to mount her to your after deck. It's also kind of funny how they put your Pom-Pom on that forward blister and the 20mm on the cigarette deck. How do you like that arrangement? Would you like them swapped?"

Turner thought about that, "Frankly, sir, having that Chicago piano covering forward along with the five inch gives us a lot of firepower up there. I think we'll leave things as-is. Another deck gun would be fantastic, though."

"Great," English said. "Done and done... now about your fish... I received a phone call from Dick Edwards the other day stating that under no circumstances are we to remove your current torpedoes and let the exploder and after body shops at them. Is that right?"

Begley shifted uncomfortably, and Turner nodded gravely, "Yes, sir."

English's eyebrows rose, "Anything special about them?"

"Admiral Edwards didn't say, sir?" Turner asked uncertainly.

"He did not."

Turner drew in a breath, "All of our remaining eighteen fish have had the Mark 6 exploder mechanism disabled, sir. It's the opinion of Admiral Edwards and frankly... myself... that the device is defective. Our fish have enough problems. And although we did have a couple of prematures last patrol, the contact exploder seemed to function properly."

English frowned, "You know what BeauOrd has to say about that, Captain."

"Yes, sir," Turner said stiffly.

English relaxed slightly and even smiled thinly, "You're not the only one who has a poor opinion of them, Captain. But Admiral Nimitz and Admiral Edwards are friends, and I'll respect his wishes. However, the six fish we're giving you *do* have the magnetic feature installed."

"Yes, sir. Thank you, sir," Turner said and came to attention.

"All right, as you were," English said. "I'd like to see you two gentlemen in my office tomorrow at fourteen hundred. Enjoy your evening. I look forward to reading your reports."

With that, English walked back up the brow and spoke to several officers and chiefs there. They came aboard and introduced themselves to Turner and Begley as the relief crew.

"I thought we'd had it for sure, sir," Begley said to Turner as they headed up the brow themselves.

"Thank God for Big Dick Edwards," Turner said as he broke off and made a beeline for his family.

Joan and the kids smothered him with hugs and kisses, and within seconds, Art Turner forgot all about torpedoes and new guns and the morale issues that had plagued his boat since Begley and Pendergast had come aboard.

CHAPTER 9

ALEUTIAN ISLAND CHAIN

MAY 20, 1942

Although it was night, what limited night there was this far north, it wasn't entirely dark. Summer was coming to Alaska, and the days were long, and the nights lit by the ghostly glow of the Aurora Borealis. It was into this gentle glow that the monster rose, her enormous bulk parting the sea amidst a five-hundred-foot carpet of froth. Once her two great backbones were clear of the sea, the monster snorted great gouts of seawater, and then a noxious cloud of exhaust gases as her six diesel engines grumbled to life.

The experimental Imperial Japanese Navy submarine carrier *Ribaiasan*, *Leviathan* in English, moved slowly ahead and turned her bull-nose into the stiff northerly breeze that blew down over the island chain, chilled to the freezing point by its Arctic origins even in late May. The great ship's electronic eyes watched, and her electronic ears listened. Finally, after several minutes, movement began on her great upper deck as hatches opened and hangar doors parted. And men began to crawl over her like ants scrabbling on a hill.

Lieutenant Commander Ryu Osaka stepped onto the bridge of the great submarine and pulled his cold-weather jacket and stocking cap close around him. The near midnight air was bitterly cold, even colder than it had been in the Kurils. Osaka *hated* the cold. Yet as officer of the deck, it was his job to oversee this evolution.

Naturally, the captain would have scheduled this when Ryu was scheduled to go on watch. Heaven forbid the slothful bastard would drag his sorry ass out of his bunk on a frigid night to get any work done. No, that was the job of his loyal and dedicated *Yakuin*... executive officer.

At least the sea was relatively calm. The fifteen-knot breeze drew with it long rolling swells of six to eight feet. Good conditions for the launching of the ship's eight bomber/fighter floatplanes. Even after several weeks aboard what, to Osaka's mind, was the oddest ship he'd ever seen, he still had an occasional bout of incredulity. Such a ship seemed impossible... and yet here she was. The expression of a military mastermind's will. Conceived by Yamamoto's genius and forged by the fire of his personality.

The ship was unlike any other submarine Osaka had ever seen or even heard of. Her hull was sixteen meters in width, of which six of those meters were consumed by the ballast tanks. And her pressure hull, ten meters at her widest point, was not circular but rather an oblate tube. Although ten meters wide, she was only seven meters in height. Yet, she could still dive to over a hundred meters thanks to her thick steel, frames, and internal support substructures along her centerline.

Although far larger and more voluminous than even the largest American fleet submarine, the boat was still essentially comprised of two decks. The hull was divided, as all submarines were, by a platform deck that separated the living spaces above from the machinery and storage spaces below. The additional space was needed for her two extra diesels and electric motors, her one extra battery and the additional fuel, both for herself and her aircraft. The greater space was also needed for aircraft ordnance and accommodations for the additional men who comprised the air wing. All in all, a hundred fifty men and ten officers made up the crew of the world's largest submarine.

In many respects, she was similar to her standard sisters, with the exception of three additional compartments, bringing the total to eleven, not including the conning tower or the two great hangars that rode upon her broad back.

There was the forward torpedo room, of course, with its eight tubes. An impressive armament, although not truly meant for prolonged ship-to-ship engagements, as the boat was simply too ungainly to be as maneuverable as the smaller Japanese and American boats. Aft of this compartment was the forward battery compartment. Larger than most, due to the oversized one hundred ninety-two cell battery, it housed the officer's and chief's quarters, ship's office, officer's head and shower, and the wardroom. This included the ship's officers as well as accommodations for the air wing commander and senior officers.

There was the control room, of course, with additional space for the radio room and an office for the air wing commander. Here, an oversized gyro compass table allowed for both plotting of attack, charting, and coordination of the aircraft.

Next came the central and after battery rooms, each with batteries the size of the forward unit. The central battery compartment was the living quarters for the pilots, all junior officers, as well as a ready room. Two hatches gave direct access to the hangars above and allowed ordnance to be passed up from their storage lockers beneath the deck. Here, ammunition for the plane's wing-mounted machine guns and additional bombs were stored outboard of the battery.

Aft from here the layout of the submarine was similar to most boats. The after battery compartment being the crew's mess, bunk room, heads, and showers. Food storage was found below decks here, as well as the small arms and deck gun munitions lockers. Next came the fuel compartment, essentially a small section comprised mostly of aviation fuel and additional water and diesel storage for the boat. The only crew accommodation here was the eight-meter corridor and the ship's laundry facilities.

There were then three engine rooms, forward, central, and after. Each housed the massive eighteen-cylinder diesels and their connected generators, auxiliary generators, and desalinators. Aft of these was the large maneuvering room where the six massive electric motors, each one half again the size of those found on most submarines, drove the ship's twin propeller shafts. Finally, there was the small air crew's quarters. Here the support crew for the eight airplanes bunked, showered, and had their head. There was some auxiliary machinery here as well as the boatswain's locker. Although the air crews and submarine crews bunked separately, they ate and socialized together in the central battery compartment.

Ribaiasan was truly a marvel of engineering. Osaka only hoped that she'd live up to the great admiral's expectations.

"Good morning, *Yakuin*," Kaigun-Shosa, Lieutenant Commander Omata Hideki, said pleasantly as he emerged from the bridge hatch and took his place beside Osaka. "Midnight on the dot."

"It's a chilly morning, Omata," Ryu said pleasantly to the ship's air wing commander, or CAG. "Enough light for a sortie, eh?"

Although both men were of the same rank, each gave the other respect for their unique positions. As the XO, Osaka was only topped by the captain. As the commander of the air wing, Hideki was in charge of the entire flight operation. Osaka liked the other man, who was about his age. Hideki seemed level-headed and was quick to praise his men and conservative in his approach to discipline. At least *his* men were spared the captain's less humane attitudes.

"A glorious day, Ryu," Hideki said with a smile. "This will give the Yankee Doodles something to think about, eh?"

Osaka chuckled, "Indeed, Omata. Although..."

Hideki eyed him and raised his eyebrows in a question, "You see a problem with this morning's assault? You know as well as I that the Americans have but a handful of men stationed on Attu."

Osaka nodded, 'Oh, I have no doubt that your eight aircraft will make short work of the radar and weather station there. No, it's the *reaction* that concerns me."

Hideki nodded, "I see. You mean that when we attack in the next few weeks, this assault will bring about a greater response than if we simply waited and attacked as planned?"

"Precisely," Osaka said. "Consider Pearl Harbor. We certainly decimated the Pacific Fleet... yet the Americans were not stopped. Their boldness in the Coral Sea is proof."

"But what of Yamamoto's plans for Midway Atoll?" Hideki asked. "Surely this will finish the job of wiping their pitiful carrier fleet off the face of the map. The Kido Butai will make short work of them. Also, if you're right, they *will* reinforce Attu... meaning when we arrive in force, there will be that many more enemies crushed. It's said we cannot lose."

Osaka shrugged, "That's the plan. I certainly hope so. If the Americans are anything, they're resilient and tenacious."

"Which is why we attacked first," Hideki said with a grin. "Here's our first bird now."

"Impressively fast," Osaka praised.

To either side of them, men were hauling out the first plane from each hangar and getting the wings, rudder, and stabilizers unfolded. Each aircraft already had its bomb, this time a three-hundred-kilo device, and its floats readied. A crane located behind the conning tower with an extendible boom would lift each aircraft. Then the crews would attach the floats and the bomb and then the plane would be set down on one of the two catapults that dominated the submarine's foredeck. Readying each aircraft took only a short ten minutes, yet it meant that each pair would have to be launched before the next pair could be readied. Meaning that it took forty minutes to get the entire complement of eight airplanes into the sky. However, Omata and Ryu were working on ways to speed the process up.

The catapults were slightly offset so that two aircraft could be readied at the same time without their wings colliding. As the pilots and their bombardiers climbed into the small cockpits, a boiler in the forward engine room built up a head of steam for both units. A signalman stood at the bow of the ship, tethered to the deck. In his hands, he held two flags up.

"Control, bridge," Osaka said into the transmitter, "increase speed to all ahead full."

Although the ship had been submerged for a considerable amount of time, none of her six engines had been put on battery charge as yet. Every ounce of speed was needed to ensure proper takeoff for the airplanes. At fourteen knots and with the headwind of close to the same, the floatplanes had an additional thirty knots of apparent wind to add to the one hundred knots that the catapults imparted. That was more than enough to get them safely aloft.

Beside him, Omata Hideki activated a heavy-duty light mounted to the forward bridge rail. The green light came on, and almost immediately the signal officer lowered his left hand, or starboard side flag. Behind the two officers, another man, the launch and recovery officer, spoke into a hand-held radio.

"Catapult one, go!" the man said.

The machine shoved the plane forward, taking it from zero to a hundred fifty kilometers per hour in only two seconds. The steam screamed as the catapult car raced forward and slammed against the stops. The floatplane soared upward, lifting off the deck well before the end of its run.

Next, the signalman lowered his other flag, and the officer said, "Catapult two, go!"

The second aircraft was hurled into the glowing sky. Already, the next two were being hauled up and their remaining equipment attached. Soon the entire complement of eight birds was aloft and slowly circling over their mother ship at a hundred meters.

"Secure the hangars and cranes!" Hideki ordered.

"Clear the bridge!" Osaka ordered.

The clamshell doors on the nearly four-meter-wide hangars were sealed, the cranes folded down, and all of the men went below. The two ranking officers went down the bridge hatch into the blessed warmth of the conning tower. Hideki continued down into the control room to oversee the plot, and Osaka stayed in the conning tower to oversee the handling of the ship.

"Helm, reduce speed to all ahead one-third," Osaka stated. "Come right to course one-three-zero. Engineer, place engines one through four on battery charge."

By slowing down and turning toward Chichagof Bay, Osaka was minimizing the ship's radar profile. Of course, if anyone on Attu was paying attention, then they'd be more worried about the eight aircraft now coming in high over the bay.

"Staying on the surface, Ryu?" came the hard-edged voice of *Kaigun-Chusa*... commander... Hiro Kajamora, captain of the submarine.

The XO turned to see the captain climbing up through the hatch from the control room. Kajamora was of medium height and build with severely close-cropped black hair and a face that somehow lacked a sense of friendliness. His mouth seemed too wide, and the long knife scar that ran from just under his left eye and curved down to the tip of his chin added to his air of sternness.

Although the *Ribaiasan's* captain spoke casually, Osaka sensed a hint of reproach in the man's question. It was no secret that he wasn't in the Yamamoto camp, and that the forty-year-old Navy veteran was out to stamp his name on the Empire's history books. Being overly ambitious, Kajamora believed the same to be true of Osaka, and this often put the men at odds. Nothing overt, they both maintained the public respect due to the chain of command... yet there was certainly an underlying friction between them and the men aboard who tended to follow or idolize one or the other of the two highest-ranking officers.

"Little risk for this target," Osaka said. "There is little or nothing on Attu now. Intelligence reports a radar and weather station, a small garrison and a pair of anti-aircraft guns, and a single six-inch naval gun mounted as a battery. And, as you know, sir... we're *supposed* to be detected."

Kajamora ordered the search periscope raised and pressed his eye to the rubber eyepiece, "Our planes, yes, Yakuin... but not this secret submarine. Command wishes only that the Ame-kohs be startled by the appearance of two squadrons of aircraft and yet baffled as to their origin."

"Of course, sir," Osaka said. "To give the Americans the impression that it's here that our attack will come, not at the island of Midway."

"So, perhaps it's best if we dive to radar and radio depth," Kajamora said a bit haughtily. "Just to be sure that our glorious admiral's plan goes well... this time."

Osaka bristled at that. This was not the first time, nor would it be the last, that the arrogant prick would hint at his true opinion of Yamamoto's skill. Pearl Harbor hadn't been the great success it was touted to be... the Battle of the Coral Sea had ended with a rather mediocre outcome. Yamamoto's mighty Kido Butai was now down the *Shokaku* and the *Zuikaku,* not to mention the total loss of the *Shoho*.

Yes, the Americans, at least as far as anyone knew, had lost both *Lexington* and *Yorktown*. That meant that only two of their three remaining Pacific carriers were in any position to defend anything. Yet Kajamora had stated on the ship's more than two-thousand-kilometer voyage to the Aleutians that he thought this plan was as hair-brained as the very ship he commanded. Not that he expressed himself in such blatant terms... that would never be permitted... but if Kajamora was good at anything, it was implying derisiveness while *sounding* correct.

"I await your orders, *Kyaputen*," Osaka said and bowed slightly at the shoulders.

"I believe I just gave it, Osaka San," Kajamora condescended.

"*Hai*," Osaka replied briskly. "Diving officer, cancel battery charge. Close main induction. Standby to dive. Helm, all stop. Prepare to answer bells on batteries. Rig out dive planes."

"Diving planes rigged," the diving officer announced from below. "Main induction closed; we have a green board, Yakuin."

"Very good," Osaka said. "Open main ballast vents. Flood safety and port and starboard negative tanks. Make your depth one-five meters. Helm, all ahead one-third."

"Answering one-third on electrical propulsion," the helmsman announced.

"Dive to radar depth, aye," the diving officer announced.

The great ship moved slowly ahead, great whooshes of air pushing geysers of seawater from the ballast tanks on her sides as thousands of tons of seawater rushed in to take its place. Below decks, near the center of the ship, her two negative tanks... necessary due to her size... were flooded to help the vessel break the surface suction and submerge. Within a few moments, her great hangars were awash, and the ship was sinking deep enough so that only her radar and radio masts, as well as her extended periscopes, peeked above the surface of the sea.

"Fifteen meters!" the diving officer reported.

"Very good," Osaka said. "Close main vents. Adjust variable ballast to maintain depth. Zero bubble on stern planes, minimal rise on the bow planes."

"Well done, Osaka San," the captain said with a small smile playing on his lips. "It is as if you haven't been away from sea for more than a year."

"*Arigatou*, sir," Osaka managed to say without hinting at his inner irritation. "Do you wish to take the deck?"

"No, Yakuin, I believe I'll go below and observe the assault," Kajamora said and slid down the ladder.

For his part, Osaka was glad to be shot of him. He activated the overhead speaker and tuned it into the radio circuit so he could monitor the progress of the flight as well. A quick glance at the dead reckoning indicator and the chart desk told him that he could maintain this course for many hours before even entering Chichagof Bay. There was no shallow water anywhere close. Submerged and running at one-third as they were, the boat was only moving at three knots anyway.

"*Aviary, Condor flight... we are nearing the target now,*" came the voice of the first squadron leader.

"*Aviary, Hawk's flight... we are nearing target also,*" this was the second squadron leader.

"*What is your status and the disposition of target, Condor and Hawk?*" Hideki was asking the two squadrons where they were and the status of the American installation.

"*Condor flight, two thousand meters... All appears quiet. We have Hawk flight on port wing. Appears... there seems to be more here than reported... multiple anti-aircraft batteries and... small harbor being built complete with supply vessel and American destroyer. Repeat, Attu is more greatly fortified than reported.*"

"*Hawk flight, two thousand meters... Confirm enemy disposition. Condor flight, please take the honor of the first attack run.*"

"*Hawk and Condor flights, Aviary,*" Hideki said. "*Understood target disposition. Hawk's flight, you will shift target to harbor assets.*"

"*Hawk flight acknowledges...*"

"*Most gracious, Hawk One... Condor flight, form up, proceed to drop ordnance on primary targets... Banzai!*"

There were a few moments of intermittent static, shouting and the roar of aircraft engines over the open channel.

"*Aviary, Condor flight! Ordnance dropped! Hawk's flight, you are clear for your attack run!*"

An acknowledgement and another burst of chaotic sound. Multiple pilots' voices screaming in excitement and announcing the drop of their bombs. Static, roaring, and then an eerie silence.

"*Report Hawk and Condor,*" the CAG ordered.

"*Aviary, Condor One,*" the Condor squadron flight leader said. "*All ordnance released. Radar installation destroyed. Confirmed hit on barracks, motor pool and docking facility. Multiple explosions... estimate seventy percent of facility obliterated.*"

A cheer rose from the control room and was joined by the men in the conning tower. Osaka distinctly heard the captain's voice rise among the cacophony.

"Excellent! Have them strafe the remaining personnel!" Kajamora ordered.

"*Aviary! Aviary!*" This was the Hawk's flight leader. "*We are taking anti-aircraft fire from the ground and the destroyer escort!*"

"*I thought you eliminated the ships?*" Hideki asked.

A pause and then Condor leader replied, "*Negative, Aviary. Confirmed hit on support vessel and pier... the DE seems unharmed.*"

There was a thoughtful pause, and then Hideki ordered, *"Both flights, proceed with exfiltration plans. We shall offer worship at the temple of the sun."*

This last was code to tell the pilots to fly a pre-established looping course out over the Bering Sea and that the submarine would rendezvous with them in several hours. Long enough to get far away from land should the American vessel get underway to try and find the aircraft carrier that must have launched the planes.

Of course, there would be no carrier. That was one of the points Yamamoto had made, and one of the *Ribaiasan's* greatest psychological weapons. She could send eight aircraft over the horizon, seemingly from nowhere, to attack a target. The planes would then vanish back over the horizon again like smoke and simply vanish.

Of course, recovery of the aircraft took more than twice as much time as launching them, as each plane must be lifted from the sea, its floats detached and then the airfoils folded so that it could be slid back into the hangar tubes.

This generally necessitated launch and recovery from several hundred kilometers away. Since the floatplanes had a range of a thousand kilometers, this was generally not an issue. This time, however, they'd launched only fifty kilometers from their target.

Kajamora's head appeared in the hatchway near Osaka's feet, "Bring us to our preset course for rendezvous, Osaka... you do remember the procedure?"

It took a great deal of willpower for the *Yakuin* not to lash out with his booted foot and smash it into the smirk that played on the captain's face. Instead, he grinned down at him.

"Of course, sir... as it was *I* who laid it out," Osaka stated serenely. "Of course, as you wished to launch so closely, we will now have to run on the surface in order to maintain the required fourteen knots of speed to make the rendezvous point in less than three hours. Do I have your permission to do so?"

Kajamora might be a snide, self-serving peacock, but he was not stupid. Although Osaka's tone had been nothing but respectful, the rebuke it contained did not go unnoticed. However, the captain couldn't openly reproach his executive officer since the words and tone had been correct.

"Very well, *Yakuin*," Kajamora said. "And since you've done such a fine job, I wish you to take *my* upcoming watch as well. To maintain the continuity of command until the evolution is completed."

"Of course, Captain," Osaka said pleasantly. "Thank you. I was going to make that request."

Kajamora frowned and disappeared down the hatchway. Osaka felt that he'd won a small victory. Kajamora had tried to punish him for his insolence, yet Osaka didn't find standing two back-to-back watches a punishment at that time. The captain, in his ill-considered way, had been correct. Osaka felt better with himself in charge of the entire mission than letting Kajamora run it in his careless way.

He'd nearly gotten the pilots killed with his inconsiderate order to strafe. It was not his place, but Hideki's. Although the American AA response would no doubt have been limited, it wouldn't do to lose a plane or two at this juncture in their operation.

"Well done, sir," the junior officer of the watch said as he climbed into the conning tower.

Osaka permitted himself a small smile. The younger man was on his side, one of the officers in his camp, and who held a low opinion of Kajamora.

"A simple operation," Osaka said lightly. "Helm, all ahead standard. Diving officer, prepare to surface the boat and rig for surface running. When we do, I want to run at four-engine speed. Put one and two on charge. I'm sure our battery levels need attention?"

"Sixty-two percent," The JOOD said.

"Very well," Osaka said.

Omata Hideki appeared in the conning tower now and stood by his friend, "Cleverly done, Ryu. You should have seen his face when he stalked forward. You really got his goat."

Osaka shrugged and, in a low voice, said, "A small victory, Omata... perhaps a little childish, but childishly satisfying."

CHAPTER 10

PEARL HARBOR

MAY 21, 1942

"Come on in, Art, Mr. Begley," Bob English said as he greeted the two officers at the heavy oaken door. "We've got quite a little pow-wow going on here."

The conference room was dominated by a large glossy table already strewn with papers. On a sideboard, a chief yeoman was setting up a coffee service. At the head of the table sat Admiral Chester Nimitz himself, with two officers, commanders both, to either side of him. There were two empty seats on the near side of the table into which English steered the two submariners. He then went and sat across in an empty seat between one of Nimitz's aides and a man in a civilian suit that Turner knew all too well.

"If it isn't Webster Clayton," Turner said. "Why am I not surprised?"

Clayton smiled, "Good to see you again, Art."

"Captain Turner, Mr. Begley," Nimitz boomed. "These are my aides, Commander John Knox, and Commander Ed Layton. Everybody get comfy; we've got a lot to go over."

"Captain Turner, I met your wife this morning," Layton offered. "A sharp lady. I think she'll add a lot to the crypto team."

Turner smiled, "Me too, sir."

"Joan is working with Ultra," Clayton stated. It wasn't a question. He wasn't even surprised. "Quite a gal that one. You fellas ought to offer her a commission."

"We are," the last man at the other end of the table said. Although he was wearing standard khakis and not his robe and slippers, Turner recognized him.

"I think you already know Commander Rochefort," Layton said to Turner.

"We've met," Turner said, shaking the man's hand. "Pleasure to see you again, sir. This is my XO, Tom Begley."

The yeoman began passing out coffee, and everyone got settled. Nimitz cleared his throat and folded his hands on top of the table.

"Let's lay it out right now," Nimitz said. "Yamamoto is coming for our carriers, and I want to know where the *hell* that's going to be. And I want to know *when* in the hell that's going to be, Joe."

This last was directed at Rochefort. The commander with the tousled hair didn't seem much discommoded by the senior admiral's tone, "I'm almost certain it's Midway Atoll, sir."

"And Washington... OP-20-G at any rate... thinks it's going to be the Aleutians," Clayton stated.

Rochefort snorted derisively.

Turner saw Layton smirk and Nimitz raise an eyebrow before asking, "Got any evidence to back you up, Joe?"

"Because *we* do," Clayton stated.

Rochefort raised his brows now, "What proof?"

"Early this morning," Clayton said, holding up a sheet of paper. "The radar station and garrison on Attu Island was attacked from the air. At least eight aircraft dropped as many bombs. Took out the radar, blew up half the barracks, destroyed a storehouse, and took out all but a single deuce-and-a-half truck. The supply ship supporting the construction of a dock facility in the harbor was heavily damaged. Salvageable... but still. The destroyer escort assigned there put to sea within an hour but so far has found no sign of a carrier."

"Was it a carrier attack?" Begley asked.

"Had to be," English put in. "How the hell else would they get all the way out there from any base they've got?"

"The destroyer would've found a carrier," Layton stated. "But they haven't seen any sign of it."

"That doesn't prove that AF is the Aleutians," Rochefort insisted. "Admiral... the way Yamamoto talks about the target... it just doesn't fit the bill."

"It would be a good place to invade the U.S., sir," Begley offered. "A foothold at any rate."

"I thought there was next to nothing on Attu," Turner observed. "Why would the Japs even bother?"

Clayton grimaced, "*Officially*, it's just a weather station... but we've been shoring it up for just such an occurrence."

"And now the Japanese have better intel on it," Turner noted.

"Either way, Attu probably will be a target sooner or later," the other aide put in, "which is why Washington thinks it's AF."

"I'm not as convinced as OP-20-G," Clayton tried to mollify Rochefort. "I know of Commander Rochefort's successes. He does have a point... but the attack on Attu has raised another issue, and it's primarily *that* which necessitates you and your XO being here, Art."

"Another secret mission, Web?" Turner asked wryly.

"Like the one where you bagged two U-boats, a tin can, and a Q-ship?" Nimitz asked with a grin. "By the way, Commander... I only saw three Nazi flags and a rising sun. How come you didn't paint the fourth swastika?"

Turner shrugged, "Well... one of the U-boats was a milk cow. Basically unarmed... I dunno, sir... seemed a little pretentious."

"I'd have painted it," Begley said. "And honestly, sir... maybe we still should."

Turner only shrugged and lit a cigarette, "So, what's the mission this time, Web?"

Clayton pulled several eight by ten glossy photos from his briefcase and passed them out to everyone around the table. Turner looked at the fuzzy images and frowned at them.

"What the hell is this, Mr. Clayton?" Knox asked.

"A whale or something?" Layton added.

"Doesn't look like anything I'm familiar with," Begley said. "Bad photography..."

"That came via a Russian spy," Clayton said. "Operating in the Kuril Island chain. What do you say, Art?"

Turner peered closer, "Well... it could be a ship... although it's sort of... is... is it a submarine, Web?"

Clayton grinned, "It is. Our intelligence says that Yamamoto is testing a new kind of boat. A submarine aircraft carrier. Even now, a class is being developed secretly in Japan."

"So, this is some kind of prototype?" Nimitz asked.

"We're not sure," Clayton admitted. "From the way my man described it... it's big. *Really* big. Those two tubular things on top are aircraft hangars."

"Aircraft...?" Begley asked in disbelief.

"My God..." Turner breathed, the full implications of what he was seeing hitting home. "The Japs could send this damned thing right up to our coast and launch attacks, and we wouldn't know about it until the damned planes flew over the beach!"

"That's precisely our worry," Clayton said. "Long term. In the short term, it's my considered opinion that Commander Rochefort is right about AF. I think the attack on Attu this morning was a red herring. I think it was *this* thing that hit them... and I think Yamamoto is going to send her our way next. He needs to finish what he started in December."

"Attack Pearl Harbor, you mean?" Begley scoffed. "Come on, Mr. Clayton. We're *ready* for it now. No puffed-up submarine with a couple of floatplanes is going to be able to finish what the entire damned Jap carrier fleet couldn't even do!"

Nimitz frowned but let Clayton reply. The Office of Strategic Services agent scowled at Begley. Rather than address him directly, however, he lit his own cigarette and looked at Turner.

"I think this boat is headed for AF," Clayton said. "To reinforce the Kido Butai. I think that in a peripheral way, Yamamoto is going to use this thing to hedge his bets. I don't know how... but that's our thinking."

"And you want *Bull Shark* to stop them," Turner said flatly.

"You do have some experience in that sort of thing," Clayton said with a grin.

"Can I bring Joanie along to take the helm again?" Turner asked with a chuckle.

Nimitz looked surprised, "What? Your wife?"

Clayton laughed, "That's right, Admiral. After rescuing Joan Turner, she was aboard *Bull Shark* for her final battle with the Nazis. Even took the wheel for a while and acted as periscope assistant."

"Hot damn!" Nimitz boomed. "I've got to meet this girl. Looks like you've got yourself a real war hero, Joe."

"True enough," Rochefort said with a grin. "She's even gotten herself a Presidential Commendation."

"Is there anything more you can tell us about this boat, Mr. Clayton?" Begley asked, trying to get the discussion back on track. He seemed to bristle whenever his submarine's previous actions were mentioned. As if his not being there were some sort of a slight on him.

"Only that she's got a very long range," Clayton said. "She's almost five hundred feet long and weighs as much as three fleet submarines. She's a monster and has six forward tubes, Art. Two AA guns and a five inch forward of her conning tower. She's probably not fast or maneuverable, but she's got some pretty sharp fangs."

Begley chuffed, "Not after *Bull Shark* gets ahold of her."

"Glad to hear the confidence, Lieutenant," Nimitz said. "If that's all, I'll let you gents get back to work. I still want proof of AF's identity, Joe. And *fast*, for Christ's sake."

Everyone rose and shook hands. Just before leaving, Clayton took Turner aside, "Good luck, Art. I think you're going to need it."

He cast a quick glance at Begley, who was chatting with Layton. Turner nodded and shrugged, "Thanks, Web."

"We'll be in touch," Clayton said. "With whatever data I can get for you. Good hunting."

———

"They made you a code cracker," Turner said proudly.

He and Joan were readying their small house for the officer's dinner party they were throwing that evening. Joan had been saving some of her ration tickets since she'd arrived and had managed to do some wheeling and dealing and obtained two huge six-pound corned beefs from the base stores along with two large stock pots to cook them in. The potatoes, carrots, and cabbage were easy to come by, vegetables not being rationed as yet. Enough to feed ten.

Although Turner wasn't much of a hand at cooking, he'd offered to go on spud patrol. Joan was preparing the two huge pots and the meat inside while he peeled almost ten pounds of taters and half-again as many carrots.

"Yeah... Joe Finnegan, remember him? I was having lunch with him and Gladys last Sunday. Turns out the crypto department has a real puzzler, and they want to try using computers... lady code breakers like they have in England... to decipher the Japanese time and date system," Joan explained.

"Well, I'll be..." Turner marveled. "So, you'll be working at the base?"

"Yes, with Joe and his entire team, including Commander Rochefort."

Turner nodded, "Well, that's great, Joanie. Look at you... submarine combat veteran and spymaster."

"So, it's okay with you?"

He looked up from his carrot, "Of course... why wouldn't it be?"

Joan shrugged, "Well, you know how a lot of men are. 'No woman of mine is gonna work...'"

Turner scoffed, "Joanie, you know I'm not that kind of man. While you're a great cook, keep a neat house, and are a wonderful mom...

you're also smart and tough. There's a lot to you, and you're certainly far more than just Art Turner's wife. If this is something you want to do, and it challenges you and lets you use your full potential... I'm all about it, honey."

She smiled broadly at him, "That's a very progressive attitude in this year of our Lord nineteen hundred and forty-two, Arthur Turner."

"Oh, I'm a terrific guy... everyone in the engine rooms says so."

They both laughed, and Joan came over and put her arms around him, "Thanks, Arty. I love you."

"I love you too, doll... now, what's the big project?' he asked after kissing her and going back to his peeling. "Or do I not have the proper clearance."

She narrowed her eyes at him, "I could tell you... but then I shall have to liquidate you!"

He sighed, "Well... okay... but it better be pretty darn interesting then."

She chuckled, "There's an impending Japanese attack coming in the next couple of weeks. The higher-ups are arguing over where they think it's going to be."

Turner nodded, "That's what I was told just before we left New London. Yamamoto wants to smash what's left of our carriers with his own. Sort of finish what he started here in December. That's your new boss's idea, too. Met him this morning at my meeting with Nimitz."

Joan nodded, "So, you already know the problem. It's our job to figure out the right answer and do it yesterday."

"I agree with Rochefort that it's Midway," Turner said. "It's pretty much a fly spec, but it's in a good location. If the Japs took it... we'd be in trouble."

Joan smiled. "The trouble is that staff wants *proof* before they commit our forces."

Turner grinned at her, "Listen to you, Captain Turner."

"That's *Lieutenant* Turner, mister... they drafted me; can you believe that?"

Turner laughed, "I most certainly can. Congratulations! By the way, did Frank and Joe's wives arrive?"

"Sure, they came over with me," Joan said. "And you'll never guess who arrived just yesterday on a liner from San Diego... April. Remember Andy Post's girl in New London?"

Turner grinned, "I do. Guess they must be serious."

"Looks that way," Joan said. "He hasn't done it yet, but April thinks Andy's going to propose."

"I hope so," Turner said. "She seemed a good fit for him. Quite a firebrand that one."

The corned beef and cabbage dinner at the Turners' started out well. With the addition of May Dutch, June Nichols, and the beaming April Olsen, the "spring girls" were back together and brought a great deal of vitality to the gathering.

Even Begley and Pendergast were on their best behavior. They smiled, told stories about their naval careers... being careful to avoid any mention of Elmer Williams, and had brought a case of beer and two bottles of wine with them.

"So, April," Pat Jarvis asked as he smashed real butter into his vegetables, "if I remember right, you were working as a secretary for a lawyer in Hartford or something, right? Do you have something lined up out here?"

"Well..." April, a tall and busty blonde about Andy Post's age and height, said a little hesitantly, "I've got some money saved and found a little apartment here with two other girls. I'm hoping to find something in Honolulu at least until Andy and I... well, until things progress."

"Oh, yeah?" Turner asked, grinning at his communications officer. "Are there signs of progress, Andy?"

Post's boyish face flushed crimson, and he cleared his throat, "Well..."

"Hey, you two get hitched, and then she won't have to search for a new job, Post," Pendergast said good-naturedly, hoisting a can of beer. His fifth of the evening.

April glanced at him, "Oh? Why's that, Mr. Pendergast?"

Pendergast didn't catch the edge in her tone, "Well, you won't need to work. I know I wouldn't want *my* wife takin' a job. Plenty to do keeping house, am I right, guys?"

Begley chuckled, but even he had sensed that his friend had tweaked the young lady.

"Guess a woman going to work kind of grates against your sensibilities, Burt?" Joan asked pleasantly but with a hint of edge in her own tone.

"Well..." Pendergast expounded, "it's just not right... the woman's place is in the home. Up to her man to bring home the bacon. Just like you and the skipper here, Joan."

"So, how was the trip over on the liner, ladies?" Jarvis attempted to deflect with a charming smile.

"No, no, Pat," May Dutch said, patting his hand, "let's hear more about a woman's role. I'm very curious to learn what the new officers have to say about it."

June Nichols blushed slightly and hid a smirk behind her napkin. Her husband aimed a knowing smile at Pat Jarvis.

"Well, Burt," April said with a frosty smile of civility playing on her full lips, "it might surprise *you* to learn that Joan and Art don't have a problem with a woman going to work. It so happens that Joanie here is working for the Navy now."

Pendergast blinked in surprise and polished off his beer, "How's that?"

"Not just working for them," Joan said with a twinkle in her blue eyes. "I'm now a Lieutenant junior grade attached to the cryptographic section. What do you think of that, Burt? How about you, Tom?"

Jarvis snickered and ate a huge bite of corned beef. Turner only watched. He was curious to see how this would play out.

"A woman in the Navy!" Burt blurted.

"Well... I'm sure it's only honorary or something, right?" Begley asked. "They don't allow women to serve."

"What about women accepted for voluntary emergency service... WAVEs?" May asked.

"Well..." Pendergast said, "that's different..."

"Well, it's a fact," Joan said. "So, I'm afraid, gents, that you're just going to have to stick that in your pipes and smoke it! Anybody for seconds?"

"Aw, hell..." Pendergast said, muffling a burp. "I didn't mean to start anything, Joan... how about another beer, huh? I'm empty. Anybody else?"

"Yeah, I could use one," Jarvis said. "Tom?"

"Sure," Begley said, sounding a bit relieved that the conversation was shifting.

"Come on, boys," Jarvis said, indicating Burt and Tom. "Let's the three of us go out in the kitchen and fetch another round. Skipper? Andy? Frank? Joe? How about you ladies? More wine?"

The tension that had been building seemed to lessen. Turner was grateful for Pat taking the men out of the room. He could clearly see that Andy Post was beginning to look irritated.

April smiled smugly as the three men left, "Woman's place is in the home...? That how you feel, hon?"

Post shook his head, "Not me, honey."

Out in the kitchen, Pat opened the fridge and pulled out a half dozen beers and a full bottle of white wine. He began to open it and speared the two men with a hard glare.

"What, you got a problem, Jarvis?" Pendergast asked. He was clearly moving well into a strong buzz.

"Yeah, I've got a problem, Burt," Jarvis said and included Begley in his glare. "Since the two of you came aboard, you've been nothing but a royal pain in the ass. And I'm telling you now, it needs to *stop*."

Begley sneered, "You're just still pissed off about that night at Lucky's. It was months ago, Pat. Hell, I ain't even with Elmer's girl anymore."

"It's not just that," Jarvis said. "You ride everybody on the boat. You criticize everyone, and me and the other officers, and quite a few of the men, have noticed that the two of you have loose tongues."

"You're talking to a superior officer, Jarvis," Begley said. "You watch your mouth."

Jarvis stepped forward and into the two men's personal space, "Like you said the first time we met, Tom... we're not on duty. We're all lieutenants here. And just among us O3s... I'm telling you this because the two of you are *fucking up* our boat's morale. You need to lighten up and get with the program."

Pendergast leaned in and glared back, "You're just pissed off cuz you didn't get Williams's slot, Jarvis. He didn't deserve it in the first place, and from what I seen... you don't either."

"The skipper has warned you both," Jarvis said evenly. "I've heard it."

Pendergast snorted, "Old Mr. Softy, you mean?"

Begley didn't agree, but he didn't protest, either.

"That's his way," Jarvis said. "Captain Turner is an easy man to work for. You do your job right and he's quick to praise. You make a mistake and he'll let it slide the first time. Give you a chance to straighten out. But I'm telling you both, you keep up the shit, and he'll come down on you like a ton of bricks. We got a good boat, and none of us want the two of you screwing it up. So, you knock off riding the men. You cut out singling out the Black men, Hispanic men, and Freddy Swooping Hawk, for that matter. You got a problem with race, keep it in your racks."

"You don't tell me what to do, gunner," Begley said dangerously. "I'm the XO in this crew, got me?"

Pendergast chuckled derisively.

"Not for long, you don't knock those chips off your shoulders. And if I have to, the three of us will go out on the after deck one evening or in a convenient alley on base, and *I'll* knock 'em off for ya'," Jarvis said. He picked up three beers in his large hands and levelled a hard look at Pendergast. "And you might want to lay off the suds tonight before you go and make a bigger ass of yourself."

With that, the big man turned and stalked back out into the dining room. The two men looked at each other and frowned.

"Think he's gonna be a problem?" Burt asked.

Tom sighed, "He's *already* a problem. This whole fuckin' boat is, Burt. But you and me... you and me are gonna fix it. We probably ought to excuse ourselves for now, though."

"This party's just gettin' started," Burt said, cracking another beer. "That April broad is a looker, huh? What do you think it'd take to get her away from that kid?"

Begley clapped him on the shoulder, "Take it easy, Burt. There'll be plenty of time to make waves, but not just yet. Let's you and me blow this snore fest and go out and have some real fun, huh? I know a great place down near the waterfront with some broads that are *real* fun."

Burt chuckled, "After curfew?"

Tom grinned, and they went back into the dining room.

"Thank you for a nice dinner, Mrs. Turner," Begley said respectfully. "I think Burt and I will shove off, though. Sorry if we overstepped our bounds any."

"Yeah... sorry if I shot my mouth off," Burt followed his friend's lead. "I didn't mean anything, April, Andy. Guess maybe I've had one too many."

"Oh, think nothing of it," Joan said pleasantly. "Thank you for coming."

Everyone said goodbye, but Turner didn't miss the hard look that Jarvis levelled at the two men as they left. Although he hadn't overheard the conversation in the kitchen, everyone had heard the hard sound in Jarvis's muffled voice. Something told the skipper that his torpedo officer had warned the two men just as he'd warned Begley... just not quite as pleasantly.

CHAPTER 11

PEARL HARBOR SUBMARINE BASE

MAY 22, 1942

Due to the situation, both the impending Japanese offensive and the desire to try and find the mysterious submarine carrier, *Bull Shark* hadn't been allowed her two weeks of rest and relaxation... again. The last time, nobody had minded. The patrol to find the Nazis had been shorter than a standard one, and the men were anxious to get out to Pearl and start fighting the "real" war.

This time, however, they weren't as gung-ho. The mood of the boat had altered considerably since leaving New London. Although everyone behaved properly and did their jobs with their usual professionalism, the overall happiness of the ship had been dampened. Perhaps not eliminated, but certainly it wasn't riding high. The skipper thought that perhaps once they heard about their mission, it might improve morale. A good old-fashioned combat patrol was something submariners lived for.

The eastern sky was just lightening from deep indigo to a softer blue as the boat left the submarine base. The men not on duty were once again lined up on deck in their dungarees in respect of the dead ships in the harbor. Hickam Field was already active, and two squadrons of

Douglas SBD Dauntless dive bombers roared close overhead as they flew out to sea on training maneuvers.

"I like the new toy," Pendergast was saying to Wendell Freeman, quartermaster of the watch.

"Yes, sir," Freeman said, concentrating heavily on the ship's progress through the harbor.

As a seaman first-class who was not yet rated, Freeman took his job seriously. He was striking for quartermaster's mate, and with the Captain and the XO on deck, he wanted to make a good impression. Anybody could con a boat out in the middle of the ocean, but here in a large and crowded harbor with winding channels, it was a challenge.

Yes, the officer of the deck had the responsibility, but it was Freeman's job to pass maneuvering orders down to the helmsman. It was also his job to gently but firmly *correct* for any deficiencies in the OODs commands, should there be any. And while Freeman liked the two new officers... they treated him well... he felt that Pendergast was a bit of a slacker. This opinion was shared by the engine snipes, too. The man seemed eager to let others do his work for him. And although Freeman himself hadn't seen this, he'd heard that the man was also quick to criticize the way others hauled on his slack.

"I say we go head-to-head against another DD topside now," Begley said from behind the two men on the bridge.

Turner chuckled politely. "Now that we've got two five-inchers, huh? Who knows, Tom... who knows?"

Ahead of them, the net tender was hauling the submarine net that blocked the harbor open for *Bull Shark* to pass out into the Pacific. Beyond, the *Perry Wilson,* an old World War One four-pipe destroyer, waited to escort the submarine out to sea.

"We've reached the submarine netting, sir," Wendell said to no one in particular, although he knew the two other officers would hear. It did have the effect of pulling Pendergast's attention back to his job, though.

"Very well," Pendergast said loftily. "Sound the acknowledgement blast."

Freeman gave the order for the conning tower to blow the ship's horn in a quick two-blast signal to the net tender. The men on the tender waved their hats in the air and whooped and whistled to the submarine and wished them good hunting.

"We're clear the harbor, Captain," Pendergast said.

"Very well," Turner replied. "Signal the DD we're ready to go to sea."

Wendell raised the signal gun to his shoulder and squeezed off the signal. Aboard the destroyer, a man on the signal bridge replied, and the sleek ship turned away, putting her stern to *Bull Shark*, and increasing her speed.

"All ahead standard," Pendergast ordered.

The order was relayed, and the submarine's big diesels growled as the boat's bow wave grew into a frothing bone.

"Helm reports speed is fifteen knots," Wendell reported.

"Very well," Pendergast said.

"Good to be at sea again, eh, XO?" Turner asked casually.

"Yes, sir, although the men might not be happy," Begley replied. "For my part, and for Burt there, too, we didn't really need any R and R."

Turner sighed, "Well... we'll get some after this patrol. Even if it's at Midway."

Down in the after battery compartment, Electrician First Class Doug Ingram was being shown to his bunk by Paul "Buck" Rogers, the chief of the boat. Ingram had come aboard that morning as a last-minute assignment to the submarine. Although he'd never served in subs before, only on surface ships, he was told by his friend, Steve Plank, that it would be better duty. The two of them had heard about the good food and higher pay.

Steve Plank was a seaman who'd recently been promoted to third-class petty, was officially rated boatswain's mate, and was going to be bunking in the after torpedo room. Steve hadn't served aboard boats either, and Doug felt it was nice to have somebody he knew among so many strange faces.

They'd both been pleasantly surprised when they'd heard that two officers they'd both served with were aboard as well. One was the XO, and one was the assistant engineer. Although Doug didn't know them quite as well as Steve, Steve had assured Doug that with Begley and Pendergast aboard, they were on easy street. Doug was glad of that. It meant fresh ground and a whole new world of prospects.

"Nice thing about this boat," the COB was saying as he pointed out the top bunk in a rack that was four high, "is you get your own rack. No hot-bunking on *Bull Shark*."

Doug was used to the stacks of bunks on Navy ships. He'd served aboard a destroyer, and it hadn't been much different. Even aboard a big heavy cruiser, the space was limited. Yet when he looked at the coffin-sized space he was to sleep in, he frowned dubiously. Rogers must have noticed and chuckled. He patted the twenty-five-year-old seaman on his shoulder. Ingram was a fairly large man. About as tall as Rogers's own six feet but not quite as bulky.

"I know it looks cramped, kid," Rogers was saying, "but don't let it fool ya. You got your own locker here, and every bunk has a reading light and its own AC vent. You'll get used to it. Couple of days and you'll be good buddies with all these guys, and you sure won't mind the chow. We got a good skipper and a good wardroom. If you're itching to fight... then you signed on the right boat."

Doug managed a friendly smile, "Glad to hear that, Chief. This is kinda new to me and Steve..."

"No worries," COB said. "I know you and Plank already know Mr. Begley and Mr. Pendergast. Our electrical officer, Mr. Dutch, is a good dude. You'll be under him, obviously. Our chief electrician's mate, Chief Harry Brannigan, can be a hard-ass, but he's fair."

"Thanks, Chief," Doug said, hefting his small seabag and looking at the tiny locker and mentally trying to figure out how to stow his gear in the bread box. As he was doing so, another young man walked up and smiled. He was a little shorter than Ingram and muscular and had jet black hair and a ruddy complexion.

"Here you go, Doug," the COB said. "This is fireman Fred Swooping Hawk. He's bunking right below you. Freddy, this is Doug Ingram. New to us and to the boats. Specializes in juice and motors. Doug, Fred here is an ace machinist, crack shot, and hell of a lookout. Show Doug how we pack a locker on *Bull Shark*, huh, Freddy? Good luck, Doug, and welcome aboard."

"Kind of a puzzle, ain't it," Rogers heard Swooping Hawk say as he headed aft. He shook his head and grinned. The kid was in for a shock, coming from tin cans to a submarine. He passed through both engine rooms where men worked tending the four massive General Motors sixteen hundred horsepower diesels and the auxiliary generator. He then passed into the maneuvering room where Ensign Andy Post leaned against the after bulkhead watching the electricians work at their panels. On the padded bench in front of the control cubicle, Chief Electrician's Mate Harry Brannigan lounged with his bare sandaled foot propped negligently against the frame.

"How's it goin', COB?" Brannigan asked when he saw Rogers duck through the forward bulkhead hatch.

"Just getting some new recruits squared away, Harry," Buck said. "Where's Mr. Dutch?"

"Forward overseeing battery inspection," Post said. "I just like the smells back here."

"Yeah, lube oil and a nice waft after somebody comes outta the head," Brannigan jibed.

Rogers chuckled, "You look like you're makin' some good music on that piano, Harry."

"Doin' my best," Brannigan said and elbowed the electrician beside him, "if'n I can get around this asshole's bulk to do it."

Sherman "Tank" Broderick elbowed him back. "You ain't exactly got a narrow ass yourself, Chief."

"You two are like an old married couple," Rogers teased. "You should think of poor Mr. Post here. Don't give him cold feet about matrimony, for Chrissakes!"

That got a big laugh from the men in the room. Post grinned broadly as Rogers walked over and stuck out his hand to congratulate him.

"How's it feel being engaged, sir?" Rogers asked.

"Crazy, Buck, crazy," Post said. "Can't believe she said yes."

"Oh, come on, sir," Brannigan said over his shoulder. "You're a great catch... just ask any of these juice jerkers."

Another big laugh. Rogers was glad to hear that. There hadn't been as much of that over the past few weeks. He grinned and ducked into the after torpedo room.

To Rogers, this was the most crowded part of the ship. Although a large space, large enough for four torpedo reloads, loading gear and bunks for a dozen guys, it seemed that every square inch of space was planned exactly... which, of course, it was. In addition to the torpedoes, the bunks and the men, the boatswain's locker took up the forward starboard corner, further eating into the space. As if that weren't enough, the small after escape trunk took up another corner.

In this space lived a dozen men, most of whom were assigned to the room during battle stations torpedo. When not in combat, though, the men stood watch at other stations doing jobs that included everything from auxiliary machinery to weapons to equipment servicing and even general housekeeping. Like every other man on the boat, the men who lived in after torpedo worked with varying degrees of dedication on studying and training to acquire their coveted silver dolphins. A pin was worn to show that they were fully sub-qualified.

Like the officer's gold version, the dolphins told everyone that a man could literally do any job on the submarine, from line handling to periscope watch, from repairing electrical and engine machinery to firing the five-inch. It was a source of great pride, and along with the submarine combat pin most everybody on board wore, along with the boat's own posted unit citation, it gave the *Bull Shark* crew a sense of unity and family unlike any other type of ship.

Now, the men who were off watch, eight in all, lounged in the room. Amazing how men could get used to the noise of engines, even two compartments away from where the rock crushers rumbled loudly. Some men lay in their bunks reading or studying manuals, and a trio was set up on stools around a collapsible table playing Acey-Deucy. One man, a medium height guy with a wrestler's build, was unpacking his seabag into one of the dozen small lockers provided to the men. He was about thirty years old and had curly blonde hair and a handsome face. The man turned when he caught sight of Rogers entering the room and stopped what he was doing, letting the bag hang on his shoulder from its strap.

Did it seem as if the man moved a little too quickly? Rogers couldn't be sure, but he thought he sensed something. He dismissed it immediately though when the new man smiled broadly.

"Come to get me tucked in, COB?" Steve Plank asked gregariously.

Rogers smiled and stuck out his big hard hand, "You got it, mate. I know we met on deck, but I figured I'd come back and do it more friendly-like. Paul Rogers. The guys call me Buck. Welcome aboard."

Plank chuckled, "Buck Rogers, huh? Thanks, Chief. Kind of a new experience for me, this submarine jazz... but I'm looking forward to it."

"Understand you worked as torpedoman aboard a tin can recently," Rogers stated.

"Yeah," Plank replied. "But it ain't the same. There you just turn your turret out and shoot them fish off. Any angle solving was done by the torpedo director, and the ship herself was aimed. Just shoot a shit-load in a fan and hope for the best! Kind of lookin' forward to learning the ropes here."

"Well, you got a good room leader in Murph," Rogers said.

"Yeah, seems like a good guy," Plank stated.

"You all set here?" Rogers asked, indicating the open locker. "I know it's not much space. We've got extra stowage in the pump room and both of the battery compartments below deck. Basically, you pack your locker, and then we stow the sea bags in the lockers there. There should be room in the after battery locker. It's abaft the cold locker beneath the mess. If not, I know we got some space in the pump room. Somebody will show you where when you're ready."

"Thanks much, Chief," Plank said pleasantly. "Think I'll find it myself. I'm the boatswain's mate... should probably do a tour above and below the platform deck so I know where everything is."

Rogers chuckled, "Steve... you're the *boatswain* on this tub. Closest thing we've had to one has been me. Your locker, in fact, is just here forward. Might want to go through it while we're en route to... wherever we're going."

"Oh," Plank said, sounding pleased. "Well, terrific. I'll do that, thanks again, COB. So, will we ever find out where we're headed?"

Rogers grinned, "When the skipper deems it necessary, he'll fill us in. Again, welcome to the *Bull Shark.*"

"Appreciate that," Plank said and went back to his unpacking.

When the broad back of the COB vanished through the compartment hatch, another smile appeared on Plank's face. This one wasn't quite as open and friendly. It might be described more as self-satisfied. Here he'd been wondering how to handle certain things, and the damned chief of the boat had laid the perfect solution in his lap. Two perfect solutions, in fact.

Because as an electrician who had knowledge of electric motors, Doug Ingram would be stationed in and have access to the motor room. This area, located beneath the maneuvering room, was where the submarine's four big GE motors lived and where they turned the two prop shafts. Not only were there tool and parts storage lockers down there, but Plank knew there would be quite a few little nooks and crannies he could use.

Between Doug's access, his own boatswain's locker, and the additional storage areas forward, Plank knew that he'd have plenty of room to set up and run his little black-market business. It didn't matter what type of ship and in what theater, a sailor was a sailor was a sailor. And all sailors liked three things above all others... dollars, drink, and dames. There was one other thing that many of them liked, especially those in high-stress environments.

Dope...

Whether it was the occasional reefer, some heavy prescription opioids, or even the hard dust, some seaman needed their fixes, and when they found out that Papa Plank could get it for them... well, that made for a very profitable little cruise indeed.

Of course, it wasn't easy. A man who wanted to run an operation like that had to be well placed, and he had to have connections. Fortunately, Steve Plank had both. He was the boatswain on a submarine... which meant that he was in charge of lines and rigging. Hardly had much use for either on a sub, he thought to himself with bemusement, so the locker would be plenty safe.

He also knew that Burt Pendergast would run interference for him. He'd done it before and had openly expressed his desire to do it again. While his pal, Begley, didn't get his hands dirty most of the time, Plank knew that he was happy to look the other way as long as he got a little grease on his palm. A few dollars here and there for the XO, and a little bread and the occasional B-girl for Pendergast, and Plank was in business.

Then there was good ole Dougie. Ingram was a decent guy, and he liked the extra pay. He was wound a little too tight, but long as he got his regular little yellow pill, he was golden. Now all that remained was to carefully vet the crew. To find out who were the guys who wanted a few extra creature comforts, who didn't care either way but wouldn't open their yappers, and who were the canaries who'd sing to the COB first chance they got. It usually didn't take long, even on a big ship with a thousand guys. On a little sewer pipe like the *Bull Shark* with only seventy dudes crammed in like sardines, Plank didn't think it'd take him a week.

One thing he probably wouldn't peddle very much of was booze. With two torpedo rooms full of weapons that ran on a hundred eighty proof alky, these sewer rats could get loaded anytime. No, this boat would probably be ripe for girly mags, pills, snort, and cheap and easy connections to broads in port. When you had to wait in line for a couple of hours at the brothels in Pearl just for a shot at three minutes with a whore, a man could get pretty antsy.

As for what men wanted at sea, Plank had a whole system set up. For the moment, though, he had only brought a small number of samples with him. Most of it was stowed under his uniform and Doug's as well. There was some in his seabag, hidden in a special secret pouch, again as there was in Ingram's. It was enough to offer samples and to figure out who the customers were on this trip. No matter what, there was three or four hundred dollars to be made on this patrol. Slip Begley his fifty, Pendergast his hundred, and then Doug his thirty percent and Plank would still go ashore in Pearl with a cool two yards in his pocket. And that would only be the down payment for next time.

On top of that, his promotion and this assignment practically doubled his Navy pay. Plus, he'd heard good things about this boat. There were medals and glory to be had, which wouldn't hurt his reputation any.

Yes, Steve Plank thought as he placed his carefully rolled crackerjack whites in what little space remained in his locker and then zipped up his duffel, he was going to *like* submarine service.

STATION HYPO: 0822 LOCAL TIME

The oaken doors opened, and the dozen or so men working in the basement offices looked up and smiled at the sight of the newcomer. She was a medium-height blonde woman dressed in a Navy female uniform. Navy blue skirt, jacket, and white dress blouse beneath with a small necktie. In her hand, she carried a large sack that brought with it the smell of freshly baked pastry.

It was hardly the first morning that the new team member reported for duty, yet to the hundred or so men in the department, she was always a breath of fresh air.

"Joanie!" Joe Finnegan said as he rose and rushed over to her from a conference table where half a dozen men sat around a heap of paper. "Did you just come from the sub piers?

"Just saw Arty and the *Bull Shark* off," Joan Turner said wistfully.

"He'll be okay, Joan," Finnegan reassured her. In an attempt to lighten her mood, he smiled and asked, "Did you brown-bag your lunch? Looks like enough to feed an army!"

Joan Turner grinned, "No, Joseph... this is a little peace offering for allowing me into your little boy's club here. Little Friday treat, you might say."

"That's very thoughtful," Finnegan said. "Let me introduce you to a few new faces. A few of these gents you already know ... here, put your bag on the table here for now. Gentleman, this is J.G. Joan Turner. She's assigned to my section and is going to help us with the mathematics of the damned Jap date codes. Joan, this new face here is Commander Wilfred Holmes, although we call him Jasper."

Holmes stood and shook Joan's hand, "A pleasure, Joan. Something smells delish in that bag... may I?"

Joan chuckled, "Of course, sir. I brought a variety of pastries from a little place right around the corner from my house. There's a couple of papaya-filled cheese Danishes in there, Commander. Plus, a bag of Hawaiian blend coffee for a little change."

Holmes's face lit up, "I *love* papaya Danish!"

"And I love Hawaiian coffee," said Commander Joe Rochefort as he shuffled out of the head, adjusting his robe. He grinned at Joan. "I like an officer who wants to make a good first impression, Joan."

Holmes chuffed, "Says the guy in his slippers whose noggin hasn't seen a comb in a week."

Rochefort waved that off, "I'm a misunderstood genius."

"You're a genius, that's undeniable,' Finnegan stated with a grin, "but we understand you fine, Joe."

"So, how did you know to bring these goodies, Lieutenant?" another man, a full lieutenant who had once been *Arizona's* band leader, asked.

"Oh, a little birdie told me," Joan said with a wicked grin. "A couple of conversations I overheard this week and a hint from Gladys Finnegan, of course."

Holmes laughed, "So, a couple of hints and you come in with powerful intelligence in order to ensure a victory... hmmm..."

Rochefort and Joan noticed that Holmes suddenly seemed lost in his own thoughts. They met each other's eye and then looked at Joe Finnegan. They waited.

"What is it, sir?" Finnegan finally asked.

Holmes's vacant expression suddenly morphed into one of gleeful and almost wicked triumph, "I'll be *damned*... I'll be God-*damned!* Joan Turner, you may have just provided the spark we need to light this fire!"

Joan looked perplexed at first, "I... I'm sorry?"

Rochefort stared at Holmes for a long moment, "What the heck are you on about, Jasper...?"

"My God..." Finnegan muttered along with several other men.

Joan's eyes went wide, and Holmes laughed out loud, "I think it's sinking in for all of you! Joan *overheard* something and then reacted to it... so suppose that my good friend and yours Isuroku did the same thing. Suppose we cable Midway and tell them to broadcast something over the radio uncoded... and then we wait and see if the Nips react."

"Jesus Christ..." Rochefort said. "That's brilliant! It's got to be something sort of... mundane, though... so that the Japs don't suspect we're yanking their chains."

"Water," Joan said and snapped her fingers. "Midway is a small atoll with no water supply, right?"

Finnegan nodded, "Yeah, they've got desalinators to make fresh water every day."

Jasper Holmes laughed again, "Right! So, we have the boys at Midway say that their desalination plant crapped out and could Pearl Harbor send out another unit on their next supply run."

"Then we listen to the JN-25 coded messages and see if any of the Japanese mention it," Rochefort said with a shake of his head. "For the love... sometimes, Joan, you get so bogged down by looking at all of the trees you can't see the forest. We've still got a problem, though. The *date*."

"What if we include a dated addendum to the Midway message," Joan suggested, pulling out her own papaya Danish. "And then if the Japanese messages contain a date code in reference to ours..."

"We'll have a base pair to match up," Finnegan said. "That might just be enough. God bless you, Mrs. Turner!"

"If this works out, Joanie..." Rochefort said with a beaming smile, "you'll get a damned medal for this!"

Joan waved that away, "It was really Captain Holmes's idea. I just shot my big mouth off. He should get the credit."

"The trouble with our business," Finnegan stated, "is that credit is hard to give... since we are supposed to be... if you'll pardon a pun... Ultra-secret."

"Whatever wins us this war," Holmes said. "That's what's important. Joan, on behalf of all these guys here... welcome to the team! We're damned glad to have you, ha-ha-HA!"

CHAPTER 12

U.S.S. BULL SHARK

MAY 23, 1942 - 0640 SHIP'S TIME

23°14' N, 162°41' W – APPROXIMATELY 665 MILES EAST, SOUTHEAST OF MIDWAY ATOLL

Tom Begley couldn't help but feel that he was in the middle of nowhere. It was something of an illusion, of course. The crossing from the Galapagos to Hawaii had been far longer than the one from Pearl to their current position. Also, they were still nearly two days run to the base at Midway.

Yet the dark, low hanging storm clouds and the rolling swells whose tops were already over his head even on the bridge, the deck of which was a good dozen feet over the waterline, seemed to close in around him and enhance the sense of isolation.

The ship was making heavy work of the fourteen to sixteen-foot rollers, many with whitecaps or their crests being blown into spindrift by the forty-knot wind. A big swell would crash into her port bow, half of it rolling down the deck before the bulbous nose of the vessel would rise and break through to the other side of the crest. With most of her bulk beneath the waves, a rounded bow with only a suggestion of a prow, the submarine bucked and plowed her way at two-engine speed through the heavy seas. It was times like this that Begley missed the way a destroyer could handle rough weather.

Especially since he was wearing an inflatable Mae West life-preserver over his foul weather gear and over this a safety harness with a cable that connected him to an eyebolt just below the forward bridge railing. Of course, he wasn't alone in this. The quartermaster of the watch, Wendell Freeman, his usual watchstander, was clipped in beside him, his rain slicker streaming with a combination of seawater and heavy tropical rain just as the XO's was. Behind and above them, the three lookouts were similarly garbed, similarly tethered but certainly *not* similarly comfortable.

As much as the constant rolling and pitching forced the two men on the bridge to stand spraddle-legged and to keep at least one hand on the teak railing, the men in the lookout perch on the periscope sheers had it much worse. Their greater height meant that the angle of heel and the centrifugal forces acting on them was greater. None of them complained, though. Each man stood his reduced lookout watch of one hour stoically, managing to scan his sector and report anything they sighted, which amounted to nothing in the current pea-soup conditions.

Begley had been pleased when he heard that Steve Plank had come aboard as the boat's new boatswain's mate. He and his junior partner, Doug Ingram, had served with him aboard an old four-piper in the Caribbean before the war. The duty had been easy, the weather good and the profits flowed. While Begley himself mostly turned a blind eye to the goings-on of the two sailors... leaving the management of their doings up to Burt... he enjoyed his share of the profits and did what he could to run interference for them. Deflecting the attention of other officers, giving Plank access to things he might not otherwise be privy to and so on.

Pendergast was the facilitator. With two officers working with him, Plank was able to run a tidy little black-market operation. Begley never really felt bad about it. It was nothing new. Sailors have been sneaking contraband aboard ship and on naval stations since the time of the

Phoenicians. It was practically the immemorial custom of any naval service.

And why not? Why shouldn't the men who served have a couple of creature comforts now and then? Was it so wrong to want to take a little hooch every once in a while? Was it so bad for men locked up inside steel ships to want to ogle a naked woman in their racks at night? Christ, was it so terrible that a guy got himself a little relaxer here and there when things got tough?

In truth, Begley cared little for the comfort or morale of the common sailor. It was simply a convenient justification for allowing the bending, stretching, and breaking of regs that, on a good station or in a good scenario, doubled his Navy pay.

He was already working on getting Plank assigned to his watch. If the two men could spend time on the bridge together in the morning watch or during the two dog watches, they could talk, plan, and certainly iron out any bugs. Ingram was another matter. Pendergast said that while he was good at finding out which of the men would be Plank's customers, he was too much a customer himself to be anything more than a convenient mule. With his position as an electric motor technician on *Bull Shark*, though, it was fortunate that they had him.

Then there was the other side of the coin... glory. Begley wanted to be promoted, to move up to a position with more power. That might be the skipper of his own boat, at least for a start. Yet, there was so much more than that. The things he could do with flag rank... and he hoped that in more ways than one, *Bull Shark* would be his meal ticket.

Unfortunately, things were not quite working out the way he'd hoped. Somehow, he'd managed to alienate almost all of the officers and a good portion of the men, especially the chiefs and LPOs. Sure, he had a few followers like Wendell Freeman, for example, but none of them were the chiefs or even the leading petties... except for Plank.

Begley was especially worried about Jarvis. Although Begley was technically the superior officer based on date of commission and his position as First Lieutenant and XO... Jarvis didn't seem to be daunted by that. He was very capable, tough, and didn't seem to be afraid that

Begley might report him or do something to hurt his career. He was also unanimously popular with the men. Pretty much all the officers were, really. That certainly went for Turner, too.

Begley just couldn't understand it. No matter what was asked of these men by Turner or Jarvis... any officer really, but those two in particular... they did it happily. Oh, sure, there was griping and bitching, and the men cursed the officers up and down when they had some unpleasant task to do... yet it was good-natured and done wryly. As if for show, but the respect and liking were always there.

On the other hand, when either he or Pendergast ordered something unpleasant done, the grumbling was real. The dislike only intensified. And even after a couple of weeks, the crew was becoming aware of the two new officers' favoritism toward certain of the crew. They'd have to be careful about that.

Begley braced himself as a particularly nasty creaming roller slammed into the port bow and heeled the ship over fifteen degrees as white foam raced up the deck and through the bridge scuppers. He would have loved to dive below this storm. And why not? They were on a submarine, for Christ's sake. But the Old Man refused, saying they needed to keep a lookout and wait for the morning Fox.

"Christ..." Begley grumbled, starting to regret his bacon and eggs... canned bacon and powdered eggs...

"Quite a ride, eh, sir?" Freeman asked with a grin.

Begley almost snapped at the man. Wasn't he feeling the least bit uncomfortable? Instead, he grinned back, "I've seen worse!"

Begley tried to focus on his thoughts and his plans to keep from thinking about his uneasy stomach. Glory... yes, the glory...

Sure, they'd snagged a pair of Jap Fubukis almost two weeks earlier, only being able to take credit for one, though. And now, if the higher-ups were right, there might be a hellacious battle around Midway in the next week. A whole Jap fleet with flat-tops and cruisers and battleships... yet the boat hadn't even gotten any medals or anything when they'd put into Pearl a few days back. Just a day or two of leave and then ship out! That was a fine how do you do. No citation, no commendation, no nothing. The captain roars into battle against a destroyer leader, *on the surface,* and command doesn't even pat anybody on the back for it.

And now this! They weren't even *headed* for Midway Atoll. The ship was on a two-ninety that would pass south of the atoll by at least three hundred and fifty miles. Pretty much headed for nowhere. He did have a small hope that if the Japs *were* going to invade Midway that their invasion force would probably come from the Marianas or even Wake Island, which was about as far from Midway as Midway was from Oahu. In that case, this plodding course at half-speed due to the sea state would eventually put *Bull Shark* into their path. That could be interesting. An invasion force would consist mostly of troop ships and some escorts. Might be a turkey shoot. Get four or five troopers, and everybody on board would get a medal. Then Begley and Pendergast wouldn't be the only officers on board without one. The Black gang and the pickle handlers would respect them then, by God!

"*Bridge, radio shack,*" the tinny bridge speaker crackled into life. "*We're receiving the morning Fox, sir... and a coded message for the skipper.*"

"Very well," Begley replied wearily. "Have the messenger of the watch alert Mr. Post, Chief Weiss, and inform the captain."

"*Bridge, radio, alert the comm officer, chief yeoman, and skipper, aye, sir.*"

Begley waited a moment as the bow of the ship rose ponderously to partially crest another heavy roller before thumbing the transmitter again, "Control, bridge... what's our speed and battery situation?"

"*Bridge, helm,*" Mug Vigliano reported in his heavy Brooklyn accent. "*Proceedin' on two-engine speed, as ordered. Bendix log indicates nine and a half knots, bridge. We're charging on batteries one and two. Mr. Dutch says we're about seventy percent.*"

"Jesus, why don't we dive and use this fancy snorkel then?" Begley cranked.

Freeman opened his mouth to explain why but shut it again. Although Begley did treat him well, he knew the man could have a short fuse and didn't like being corrected. Instructing him might also lose the favor he'd seem to earn.

Begley must have noticed and chuckled softly, "I know, Wendell, I know... the ball valve moves around too much in big seas and chokes out the diesels. Just grumbling."

"Yes, sir," Wendell said and smiled.

"*Bridge, control room,*" this was the skipper's voice.

"Go ahead, sir," Begley replied.

"*XO, order number three onto battery and proceed at ahead one-third,*" Turner said. "*Let's get these batteries stuffed and then dive under this slop. Once Joe reports a full charge, clear the bridge, and order a dive to a comfortable depth. Then report to the wardroom; we've got some things to discuss.*"

Begley and Freeman exchanged a glance before Begley said, "Aye-aye, sir."

A half-hour later, five wet and grateful men descended into the conning tower and then into the control room where they shed their rain gear, and it was hung up down in the pump room to drip dry. All five men were allowed to go to grab a quick shower and change into dry clothes and get something to eat. Begley turned the watch over to Nichols and Post, the two most junior officers, and headed into officer's country.

Turner, Jarvis, Dutch, Pendergast, and even the COB were already seated around the wardroom table when Begley arrived. He slid into his customary place at the foot and accepted a cup of coffee from Carlson.

"Welcome to the party, XO," Turner said.

"Thanks, sir," Begley replied. "We're at one hundred feet, cruising at two-thirds, making turns for five knots. Should give us plenty of time for the weather to clear and make decent progress to... wherever."

Jarvis cocked an eyebrow but said nothing. Turner sipped his own coffee and looked down at a message flimsy on the table in front of him, "Well, we've got some things to discuss, gentleman. I'd like to have Frank and Andy in here, but somebody's got to mind the store. We'll make sure they're briefed later... okay... Tom and I already know about one of these items. We were briefed in Admiral Nimitz's office the other day. The Japs have created some kind of Frankenstein's monster. Here's a crummy photo."

Turner pulled one of the large blow-ups they'd seen the other day and passed it around the table.

"Is this... a submarine?" Rogers asked.

"Apparently, it's a submarine aircraft carrier," Turner explained. "Yamamoto has some pretty far-out ideas. An... acquaintance of mine, Mr. Webster Clayton, informs me that the Japanese are designing a boat they're labeling the four hundred series, but they're years away. This thing, though, has apparently been built and is even larger than what the Japs are drawing up. She's five hundred feet long and must displace... eight thousand tons or more."

"Jesus Christ..." Joe Dutch emoted.

"So, she's got what... floatplanes in these bulges on top?" Jarvis asked.

"Apparently, they're two hangars," Turner said. "Eight Aichi floaters in total, with bombs and machine guns. Clayton believes this thing attacked the Aleutians early this week and all but wiped the station there off the island."

"So, we're supposed to find her and sink her?" Pendergast asked.

"Seems like that's becoming our job," Jarvis opined. "Goin' after specialty ships."

Begley chuffed.

"It does at that," Turner said. "Okay, that's item number one... the morning Fox isn't anything particularly interesting... however... as some of you may know, ever since the Battle of the Coral Sea, command has been planning for another Jap offensive. One designed to wipe our remaining Pacific carriers... minus *Saratoga*, of course, since she's still on the west coast being repaired... to wipe *Enterprise*, *Yorktown*, and *Hornet* off the face of the sea. They're sending the rest of the Kido Butai, their carrier fleet, along with escorts and an invasion fleet to a specific target. The idea is to draw us in and smash us to bits."

"Good God..." Pendergast breathed.

"However, we have a few advantages," Turner went on. "The Ultra program has at least partially deciphered the IJN's code system, JN-25B. We have an idea of what they plan, but the plan only refers to a location they call AF."

"Where the hell is AF?" Rogers asked.

"The crypto gang is split on that one," Turner said. "Washington apparently believes it's the Aleutians, Station Kask believes it's Port Moresby again, and our Pearl group is certain it's Midway. All things considered, I agree with Station Hypo."

"But Midway is just a flyspeck of nothing," Begley pointed out.

"Well, Tom, as it was expressed in the meeting," Turner put in, "it's strategically important for both sides."

"It'd be a great place for the Japs to launch attacks against Hawaii," Jarvis stated. "And in our case, with the sub base being set up there, it extends the reach of our boats another eleven hundred miles further out from Pearl. Makes sense to me."

"I don't know..." Pendergast said. "The Aleutians *are* technically American soil. Taking a couple of those outer islands would give the Japs a foothold on our back doorstep and a good place to attack Russia... or keep *us* from invading the Kurils. Hell, long-range bombers might even be able to reach the coast of Washington or Oregon for that matter."

"Good point, Burt," Begley praised.

"It is a good point," Turner stated. "And Clayton feels that the Japs *will* attack Attu and maybe Kiska... even Dutch Harbor. But that notwithstanding, the big target is still Midway."

"So, are we going to lie in wait for the Jap fleet?" Begley asked hopefully. "Sink a few carriers before they get here?"

Turner chuckled, "If only... not as yet, at least. Command wants proof, and the message Weiss and I just decoded states that Ultra has a plan to learn for certain. Our job is to be on the surface and as close to Midway as we can by twenty hundred local time. At that time, we're to be on the surface and listening for radio broadcasts from both Midway and anything from the Japanese. Whatever happens after that will determine what our fleet does and where we'll be going."

He picked up the hardwired phone hanging on the bulkhead near him and ordered the helm to change course to three-three-zero. He hung up and sighed.

"I'd like to get at least another hundred and thirty miles before sunset," Turner explained. "We'll give the storm another couple of hours to abate, see how it is on top, and then run on the surface at about fifteen knots, charging with one engine."

"What's the plan to discover the Jap target?" Pendergast asked.

"I'm not sure," Turner stated. "Command doesn't even want to say with code. But the message says that we'll know, and more importantly, *they'll* know."

"This is gonna be big," Jarvis opined.

"Might even get another bronze star out of it," Begley sounded jovial with the tease, but Jarvis frowned.

"There will be enough glory to go around, I'm sure," Turner said with a sigh. "Let's just hope we live through it."

CHAPTER 13

500 MILES EAST, SOUTHEAST OF MIDWAY ATOLL

The late tropical evening was a stark contrast to how the day had begun. The sky was nearly free of clouds, and a fat yellow sun hung low over the western horizon. The sea, although still bulging with long swells, was no longer violent and foaming. The steep white caps had given way to a leisurely long roll that promised a calm and pleasant night upon its surface.

That semi-tranquil surface was suddenly broken by a massive steel machine that broke through from beneath. First its variety of masts, then its central bridge and conning tower, the formidable shapes of her guns and finally the long, slender hull. Behind the conning tower, the four diesel exhausts belched puffs of spray and smoke as the powerful engines rumbled to life. On her bridge, men began to appear. Three scrambling up the latticework of the periscope sheers and two others standing beside one another on the small bridge at the forward end of the deck.

"Control, bridge... trim dive complete. Well done. AOOD, Captain Arthur Turner announced over the bridge speaker. "Give me a full sweep on both radars. Let's run on three engine speed and charge on two. Lookouts?"

Above and behind Turner and this evening's quartermaster of the watch, Chief Paul "Buck" Rogers, , the three lookouts scanned their sectors first with the naked eye and then with their powerful, wide-angle and nighttime enhanced Bausch and Lomb 7x50 binoculars. Seeing nothing out to the horizon, they reported such to the bridge.

"*Negative contact on the Sugar Jig... negative on Sugar Dog,*" Ensign Andy Post reported.

"Very well," Turner said. "Maintain heading."

Turner pulled a pack of Lucky Strikes from his duty shirt, which he now wore unbuttoned over his T-shirt. With the submarine in warm Pacific waters and climates, the uniform of the day for everybody was sub sandals, shorts, and T-shirts. Officers and chiefs sometimes wore their khakis open, but Turner didn't require it. Men were even allowed to go shirtless if it got hot below on a dive or if they were up on deck during the day. In that event, however, they were required to slather on suntan lotion.

Submariners were notoriously white. Even the darker-skinned Black, Hispanic, and Native American sailors turned paler inside their sewer pipe. They were encouraged to go topside and get some sun whenever possible, the light helping their bodies to produce vitamin D. However, they were constantly cautioned by Henry Hoffman, the boat's pharmacist's mate, to be careful about burning.

Turner held the pack out to Rogers, who took a cigarette as well. Turner snapped his zippo and lit both of their smokes.

"Nice change from this morning," Rogers said absently.

Turner drew on his butt and nodded, "Yeah, nice and calm, and a light breeze blowing."

Hanging in his perch on the after side of the sheers, boatswain's mate Steve Plank smiled to himself. The skipper and COB were right; it was a pleasant evening. What was more pleasant still was that the rough morning had already born Plank some ripe fruit.

Several of the lookouts and some of the new hands had not enjoyed the rough weather and had thanked their lucky stars when the ship had finally plunged below the roiling storm to once again cruise placidly in the tranquil depths. Thanks to some careful listening and a couple of little hints from Doug, five of the men aboard had been given something to ease their minds a little.

Among Plank's gear, stowed carefully in his sea bag's hidden pocket, were packets of what he liked to call "the big three." He'd made sure that Ingram now had a small number of each to pass out to anyone interested by way of free samples.

For times like during the bad weather or heavy combat or stress, Plank could provide the men with what were commonly known as "Blue Amies." These were legal prescription Amytal capsules... not legally obtained, however, and certainly not allowed to be used except when given by a certified medical officer or corpsman. When the men needed a pick-me-up, Plank could be right there with Benzedrine, which was a common amphetamine, or speed, known as "Bennies." Finally, if and when the guys needed something a little extra, there were several tiny paper-wrapped packets that resembled the popular BC powder. However, unlike the powdered aspirin that could be purchased instead of capsules, these little folded paper packets held a different kind of powder. Cocaine.

Most of the men that Plank sold to generally liked the Amies and Bennies over the cocaine. There was a strong stigma attached to cokies, yet the pills that Plank pushed were not only available in pharmacies all over the country, but they were also both even prescribed by Navy doctors. Naturally, this was done carefully, and under supervision, so Plank's position was that of a guy who could give you just a little extra when you needed it.

And now, thanks to the storm, at least five of the *Bull Shark's* crew had already had a morning date with Amy. Plank had a very small supply of everything, but he made it a policy to give out two freebies before saying that he had to charge the man for his next one. He was reasonable about it, though. Only fifty cents a pop or a dozen for a five spot. Plank also made it clear that only he or Doug would give out the doses one at a time. He stated that because his father was a pharmacist, he knew how to be careful with the drugs. This gave him even more credibility and set him up as a guy to be trusted.

"*Bridge, radio,*" Andy Post's voice announced over the speaker. "*We're intercepting a broadcast on the wideband, and I think it's from Midway, sir.*"

"Here we go..." Turner muttered. "Pipe it up here, Andy, and please take notes."

The speaker crackled and popped with atmospheric interference over the open channel. Then a voice began to speak, "*Station Hypo... Station Hypo... Naval Air Station Midway here, come in please...*"

Another crackle, and then the radioman repeated the call. After a moment, another voice joined in.

"*Hypo here, Midway, we read. Go ahead. All well?*"

A short pause, "*Hey, that you, Marty...? Yeah, mostly quiet out here.*"

"*You fellas enjoying the beach, Phil?*" Marty, the Pearl Harbor radioman, asked jovially.

Phil laughed sardonically, "*Might as well... 'bout the only water we might see for a while.*"

"*Huh?*"

Phil sighed, "*One of our water makers shit the bed, Phil. The other one's gettin' cranky, too. Can you believe this crap? It's awful dry out here without those gadgets.*"

Another pause, "*That sounds like a problem, buddy. Can you guys fix them?*"

A scoff, "*The guys are tryin'... but we're just a ragtag bunch of flyers and Marines out here. I think we're gonna need some help on this one.*"

Marty laughed, "*Okay, pal... I'll pass this along to the powers that be. I'm sure we can get you a couple of new desalinators on the next supply run. Maybe send a big fat PBY out there with some spare parts for now. Just be thankful you're way back from the fighting, huh?*"

"*Blessing and a curse, Marty,*" Phil said. "*Okay, that's about it. Captain Simard will have me send out more info on the next coded broadcast.*"

The speaker crackled and then shut down. Buck and Turner looked at one another with wide eyes.

"You think the Japs heard that?" Buck asked.

"I can't imagine they didn't," Turner said. "It went out on the AM band and uncoded. Guess we'll see."

———

Sixteen hundred miles west of the *Bull Shark*, a little more than halfway between Midway Atoll and the Japanese-held islands of Guam and Saipan in the Marianas, another radio set was tuned into the Midway broadcast. Ryu Osaka stood on the *Ribaiasan's* bridge listening to the staticky conversation between the Midway radioman and his counterpart at Pearl Harbor. Being one of the few officers who spoke English, it was Osaka's job to monitor any enemy transmissions that might be intercepted. Not even the ship's captain could do so, very much not to his credit in the mind of the XO.

Omata Hideki, however, was one of the few. The submarine carrier's CAG stood beside his friend and listened to the inane chatter that contained so much useful information. Both men chuckled when the transmission ended.

"Such a lack of discipline!" Hideki stated with a head shake.

"Indeed, my friend," Osaka commented. "We must report this to headquarters immediately. The occupation force must be notified to bring water purification equipment with them."

"Of course, *we* will do so in code," Hideki observed wryly.

Both men chuckled once again. They watched as the flight deck officer, tethered at the ship's bow, waved his flag overhead once again, and the last of squadron one's Aichi floatplanes was catapulted into the late afternoon sky.

"Can you imagine it, Ryu?" Hideki said as the plane arced upward and turned onto its assigned patrol route. "When our Kido Butai reaches the battle zone in a few days... four great carriers... *hundreds* of airplanes! It will be one more in a series of tremendous victories!"

"It's said we cannot lose," Osaka added. "Such confidence is...

perhaps incautious."

"You don't believe we shall be victorious over the American fleet, whatever it might contain?"

Osaka sighed lightly, "My friend... I served with the great admiral for over a year. While he is brilliant, he's also a realist. Even though it was his plan to attack Pearl Harbor, he still maintains his doubts."

"How so?"

"That we've initiated combat with an intractable enemy whose industrial might is enormous," Osaka explained. "And that even if he can draw the remaining Pacific carriers into battle and crush them *entirely*... it won't be long before they're replaced. In essence, we sink one, and they come back with two."

"Surely it's not that bleak," Hideki argued. "The Americans have what... five large carriers all told? *Lexington* was sunk in the Coral Sea last month, *Enterprise* and *Hornet*... such names... and the *Saratoga*, which at last report had to go back to their west coast for repairs. We believe we sunk the *Yorktown*, and the *Ranger* is certainly in the Atlantic."

Osaka nodded, "And they have another, the *Wasp*, although this one is not quite as large or capable as the others. I believe they have several light carriers as well, but they're in no position to assist Midway."

"And we have our two light carriers and their task force headed to the Aleutians as we speak," Hideki said. "Not to mention the *Zuikaku* and *Shokaku*, which once repaired will take their place once again in our mighty Kido Butai!"

Osaka smiled indulgently at his friend's enthusiastic confidence in their Navy. It was certainly founded in truth, to be sure. The IJN was the largest and most advanced on Earth. That couldn't be denied... but as Yamamoto continually pointed out, the Japanese belief in their invulnerability could lead to mistakes.

"Quartermaster, order helm to all ahead one-third," Osaka ordered into the bridge transmitter. "Assistant duty officer, please note that squadron one has been successfully launched and is assuming patrol sectors."

From the bridge hatch, Captain Kajimora emerged with a smile playing on his features. He stepped over to the two officers, nonchalantly shouldering the quartermaster out of the way. He pulled a new pack of Golden Bats from his uniform pocket, carefully removed one and lit it with a gold-plated Zippo lighter with an American flag etched into its face. Kajimora claimed he'd taken it from an American sailor following a fight in which the sailor tried to escape after being pulled from the sea.

Osaka doubted the tale, having some inside knowledge as to Kajimora's whereabouts during the conflict in question, and Kajimora was nowhere near the battle of Rabul. Kajimora probably knew that Osaka knew that as well. The man would've had his first officer looked into.

Yet the captain continued with the blatant falsity, as if daring the Yakuin to speak out. Osaka would not, of course. First of all, because he couldn't produce any proof that Kajimora was lying. Second, because his position demanded that he maintain loyalty to the captain regardless of his personal feelings. Further, Osaka was a man who believed in the ancient bit of wisdom that stated that if given enough rope, a man would eventually hang himself.

"So, what do you make of the intercepted American radio transmission, Yakuin?" Kajimora asked once his cigarette was lighted and smoking.

"Quite interesting, Captain san," Osaka said neutrally.

"And you, air wing commander?"

Hideki shrugged, "Useful. To us, that is."

"Indeed?" Kajimora asked casually, although Osaka had served with him long enough to detect the subtle hint of annoyance in his tone. Kajimora couldn't speak English and therefore had to have the message translated for him. This did not sit well. "In what way was it interesting and useful, gentlemen?"

"Midway Naval Station is suffering damage to their water purification systems," Osaka said but elected to say no more without being asked. He knew this would irk the captain even further, and the XO rather enjoyed it.

"They're asking Pearl Harbor to send new machines and spare parts," Hideki offered. "This is perhaps a concern for our invasion forces, sir."

Kajimora puffed thoughtfully on his smoke for a moment, as if in deep contemplation. This was something he did that got under Osaka's skin, although the XO was too careful a man to let that show.

Kajimora was a stupid man whose imagination went no further than his next visit with a favored geisha. Yet he was good at feigning intelligence, as if aping the behaviors and mannerisms of smarter men. Worse than a stupid man in a position of authority was one who was cunning. A cunning man could hide his shortcomings and often over-compensated with arrogance.

"So, we must inform our great commander, Admiral Yamamoto," Kajimora finally said. "So that he may instruct the invasion force to bring additional equipment. A very lucky stroke, this careless trans-mission."

"Yes, sir," Osaka agreed.

"Excellent," Kajimora said. "I shall send the coded message immedi-ately. Hopefully it will reach the flagship or at least *someone* capable of making the decision before Yamamoto's radio silence order goes into effect."

With that, the captain flicked his nearly dead butt over the railing where it landed on the deck only inches from where a crewman was mopping up a small aviation gas spill. Osaka cringed, as did Hideki. Once again, Osaka amused himself with the mental image of the stupid bastard who commanded this most brilliant submarine swinging by his neck from one of the recovery booms.

"So, he takes the credit," Hideki said sourly.

Osaka treated him to a sliver of a smile, "Does he? We have listening stations all over the Pacific. At best, our illustrious captain will simply be re-confirming what our intelligence division already knows. Let us hope for his sake that he doesn't try to add anything to his report that might seem to our superiors to be self-aggrandizing."

Hideki chuckled softly, "Let us hope not."

The quartermaster, although maintaining a correct posture of attentiveness to his duties and not to the officer's conversation, nevertheless smiled to himself as well.

———

Not far away, no more than a few nautical miles and a hundred feet below the surface, another man was thinking about paying out enough line to hang someone. His submarine, a post-Great War S-boat, S27, cruised along silently on her intercept course for the odd ship they'd almost run aboard before the lookouts and the sonar operator discovered her.

Now, S27 slunk slowly toward her quarry. At only four knots, it would take the better part of thirty minutes to cover the slightly more than four thousand yards between the submerged boat and the... whatever it was. Nobody aboard quite knew.

That included the old boat's captain, Lieutenant Commander Owen March. He simply stood by his periscopes and waited until the submarine could close the distance enough to go up to periscope depth and take a look.

The lookouts had spotted aircraft on the horizon, which had prompted a rapid dive. However, passive sonar detected a ship with twin slow screws moving northeast at fourteen knots. It could only be an aircraft carrier or seaplane tender... but what the hell was it doing out in the middle of nowhere?

The nearest bit of Japanese territory to their current position was Wake Island. It wasn't too far to the south... but still...

"What's happening with our target, sonar?" March asked impatiently, willing his boat to move faster through the water.

Not that it couldn't, but any faster and they'd surely be picked up even on passive sonar this close. Assuming the ship they were tracking even had sonar.

"Nothing's changed, sir," the technician stated. "Still headed northeast... no, wait... screw noise diminishing. Assess reducing speed, sir."

"After launching aircraft," March muttered, tapping his chin. "XO, how many birds did the lookouts sight?"

The executive officer was a middle-aged lieutenant commander who, although a decent submariner, had never quite managed to distinguish himself. He'd been serving aboard pig boats now for twenty years and so far, rising to the second in command of an old rust bucket like S27 was the best he could do.

"Four," Wayne Dawker replied, looking at his notebook. "Headed off in different directions."

"Definitely Nips, though?" the captain asked.

"Oh, yes, sir," Dawker replied with enthusiasm. Although not wildly successful and still an O4 at forty-three, Dawker wasn't a bitter man. Now that war had broken out, his chances had certainly improved. "Looked like Aichis, and they all had rising suns painted on 'em."

"Excellent," March said, rubbing his hands together. "Well, whether it's a seaplane tender or Jeep carrier, Wayne, we're gonna bag us a Jap this evening. Phone talker, forward room, open all outer doors. Let's set the depth on the fish to six feet."

Dawker grinned, slung the IsWas around his neck and dropped down into the control room. S27 didn't have a fancy new TDC like the big fleet boats. All they had were the old but tried and tested methods in use since the last war. A party to plot the movements of the targets and the IsWas, colloquially known as "the banjo." The banjo was a series of celluloid discs that could be independently spun and used as an angle-solver in order to determine gyroscope settings for the torpedoes. They'd have to be called up to the torpedo room and set manually, but it was a solid method, if a bit time-consuming.

"Estimated range now two-four-zero-zero yards on target," sonar reported. "Still moving at same course and speed... bearing approximately three-zero-zero to three-three-zero, Skipper."

"Okay, here we go," March said. "Let's pray these damned torpedoes don't fail us... helm, come left to course zero-five-zero, all ahead standard. Diving officer, bring me to periscope depth. Up attack scope."

Orders were acknowledged, and the submarine's electric motors whined as they spun up to increase the boat's speed from four to six knots. The ship rose gently to fifty-five feet, and the slim attack periscope broke the surface.

March had to blink his eye once or twice to adjust to the bright pre-sunset light. He turned the scope back and forth, and then he saw their quarry.

"What the hell is *that?*" he asked himself. Perry, grab the recog book and take a look at this thing..."

Perry Medhouser, the boat's torpedo and gunnery officer, picked up the Japanese ship recognition book from the tiny chart desk and peered through the periscope. He stepped back and gave his captain an incredulous look, "Sir... I've never seen anything like that... whatever it is."

"I'd say it's a submarine," March opined.

"Yes, sir... but with some kind of long tubes on its deck," Medhouser added with a shake of his head. "Maybe some kind of seaplane garages?"

March chuckled, "It's a goddamned Jap submarine aircraft carrier! What a screwball idea... Well, we're gonna sink it, and then we're gonna report it. Got your camera, Perry?"

Medhouser grinned and pulled his Kodak from a small locker and pressed the lens to the periscope eyepiece. He snapped off several shots, "Got him, Skipper."

"Okay, great," March said. "We've shot him with a camera, now let's try it with pickles. Standby for final observation."

Medhouser took the phone talker's sound-powered telephone from around the young seaman's neck and hung it on his own.

"Okay... constant bearings... mark!" March announced.

The seaman who'd been the phone talker now shifted to periscope assistant. He read the bearing off the ring.

"Angle on the bow is two-one-five port," March said, fiddling with the handles and knobs on the periscope. "Range... Christ, I don't know, but sonar's estimate sounds close... Hell, let's use thirty-five feet for the mast heights... range, mark!"

The periscope assistant frowned at the stadimeter scale and shrugged, "Uhm... one-eight-zero-zero, sir."

March chuckled, "Know how you feel, Baker... down scope!"

"Desired firing range?" Dawker asked from below.

"Let's get in pretty tight," March said. "Eleven hundred yards should do it. We'll fire a full spread, Perry. No sense in taking chances. Give me a five-degree spread on our fish. Order of tubes is one, two, three, and four."

"So, all of them, then," Medhouser said with a wry grin.

"Nobody likes a smart-ass ensign," March stated.

"I'm a Lieutenant, sir."

"Nothing's forever, Perry."

Soft chuckles rolled through the conning tower and the control room. It felt good to laugh in a situation like this. March and his crew hadn't had many opportunities like the one they were now presented. It was making everyone a little giddy.

The Pacific Ocean, especially in the tropical latitudes in which the two submarines found themselves, was quite clear. The visibility could be well over a hundred feet, even in late afternoon. This was highly unfortunate for the American submarine because, at periscope depth, her dark hull was clearly visible from above.

One of the Aichis did not continue on her assigned patrol loop. She sighted the enemy submarine as she passed, and rather than turning and attacking, the pilot flew on, reporting what he'd seen to his carrier. He flew over the horizon and then banked around to come up on the estimated track of the skulking Yankee boat.

As he homed in from two thousand feet, the pilot clearly saw the slim black shape of the submarine and the thin line of foam from her periscope cutting the surface as she turned to pursue his home ship. The pilot was carrying two, one-hundred- and fifty-kilogram bombs. He angled downward steeply, lining up the submarine in the crosshairs painted on his windscreen.

The only warning the S27 had of the air attack was the splash of the bomb as it dropped into the sea just forward of the boat's bulbous bow.

There was simply no time to prepare nor to evade. The bomb exploded virtually on the ship's bow, and the devastation was immediate and mortal.

The concussion instantly blasted away fifty feet of her wooden decking. Several aged welds along the ship's frames were ripped open, and water began to pour into the torpedo room. This in and of itself wasn't enough to doom the ship... however, the sympathetic vibrations caused by the tremendous concussion wave set off one of the reload torpedoes. The Mark 14's Torpex warhead ignited and turned the forward room into an instant hell, killing every man there and blasting open the side of the ship like a tin can.

Thousands of gallons of water rammed into the submarine and began to drag her bow downward so fast that no compensation from the high-pressure manifold nor the trim manifold could render any aid. Worse still, as the water blasted through the open compartment doors and began filling areas aft of the destroyed torpedo room, the second Japanese bomb struck just abaft the conning tower and ripped her open again.

Most of the crew of the S27 died in the first ten seconds of the attack. For those dozen or so farthest aft who'd been spared the devastating explosions, their death came as the submarine plunged into the abyssal depths more than two miles below. Whether they drowned, were burnt alive as what air remained compressed and super-heated, or were crushed when the pressures overcame the steel of the submarine and flattened her, it didn't matter. They were gone in less time than it took to describe their demise.

On the bridge of the *Ribaiasan*, Ryu Osaka offered Omata Hideki a celebratory cigarette. The two men watched as a ball of water, smoke, and debris shot into the air less than half a mile from their port quarter.

"You see, my friend," Osaka said, lighting Hideki's smoke, "give them enough rope."

"Banzai," Hideki said calmly and inhaled deeply.

CHAPTER 14

BATTLESHIP YAMATO – HASHIRA JIMA ANCHORAGE

MAY 24, 1942 – 0815 MIDWAY TIME

Admiral Isoroku Yamamoto stood in his private office and stared down at the logistics table that was by far the most dominant feature in the large cabin.

This special table, which he had built, and which was painted blue and marked with black lines of latitude and longitude, gave him a bird's eye view of any operation he commanded. The table, nearly ten feet on a side, could be outlined with a variety of numbers to indicate grid points, as well as small bits of brown felt to illustrate landmasses. The most dominant feature of the table were the dozens of toy ships that sailed upon its painted surface.

Currently, there were two small circles of land at the table's southern edge. On each, two small airplane models sat. This represented the American base at Midway. Sand Island and East Island and the airplanes currently known to be stationed there. Also placed on the table far to the "east" were a number of ships representing the American fleet, or what was known of it? A fleet that Yamamoto hoped would be drawn out into his trap when the Kido Butai began their assault on Midway.

Two tiny aircraft carriers, eight cruisers, and fifteen destroyers were all clumped together, representing what the IJN knew of the American forces that could be employed against their own. What no one in the Navy knew, including Yamamoto, was that the *Yorktown* had not been sunk in the Battle of the Coral Sea. They didn't know that even at that moment, the ship was being repaired and would be put to sea as Task Force 17.

Yamamoto was no fool, however. He knew that the Americans had other carriers. *Saratoga* and *Wasp* were both stationed in the Pacific. The former was suspected to be in dry-dock in San Francisco, and the other's whereabouts were unknown. He, therefore, placed another tiny aircraft carrier model, red like all of the enemy ships, along the edge of the board as a possibility. Even with three carriers... hell, even with *four*, the American forces were pitiful indeed when stacked up against the white armada set up on Yamamoto's side of the board.

The IJN, in fact, had four fleets assembled and already prepared to get underway, including the world's mightiest battleship on which the admiral now stood. The first of these groups, the fifth fleet, was headed for the Aleutians. He smiled to himself as he thought of his secret weapon performing a night raid on Attu. However, the main force, two light carriers, four battleships, eight cruisers, and four transports, along with a screening force of no less than twenty-five destroyers, would attack Dutch Harbor on the same day that his mighty Kido Butai struck Midway.

His main force, the great mobile force of the four carriers *Kaga, Akagi, Soryu,* and *Hiryu,* would soon be steaming for Midway. These four white ships were surrounded on the board by two battleships, three cruisers, and a dozen screening destroyers. Once this force obliterated the air force at Midway, a second fleet, sent from Saipan, would arrive and invade the island. This fleet consisted of a light carrier, two battleships, ten cruisers, and twenty-one destroyers. They would accompany the five thousand men aboard the eleven transports. Part of this fleet would also be sent from Guam, those ships to act as bombardment vessels before the troops were landed to seize the island from what American Marines remained.

While his former aide Ryu Osaka shared Yamamoto's thought that the Japanese people were growing too complacent in their belief that they were invincible... the venerable admiral had to admit that when one looked at the operations board and saw the enormous forces at his command against the pitifully small forces at Nimitz's... it was easy to believe in one's superiority.

A soft knock came at the hatch that led into the corridor outside Yamamoto's "war room." The door opened, and Rear-admiral Matome Ugaki stepped in. The junior officer closed the door quietly behind him and waited in respectful silence, holding several message flimsies in his hands.

"Please come in, Matome," Yamamoto said and smiled a kindly smile at his chief of staff and friend. "You know you must never stand on ceremony with me."

Ugaki bowed at the shoulders, "I wouldn't presume to interrupt such important contemplations, sir."

Yamamoto chuckled with just a hint of irreverence, "Important... perhaps, my friend. Yet... yet certainly not worthy of an emperor's consideration. Not for you, at least."

"A very impressive collection," Ugaki said, waving his papers at the war board. "We outnumber the Americans four... perhaps five to one. It is what I believe is known in the United States as a... turkey hunt."

Yamamoto laughed then. Not a big belly laugh, but hearty if a bit sardonic, "Turkey *shoot*... and you have, in your usual intuitive way, Matome, struck on the very point upon which I was pondering. The divine superiority and invincibility of the Japanese... certainly the Imperial Navy."

Ugaki could see that his friend was feeling a bit maudlin this morning. Perhaps this was inevitable, considering what was happening in Yamamoto's personal life. There were three oil paintings hanging in this room, dominating one of the windowless bulkheads. They seemed oddly out of place among the other large maps and charts and the large chalkboard on one. There was the ubiquitous portrait of Hirohito, of course. There was one of Yamamoto's wife, Reiko, naturally. This one seemed oddly dull, however, as if the artist who'd painted it somehow knew of the admiral's true feelings for the mother of his four children.

The final image, though, was, by comparison, a bright and cheerful one. That of a smiling woman named Kawai Chiyoko. Chiyoko was Yamamoto's favorite geisha. A woman somewhat younger than he and whose kindness, gentleness, and caring filled the admiral's heart. So grand and so close was their connection that it was hardly even considered to be a pretense of a secret among those who knew him.

Of course, that was one factor currently adding to Yamamoto's gloom. Chiyoko had been ill lately, more than once seemingly on the point of dissolution. Without her near, at least when Yamamoto was in Japan, his moods were often reserved at best.

"What have you there, Matome?" Yamamoto asked.

"Several things I think may bring good cheer, sir," Ugaki said, stepping forward and handing one of the messages over.

"Are we in need of good cheer, my friend?" Yamamoto asked wryly.

"It can never hurt... this one is a summary from a message we intercepted last evening. Midway's seawater evaporators are breaking down."

Yamamoto nodded, "Naturally. No doubt they're overtaxed on such a barren sand heap so over-burdened with men. Please inform second fleet of this. They should take such equipment and repair parts with them. Any word from our submarine pickets?"

"Not as yet, sir," Ugaki said. "They are no doubt still running for their assigned patrol areas."

Yamamoto sighed, "Indeed... well, we'll simply have to wait to hear from them. I would have liked this better if our seaplane raid to Oahu had been completed."

Ugaki snorted, "Yes, sir. It was simply bad luck that the damned Americans stationed a seaplane tender at French Frigate Shoals."

Yamamoto sighed, "All of this we know, Matome. Nothing particularly cheering here... anything from our young friend, Osaka?"

Ugaki smiled, "As a matter of fact, yes, sir... well, from Kajimora in point of fact. This message has just been decoded."

Yamamoto took the paper and read. He laughed with good cheer at first and then sardonically later, "You have read this, I'm sure."

Ugaki nodded, "Yes. One of their Aichi eliminated a Yankee submarine. Possibly an S-class, based on the size. That leaves, at least temporarily, a hole in their own submarine patrol routes."

"Yes,' Yamamoto said. "And Kajimora also includes his... *assessment* of the situation. Fool... he actually tries to take *credit* for the idea of including desalinators in second fleet's cargo. He even intimates that his sinking of that S-boat may be the very pinnacle of our success."

Ugaki chuffed, "Yes, it certainly reads that way. No credit to his officers. Certainly, none to Osaka or Hideki. Nothing even for the pilot who actually *sank* the submarine. Do you think he's going to be a problem?"

Yamamoto smiled thinly. Even his trusted chief of staff and friend, Matome, didn't know the full extent of Yamamoto's plans for the secret submarine carrier.

"I do, Matome, I do."

CHAPTER 15

STATION HYPO, CRYPTOGRAPHIC SECTION

"By God... that's it!" Joseph Rochefort, in an uncharacteristic display of emotion, leapt to his feet and waved a piece of lined paper over his head. "Listen up, everybody! We've got them! We've got the Jap right where we want him!"

"You've confirmed AF?" Joe Finnegan asked excitedly.

"You're shittin' us!" Jasper Holmes whooped.

Joan Turner, who was steadily scribbling away amongst a loose collection of notes and slips of paper at her small desk, looked up and blinked. Everyone in the basement room, over a hundred men and her, stood and began to applaud.

Rochefort held up a hand for quiet, "Don't clap for me, everyone... if you're going to applaud, applaud yourselves. Here's what we've been busting our hump on for weeks now... From: Admiral Yamamoto to commander second fleet. Re: AF... proceed as planned with following addition. Take aboard three industrial water purification plants. AF reports water shortage due to equipment failure. Immediately confirm receipt and feasibility, blah, blah, blah..."

"Hot damn!" someone shouted. "What do you think old Layton will make of this?"

As if the man had conjured him, the heavy door to the crypto office swung inward, and Commander Ed Layton walked in, shaking hands with the Marine sentry who'd opened the door for him.

"Well, Ed," Rochefort said nonchalantly, exercising a bit of wit. It was suspected that the oddball, seen most often in his robe or his smoking jacket, didn't even have a sense of humor. This was untrue; however, it was simply that Rochefort was generally too overworked and harried to let it show very often. "What brings you down to the dungeon, eh? Buying us all lunch at the O-club, perhaps?"

Layton cocked an eyebrow at his friend, "There some reason I should, Joe?"

A few snickers and even a chuckle or two floated around the room. Joan Turner watched with bright-eyed interest. The attitude in the cold basement room was often tense, yet the people there did their best not to let tempers flare or feelings fester. It was good to see their leader having a bit of fun.

"Oh, I think there is," Rochefort said, waving his message flimsy casually. "But before I tell you, I want to know what it's worth to ya'."

Layton frowned, "Joe, are you aware that the USS *Yorktown* is almost ready to put into dry-dock to rush back out to rejoin task force sixteen upon *your* recommendation? Are you aware that the ship is still full of holes, and dudes will be hanging over the side on platforms and safety lines painting, drilling, and *welding* while she puts to sea? Do you realize that within a few days, our Pacific fleet is going to come under a massive Japanese assault? Do you think this is a time to joke?"

Rochefort suddenly seemed to turn serious. He glowered at his friend for a long moment before the twinkle returned to his eyes, and he smiled and handed over the message, "Okay, okay, sourpuss. As a matter of fact, *I* do know all of that, as do my people here. *We* know more than any of you folks over at staff. Read it and weep, pal."

Layton did just that. He quickly scanned the message, his eyes nearly bugging right out of his skull, read it again more carefully and whooped in delight. He laughed heartily with such elation and relief that his eyes watered.

"Christ, I was only kidding," Rochefort teased, smiling all the way across his rumpled face. "Don't have to get all weepy about it."

"Joe! You son of a *bitch!*" Layton cheered. He clapped Rochefort on the shoulder, then spun him around and kicked him squarely but, not too hard, right in the ass. "There's your reward! Ha-ha-ha-HAA! We've got to show this to the Old Man, pronto. And if I have anything to say about it, there will *indeed* be a little something in all of your envelopes. Only thing I don't see here are dates."

Rochefort's good mood cooled a bit, "Yeah... we're still working on that. Mrs. Turner there says she's got a bead on it. Was her idea to include date and time info in our uncoded broadcast, and she's comparing character sets now and working up mathematical probabilities."

Layton walked over to Joan, "How's it going, Joan?"

Joan shrugged, "It's a bear, Commander. Yet I think I've got it nearly licked. Funny, though... there are a couple of dates here. Also, a couple of different locations. There's AF, of course, which we now are certain is Midway... then there's AG... the date and times seem slightly different, though."

Rochefort appeared at Joan's desk accompanied by Holmes and Finnegan. In particular, the three men felt a sense of propriety for Joan. As she was new and had already proven herself, they felt somewhat protective of her.

"OP-20-G still maintains AF is the Aleutians," Layton said.

Rochefort snorted, "What those gents know I wouldn't pay a plug nickel for, Ed! We *know* that AF is Midway. AG is probably the Aleutians. Message traffic and the bits and pieces we've gathered point to it... but I still say that attack is a ruse to pull our guys away from the real target."

"I tend to agree with the Commander, sir," Joan told Layton. "Look at this... oh, Joe, do you have it?"

Finnegan went to his desk and retrieved the information Joan was seeking. He showed the list to Layton, "I think Lt. Turner is referring to the task force assigned to AG, Ed. Look... two carriers, *Junyo* and *Ryujo*, neither one a fleet carrier. Couple of battleships, cruisers, and a hatful of destroyers."

Layton scowled at the list of ships, "Still... pretty big fleet for the Aleutians. There's nothing out there besides Dutch Harbor. There's that Kiska with a weather station on it. And Attu... which the Japs bombed already... for that they need forty ships?"

"Yeah, but the Kido Butai is headed for AF!" Rochefort insisted. "And another fleet is, too. To hell with the Aleutians."

Layton chuffed, "You go tell that to Nimitz, Joe."

"Let's go, then," Rochefort said. "We'll take Joanie here. She's already got the date and times narrowed down."

Layton looked at Joan. Joan drew in a breath and sighed, "I'd be happy to brief the Admiral, sir, if it came to it."

"Okay," Layton said. "He's touring the dockyard now... let's say after lunch? 1315 or so? That'll give our new star Lieutenant J.G. here time to work on her figures, and there just might... *might* mind you... be time for you to take a long hot shower, Joe. It's been quite a while, I'd guess."

That produced a round of partially subdued laughter. Rochefort, though, in his usual collected way, only shrugged, "You want clean pits or Jap message traffic decoded, Ed. Can't have both."

"Long as you come out smelling like a rose, Joe, I'm happy," Layton said as he walked toward the security desk with Rochefort's message in his khaki coat pocket. The Marine opened the door for him, and he turned back. "I meant that literally, Commander."

After the chuckles had died down, Rochefort went to stand by Joan's desk again. He was just about to ask her about her progress and offer to help when a young petty officer stood from his small station. He pulled off a pair of headphones and set the radio receiver on loud-speaker. The set was tied into the base's own receivers and allowed the Ultra team to listen in on message traffic and get first dibs at cracking any Japanese transmissions.

"Sir... uhm... can I get your help on something?" the twenty-one-year-old man asked.

Rochefort smiled indulgently at Joan and strolled across the large room, "Sure, Wally. Whatcha got?"

"Uhm..." Wally said nervously. He wasn't used to dealing with so many officers in one place.

"Take it easy, son," Rochefort said kindly. "You know the deal down here. When we're in the dungeon, we're all on the same team. It's Wally and Joe down here. Never mind all that rank and protocol foolishness. Now, what's eatin' ya?"

Wally smiled thinly, "A new message, sir... uhm... Joe. But it's partially in teletype and partially in voice... but of course, the voice is all Japanese. I've written it all down, but I can't make heads or tails."

"Okay," Rochefort said. "Send the signal groups over to our decoding team. Joe Finnegan will take that. As for the voice stuff, let me have a gander..."

Rochefort examined the message. It was brief, but he read it aloud, translating it as he did so: "Congratulate... *Leviathan?* Yes... *Leviathan* on eliminating U.S. submarine. Maintain station... will be radio silent until operation at AF... will contact... sending support. That's it. Hmm... interesting... Jasper, have we lost a boat recently?"

Holmes lit a cigarette and leaned back in his chair, "I'm not sure... not in the past couple of hours, anyway. But the evening reports will tell. Why? What's *Leviathan?*"

Rochefort frowned, "Not sure... although I think I'll take this to the meeting later. Joe, can you work out those code groups in the associated message by then?"

Finnegan walked over and picked up the sheet Wally had worked on, "I'll give it a go."

"Great," Rochefort said. "Good work, Wally. Keep your ears open. Joanie, any chance you'll have more of that date info in the next couple of hours?"

Joan frowned, "I hope so, Joe... God, it's right in front of my eyes... I can *almost* see it..."

"Don't work yourself up, now," Rochefort said. "Just take it one group at a time. Best thing is not to overthink it and not to get frustrated. Trust me, I speak from experience. Just work the problem, and I promise you; the solution will come."

————

And it had, or mostly.

The date information that Rochefort, Layton, and Joan Turner brought to Chester Nimitz's office wasn't exact, but as Rochefort indicated, was close enough for jazz.

This didn't exactly help his case. Although Joan, at the insistence of some of her teammates, had convinced Rochefort to wear a coat and tie, the man's acerbic nature, acerbic when he was sure of himself and being challenged, dulled the effect slightly.

Also in the meeting was Webster Clayton. He carefully examined the data that the Ultra team had compiled and nodded grimly, "I think you're right, Commander Rochefort. And I think that Mrs. Turner's dates are fairly close, as well. The Japanese will attack Midway Atoll on either June third or fourth. No doubt in my mind. Washington still insists it's the Aleutians, though, Admiral... something must be done on that front."

"We've got some cruisers and destroyers up there," Nimitz said. "We've got units at Dutch Harbor and nearby... that should be sufficient. I'll try and route a few more ships as well. Will that satisfy your bosses, Mr. Clayton?"

Clayton nodded, "I think so, Admiral... and now that we *know* where AF is and when it's to be attacked... we can set a trap for the Japs. Turn the tables on them. There's one thing that bothers me, though... this other communique from Yamamoto to this *Leviathan*. I'm not entirely sure, but I think *Leviathan*, or *Ribaiasan* in Japanese, is our submarine carrier. And from what I understand... she's directly in line between the Japanese invasion fleet and Midway. I need to get out there, Admiral. Is there any way to do that?"

Nimitz nodded, "Certainly. We've got a group of B-17 Flying Fortresses arriving shortly. I'm sure they can squeeze you in when we send them out to Midway. But why the urge to go, Clayton? Want to stand a post with the Marines out there?"

Clayton chuffed, "I would... but that's not it, sir. It's *Bull Shark*."

Joan's eyes lit up, and she leaned in closer. Clayton smiled thinly at her.

"*Bull Shark?*" Nimitz asked. "What about her?"

"She's my ace in the hole against this monster sub of Yamamoto's," Clayton said. "And the last time I sent her against a special adversary, I wasn't there... in fact, Mrs. Turner here was. Even took the helm during the final battle with the Germans. Well... I want to get Art Turner out to that *Leviathan*, and I want to be there when he does. I want that boat, Admiral."

Everyone looked at Clayton as if he'd gone mad. Nimitz leaned closer, "Are you saying you want to be there when she's sunk... or you want to acquire her, Clayton?"

Clayton set his jaw, "Preferably the latter, but I'll settle for the former. But I believe I need to be on the scene."

Nimitz nodded, "The Army Air Corps will see to that. As for the *Bull Shark*... she's a few hundred miles from Midway, if I'm not mistaken. She can be there tomorrow, I'd think. But that pulls her away from your target, Mr. Clayton."

"I know, sir... but I owe it to Art Turner... and Joan here."

Joan smiled at Clayton, "You don't really, Web."

Clayton chuckled, "It was my carelessness that allowed Milly Allman to slip past our screens, Joan. I should've known she was a Nazi spy the moment I found out she was on that freighter that got torpedoed... and as a result, you were kidnapped, for Christ's sake! If anybody should be in the hot seat this time... it's me."

All of the other three men were staring at Joan now. Each one knew a little about her stint aboard her husband's submarine, but she'd never related the entire story.

"Good lord..." Nimitz said with a smile playing on his lips. "No wonder they wanted you so bad, Lt. One day, you'll have to tell the whole story. All right, Clayton, we'll make it happen. Ed, please send a coded message to Captain Turner and order him to hightail it to Midway. Hopefully, he's got his radio antenna exposed. If not... we'll figure it out. Good work, all of you. Thank you."

"Well, how do you like that?" Layton said as he walked Rochefort and Joan out. "An intelligence man going to fight. What's the world coming to?"

"Let's hope it's not a trend," Rochefort said with a lopsided smile tugging at the corner of his mouth. "I'm a horrible shot."

"Good luck, Web," Joan said as Clayton exited the admiral's office after them. She hugged him quickly and stepped back. "Give Art my love."

USS BULL SHARK - 285 MILES SOUTH, SOUTHEAST OF MIDWAY ATOLL

"Is this for real?" Art Turner asked as he studied the message flimsy in front of him.

Chief Yeoman Clancy Weiss grinned, "Seems so, sir... Mr. Post and I decoded it three times to be sure."

"Christ on a crutch... okay, thank you, Yo," Turner said, and drank some coffee.

Around him, all of the men in the wardroom, including Begley, Nichols, and Joe Dutch, waited impatiently. Even Eddie Carlson stood by in his pantry, holding the coffee pot and looking eager to pour. He had several bets going, and what he heard next could add fifty bucks to his wallet or take away a couple of months' pay.

"CincPac has ordered us to proceed to Midway," Turner said, pushing the flimsy across to his XO. "We're to put into the base and receive a passenger with special information. There's an impending attack, and Ultra has confirmed that it's Midway. Projected hostilities begin around the second, third, or fourth. We're to receive secret op orders when our passenger comes aboard."

"Jesus..." Nichols muttered. "What kind of attack?"

Turner inhaled deeply, "I'm not a hundred percent sure, Enj. Big

Jap fleet is coming, though. Flat tops, battlewagons, cruisers, tin cans, and probably subs, too. That's not including the invasion fleet. The works."

"Sounds like an opportunity," Begley stated with a predatory gleam in his eye.

"For both sides," Dutch said without quite as much glee.

"Well, we go where we're needed," Turner said. "I think I have an idea of what's going on. I think you do, too, XO."

"That Jap sub carrier!" Begley said with even more enthusiasm. "I bet somebody got a line on them... still, I'd hate to miss the big to-do just to go chase down some whacky boat, sir."

"Yeah, you don't get a silver star just for sinking one boat," Dutch opined.

Begley shot him a look but said nothing. The dig was subtle, but he'd picked up on it.

"We're not out here for medals," Turner stated firmly. "We're out here to beat the Jap and beat him we will."

Eddie Carlson nodded imperceptibly and smiled slightly as well. Although he certainly agreed with the skipper's words, he'd also just won fifty bucks.

The nine B-17's sat in a long row on the tarmac at Hickam Field, each plane's four engines already rumbling and their ground crews finishing their final checks and removing the wheel chocks.

Webster Clayton, now dressed in unmarked Navy khakis, headed for the first aircraft in the line. He carried a small knapsack with a few changes of clothes, toiletries, and a few other odds and ends. It was made clear to him that aboard *Bull Shark*, he'd have little room for luxuries. He'd known that already, of course, having visited the submarine back in April.

Beside him walked another man in khakis. Unlike Clayton's uniform, this one was decorated with a lieutenant commander's oak leaves as well as a submarine combat pin below a set of gold dolphins. The man's prominent square jaw gave him something of an air of sternness, but his ready smile revealed the true friendly personality that lay beneath. The officer was in his mid-thirties and had joined Clayton for the walk out to the plane, informing him that he was assigned TAD to Midway for the duration of the battle before being returned to Pearl for further submarine assignment.

Dudley Morton grinned at Clayton as the two men walked across the hot tarmac, "So, what's a civvy doing flying out to the middle of a potential war zone, Web?"

Clayton chuckled softly, 'I'm not your ordinary civvy, Dudley."

Morton nodded, "Just call me Mush. Everybody does. What's that mean? You some kind of private contractor or secret agent, maybe?"

Clayton winked, "That's classified, Mush."

Morton laughed, "Okay... an OSS man, huh? Can I assume by the plain uniform that you're meeting a ship out there?"

"You sure ask a lot of questions, Mush," Clayton said as the two men approached their aircraft. "What about you?"

"Advisor," Morton said. "To Captain Simard. Try to help figure out what the Jap might do with his submarines. Ever been aboard a sub, Web?"

"Indeed, I have," Clayton said, returning the salute of the Army corporal who took his and Morton's seabags. "The SS-333. *Bull Shark.* Art Turner's command. Ever meet him?"

Morton grinned, "Old Anvil Art? Sure, I know him. We crossed paths once or twice while I was commanding an R-boat out of New London. Before that, too. Was one of his trainers at PXO School. Good man. Sharp, tough, and level-headed. Heard about that operation with the Krauts a month back. Pretty impressive. That who you're going to meet?"

Clayton shrugged, "As a matter of fact, yes."

The two men climbed inside the big bomber and were shown to a couple of folding canvas rumble seats.

"Sorry we don't have anything more comfortable, sirs," the corporal said wryly. "It may be a rough and bumpy flight... but at least it'll be long."

After running for over a day at a modest pace through thankfully moderate seas, the USS *Bull Shark* came within sight of the southern passage through the reef at Midway Atoll. It was summer, and the days thankfully long, so there was just enough daylight left for the boat's captain to be able to con her in. The PT boat that met them and led the way helped, but Art Turner always preferred to rely on himself whenever possible.

"Pretty dark," Begley said from behind Turner. "Thank God the swells aren't too high..."

"I can see them breaking to port and starboard," Buck Rogers was saying from beside Turner.

"Just enough light," Turner said. "Plus, our friends in the patrol boat know the way."

"Let's hope so..." Burt Pendergast said from beside Begley.

He wasn't quite sure of the reason, but Turner had noticed that Pendergast had changed slightly since they'd left Pearl. His stiff-neck attitude was still there, but he seemed... anxious. Turner knew that he hadn't been the only one to notice. Pat Jarvis had mentioned it earlier during his afternoon watch. It was probably nothing, just early-patrol jitters from a man who was still getting used to submarine life.

Of course... Pendergast had seemed fine... fine for him... on their way out to Pearl. It wasn't totally uncommon, either. Several of the men had caught the nervous disease. They'd gotten some new hands at Pearl, and the storm two days before had shaken a few of them up. Especially those who'd had to stand lookout watches during the hardest part of the blow.

They'd get used to it. Certainly, once the ship was embroiled in another fight, the din of a heavy storm at sea would be nothing in comparison to a depth charge attack.

As the submarine neared the narrow passage through the reef, the yawing became more pronounced. Rogers had the line handling party standing by below so they wouldn't be imperiled by any rough channel passage. It wasn't bad, but without any lifelines on the main deck, a man could slip or stumble and go over the side in a blink.

"We're through!" Rogers announced almost unnecessarily. The motion of the waves almost immediately dropped to a calm once the ship's stern passed through the roiling eddies of the reef break. They were now in the placid waters of Midway Lagoon.

"Well done, quartermaster," Turner said, patting Rogers on the shoulder. "Go ahead and station the line handlers. I'll con her in. Unless you'd like to have a go, Mr. Pendergast?"

"Me, sir?" the engineer asked.

"You, sir," Turner said with a smile. "Got to earn those dolphins before you qualify for command. Ever con a boat into a new dock before?"

"Uhm... no, sir," Pendergast said, trying to maintain a professional calm. Turner detected his anxiety beneath, however.

"First time for everything, then, Lieutenant," Turner said, stepping back so Pendergast could take his place. "Don't fret too much. This is an easy docking. Just follow the PT boat in, and you'll slide right into the slip."

Pendergast drew in a breath and stepped forward, "Aye-aye, sir. I have the con."

Just then, Pat Jarvis, Joe Dutch, and Andy Post came up through the bridge hatch to watch the docking. Although they stood back on the cigarette deck away from the bridge, Pendergast knew they were there. He knew they were watching him... judging him...

"Helm, bridge... slow to ahead two-thirds," Pendergast said into the transmitter.

"Maneuvering answering all ahead two-thirds," came the tinny and disembodied voice of Wendell Freeman, steersman of the watch.

Above the officers in the periscope sheers, the three lookouts were watching as well. Doug Ingram had the stern sector, Freddy Swooping Hawk the starboard, and Pete Griggs, torpedoman, had the port. All three men felt a little uneasy about the docking. Not that there was any real danger, even if the second engineer did screw up. Yet it was dark, and their boat's reputation was at stake.

Also, Doug Ingram knew more about Pendergast than the other two sailors and had more reason to worry, especially lately. Pendergast was not doing well with sea duty, especially since the storm. He'd come to Steve Plank that morning and asked for a handful of Amies, and Doug had been the one to supply them. Just before they'd come on watch, the lieutenant had inquired about getting more.

Doug had given him three, which was enough to sedate a grown man for up to twenty-four hours... and Pendergast already needed more? That was always a danger in their business, Ingram knew... but for an officer to start using so hard so fast... an officer who knew about Plank's black-market scheme... it gave the electrician several vague causes to worry.

Fred Swooping Hawk was only mildly concerned. The passage through the reef had been a little hairy, but he trusted Turner, and he also trusted the COB, both men at the con during the passage. Yet, the two new officers were another matter. Begley was a bigoted prick, and Pendergast was that and then some. Swooping Hawk also thought the man was incompetent.

Then there was Griggs. He had become one of Plank's customers through Doug. Although he was more a Benny man, he'd popped an Amy after the storm, too. He hadn't expected to go on watch, having been chosen as a last-minute replacement for Johnny Wexler, a torpedoman from the after room who'd come down sick just before the change of the watch.

Unfortunately, Griggs had just come off a grueling couple of hours in his room. Sparky had ordered that they pull and routine all six fish in the tubes and wanted it done before the boat reached the reef. Wanted to make sure everything was ship-shape in case they were inspected when they pulled in. So, it had been pull, inspect, oil, lube, reload, and polish the room, the racks, the reloads, and the officer's head to a Sparky Sparkle. Now here he was, standing a lookout watch when he planned to be in his rack, or at least be in it after *Bull Shark* tied up.

Luckily, though, old Doug had come through. Said he had just the thing for an overworked sailor. Gave him what he said was headache powder and winked. Griggs said that he didn't have a headache. Doug had only smiled and said there were all sorts of headaches, including officers and chiefs who didn't think of a man's comfort after a long day.

Griggs had taken the powder and snorted it, understanding what it really was. He'd never been a cokie, nor even a druggie, but he'd tried a few things in his day, including jujus, which he preferred but which was impossible aboard a submarine. So now, he felt energized and bright-eyed. Great for duty, but he also kept thinking that somebody would notice... that somebody would ask why a man who just put the forward room through the wash and rinse cycle would be so chipper. Would the captain notice? The COB? Certainly, the XO or Pendergast... those two hard asses didn't let anything slip.

As it turned out, there was no reason for worry, at least not much. Pendergast conned the sub up to the dock, and the lines were thrown. Although he was sweating more than what seemed usual even on a near June evening in the near tropics, Pendergast played it off well.

"Good work, Mr. Pendergast," Turner said.

"Captain, permission to take the brow?" Rogers asked from the main deck.

"Permission granted," Turner said, gazing across the expanse of water between the submarine's hull and the pier. On it stood four men, two of whom he knew. One of the men was a civilian standing behind a movie camera on a tripod with bright lights mounted above it.

"Just the single brow, Captain!" the senior officer of the three, Captain Simard, stated. "No phone, electric, or water lines, either. This is a short stop. Permission to come aboard?"

"You're welcome, Captain," Turner said, casting a quick glance at Pat Jarvis as he went down on the main deck to greet his guests.

Simard led the other two officers Turner knew over the gangway, and they saluted the flag. Then Simard shook Turner's hand.

"Welcome to Midway, Captain. Sorry it's got to be a brief visit this time," Simard said. "Pleasure to meet you. I believe you know these two gents."

Turner smiled, "Thank you, sir... likewise. Yes, I certainly know Mr. Clayton here. And that's not the glass-jawed Mush Morton I see on my deck, is it?"

Morton grinned broadly, "Good to see you again, Anvil. Boat looks great. I see you've got a handful of flags already painted... four Nazis and a rising sun. Not bad for a boat only been off the ways for four months."

"I'll say," Simard said with a smile of his own. "Can we get the nickel tour?"

"Of course, sir," Turner said, eyeing Clayton suspiciously.

"I'd like a word with Art first, Captain, if you don't mind," Clayton stated.

"Mr. Begley," Turner turned and addressed the cigarette deck. "Would you conduct the Captain and the Commander here on a turn through the boat?"

"Of course, sir," Begley said formally. "Sirs, if you'll come forward, we'll go down into the forward room..."

"Surprised to see you here, Web," Turner said. "How's Joanie and the kids?"

"They send their love," Clayton said with a grin. "That wife of yours is doing very well in her new job. She's partly responsible for Ultra figuring this thing out. But we've gotten some more news on the Jap sub carrier... and I thought I should tell you in person... not like last time."

Turner smiled thinly, "Web, you're a civvy. Nobody expected you to go to sea with us and hunt down those Huns."

Clayton scoffed, "No... but nobody expected a young mother of two to be *taken* to sea and then to be aboard during a damned battle."

He drew in a breath and sighed. Turner reached out and squeezed his shoulder, "Take it easy, Web. What's done is done... by the way, who's that guy with the movie camera?"

Clayton smiled too, "Thanks, Art... I appreciate that. That guy, by the way... ever see *Stagecoach? The Grapes of Wrath?*"

"Yeah, both."

"That's the guy who directed them. John Ford," Clayton explained. "He's here to document the battle. I said I thought it'd be okay if he got some footage of you guys pulling in and out. Now listen, Art... I've got some news on that submarine. I think I know where she is right now, and I think we can get there in a couple of days. Maybe get her before the big battle. However... I believe she may be escorted. She's right in line between here and the invasion fleet... which means by the time we intercept, she might not only have a destroyer escort but a whole invasion convoy to cover her, too. It's dangerous as hell... so I'm coming along for the ride."

"Web... that's not necessary," Turner said. "We can handle things on our own. It's our job."

Clayton drew in a breath, "I want the boat, Art."

"You mean... to *capture* this thing?" Turner asked. "That's... well, it's ambitious, Web. Almost impossible. We have to figure that they'll have more men aboard a sub that size and in order to subdue her enough to get our guys aboard, we have to damage her without using torpedoes."

"I'm not saying it's all or nothing," Clayton insisted. "But if the opportunity arises... it might be doable. Remember, I've got contacts in Southeast Asia. I think we may even have an asset already on the boat."

Turner's eyes widened, "A spy? Why the hell didn't you say so earlier?"

Clayton pulled a cigarette from a pack in his duty blouse and lit it, "I'm not entirely certain. But we've got a few Japanese Americans who were over there before the war began. Most are simply victims of circumstance and have probably been pressed into the Imperial Japanese service or merchant service. However, we do have several confirmed OSS assets over there. One, in particular, I don't know his name... only know him by his code name... is in the IJN. He was funneling information to us up until that big monster surfaced in the Kurils. I have reason to suspect he's aboard her even now. If we can get close enough, it could be that I can activate him, and he might help us to disable the ship. It's a helluva long shot... but I think it's worth taking."

"Good Christ, Web..." Turner muttered and shook his head in bewilderment. "You and your damned cloak and dagger nonsense..."

Clayton smiled indulgently, "I know, Art... but hey... it *did* win you a Navy Cross last time."

Turner drew in a breath, "Well, all right, Web. But my two officer's staterooms and the chief's stateroom are full. However... I've got a fold-down bunk in my cabin that's not being used. You can bunk with me. Go on below and stow your bag. Welcome to the submarine Navy."

———

Bull Shark stayed at the Midway dock for just over thirty-six hours. Barely long enough for a fuel truck to top off their diesel tanks, to swap out some movie reels, and for the men to stretch their legs for a few hours in Goonieville. John Ford, the movie director, was allowed to come aboard the boat and speak to a few of the officers and men. He said he wasn't sure if the interviews would make it into the documentary, but he'd certainly try his best.

At 0230 on the morning of May 28, the submarine was once again being led through the southern passage and out into the rolling swells of the Pacific. Once clear of the reef, Lieutenant Pat Jarvis, who was OOD for the middle watch, ordered the ship onto a course of two-four-zero on all four engines. He had the engines on an 80 / 90 split, and the submarine ran in the general direction of the Mariana Island chain at eighteen knots.

If Clayton's coordinates were correct, and if the big submarine carrier was holding station, it would take the *Bull Shark* the better part of sixty hours to reach the position. Of course, if they had to dive during the day, that timeframe would lengthen significantly. That also meant that if Ultra's date for the Japanese attack was correct, then the submarine would reach the location of the *Leviathan* as late as the first of June. They'd never get back to Midway in time to take part in the battle.

Clayton said that he doubted that would be the case. Since the sub carrier was lying directly in the path of the oncoming Japanese invasion force, then she'd no doubt proceed with them when they met up. In that likelihood, then, the lone American boat would meet the entire force a bit early. Which meant they could run up to them or lie in wait themselves, perhaps thirty-six or forty-eight hours out from Midway and ambush the entire fleet. That would put *Bull Shark* six or seven hundred miles from Midway and might allow them to coordinate with the proposed B-17 scouting attacks.

Although they didn't know all of the details, the crew was beginning to get a pretty good idea of what was going on. This was due in no small part to Eddie Carlson, whose unique position gave him a lot of poop from the wardroom. The lookouts, the radiomen, the watchstanders in the conning tower, and the control room also contributed. It was impossible to keep anything secret in a three-hundred-and eleven-foot cigar tube, after all. Carlson, for example, would keep his mouth shut if asked, but the officers also knew when to let things slide. An informed crew was a good crew.

In the portside bunking area aft of the mess, Doug Ingram was readying to climb up and into his rack. He saw that Freddy Swooping Hawk had his little reading lamp on and was engrossed in a comic book he'd acquired from a Marine at the Midway dock in exchange for one he'd finished reading the day before.

"Hey, Freddy," Doug said quietly but casually, "you readin' a Lone Ranger?"

The Navajo looked at Doug and smiled, "Sure, why not?"

"Well... I dunno... thought maybe that might bother you or somethin', on account you're an Indian and all."

Fred only shrugged, "Nah... besides, the Lone Ranger respects Tonto. Values him and treats him as a friend. Kinda nice."

"Yeah..." Doug said wistfully. "It's nice havin' friends..."

Fred lowered the comic and gazed at Doug, "Somethin' botherin' you, Doug? You got friends. How about Plank?"

Doug shrugged, "Steve's... a good guy, but he's more like a big brother or somethin', y'know? We're not... not on the same deck, if you see what I mean."

Fred nodded, "Sure, I see. But hey, we're friends, aren't we?"

Doug smiled, "Yeah, Freddy. Even though we only known each other a couple of days and all. Spend a few hours in the perch with a guy and you either love him or hate him, I guess."

Fred chuckled, "That's true. That all that's eating you?"

Doug drew in a breath, paused, seemed to come to a decision and continued, "You ever... ever get scared, Freddy?"

Swooping Hawk had seen this before. Although Ingram was no stranger to shipboard life, he was new to the boats. It could be a bit jarring for some men at first.

"Sometimes," Fred admitted. "I've been aboard since before we were put into commission. A plank owner, in fact. Had a few tough moments on that last patrol. Plus, on the way out here, we mixed it up with a couple of Jap tin cans. On the surface and everything. That'll tighten your belly for sure. You scared, Doug?"

"Aw, hell..." Doug tried to bluster. "Me? Nah... not really... plus... well, if I ever do get scared... I got a little helper gets me through it."

Fred looked askance at the other man, "Helper? What've you got a secret stash of glug-glug on board? Maybe break into the torpedo alky once in a while?"

Doug chuckled, "Nah, nothin' like that... well, no more'n the other guys. But y'know... sometimes you get nervous or feel a bit anxious or whatever... so you need a little somethin' to get you over the hump, is all."

"Oh, yeah?" Fred asked with interest.

"You ever feel like that?" Doug asked. "Like you might need a little somethin' to take the edge off... but not cloud your brain like booze?"

Fred shrugged, "Maybe... what do you mean?"

"Well, I like these," Doug said, holding out his hand and showing Fred the two small bullet-shaped blue pills. "Docs prescribe them for tension and stuff. Helps you sleep, but not really a knockout drug. Just a relaxer."

"Docs give them out?" Fred asked, eyeing the pills.

"Yeah... but I can get 'em without that," Doug said. "I know a guy who knows a guy, y'know. Anyway, I'm about to hit the rack, and I'm gonna take one. Thought maybe you'd like one for yourself."

"And you say they're safe?" Fred asked.

"Oh, sure!" Doug said. "Just a relaxer. Amytal they're called... Amies or Blue Amies for short. Hell, several of the guys aboard eat one once in a while. No big thing. Like I say, they let you relax and don't fog your head like liquor."

Fred shrugged, "Okay, what the hell. Might make it easier to sleep when it's rough or when we're diving, and it's hot."

Doug smiled and handed an Amy to Fred. He swallowed his own and then held out a coffee mug of water. Fred swallowed the pill, said thanks, and went back to his comic.

Doug climbed up and into his rack and got settled in, adjusting the little AC vent. Yet another potential customer for Plank. It kind of made Doug feel good that Fred wanted the pill. It sort of made him feel a little better about downing them himself, now that a friend and a guy on his own level was taking them, too.

In the lowest bunk, Sherman "Tank" Broderick lay on his back wide awake. He'd drawn the curtain and tried to read, but that hadn't helped. So, he just resigned himself to waiting for sleep to overtake him. Sherman was a big man, thus the nickname, and while the bunks were pretty comfortable, especially with the individual air conditioning vents, they were only just big enough for his wide shoulders to fit in. He often had trouble sleeping for one reason or another.

Tank couldn't help but overhear the conversation above, as Doug Ingram's knees had only been a few inches from his face. Although he hadn't seen what Ingram had given Fred, he'd picked up enough to figure it out. Some kind of pill. Probably a sedative of some kind. Clearly not allowed by the regs and not given out by Hoffman, the pharmacist's mate.

Tank had seen it before. Seen it on surface ships, on bases, and even in the submarines. Some guy with a little stash of pills or who could get you cheap alky ashore or maybe a date with a *real* friendly broad. For the most part, it was harmless... but on a submarine, where every man depended on another... Tank never liked it.

Tank also suspected that Ingram wasn't the main man. He just didn't have the... savvy... grit, maybe? No, he was the frontman. The salesman. Somebody else was backing him, that was for sure. Could be Plank. New boatswain's mate who had access to areas of the boat where he could hide a stash. It could even be one of the officers. Tank had seen that before, too.

The real question was what to do about it. Tank had no problem with a guy kicking back and letting his hair down on shore. Hell, he was a hard-drinking, red-blooded male himself. Liked fast women and easy booze... but not on duty. Not in a *fuckin'* war zone, for Chrissakes. Ingram had said a few other guys were using, too... that's how it always went. Couple free samples and then the selling.

Still... Sherman Broderick's mother didn't raise no stool Pidgeon. He wasn't gonna run to the COB and rat Ingram out. Not only did it go against the grain, Tank *liked* the kid. He was good-natured and did his duty. And he probably felt he was really helping the guys out with his *product*.

Tank sighed. He'd have to think of something. Just one more goddamned thing to keep him awake off watch... join the Navy they said... see the world they said... then they lock you up inside a cigar tube full of diesel fumes, stinky pits, and egg farts. As if that wasn't bad enough, now Tank had to put up with dopers.

His wry smile still showed on his face when sleep snuck up on him only five minutes later.

CHAPTER 17

MAY 30, 1942

500 MILES WEST, SOUTHWEST OF MIDWAY ATOLL

T he sun had yet to make its appearance in the eastern sky. Although false dawn was beginning to turn the sky behind the *Bull Shark* a deep indigo. The boat plowed ahead at a moderate sixteen knots. In the lookout perch on the periscope sheers, three fresh lookouts had just been posted, their bellies full of coffee, ham, and eggs, and their eyes sharp. Above them, at thirty-minute intervals, the SD air search and SJ surface search radar heads would power up, sweep through a complete circle, and then power down. On the bridge, two men stood quietly, both tired and ready to go off watch.

In the wardroom, the captain, first engineer, and the electrical engineer were sipping coffee and eating their own plate of ham and eggs. Along with this was a plate of cheese Danishes, freshly baked during the middle watch. The Danishes were filled with a fruit compote made from random frozen fruits and were popular among all of the men.

In the torpedo rooms, men were getting out of their racks and getting them squared away in preparation to go on watch. They knew better than to leave a rumpled bed with the eyes of Walter Murphy and Walter Sparks to find them. They combed their hair, read the plan of the day tacked to the small bulletin boards, and moved toward the after battery compartment to join their fellows who bunked there for breakfast.

At the moment, neither leading petty could be found in their respective rooms. They were huddled together in the chief's quarters in the forward battery compartment along with the chief of the boat and the pharmacist's mate, Henry Hoffman. The four men spoke in hushed voices, the only thing between them and the ears of the officers in the wardroom and any crew moving through the passage being a thin baize curtain.

"I don't want to make a big deal of this," Paul "Buck" Rogers was saying. "It's a couple of minor things... but you know how that goes, boys. Even a small leak can sink a ship."

Murph nodded, "And I think we got a couple of small leaks, Chief."

Sparky, who was less sanguine than Murph, harrumphed, "Couple of goddamned gold-brickers is more like it. Wexler takes sick at the last minute and then my man Griggs has to go on watch and pull double duty? Bunch of bullshit."

"Yeah, and what's up with Grigsy lately, Sparky?" Murph shot back, annoyed now. "Kid's dumpy one minute and peppy the next. Maybe somebody's got the key to your alky locker."

"Hold on," Rogers said, holding up a hand. "Let's not start bickering and chewing each other's ass off. That ain't gonna solve anything. I like friendly competition between the rooms, but no real hard feelings now. I'm not blaming you two fellas any more than I'm blaming Harry or Mike for the few defaulters in their compartments, either."

Murph and Sparky looked a bit sheepish and grinned at one another.

The COB looked to Hoffman, "What do you think, Hank? Seems like ever since we left Pearl, we've got half a dozen guys that are suddenly slackin' off or just acting... odd."

Hoffman frowned, "I examined Wexler. There was nothing wrong with him that I could see. Temperature and reflexes okay, good color... in my opinion, either he just had a belly ache, or he's a loafer."

"What about the rest?" Rogers asked.

Hoffman shrugged, "I couldn't say. Probably got a few new members of the brush-off club aboard. Always happens when new guys put to sea. Lot of women don't want to wait."

"That's true," Murph put in. "Always a load of coffee coolers and sack rats first week or two until we get them with the program."

Sparky chuffed, "Ain't gonna be none of that in my fuckin' room. Last thing we need is for the fuckin' Old Man to start riding our asses about this."

"You know that's not his style, Sparky," COB admonished gently.

"Shit, Buck, I know that... I ain't bad-mouthing the skipper," Sparks said, holding up a hand. "Just the opposite. Our captain knows how to let us handle the men. Knows when to pay out some line and let a guy get his head on square. But if he starts coming to *us* with somethin'... then we screwed up is all I'm sayin'."

Murph nodded, as did Hoffman.

"Yeah, that's right," COB said. "As of now, he hasn't spoken to me about it, but you can bet your asses he sees it. In my opinion, and what do you think of this, Doc...? I think we've got some dopers aboard."

"Shit..." Sparky drawled out a groan.

Murph scowled but didn't disagree. Hoffman tapped his chin lightly and then nodded slowly, "I hate to admit it, Chief... but you might be right. With the war now six months old, medical, and even BeauPers, is taking note of some of this stuff. I read a thing while we were in Pearl about drug use becoming more and more prevalent among fighting men. Not just in our service, either. And not just the hard shit like coke or heroin or even guys smoking sticks of tea... it's prescription stuff. Most common things are sedatives and amphetamines. Basically, downers and uppers. Some of it's even sanctioned... but not in the Navy."

"Damn well told," Murph grumbled.

"Last thing we need are guys all hopped up on goofballs or whatever," Sparky intoned. "It's one thing to get shit-faced on leave; it's another to start fuckin' around on a ship, specially a fuckin' submarine. It puts everybody's life in danger."

Rogers nodded, "I agree. And I agree with you, Hank. I've seen this before. So far, I think it's pretty mild... but we need to keep our eyes open and watch for the signs. I'm gonna have this same talk with Brannigan and Duncan, too."

"Who you think is the pusher?" Sparky asked. "There's always a guy brings the shit to sea, right, Hank?"

Hoffman shrugged, "Probably. I'm not an aficionado on dope use... but I'd say that's right. Either that or somebody's breaking into my medicine locker... but I doubt that. That's hard to do, and the only key is around my neck."

"It's got to be one of the new guys," Murph opined. "This shit didn't start until we left Pearl."

Sparky nodded vigorously, "That's right! Maybe you oughta have a talk with *them*, Buck. Put a scare into em'... or I'll do it if'n you want. I'll scare them shitbirds so bad they won't take an aspirin for a headache afterward."

Rogers grinned, "Not yet, Sparky. I'll make some... discreet inquiries. Don't want to start throwing any blanket parties yet. Anybody got any idea on who it might be? There's at least one guy with the stuff, maybe two."

Everyone fell silent. Finally, Murph drew in a breath and reluctantly said, "The only guy who's got the freedom would be our new boatswain's mate, Steve Plank. Lives in my room."

"Shit," Sparky said with a shake of his head. "I dunno, Murph... he's a good dude. Does his duty and seems friendly and like a straight shooter."

Murph shrugged, "Yeah, I know... always ready to pitch in... he doesn't seem the type..."

Rogers frowned, "But that's the perfect type. Problem is I don't want to start a witch hunt here. I don't want to start suspecting guys for no reason. Morale on this boat has been bad enough since... since we left New England. Let's not make it worse. We just keep our eyes open and ears to the ground."

"Maybe the men can help," Hoffman suggested. "One of them will surely report something. Not everybody approached about taking dope wants it."

The COB sighed, "Maybe... but sailors are a funny lot, Hank. Nobody likes a fink. And popping a pill or taking a little snort of hooch off-watch now and then ain't a big deal to your sailor... even a submarine sailor. What we do is find a couple of guys we *know* we can trust and hint to them that we'd appreciate anything weird they notice being reported. Could you do a piss test or something, Hank?"

Hoffman snorted, "Out here? Hardly. I don't have the chemicals to test for dope or anything."

"Yeah... but the men don't know that," Sparky said with a wicked grin.

Rogers nodded, "Interesting... okay, let's hold off on that. Because if we suddenly announce a boat-wide tinkle party, then everybody's gonna know something's up. I'd like to nip this in the bud before the captain sniffs it out. Okay, guys, enough of this shit, let's get back to work, huh? I heard a rumor there's a fuckin war on someplace."

In the wardroom, Captain Turner was pondering the same situation. His lofty position as the high and mighty captain did not preclude him from seeing what was right under his nose. Maybe on a battleship or a carrier the skipper could be unaware of what was happening half a dozen decks below him, but on a submarine, that just wasn't possible unless the skipper was a complete moron.

He'd seen the signs of something being off with several of his men. He wasn't sure what it was, exactly, but he knew something was odd. Partly, he chalked it up to the morale issue with his new officers. Pendergast and Begley had drastically altered the atmosphere aboard his boat. He did not like it. He missed the way things were before. Missed Elmer Williams's quiet competence. Missed the way the officers and men had fallen into a well-oiled groove. Even so far as to joke around with one another.

Before the change, Turner would take a turn through the boat and shoot the shit with the crew. There would be smiles and laughter and a little good-natured ribbing. The men felt comfortable talking with him, and yet they respected him as well, and he them. Now, when he toured the submarine, Turner felt the tension. Felt that a barrier now stood between himself and his men.

On the surface of it, he and they knew why. The people's displeasure wasn't aimed toward him... at least not entirely. They knew that the new officers had a different way of doing things. Yet they also knew that as the captain, the ultimate responsibility was Turner's. Sure, he couldn't control who got assigned to his boat, but they knew that Turner was a man who would kick some ass when required... so why wasn't he straightening the XO and second engineer out?

He was aware that Pat Jarvis had made an attempt. He, Pendergast, and Begley had some sort of private talk at Turner's house, and the two officers left shortly afterward. The trouble there was that they were all the same rank, and Begley was senior to Jarvis as the XO.

Turner had tried the carrot with Begley as well. It seemed to work after the brush-up with the *Fubukis*... but that hadn't lasted. Things were back to the way they'd started and, in fact... a little worse.

Although Begley seemed a reasonably competent submariner, he lacked something when it came to leadership. That was unfortunate because Pendergast's attitude seemed to have degraded over the past few days. Turner needed Begley to take his friend in hand. Otherwise, it'd be up to him or Jarvis, and while the thought of the big torpedo officer smacking Pendergast upside his thick noggin was amusing, Turner wanted to hold that back as a last resort.

Perhaps all that was required was a battle. That had certainly knit the crew together when they were new. It had worked temporarily near the Galapagos, but maybe another major engagement might stitch the wound in *Bull Shark's* morale.

The curtain slid aside, and Web Clayton entered, rubbing sleep from his eyes. He took an empty seat and smiled gratefully at Carlson, who set down a cup of coffee in front of him.

"Welcome back to the land of the living, Web," Turner said with a smile. "Feel like breakfast?"

"I think so," Clayton said. "And a smoke. What are you gents up to this morning?"

"Skipper and I are about to go on watch," Post said. "Otherwise... I think we're all wondering about this big dust-up with the Japs that's coming."

"That and about this mystery submarine we're supposed to be chasing," Nichols added.

"I think we should tell the men what's going on," Turner said to Clayton. "Fill them in and get them up to speed."

Clayton drew in a breath and let it out slowly, "Usually, in my line, Art, we play it close to the vest."

Nichols smirked, "Who are they going to tell, Mr. Clayton?"

Clayton chuckled, "That's true. By the time any of these boys can tell anyone what they've been up to..., it'll be over."

Turner nodded and smiled indulgently, "They call this the silent service for a reason, Web. Submariners don't make a lot of chin music about what they do, not even to impress a woman... at least not anything that's classified. A submarine is a special unit, a unit that works on trust as much as discipline."

He saw Post and Nichols frown slightly at that. He knew they were thinking about what he'd been thinking about. About how that bond of trust, while not broken, was being strained.

"Okay," Clayton said. "You're probably right. At least insofar as the operation at Midway and the *Leviathan* goes."

Turner nodded, "I'll make an announcement over the 1MC in a bit. Do you think your people will have any more info for us this morning, Web?"

Clayton shrugged, "Certainly not over the fleet broadcast. I've asked Commander Rochefort and his team to pay special attention to anything regarding Yamamoto's pet project."

"Rochefort..." Nichols said. "He's that weird guy who wears his bathrobe to work, right?"

Clayton chuckled, "The same. Very good man, though. Speaks Japanese like a native and has a real head for puzzles."

"Let's just hope the Nips don't have their own bathrobe guy," Post said glumly. "This code-breaking stuff goes both ways, doesn't it? We all know firsthand how easy it is to spy on us."

Clayton frowned, "Yeah... but it's different with the Japanese. Maybe it's even racially motivated. It's one thing for a Milly Allman, a blonde, White woman, to be a German spy. It's another for some man or woman from the Midwest or whatever to work for the Japs. We've got the same problem, obviously. Still, we can only control what we control."

"Exactly," Turner stated, draining his coffee mug. "I'm going to keep us running on top for the duration. Unless we get forced under, I want to close with this Jap sub. If you're right, Web, that could be this time tomorrow or tomorrow evening. If we don't spot them by then, I'll probably dive and lie in wait unless we get other information. Personally, I'd like to sink this sub carrier, maybe a few dozen Jap transports, cruisers, and a carrier, and then get back to Midway and blow up the Kido Butai."

The men, including Carlson, all laughed. Nichols shook his head, "Okay, that takes care of this week, then what?"

Another laugh. Turner stood, "Oh, figure we'll be in the Imperial Palace by July... Frank, your rock crushers okay with this much running?"

Nichols waved that off, "They're good solid GM diesels, Captain. They love having a load on 'em."

"Great. Okay, Andy, let's go mind the store," Turner stated. "Web, you want to join me on the bridge for a while? Nothing quite like a sunrise at sea."

700 MILES AHEAD OF *BULL SHARK* AND 12 HOURS LATER...

"Contact on echo ranging!" the young sonarman said a bit too excitedly. "Fast screws bearing one hundred and fifty degrees!"

Captain Kajimora inhaled deeply and flicked the long ash from the end of his cigarette. It fluttered to the deck, disintegrating as it fell in almost languid slow motion. He sighed and tried to make himself comfortable in his position leaning against the search periscope's barrel.

"Please endeavor to contain yourself, sonarman," Kajimora said negligently, almost uncaringly, as if he hadn't just been told that a ship was bearing down on his submarine. "What is the range and speed?"

The young man pressed a hand to his earphones and tapped the other against his leg for a few moments. Kajimora resisted the urge to snap at him. This was information he should have already had or at the very least been calculating as he made his contact report.

Finally, the sonarman said, "Range is twenty-four thousand meters... speed twenty-five knots. Possible destroyer, sir."

"Do you hear that, Yakuin?" Kajimora called down the open hatch to the control room. "We appear to have a guest."

Osaka's head appeared in the wide hatchway, "I believe they are right on time, sir."

"How do we know it's not an American...? Or perhaps an Australian searching for his lost kangaroo, eh?" Kajimora quipped.

Osaka smiled and joined in the polite chuckling before saying, "I believe this is the escort we were promised, sir."

"Of course," Kajimora said, lighting another Golden Bat. "We can always rely on the Great Yamamoto to be prompt."

"Yes, sir," Osaka said neutrally.

"Shall we surface and surprise him?" Kajimora said. "Or perhaps have a bit of fun at his expense. Wait until he passes and surface in his wake, eh?"

Osaka bowed at the shoulders, "It is as you wish, sir."

"But what do you say, executive officer?" The captain needled.

Osaka drew in a breath, "It is perhaps unwise to tease a destroyer, sir. I think that their captains are perhaps a bit edgy these days and might fire on a submarine and ask of our identity later."

Kajimora laughed, "Yes, most wise, Yakuin. Best not to poke the tiger when you've got him by the tail. Very well. Diving officer, prepare to surface the boat. Ryu, would you please send for flight leader Hideki. Perhaps we might launch a scouting sortie since we're going to surface in any case. Also, have the radio room standby to hail the destroyer and make the recognition signal, please."

"Hai," Osaka said and vanished.

Kajimora sighed. All of this sitting around and waiting, hiding in the depths when the sun shone just on the nearly impossible chance that an enemy might wander by was beginning to try his patience. Here he had this magnificent monstrosity of Yamamoto's genius, and what had they done with it thus far?

A pitifully easy raid on an island that had next to nothing on it. A few shacks, a dock, and a couple of ships there to set up an American base. So much the better when the *real* invasion came... yet where was the action? Where was the glory?

Kajimora sighed. It was to be found two thousand kilometers away on a speck of dust the Americans crawled over like beetles on shit. And while the mighty Kido Butai went in to smash the Americans to bits, Kajimora's secret weapon sat in the middle of the Pacific, waiting for a pack of merchant transports to sail by.

Pathetic... ridiculous...

Kajimora almost labeled it as cowardice. Even in his own thoughts, however, he wasn't quite prepared to go that far in judging Yamamoto. The events of the next week would tell, of course. Should the revered admiral be successful... then Kajimora would be the first to applaud his efforts. Should things go awry on the other hand... time would certainly tell.

Kajimora wasn't a superstitious man, indeed far from it. At least this is what he told himself. Yet he was wise enough, as he also told himself, to realize that often one's innermost thoughts and feelings could show on one's face, and that wouldn't do under the circumstances. Not with Osaka watching his every action.

Once on the surface, Kajimora went up onto the bridge and breathed in the fresh evening air. There was a good two hours of daylight left. Plenty to launch his birds and even recover them a bit after sunset. Kajimora watched as the big destroyer drew closer. No, not a destroyer... a larger ship. A light cruiser by the looks of her. A formidable escort and one that could add at least one floatplane, possibly two, to the squadron.

"And with a full *Kaigun Chusa* in charge to argue with me and try to take control of my operation," Kajimora grumbled under his breath.

The quartermaster of the watch held up a pair of binoculars, "Ship is signaling, sir... Light cruiser *Nikatoni*... Commander Taji Pendo commanding... sending radio frequency and requesting voice communication, sir."

"Acknowledge with signal gun," Kajimora said and depressed the bridge transmitter button. "Radio, bridge. Contact escort on the short range. Use frequency..."

He looked to the quartermaster, who repeated the radio setting into the transmitter. After a moment, a gruff-voiced man came over the transmitter.

"*Captain Kajimora, I am Captain Taji Pendo. It is a pleasure to make your acquaintance,*" the other captain said. "*Admiral Yamamoto and Admiral Ugaki send their compliments.*"

"I am honored, Pendo san," Kajimora replied politely. "Do you have new orders or information from the fleet?"

"*Nothing new,*" Pendo replied. "*As you are no doubt aware, a large operation is soon to begin. Admiral Kondo's invasion force is several days behind us. I believe that you have been requested to wait for them and escort them to the battle. However, as we seem to have a few days at our disposal... I do have a suggestion.*"

Kajimora waited.

"*We are to provide surface support for you and to join the escort of the invasion force,*" Pendo continued. "*However, I and my crew would appreciate a bit of action. Perhaps we might scout ahead somewhat and see if we might find an American submarine or picket ship and pay them a compliment.*"

Suddenly Kajimora's suspicions were allayed. He smiled, being pleased that this cruiser commander's thinking was in line with his own. Perhaps this would go well after all.

"I'm of your thinking entirely, Captain," Kajimora said. "I was about to launch a reconnaissance flight to scout ahead. As it will be dark soon, perhaps we can run through the night and perhaps the next day and get another five hundred kilometers closer by this time tomorrow evening."

"*Agreed, Captain,*" Pendo said. "*I have two Aichi floatplanes aboard and ready to fly if you wish to forego your launch operations... although I would be fascinated to see that. That vessel of yours is quite unique.*"

Kajimora smiled, "Perhaps that would be the best course, Captain. If you'd care to launch a boat, I'd be happy to provide you with a brief tour and perhaps treat you and your first officer to a meal."

"*Excellent!*" Pendo said. "*Then it shall be as you say. I and my Yakuin will arrive shortly.*"

Kajimora ordered the helm to ahead slow. Although the transfer of a boat to and from his submarine would waste a half hours' time, Kajimora knew that engendering goodwill with his new partner was important.

"Conning tower, bridge," Kajimora said, a smile playing on his thin lips. "Is the executive officer there?"

A pause, and Osaka replied, "*Bridge, I am here.*"

"Good, Yakuin," Kajimora said pleasantly. "Please make preparations to receive two guests. We'll be showing them our boat and dining with them. Oh, Ryu... please make a note in the duty log that sonarman Weduko is on report. His contact report was flawed, and this must not be allowed to go uncorrected. We shall have a punishment hearing once we're underway again."

Another pause while Osaka no doubt seethed. A captain's mast was a severe step for simply failing to report three screws rather than just that they were light and fast. However, discipline was all and the snot... one of the XO's pets... wouldn't again be lax in his reporting. The rebuke had a two-fold effect. It would force Weduko to be more attentive when on duty, and it was also an unspoken reproof aimed at Osaka.

"*Aye-aye, sir,*" was all Osaka said.

Kajimora chuckled and rubbed his hands together, thinking about what adventure might be waiting for him just over the horizon.

CHAPTER 18

JUNE 1

750 MILES WEST, SOUTHWEST OF MIDWAY ATOLL

Three thousand meters above the azure surface of the Pacific, a pair of Aichi E16A floatplanes moved north of east at a cruising speed of two hundred knots. Known by their Japanese makers as the "Auspicious Cloud" and less poetically by the Allies as the "Paul," the E16A was a versatile aircraft with a splendid track record. Well-armed and able to carry half a ton of bombs slung between its floats, the plane was well-suited for naval operations as either a scout or an aerial assault plane.

The two aircraft were fifteen kilometers apart, just close enough to be seen by one another as dark specks against the sky. At their current height and distance apart, the aircrews had an observation sphere of no less than eighty kilometers. It was only a mild surprise, therefore, when the northern of the two spotted something white against the blue far out to the horizon.

As per their op orders, the airplanes slowed to just above a stall speed and reduced their altitude to only two hundred meters above the waves. This effectively put their target over the horizon and would give them plenty of time to make a report without being spotted or tagged by enemy radar.

"Warrior Wing one to Fuji," the pilot of the northern plane said into his radio. "Have spotted unknown vessel on horizon. Seems to have a bow wave, estimate speed of fifteen knots or better."

There was a burst of static before the mother ship, the light cruiser *Nikatoni*, trailing the scout craft by a hundred kilometers, replied, "*Warrior Wing Two, do you confirm?*"

The other aircraft replied that they had not. This meant only that there had been enough of the curvature of the Earth to obscure the target from their position. A good thing, as the target was doubtless unaware that they'd been spotted.

"*Warrior Wing flight, Fuji,*" the cruiser came back. "*Excellent. Maintain station and make observation of target every ten minutes to determine course and speed. Take all measures to avoid detection. Will advise.*"

The flight leader acknowledged, and the two aircraft closed formation and began a series of long and lazy circles. At seventy knots, they could orbit the area for several hours, conserving fuel and popping up to peek over the horizon at the approaching ship. There was no guarantee that they wouldn't be detected, but by the time their fuel began to run low, the cruiser and carrier would be close enough to engage the target. Theoretically, the two IJN ships and the American... it was improbable that the ship was anything else... were closing the range at something like twenty-five knots. This meant that they'd meet in little more than two hours.

The Aichis made two more observations before Warrior Wing Two determined that the approaching ship was an American submarine running on the surface. Classification unknown, but she did seem large. That could only mean one of the new fleet submarines. This was reported back to the cruiser. Upon the next observation, however, the submarine seemed to have disappeared.

"*Warrior Wing Flight,*" the cruiser replied tersely after this report. "*Assess the enemy has spotted you and dived. We are approximately thirty minutes from your position. Proceed back to Fuji for recovery. Kaiju will soar.*"

Essentially, turn tail and get back here, and the submarine carrier will launch an assault. As the two Aichis were armed only with ammunition for their machine guns, this was sensible. If the enemy *was* an American fleet submarine, then they would be heavily armed and might be able to shoot down the floatplanes before they could get in close enough to do any harm with wing cannons.

———

"Periscope depth!" Nichols called out from his station in the control room and over the gonging general alarm.

One of the lookouts had reported sighting a pair of aircraft low on the horizon. Almost simultaneously, the half-hourly SJ radar sweep had detected them as well. At a range of twenty-eight thousand yards, the aircraft had only been visible for a moment before they vanished both from human sight and from the light beam of the unflinching electric SJ eye.

Begley had immediately ordered a dive and for general quarters to be sounded. The boat was well over seven hundred miles from Midway now, and with every mile further out, the odds of running across a Japanese vessel grew. He'd initially activated the snorkel. The *Bull Shark's* secret weapon, an experiment derived from a Scottish scientist's tests just after the First World War. However, Turner had ordered it lowered and the submarine put on battery power. Although a great way to maintain speed at periscope depth or shallower, the thick pipe of the snorkel had the same disadvantage as the periscopes... more so, in fact. It left a nice frothy feather line on the surface that would be easy for an airplane to spot while the sun shone.

"Captain has the con. All ahead two-thirds," Turner ordered as he went up the ladder into the conning tower. "Open the outer doors on all torpedo tubes. We're far too distant from any landmass for those two planes to come from anything but a ship. XO, I'll run the attack; you run the scopes. Mr. Pendergast, take over the plot."

Normally Turner would handle the approach and the attack

himself. However, he felt that if Begley got in on the action, it'd not only create more unit cohesion but would give the XO that much more practice. It would also leave his, Turner's, mind free to maneuver his ship for the best possible position. As yet, they didn't know what their foe was, but he felt sure they'd soon find out. He also felt sure that his foe already knew he was out here.

In the forward torpedo room, Sparky stood between his torpedo tubes and glared at the reload gang. Tommy Perkins stood at the center of the room along with Perry Wilkes. The two petty officers each supervised a side, making sure their reload gangs were ready and worked while Sparky oversaw firing procedures and kept a weather eye on everyone.

"Phone talker," Sparky called back to the kid standing by the watertight hatch. "Control room, forward torpedo. All outer doors open."

The kid repeated the message and called out that the conning tower had acknowledged. At the moment, there was nothing for the men to do. There were already six torpedoes loaded, and no reloading would be done unless and until the fire control officer or captain ordered it. The tailing tackles, or tagles, were already rigged, and men stood by the fish in their racks and on the skids, ready to throw off the tie-downs and rig them to be hauled up and onto the rollers and into their respective tubes.

"New kid," Sparky barked at a young seaman apprentice who'd signed aboard at Pearl.

"Name's Parker, sir," the kid who was still young enough to sport a few pimples on his smooth face said and shifted uncomfortably.

"I know your goddamned name, *Eugene!*" Sparky snapped. "You think I don't know the boys in my fuckin' room? And who you callin' sir, boy? See these chevrons here? Know what they mean?"

"Uhm... yes, is—Sparky," the kid flummoxed. "Means you're a PO1 and that other patch says you're an LPO."

"Means I'm workin' Navy, Parker," Sparks glowered. Although Parker didn't know it, the more seasoned men in the room knew that Sparky was riding the kid for a reason and was only playing at annoyance. "Just like you. Now, what's *next?*"

Parker cleared his throat, "We await orders from the bridge to set depth and speed spindles."

"The *bridge?*" Sparky exclaimed, throwing up his hands. "This look like a fuckin' tin can or some big comfy cruiser, Parker?"

Everyone laughed except Parker, who flushed beet red. His last and only assignment thus far had been aboard a destroyer. He had at least been in the torpedo gang.

Sparky grinned at the kid and stepped forward to pat him on the shoulder, "Take it easy, Parker. Just havin' a little fun with ya'. This ain't like a tin can, though. Things can get mighty tense down here, and you gotta be able to handle it. If you can't handle gettin' barked at by a hard-ass room leader like me, then you're gonna shit your drawers first time we get ash-canned. Ain't that right, Grigsy?"

"Sure is, Sparky!" Grigsy almost shouted with enthusiasm. "But the difference between bein' barked at by Sparky or by a depth charge ain't much to worry about."

That got another laugh, and this time Parker joined in.

At the other end of the boat, Walter Murphy was assembling his men in a similar fashion. With the addition of Steve Plank, the submarine's de facto boatswain, he had an extra hand for once. Although, like his friend Ingram, Plank had never served aboard a submarine, he had served on a tin can and knew something about torpedoes.

What was also cheering Murph up was that Johnny Wexler was off the sick list and back at his station, ready to heave on the tagle should the need arise.

The only fly in Murph's ointment was that now Jack "Smitty" Smith didn't quite seem himself, either. He stood by the compartment air salvage controls, ready to manually alter the room's air supply and pressure as well as heave when required. Yet the man seemed jumpy, as if he had ants in the pants. Sure, Murph had only known the man since late last year when he'd signed aboard *Bull Shark* while she was still being built at Groton. But in the months since, Smitty had always been a steady rock. Yet, for the past week or so, he started acting odd. Glum, self-absorbed and sleeping oddly. Murph had tried talking to him about it, and all Smitty would say is that war sucked shit, and that he didn't want to talk about it.

Probably lost a girl. What else could it be? There was no way Smitty was a pill popper.

"Think we're really gonna use up all these fish, Murph?" Plank asked.

Murph chuckled, "This Old Man loves to scrap, Steve. Ain't that right, Mr. Post?"

Andy Post was stationed in the maneuvering room forward of after torpedo. He generally made a habit to hang in one compartment or the other by the open hatch. Should they seal for a depth charge attack, he'd station himself in the after room.

"Christ, Plank," Post said with a crooked grin, "we've been on this boat maybe four months now... hell not even... and we've been in what, four scraps, Murph?"

Murph grinned at Post. Both men knew damned well it had been five. But Post was letting Murph brag a little.

"Hell, sir, it was *five*," Murph boasted. "That Kraut mouse trap off Virginia, traded blows with that special Nazi tin can off Jacksonville, took down one of their milk cow subs between the Bahamas and Bermuda... then there was the big dust-up off Cay Sal Bank. That German light destroyer, another U-boat, and that spy freighter. Now *that* was exciting, boys!"

"Yeah, nearly flooded the room," one of the reload gang joked. "Mr. Post here had the idear to hook the tagle to the inner door on number ten, and we all heaved her closed. Member that, Smitty?"

"Yeah..." Smitty said. "Real kick in the pants."

"Oh, and we tangled with a couple of Nip Fubukis near the Galapagos a few weeks ago," Murph enthused, noting but not acknowledging Smitty's gloom. "Ever seen one of them, Steve? Big fuckers... fast, and they were carryin' seaplanes that dropped a goddamned egg on us, ha-ha-HAA!"

"Yeah, this old man's a real slugger, you'll see, boatswain," another man jibed. "By the time we put into Pearl again, you're gonna have one of these combat pins too."

Thirty miles westward, Ryu Osaka and Omata Hideki once again stood on the bridge of *Ribaiasan* monitoring the deployment of aircraft. The ship was pointed to the southeast to take advantage of the ten-knot breeze. That combined with her fourteen knots of flank speed was hardly a gale, but one of the Aichis best attributes was that it needed little to become airborne.

The FDO waved his flag, and first the starboard, and then the port floatplane was accelerated to over a hundred fifty kilometers per hour in less than two seconds. The booms already had the next two planes ready, and they hoisted them onto the catapults.

"The last two," Hideki said. "Thirty minutes. I believe that's a new record, Ryu."

"Excellent, Omata, the Emperor will no doubt be pleased," Osaka said.

"And what of our illustrious captain?" Hideki inquired with a wry smile.

"Oh, I'm sure he is nothing short of ecstatic."

Off to port, headed east by north, the light cruiser *Nikatoni* was already at full speed after having recovered her two scout birds. The ship would intercept the submarine and keep her occupied while Kajimora's two squadrons launched and assembled. The carrier herself would then follow in *Nikatoni's* wake and enter the battle zone to further trap the American if the submarine wasn't already destroyed by then.

"Naturally he'd rather be driving into combat directly," Osaka observed. "Submarine to submarine. However, he knows that this vessel's primary mission is to launch and recover her aircraft. Undersea warfare is secondary."

Hideki nodded, "I would be interested to see how she does, however."

"Perhaps you'll get your chance," Osaka commented. "What is your plan for the air wing?"

"According to the captain, we will run on the surface until we sight the cruiser again," Hideki stated. "Then submerge to radio depth so that I can maintain contact with the squadrons. I've instructed them to fly low, no more than twenty meters over the deck. This will hide them from the American radar until the last possible moment."

Osaka nodded, "Most clever."

The last two floatplanes were locked into the catapults that ran forward on *Ribaiasan's* broad foredeck. The flag swooped, the steam screamed, and the cars rumbled down the deck as the airplanes shoved their throttles to the stops. With the final two aircraft aloft and forming up as they circled the carrier, the two officers left the quartermaster on the bridge and went down into the conning tower.

"A successful launch?" Kajimora asked as he mounted the ladder to take the bridge. He insisted that it would be he who ran this attack.

"All aircraft aloft, Captain," Omata said. "We are proceeding to flight control."

"Very good," Kajimora said and then smiled at Osaka. "Let us see if we can't deprive the Americans of another asset, eh, Yakuin?"

"Indeed, sir," Osaka said.

Down in the oversized control room, there were two plotting parties assigned. One to the large chart on the master gyro-compass table who would be assigned to track the American submarine. Aft of this and closer to the radio room, another table was set up for an additional plotting party to track the aircraft. This party had a different methodology, however. The aircraft moved too fast to chart and plot their exact positions as the target plotters could do with surface and submerged ships. Instead, a copy of the main plot was laid out, and the table was divided into grid sections. In these sections, small metal iconized airplanes could be moved about according to their reported positions, and the air wing commander would have an up-to-date visualization of where his aircraft were.

Hideki and his assistants began to position the tiny aircraft in two groups of four and move them toward the hypothetical position of the enemy.

Everyone in the control room felt the mild centrifugal force as the captain ordered a hard left rudder at flank speed. Like all ships, *Riba-iasan* leaned *away* from the turn. The ship was bulky and did not maneuver very quickly. Even at fourteen knots, her flank speed, she took more than a minute to turn through ninety degrees and steady up on the course the cruiser had taken.

"Not exactly a fighter plane," Hideki said wryly.

Osaka shrugged, "No... but that is not her purpose. In spite of that, however, we do have a considerable armament of torpedoes. This will indeed be an interesting exercise."

"Contact!" Chet Rivers called out from his sonar station. "Light, fast screws ahead, sir. Estimated range is twenty thousand yards... sounds like three screws, sir. Assess light cruiser. She's moving toward us at twenty knots, it sounds like. I'm not a hundred percent on some of these figures as yet, though."

"Slow to all ahead one-third," Turner stated. "Helm, right standard rudder. Let's move out of her way and see if she notices us."

"Maneuvering answering one-third," the duty helmsman, Dick "Mug" Vigliano, said in his Bronx accent. "My helm is right standid."

Bull Shark turned easily toward the north, moving at a leisurely three knots. That would put the submarine a good mile or more off the cruiser's port beam by the time she closed the ten miles between them.

Turner knew that the cruiser wasn't alone, too. She'd launched two scouts, and the likelihood of their being out there was still quite high. It wouldn't do to get caught blind and have them drop a couple of bombs on his roof.

"Grab a quick observation, XO," Turner said. "Diving officer, take us up to radar depth. Ted, once up there, give me a quick sweep with the Sugar Dog. Mug, steady up on course three-three-zero."

"Radar depth, aye!" Nichols called out from below.

"Tree-tree-zero, aye," Mug acknowledged.

The boat eased gently another twenty-five feet toward the surface and levelled off. The men at the bow and stern planes operating their wheels with extra care. At the high pressure, service air and trim manifolds, the COB, Ralph Hotrod Hernandez, and assistant ship's cook Bill Borshowski stood by to manage the dizzying array of ballast tanks, flood valves, and pumps all over the ship that could alter her buoyancy. Joe Dutch, as second engineer, was also the diving assistant in charge of the ship's trim during battle.

"Radar depth!" Nichols reported.

"Sugar Dog active..." Balkley stated.

"I've got nothing up top yet," Begley said, turning the attack scope in a circle and using the right handle to adjust the lens angle. "Looks all clear, sir."

"Negative contacts," Balkley reported.

"Very well," Turner said. "Pat, let's set—"

"Aircraft!" Begley said excitedly. "Jesus Christ! Four... no, six... no, *eight!* Eight float planes coming up over the horizon... God, they're close!"

Damn SD... "Ted, switch to the Sugar Jig, fast!" Turner snapped. He saw where Begley was pointing, and it was a few points off the port bow, and he was swinging aft. "Sweep, zero-zero-zero to two-seven-zero, pronto!"

Balkley worked his gear. On his scope, eight spikes appeared, "Sir... eight thousand yards!"

The aircraft must have been skimming the waves not to appear until that distance, even at radar depth. If they were traveling at anything close to maximum speed, they could be over the boat in less than two minutes.

"Down scope!" Turner ordered. "Emergency deep! Hard dive, Frank! Now! Flood negative, flood safety... Thirty degree down bubble!"

CHAPTER 19

As the boat angled downward steeper and steeper, Turner couldn't help but feel that he'd walked into a trap. This was ridiculous, of course. The Japanese had no foreknowledge that *Bull Shark* would be out where she was any more than he had any knowledge that they'd be out there.

Then again... that wasn't exactly true, was it? After all, Webster Clayton *had* told him that the *Leviathan* would be on the route between Midway and the Marianas. Still, just because he'd been spotted by a couple of birds and then more showed up from over the hill didn't make it a setup.

Turner flipped the switch that would activate the 1MC and spoke into the handset, "Mr. Clayton, please come to the conning tower. Talk to me, Chet."

"Still tracking the cruiser, sir," Rivers reported. "She's still heading about sixty degrees or so... maintaining speed. I can also hear the floaters overhead. Can't give you much data on them, just that they're low and I can hear their engines."

"Any chance they sighted our scope?" Jarvis asked from his station at the TDC.

Begley nodded in agreement and looked to Rivers also.

Rivers shrugged, "I couldn't say, sir... sirs... least not yet. A little time will tell, though. For instance, if the prop sounds stay fairly close and if the ship up there alters course toward us... oh, Jesus! Splashes!"

"Depth now one hundred and fifty feet," Vigliano reported, reading the depth gauge indicator at his station.

"Rig for depth charge!" Turner ordered. "Mug, left full rudder! Bombs, Chet?"

"I'd say so, sir... four of them damned near right on—"

Outside the ship, four five-hundred-pound bombs detonated fifty feet below the surface. The world in and around the submarine was saturated by a near-deafening roar that seemed to come from everywhere at once. Powerful concussion waves raced through the water to hammer the submarine from both sides and from the top, rocking her like a baby cradle and shoving her twenty feet deeper in the water column.

Inside the boat, cork insulation dislodged and fluttered around the compartments like gray snow. Several light bulbs burst along with glass from instrument readouts, throwing up small bits of sharp glass that gave one, or two, men minor cuts on their hands and faces. Anyone not seated was flung sideways to the deck or had to clutch onto something to prevent it.

"That was a waste," Murph said casually in the after room. "Fuckin' Jap planes just dropped half their load on us, and it wasn't even close. Hope the canned morale is good tonight to make up for this yawn fest. Show me Hedy Lamar or Veronica Lake, and *now* we're talkin' excitement!"

"What're you shittin' me, Murph?" Plank asked, trying to conceal his unease with affected good humor. "How about Lauren Bacall?"

Andy Post slammed the hatch shut, sealing himself in the after room, "Oh, don't worry about it, Plank. Murph here doesn't even get excited unless we get a few dozen tooth shakers bouncing off our deck."

"Yeah, if Murph here ain't worried, then you don't need to be either, Steve," Wexler said wryly.

Plank shook his head, "Christ... join the subs, they said... good chow, movies every night, and air conditioning, they said... fuck me...”

Nearly three hundred feet away in the forward room, Eugene Parker was clinging to one of the bunk support uprights. His eyes were wide and his face blanched, “Oh, God... oh, God...”

“Easy, kid, easy,” Tommy Perkins said from beside him in his laid-back California twang. “Those weren’t depth charges, and they weren’t even close. I know it’s scary your first time. We didn’t have time to do an indoctrinal depth charging before leaving Pearl... but you’ll be all right.”

“A what?” Parker bleated, trying to focus on asking a question and not peeing his shorts.

“That’s where one of our tin cans drops a couple of ashcans a hundred yards away,” Sparky explained, appearing at Parker’s side seemingly from nowhere. He laid one of his big hands on the kid’s shoulder and was speaking in an uncharacteristically soft and gentle tone. “It’s not much different than what just happened. Kind of gives you a taste of it. So’s you know that it ain’t the end of the world when them fuckin’ Japs start dropping on you. Believe it or not, Eugene, the odds of a boat being sunk by charges is small. Yeah, we might get rattled a bit... but we’ve been through it before, and this boat’s still going strong, right, Tommy?”

“Exactly, Sparky,” Perkins said, his surfer voice calming the young man somewhat. “We been through way worse. Believe it or not, you’ll get used to it. It’s okay to be scared; just don’t let it take over, okay?”

“Okay...” Parker said.

“Tell you what, kid,” Sparky said. “On account we’re now riggin’ for depth charge, the Old Man done turned off hydraulic power. That means we gotta turn the fuckin’ sound heads by hand. You got some height on ya’, why don’t you take the JP Head wheel up there. Be good practice and build you some sex muscle.”

“Sex muscle?” Parker asked as he moved forward and took the manual sonar head directional wheel above him.

“Yeah,” Perry Wilkes commented. “Buff up them arms. Girls like that.”

“Sure do,” Sparky said. “Time we get back to Pearl, me and Tommy and Perry here know a joint where they got some real go-getters. Shit, kid, they's one broad when she sees some bulging biceps on ya', she'll throw you a five-spot just so's you let her chew on your pecker! Ain't that right, Perry?"

"Jesus Christ, Sparky!" Wilkes said and burst into laughter along with everyone else in the room, including Parker.

———

"Guess they know where we are," Jarvis quipped as he brushed cork dust from his black hair.

"How?" Begley inquired to no one. "We were over a hundred feet down...?"

Turner chuffed, "In these clear waters? They can probably pick us out down to two hundred feet. Mug, meet her... ah, Web, welcome to the party."

Clayton came up through the hatch and joined Turner at the bridge ladder, nearly white knuckling the rungs, "Gee, thanks, Art."

"Hey, you wanted to come," Turner said and chuckled. "Said you thought it'd be duck soup."

"It isn't?" Clayton tried to brazen.

"So far," Turner said. "But it looks like the Japs have found us. Eight floatplanes up there... think they're from our quarry?"

Clayton sighed, "Either that or a seaplane tender... but I doubt it."

"Me too," Turner replied. "Chet, how about that cruiser?"

"Still on the same course," Rivers said. "Although her screw noise is diminished... turn rate indicates a speed of eight knots... hold on! Aspect change... she's turning toward us."

"Now passing three hundred feet," Mug reported.

"Frank, level us off at four bills," Turner called out.

From outside, a faint and spectral whine began. A high-frequency beam of sound was probing the depths. No one needed to hear the report that Rivers delivered next.

"Echo ranging from the cruiser," he said glumly. "Not close yet, but

I think they're homing in. Bearing two-six-zero, range fifteen hundred yards."

"Dammit!" Pendergast cranked from his position at the master gyro table. "With those slants flying around up there with bombs slung, we can't go shallow enough to fire back!"

He was leading the plotting party and doing some calculations. *Bull Shark* was traveling west at three knots, or about a yard and a half per second. The cruiser, if she maintained her speed, was moving north at about four yards per second. In six minutes, she'd be over the submarine's current position. In that same time, *Bull Shark* would be less than five hundred yards off the cruiser's port side. That was assuming that by then the surface ship's sonar didn't peg the boat.

"We *could* go up to a hundred and fire," Hernandez offered.

Pendergast scoffed, "Oh, yeah, Hernandez? And get whacked by a couple of five-hundred-pound bombs? Yeah, they can't set the depth that they go off, but they still sink fifty feet or so before detonating. Hell, they could let 'em go from higher, and they'd come deeper, I bet."

"Four hundred feet," Nichols announced. "We could handle that, though, Burt."

Pendergast laughed sardonically, "Yeah, and then the fuckin' cruiser would be on us dropping ashcans at our depth. Probably tear us open like a can of Spam."

"Oh, quit being such a dead battery!" Nichols shot back. He tried to make it sound light-hearted but didn't entirely conceal his irritation.

"Let's cut the chatter down there," Turner said firmly. "Mind your duties."

He hadn't liked the sound of Pendergast's comments. The man was probably scared and trying to cover with gruffness. It wouldn't do for an argument to break out during an attack.

Ping... ping... ping...

"Range is now seven hundred yards," Rivers said quietly.

"Phone talker, all compartments... rig for silent running," Turner said. He wanted to order up more speed as well, but that would only create more noise.

Although submarines were designed to be very quiet, there was only so much that could be done. One major problem they all had was that the propeller shafts were attached to reduction gearing. This gearing reduced the high speed of the motors to turn the propellers at a lower rpm. This meant that a larger propeller didn't have to spin at high speeds to achieve higher speeds. It was efficient, but unfortunately, the faster the electric motors revved, the more noise the boat made.

Three knots was pretty close to the right balance between speed and silence. Any slower, and the boat just wouldn't move away from her pursuer fast enough to get away. Any faster and the additional noise helped her pursuer to track her through the depths.

Whoosh... whoosh... whoosh...

The sound of the cruiser's screws echoed through the water, growing louder and louder by the second. Between that sound and the incessant spectral pinging of sonar, it was a wonder more submariners didn't flip their lids.

"Any sign of a halocline, control room?" Turner softly called down the hatch.

"Negative," Pendergast replied. To Turner, he sounded almost resentful.

"We only need to hold out for another hour and a half or so," Begley stated quietly. "It'll be dark soon, and everybody knows the Jap can't see for shit at night."

"Even if he can," Jarvis stated, "those planes won't be able to spot a submarine underwater. We'll have the advantage then."

Turner nodded silently. That was true. Although he wasn't sure about Japanese eyesight. That was something of a stereotype perpetuated by propaganda posters of the Japanese Prime Minister, Hideki Tojo. In the images, the caricature of Tojo wore thick Coke-bottle glasses and had enormous buck teeth. In truth, however, the IJN and their Kido Butai carrier fleet had already demonstrated remarkable skill both during the day and at night.

Interestingly, Begley had seen that for himself just a few weeks earlier off the Galapagos. The XO was probably only trying to make the men feel better, but still...

No matter what, however, it would be impossible for human eyes to see a submarine even at periscope depth after dark, with the exception of the feather line made by a periscope, of course. In the warm summer Pacific tropical regions they were now in, phosphorescent plankton was plentiful and could turn any wake into a glowing chalk line across the black sea.

Ping, ping, ping...

Whoosh, whoosh, whoosh...

The ghostly high-pitched sound beam reached out for them, its eerie reverberation unnerving in the silent tube that was the submarine. Most of the men were now inured to it, having experienced this type of combat more than once on *Bull Shark's* first patrol. Some, however, who were both new to the boat and to the boats in general, were cringing in expectation. The fact that the screw noise of the cruiser was beginning to drown it out was by no means a comfort.

"Helm... left thirty... come to course two-three-oh," Turner whispered to Vigliano. "Let's see if we can get past him before he tags us."

"Aye-aye, my helm is left thirty," Mug whispered back. After a few moments, he centered his wheel. "Sir, helm is steady on course two-three-zero."

In the maneuvering room, Chief Harry Brannigan lounged on his bench before the control cubicle. His air of nonchalance was important for the men stationed in the room with him. These guys would be responsible for throwing breakers, manually operating electrical systems, and even moving through the boat with repair parts. They needed an example.

That seemed especially true for Ingram. The kid was nervous; anybody could see that. He stood by the deck hatch with a tool belt strapped around his waist, ready to descend into the motor room if necessary. The kid looked fidgety and twitchy and seemed a little pale.

Brannigan thought of posting him beside himself at the cubicle. It might make the kid feel better to be by his chief and to have a sense of control that came from operating the levers and switches that drove the submarine. Unfortunately, he wasn't yet checked out on the gear, and Brannigan needed experience at that moment.

"Oh, man," Brannigan said casually and only loud enough to be heard in the compartment. "I remember this one time, back when I was posted on a tin can... we was playin' a wargame, and us and another destroyer had to hunt down this S-boat, right... we circled and criss-crossed and pinged the bejesus out of that ocean, and you know what happened, Ingram?"

"Uhm... you nailed him, Chief?" Ingram replied just a bit shakily.

Brannigan laughed quietly. In spite of the order for silent running, he knew that this little light-hearted conversation was sorely needed at that moment, "Hell no! The son of a bitch evaded us. You believe that? One of them old boats, can't hardly go down to three hundred and that being past their test depth... and he got away. Know how?"

"Found him a layer," Electrician's mate Paul Baxter chuckled from the ICS master circuit board.

"Damn well told," Brannigan said with a chuckle of his own.

"Tell us, teach, what *is* a layer?" Chief machinist's mate Mike Duncan asked from where he lounged against the forward hatch. With both engine rooms shut down for the dive, he had come back to maneuvering to offer a hand. He often did this, since many of his own motor macs were used for the torpedo reload gangs anyway.

Brannigan chuckled, "Why, thanks for askin' Mikey... For you new kids, a layer, or *halocline*, is where the salt is a bit thicker in the water. See, the ocean ain't just a single body of water. You think of it like layers. Like pancakes. Well, when one of them pancakes is saltier than the others, or less salty, it changes the density and the temperature of the water. That bounces sound beams off like a solid wall. A boat gets *under* one of them... and it's Harry fuckin' Houdini!"

"Are we in one of those things now?" Ingram asked hopefully.

Ping-whoosh, ping-whoosh, whoosh...

"Not yet," Brannigan stated. "But if you listen close, you can kind of tell where the ship is by where the sound of the pinging and the props is. A few minutes ago, it was comin' from our port quarter. Sound now like it's forward of amidships. The skipper's turned a little south, so he can slip past the cruiser. You keep listenin' and you'll hear them sound beams moving aft. Don't worry about it. Even if they tag us, the skipper will drop us down. Bound to be a layer down there somewhere."

"How deep are we now?" somebody asked quietly.

"Dunno," Brannigan said. "But this boat's been down to six bills. Hell, I seen the test depth in the control room and the tower. We marked her at six-fifty! And that ain't even as deep as she'll go. I'll bet we could get down to eight hundred and be okay."

"Eight *hundred* feet... Jesus..." Ingram muttered.

Surreptitiously, he reached into the pocket of his shorts and pulled out an Amy. He pretended to cough and slipped the sedative into his mouth and dry-swallowed. He did this just in time because the next sound they all heard was not comforting. The eerie pinging grew louder, shriller, and then struck the hull with a resounding gong, as if somebody had dropped a hammer over the side and it had bounced off the pressure hull.

"Christ..." Turner groaned. "Hard left rudder, Mug! All ahead full."

"Here she comes!" Rivers quietly exclaimed.

Now the sound of three churning propellers began to grow and overshadow the sound beams once again... with the exception of the ponging as the sonar waves struck the boat, of course.

Whoosh, whoosh, whoosh, whoosh, whoosh, whoosh...

"Splashes!" Rivers gulped. "Two... six..."

The screw noise passed overhead and began to diminish. Long and agonizing seconds later, in the dead silence that pervaded the boat inside and out, a series of six clicks were heard as the depth charges' hydrostatic pistols engaged and initiated the internal charges and then...

The six explosions roared and thundered like doomsday. So loud and so close were they that it made what came before seem almost soothing by comparison. Repeated pressure waves slammed the submarine, shoving her bow first one way and then another, her stern left and then right and rocking her like a hobby horse. Inside, cork insulation once again rained down, and dozens of lightbulbs exploded, gauge glass shattered, and men were tossed asunder.

Even with all of that, however, the net effect was poor. The charges hadn't been set deep enough, and the damage to the boat was superficial. Of course, the damage to frayed nerves and human constitutions was greater, and yet once having been experienced and survived, men were usually stronger from the break.

"Phone talker, compartment by compartment," Turner ordered softly. "Rig battle lanterns. Frank, take us down to five hundred feet. Mug, back us down to one-third again and make turns for four knots."

"Maneuvering answering four knots," Mug stated.

"Make my depth five-zero-zero feet, aye," Nichols called up from the control room.

"Buck, blow bow buoyancy," Turner ordered. "Nice and slow, though. Burt, you're gonna have to compensate. Planesmen will have to work a little harder with that positive buoyancy. Any thermals?"

Above them, the churning screws of the cruiser were returning, along with their sound beams. No one truly required Rivers report to that effect.

"Splashes..." the sonarman announced. "Four... six... no eight this time!"

"Hang on!" Turner said and gripped the bridge ladder.

Next to him, Webster Clayton's eyes were as large as saucers. Turner reached out and squeezed his shoulder. The OSS man smiled thinly and gave a thumbs-up. So far, he was holding up. Turner had to admire his fortitude.

Outside, in the heavy quiet of the sea, eight rapid clicks could be heard through the hull as the depth charges initiators fired and then...

Once again, the world exploded around them. Once again, *Bull Shark* was swatted by a giant's fist. She rocked and rolled and bucked like an enraged thoroughbred, sending men sprawling, shattering more lights and causing several control boards to spark and smoke. Dozens of electrical breakers tripped, and the smell of ozone in several compartments forced men to try and muffle heavy coughs into their T-shirts.

Although the charges certainly rattled the sailor's teeth, they weren't close yet. The depth charge team or the commanding officer of the cruiser wasn't very experienced. The tooth-shakers had gone off at three hundred fifty feet, gratefully limiting their effectiveness.

Within seconds, breakers were being reset, and men were picking themselves up off the deck. There were bruises, scrapes and a few hard lumps, but no bones had been broken, and no serious injuries had to be reported. The robust submarine was in the same general condition. Minor damage that amounted more to annoyances than any real threat to the ship.

Turner glanced at his watch. It was eight-twenty-five. They'd been under for over an hour and a half, and the sun had set by then. Full dark would come within the next twenty or thirty minutes. Full dark, and then *Bull Shark* could rise from the depths, her figurative jaws wide, and her metaphorical teeth sharp and ready to once again become the hunter.

"You see that, Parker?" Sparky was saying from where he stood braced between his tubes. "Couple of ashcans ain't shit. They wasn't even close."

Parker only shook his head and clutched the wheel above him. He slowly turned the JP sound head mounted above the hull and stood by to train the device where Chet Rivers or Mr. Post would order, "If this is your idea of no big deal, Sparky... I sure as shit don't wanna find out what makes you clench your butthole."

Everyone laughed, muffling the outburst with convenient hands or shirts. Sparky grinned.

"I knew I shoulda joined the circus," Murph said as he stood between the torpedo tubes in *his* room.

That got a laugh from most of the men. Smitty was still frowning, though.

"Hell, Murph," Post said from beside the room's phone talker. "I think you're right. I'm sure shoveling elephant shit is way more exciting than this, huh?"

More laughter. Even Johnny Wexler smiled this time.

"What'd I tell ya, kid," Brannigan said to Ingram, who sat on the deck and clutched at the grating over the motor room hatchway. "Just another day at the office."

By now, the sedative Ingram had taken was beginning to take effect. Although he was still scared shitless, the razor's edge of the fear had come off. He managed a fake smile, "Yeah, the office... 'cept I gotta look at all you mugs instead of the legs of some pretty young secretary."

Chuckles floated around the compartment. Brannigan smiled to himself. High spirits and good humor were a great tonic for fear.

That was good because the men of the USS *Bull Shark* would need all of that tonic they could stand shortly. In the conning tower, Chet Rivers reached up and pushed the cups of his headphones tighter over his ears. He adjusted the gain setting on his equipment and frowned.

"Something, Chet?" Turner asked, bending close.

"Can you order the forward room to train the heads to about... zero-nine-zero... or maybe a bit forward, sir?" Rivers asked, still frowning.

Turner did so and ordered Vigliano to steady up on one-eight-zero. After a moment, Rivers cursed under his breath.

"Slow light screws, sir," Rivers finally announced, nodding to himself as if confirming something. "Ten thousand yards... bearing zero-eight-zero... making turns for... hmm... I think about fourteen knots."

"Ten thousand yards?" Begley snapped. "That's awfully close, mister! Why didn't you report sooner?"

Rivers shrugged, "Sorry, sir... with the noise of the ashcans and the cruiser's screws, I couldn't hear him earlier."

"What's all that mean?" Clayton asked.

Turner drew in a breath and turned to him, "Light slow screws indicates a ship with reduction gearing. Probably a submarine. And being this close to a cruiser with eight birds aloft... I'd say, Web, that we've found your *Leviathan*."

"Or *she* found *us*," Pat Jarvis cranked.

CHAPTER 20

"More active pinging, sir," Rivers reported. "Faint though... must be from the second contact."

"He must be running on diesels..." Turner mused.

"Based on his speed and noise, I'd say so, sir," Rivers replied.

"If only that damned cruiser would give us enough space, Goddammit!" Begley cranked. "We could rise and get a shot off."

"Wish we could do *something* instead of just *taking* it..." Pendergast growled from his plot in the control room. "Jesus..."

Bull Shark had been down for just over two hours now, and the temperature gauges were already reading in the mid-eighties. The humidity was rising too, and most of the men were sweating. Many of them had already removed their T-shirts, including Mug Vigliano, who'd laid his over the backrest of his chair. Moist heat and continuous depth charging could very easily fray the calmest tempers.

"Mug, make turns for two knots, come right and steady up on two-eight-zero," Turner ordered. "Pat, tell the rooms to standby. In a few minutes, we're gonna rise to a hundred feet and shoot."

Jarvis grinned and spoke into the sound-powered battle telephone now hung around his neck.

"If this works out, we'll set the depth spindles on the after tubes to six feet and the forward to three," Turner said. "That may change, though."

Ping... ping... ping, ping... pong!

The cruiser had located them again. Even from five hundred feet down, the crew could hear the sound of the ship's screws getting closer. Begley cursed under his breath, and Pendergast slammed his fist on the master gyro table. The rest of the men were none too happy either but took it with a bit more aplomb. At least around the officers.

"Splashes," Rivers intoned. "Eight... Geez, they must have two Y-guns as well as racks up there..."

It took over a minute for the depth charges to sink to *Bull Shark's* depth. This time, somebody aboard the cruiser had gotten it right. The charges blasted holes into the water at five hundred feet, the depth so great that each explosion generated several shockwaves before the expanding gas of the bomb was able to reach the surface and eliminate the pressure. These waves slammed into the submarine and twisted her back and forth, up and down, and anything that wasn't secured went flying. What light bulbs were left exploded and plunged compartments into darkness. Cork flew through the air like driving sleet, and men were tumbled about like socks in a dryer. Now, pipe fittings, valve stems, table edges, furniture supports, and more became a danger to fragile human forms.

In the after torpedo room, Steve Plank was tossed across the compartment. He struck one of the bunk supports, and the edge of a bolt that should've been capped tore a six-inch gash in his upper arm. In the motor room, a lube oil flask cracked, spraying number one and two electric motors with lubricant. In the after engine room, two men were jerked from their positions. Unable to hang on, Mike Watley was flung against the number three diesel, at least that of it which stuck up above the platform deck, and was knocked unconscious. Chief Mike Duncan moved to help him and was himself smashed into the same engine head, breaking his left wrist.

There were several minor injuries in forward torpedo as well.

However, Sparky had most of the men climb into their racks to ride out the roller coaster. Eugene Parker literally hung from the JP wheel, his legs swinging wildly as he rocked like a pendulum in the darkness. One of his flailing feet struck Perry Wilkes directly in the crotch, causing him to gag and curl up on deck in agony.

In the after battery compartment, Joe Dutch, who was DCO, coordinated injury and casualty reports. Pharmacist's mate Henry Hoffman was there, ready to move forward or aft to attend to any injured man. Eddie Carlson, Henry Martin, and Leroy Potts, the ship's baker, were stationed there as well to act as loblolly boys and assistants. All of these men sat at the mess tables, being able to steady themselves against the bucking of their submarine.

"Christ, we've got reports coming in from just about every compartment, Hank," Dutch was saying. "Got a bleeder in the after room, a head wound and broken arm in after engine, and a few minors in the forward room. Think you guys can handle that? So far, no ship casualties, thank God. Take battle lanterns with you and pass them out, too."

Hoffman tapped Carlson and Potts, and they headed aft for the watertight door to the forward engine room. Henry Martin grabbed a first-aid kit and went forward.

"Conning tower, crew's mess," Dutch said into the sound-powered telephone he wore. He reported what he'd heard so far. "How's everybody up there and in the control room?"

Even as Martin opened the watertight hatch, he was bowled aside by Burt Pendergast and Ralph Hernandez. The two men were carrying a limp burden between them, and to Dutch's horror, he saw that it was Art Turner. Martin gaped for a second but went through the door on his errand.

"It's the skipper, sir!" Hotrod announced shakily. "He was tossed down the conning tower hatch!"

Dutch watched as the two men stretched Turner out on a mess table. The captain's face was a bloody mask.

"I think he might've screwed up his ankle, too, Joe," Pendergast said, sounding uncharacteristically concerned. "He hit weird and yelled out before smacking his forehead on the ladder and crumpling to a heap.... Where's the Doc?"

"Aft," Dutch said tersely. "Jesus Christ... any more up there?"

Pendergast shook his head, "Some cuts and bruises. Martin can tackle them when he comes aft again. I've got that Mr. Clayton guy doing a little first-aid. It'll do. You okay back here, Joe? I gotta get back to my plot."

"Yeah, we're fine, Burt," Joe said, suddenly wishing he'd opted for more first-aid training.

Pendergast nodded and vanished through the hatch. A moment later, Hoffman led Chief Duncan into the mess, followed by Carlson and Potts, who carried Mike Watley. Behind them, Steve Plank walked, holding a rag to his right forearm.

"Oh, Jesus..." Hoffman exclaimed when he saw Turner.

"Hit his head and maybe busted an ankle," Dutch said.

Hoffman moved to Turner and examined him quickly, pulling a clean rag from a bin and wiping Turner's face. This revealed the four-inch split just below his hairline. He then gently removed the skipper's sandals, and everyone could see the angry purple bruising around his left ankle.

"Okay... the cut is superficial," Hoffman was muttering. "I don't see any sign of a fracture... let me attend to Watley first. He may have a depressed fracture... Eddie, Leroy, can you get Plank fixed up? Wash, sanitize, and stitch..."

In the conning tower, Tom Begley had suddenly gotten exactly what he'd wished for. He stood at the bridge ladder where Turner had been standing a moment before and looked around. Everyone was looking back at him, with the exception of Chet Rivers, who was listening to his sonar set and watching the Magic Eye display intently. Vigliano kept casting glances over his shoulder at the XO. Ted Balkley, having nothing to do for the moment, sat at his radar screens and frowned. Wendell Freeman was positioned at the small chart desk and dead reckoning indicator, making notes on a maneuvering board. He smiled reassuringly at Begley.

Then there was Pat Jarvis. The torpedo officer's face was expression-less, but Begley knew how he felt. The two men had not gotten along since they'd met, and nothing since had improved that situation.

"You all right, Lieutenant?" Webster Clayton asked from beside him.

"I'm fine, Mr. Clayton," Begley said.

"You're in command now, Tom," Jarvis said neutrally.

"I'm aware of that, gunner," Begley said stiffly.

Jarvis waited.

"We've got to end this," Begley announced. "Diving officer, make your depth one hundred feet. Helmsman, increase speed to all ahead two-thirds."

"Recommend we go deep and try to find a layer, Tom," Jarvis said again, sounding bland, as if he were struggling to keep the emotion from his voice... which of course he was. "We're in a bad spot to start shooting."

"Did I ask for your opinion, Jarvis?" Begley snapped.

"I'm your XO now," Jarvis said, not entirely successful in hiding his own pique. "It's my job."

"I'm getting tired of being tossed around and doing nothing about it," Begley replied. "Carry out my orders, Vigliano. You too, Frank."

Jarvis stood and came over to where Begley and Clayton were stand-ing. He leaned in close so only the other two men could hear, "You're making a mistake, Tom. That cruiser has already dropped almost thirty ashcans on us. She can't have much more. But that other ship is out there, and who knows what she's got? Depth charges? Or maybe they can load up their floaters? This isn't the time."

"I agree with Mr. Jarvis, Mr. Begley," Clayton offered. "We don't know what we're facing with that super-sub."

Begley glowered at the two men, "Just because you're *scared*, Pat, is no reason to slink away and hide. As for you, Mr. Clayton, you're not an officer aboard this ship... hell, you're not even in the fucking Navy! It's nighttime now and those slopes can't see shit in the dark. This is our best chance!"

"There's a fine line between brave and *stupid*, Tom," Jarvis growled. "And you just crossed it. This isn't a dick-measuring contest. You're gonna get us all killed. We've already seen that the Jap can not only fly at night but do so well. And as for Mr. Clayton here, he knows more about this Jap sub than anybody."

"It's a ship," Begley stated. "We can deal with him like any ship. Active pinging or not, he's running on top at high speeds. Now back the hell off!"

Jarvis met Begley's eyes and held the man's gaze for a moment. The big torpedo officer's blue eyes were cold. He moved away and sat at his TDC, fuming.

Clayton shook his head and went down the ladder into the control room. If he couldn't be of help up there, he'd go check on Art.

For Begley's part, he was glad to be shot of the man, "Status, Vigliano?"

"Sir, my course is two-eight-zero; my engines are all ahead two-thirds. We're making five knots," Mug replied stiffly.

"Rivers?" Begley asked, annoyed at having to inquire.

"The cruiser is making a turn astern of us," Rivers stated. "Estimate three hundred yards and opening. Second target is now... five thousand yards off, dead ahead. Not slowing."

"Excellent," Begley gloated. "We leave the cruiser stewing in his own juices long enough to send a few fish his way, and at the combined closing rate, we should be in firing range of the *Leviathan* in about twelve minutes."

"Yeah, if we live that long..." Balkley muttered under his breath.

"Now passing four hundred feet," Vigliano stated.

"Torpedo officer, when we get to one hundred, I want an after torpedo solution on the cruiser," Begley said.

"And just what should I use as targeting data?" Jarvis asked. He'd almost added, "ya' moron," but managed to contain himself.

Begley scowled and then chewed on his lower lip for a second, "Very well, XO... diving officer, revise depth to periscope. I'll make an observation and give you some data, Mr. Jarvis. Will that make you happy?"

"Ecstatic," Jarvis muttered, beginning to crank information into the torpedo data computer. "Can you give me anything now, Chet?"

"Yes, sir... cruiser bears approximately one-six-zero," Rivers said. "But the bearing isn't constant."

Jarvis sighed and entered that information. Into his telephone he said, "After room, conning tower. Set depth spindles on all torpedoes to six feet. Speed is high."

"Now passing two hundred..." Vigliano announced.

"Okay, here we go," Begley stated excitedly, even going so far as to rub his hands together. "We'll get targeting data and shoot and then go back down, Frank. Be ready to dive her fast. You focus on your solution, Jarvis... okay, get ready..."

"Range to cruiser now six hundred yards," Rivers announced. "The other vessel is three thousand yards off our bow, sir... oh, I think she's cutting her diesels. Sounds like she's slowing."

"Any sign of the planes?" Begley asked.

"No, sir," Rivers stated. "I can't hear them at least."

"Periscope depth!" Nichols shouted from below.

"Up search scope!" Begley ordered.

Ted Balkley, who was acting as periscope assistant, looked at him, "Search, sir?" Not attack?"

"Need the better optics," Begley said.

Balkley did as ordered and raised the scope. The XO snapped the handles down and spun to face aft.

"Got him! Got that fucker! Okay, get ready, gunner... final bearing... mark!"

"One-six-five," Balkley read off the bearing ring.

"Range is... six-eight-five yards," Begley and Balkley reported. "Angle on the bow is zero-three-five starboard!"

Begley watched the ship in his scope for a few more seconds. Rivers had been right; it was turning. He reported this to Jarvis and ordered a five-degree spread.

"Down scope, sir?" Balkley asked nervously.

"Just a sec... yeah, down scope!" Begley ordered.

"Shoot!" Jarvis stated.

"Fire seven," Begley announced. He waited six seconds between each order. "Fire eight... fire nine... fire ten!"

————

A thousand feet above the dark Pacific, the four aircraft of Condor Flight were circling in a wide arc between their mother ship and the cruiser. Falcon Flight had already dropped their bombs and was circling at five thousand feet to act as a combination combat air patrol and cover for the Aichis below that still had bombs.

Condor Flight Four's observer was carefully scanning the ocean between the two surfaced ships. It still amazed him how massive the *Ribaiasan* truly was. Longer even than the light cruiser, her bulk and odd configuration were clearly visible on the sea even at night. Suddenly, perhaps five or six hundred meters from the cruiser and stretching out in a line between her and the carrier sub, a thin line of phosphorescent foam appeared.

"Periscope!" the observer shouted unnecessarily loud and pointed.

"I see it," the pilot, a seasoned flyer whose notorious patience had saddled him with this particular excitable but competent observer. "Raptor Nest, Condor Flight Four... located enemy periscope wake. Appears to be headed directly for you."

A moment passed before Commander Hideki's voice filtered over the radio, "*Good sighting, Condor Flight Four. Permission to attack. Condor Flight, number four will take the lead. Attack in turn after effectiveness of initial weapon.*"

The pilot banked his aircraft and turned so that he was approaching the submarine from its bow. Even as he lined up, he could see that the line had stopped moving. The boat had lowered its scope. It wouldn't save them, however. His mathematical mind had already calculated the various speeds involved, and now he dove his aircraft, lining up the crosshairs on his windscreen at a point ahead of where the line of foam ceased.

"Banzai!" the observer shouted in triumph as the two hundred-fifty-kilogram bomb was released and plunged into the black ocean below.

———

"Ha! Bring us down to two hundred feet, Nichols, and smartly," Begley ordered smugly.

"All fish running hot, straight, and normal," Rivers announced with a smile playing on his lips. His face then went white. "Sir! Sir! Incoming aircraft noise!"

Begley's stomach lurched, "Frank! Full down angle on the bow and stern planes! Take us deep! Helm, all ahead full! COB, flood—"

Begley had been about to order the bow buoyancy and negative tanks flooded in order to speed up the dive. The ironic interruption of the bone-jarring explosion over the afterdeck was the only thing that saved the submarine from an uncontrolled dive that would likely have doomed her.

The bomb detonated only twenty feet above the after main deck. Much of the concussive force, as with all underwater detonations, was forced upward as the sphere of expanding gases sought release from the pressure of the sea. Being close to the surface, therefore, much of the explosive force burst from the surface in a dramatic Hollywood-esque ball of foam. However, enough of the energy remained below to smash into the upper surface of the boat, dislodging forty feet of deck planking and cracking a weld at frame one hundred and four. The crack was only a few inches long and no wider than a finger, but it allowed a noticeable amount of seawater to spray into the maneuvering room. Further, a pipe fitting in the overhead burst, sending even more seawater spraying down on the men and the electrical gear. It wasn't a major leak, perhaps a few gallons per second, but it could and would accumulate given enough time.

Fortunately, the boat's electrical systems were secured against such occurrences, at least to a degree. However, as water flooded in, it made its way through the grating in the deck and began to fill the motor room. That would eventually be a problem.

"Phone talker!" Brannigan shouted. "Report to the DCO that we've got a casualty back here. A seawater line is busted, and we've got an upper hull leak!"

Doug Ingram only stared with wide and disbelieving eyes as a small waterfall cascaded down into the room and nearly on top of him. He thought that it might be his fear-fueled imagination, but he could swear that the stream was growing stronger by the second.

This was, of course, what was happening. The submarine was driving herself down into the darkness. With each foot of depth, the ocean pressure on her hull increased by a little less than half a pound per square inch. The higher the pressure, the stronger the inflow of seawater would become.

———

"Ha!" said Condor Flight Four's observer. "I believe we hit him!"

The pilot grinned, and then it faded into horror as a bright flash caught his eye. He looked over to see an explosion along the side of the cruiser's bow.

Of the four fish fired by the American boat, three had gone wide, the second that had been fired missing the stern of the cruiser, thanks to her turn, by no more than twenty meters. The fourth torpedo, however, had been right on target. It angled in and would have struck the ship a hundred feet from her cutwater, blasting the bow off and dooming her. Instead, though, like the Japanese bomb that had exploded near but not against *Bull Shark's* hull, the six-hundred-fifty-pound Torpex warhead prematurely detonated five yards from the ship.

Although not fatal, the explosion was close enough to blast open a substantial portion of the hull below the waterline.

The *Nikatoni* was an older ship, having been riveted rather than welded. The force of the explosion sheared off several dozen rivet heads, allowing two seams to open to nearly a foot across and bending a hull plate inward. The compartment had to be abandoned and sealed off. The ship wasn't going to sink, but she was also slowed down considerably until a more permanent solution could be found.

The cruiser came to a full stop and silenced their echo ranging. The sub carrier slowed and came to a stop a thousand yards away, her passive sonar listening as she began the process of recovering her aircraft. And below them, plunging headlong into the crushing deep, *Bull Shark* reduced her speed, turned toward the south and sought the protection of a thermal layer.

CHAPTER 21

"Depth now four hundred feet," Frank Nichols said from his position standing behind the men at the air manifolds. "How deep do we go, sir? There is that casualty in the maneuvering room to think about. We've also got some ruptured fittings in a couple of other compartments too…"

Above and slightly to the north, the active pinging had ceased. Everyone had heard the concussive *crack-boom* of A Torpex explosion above them. Rivers couldn't confirm a hit, but he thought it might have been a close premature.

"Get us under a layer," Begley stated, not with quite as much grace as he might.

Pat Jarvis glanced sidelong at the XO. He didn't like what he saw. Perhaps he was only projecting… but Begley seemed rattled. Although it was hard to tell, what with the temperature approaching ninety, but the man seemed to be sweating profusely. They were all sweaty, but Begley's khaki uniform blouse was practically glued to his back.

"DCO, conning tower," Jarvis said into his telephone set. "How's that situation in maneuvering, Joe?"

A long pause and then Harry Brannigan came back over the system,

"*Conning, maneuvering. Getting worse, Mr. Jarvis. We're getting a patch on the pipe now. That's the easy one. But I think we've got a direct leak near frame one-oh-four. A burst weld. Water's coming in pretty good, getting worse with pressure. Might have to shut the motors down soon. Can we get the pumps going and try to jump on it, sir?*"

Jarvis frowned and reported that to Begley. The XO shook his head no as if this would prevent the situation, "We need the drive to alter depth... otherwise, we're gonna have to use the air in the tanks to blow the MBTs and the FBTs... not to mention the other tanks if we can't get that leak stopped."

"If we can't get that leak stopped, it won't matter," Jarvis said sternly.

"The drain or trim pump makes a racket, though..." Begley said.

"Depth now five hundred," Frank said. "No halocline indicated yet, sir."

"Sir, should I reduce speed?" Vigliano asked. "We're eatin' a lotta juice at this rate."

"Did I order a new bell, helmsman?" Begley lashed out. "Mind your fuckin' station and I'll let you know when I want you to do something."

"XO, the leak?" Jarvis asked, holding onto his patience by fingernails.

"I'm thinking, Goddammit!" Begley said, white knuckling the ladder.

Jarvis stood and moved closer, getting right into the smaller man's face, "Snap out of it, Tom. You're the captain right now. Pull your head outta your ass and make a decision... or let me do it for you."

"I'm the senior officer here, Jarvis," Begley growled. "I'm getting tired of your mouth. I know you want command and—"

"Listen to me carefully, you stupid *shit*," Jarvis said in a quiet and deadly tone. "What I care about is the safety of these men and this boat. I don't give a *damn* what you *think*, what you *feel* or what you *want*. Unless it deals with this boat and the men aboard. Now either start being the CO, or I'll knock you on your ass and tie you into your fuckin' rack!"

It was at this point that Web Clayton decided to come back up to the conning tower. He saw the two men squared off and heard the anger in the big gunnery officer's tone. He may not know much about submarines, but Clayton knew that if this got out of hand, it could mean the loss of lives or the entire ship.

"Gentlemen," Clayton hissed. "This isn't the time for a pissing contest. These men need you. Now, what are we going to do about this?"

"Old Jarvis here wants to blow most or all of our six-hundred-pound air supply to pressurize the maneuvering room," Begley said.

"Doesn't that make sense?" Clayton asked. "Won't greater internal air pressure counteract the sea pressure from outside?"

"Yes," Begley admitted if grudgingly. "It also means pressurizing the surrounding compartments so that men can get in and out of the affected one. It might mean pressurizing the entire boat, for that matter."

"That'd be a good thing, though, right?" Clayton asked. "All that air pressure would help us stay neutral or rise even if we lose power, correct?"

"Not exactly," now it was time for Jarvis to admit something. "All the air we've got is already aboard. What buoyancy it provides is already being applied. Spreading it out into a greater volume helps a little... but the real problem is water. It's the weight of the water that draws us down. Our air is used to lighten the ship... to push water out. If we need to blow the ballast tanks, we need the high-pressure air to do that, especially the deeper we go. It's sort of a balancing act."

"There's only so much air to go around," Begley stated coldly.

"Yeah, but there's an unlimited supply of seawater," Jarvis said tersely. "The longer we wait, the more comes into the maneuvering room. We lose that room, we lose motive power and just about every major electrical circuit on the ship."

"Then pressurize maneuvering," Clayton said. "Or activate the pumps!"

"My decision," Begley retorted.

"Then make it," Clayton said. "Or I'll place you under arrest for endangering a top-level intelligence operation."

Begley stared at him, "Bullshit."

Clayton stared right back, "Try me, Lieutenant."

"So, this is how we operate now?" Begley hissed. "You don't like your CO; you just bully him into getting your way? Threaten to sic the spooks on him?"

"Tom, I'm trying to get you to act before the goddamned ship goes down!" Jarvis snapped. "For Christ's sake!"

"Fine, go handle it, Jarvis," Begley grumbled. "You won't be needed up *here* anytime soon. Maybe had you actually *hit* that cruiser, we might *already* be in good shape. But hey, don't let *your* conscience bother you."

Jarvis only snorted in derision and dropped down the ladder. Clayton followed him. Jarvis spoke into his sound-powered telephone, "Maneuvering, permission to release air through the salvage system. Pressurize your room; we're already at..."

"Six hundred feet, sir," Nichols said, meeting Jarvis's eyes.

"Activate the drain pump," Jarvis said. "Let's get some of that water out."

Nichols tried. He flipped switches and turned back to Jarvis, his face pale, "Drain pump is non-responsive."

"Trim pump?" Jarvis asked.

Nichols drew in a breath, "The valve line-ups are all wrong. I'll need to get somebody down in the pump room to work on that... but that does mean we won't have use of that pump for trimming."

"Get started on it, Frank. Trim us as best you can," Jarvis ordered and turned to Tank Broderick, who was manning the bow planes. "Tank, I need you to go down into the pump room and handle the pumps and bilgeways," Jarvis stated. "We've got to get the water out of the motor room so we can restore propulsion. I'd rather do as much manually as we can to save on battery."

For some time now, *Bull Shark's* hull had been creaking and now began to groan. They were approaching the boat's test depth. That depth at which problems began to occur and the hull integrity began to show signs of weakening. It wasn't the deepest she *could* go, just the deepest she'd gone and still remained fully functional.

Pendergast looked up at Jarvis, then down at his plot and up again. The look on his face was hard but otherwise unreadable, "You ought to give him a chance, Lieutenant."

"I am, Burt," Jarvis said. "And he's blowing it."

"Seven hundred feet!" Nichols called out and looked to Jarvis.

There was a general sense among the officers, chiefs, and most of the men, that now that Turner was down for the count, Pat Jarvis ought to be in charge. He was tough, brave, and competent. Everyone liked him. They felt he was tough but fair and definitely preferred to smile and shoot the shit rather than dress down. However, regs were regs, and for the moment, there was only so much that could be done.

"*Ay, dios mio!*" Hotrod announced in quiet joy. He pointed at the Bathythermograph where the stylus was beginning to trace an erratic pattern. "Look!"

"Thank Christ..." Jarvis muttered. "Where are we, Frank?"

"Seven twenty," Nichols said nervously.

"Okay, level us off at seven fifty," Jarvis ordered. "Buck, Hotrod... the two-twenty-five air supply isn't gonna do it. We need more air from the six hundred for the salvage air supply. Otherwise, that maneuvering room is gonna—"

The lights, what few lights were on after having their bulbs replaced twice, flickered, and then died. The only light in the control room and the conning tower was the pale-yellow glow from the battery-powered battle lanterns. After nearly three seconds, the main illumination came back, but at a noticeably reduced level.

"Jesus..." Clayton muttered.

"All compartments except maneuvering," Jarvis spoke into his telephone. "Open the watertight doors and flappers. Make reports from forward aft to control. Mr. Pendergast is AOOD. Maneuvering, I'm headed back."

Another sound reverberated through the ship. No, not a sound...

more the lack of a sound. Even as Jarvis and Clayton ducked to go through the hatchway to the after battery compartment, Jarvis heard somebody behind him announce that propulsion was offline. The water must be flooding the motor room...

As they passed through the crew's mess, Jarvis briefly stopped to take a quick look at his captain. Hoffman had mopped the blood from Turner's face and was in the process of stitching the cut on his forehead.

"How goes it, Mr. Hoffman?" Clayton beat Jarvis to the question.

Hoffman frowned, "I think he's just out from the bonk. Pretty sure his ankle isn't broken... maybe a hairline fracture, though, but I don't have an X-ray machine aboard."

Jarvis looked around at the other men in various states of repair, "How about you, fellas?"

Steve Plank held up his bandaged arm and grinned, "Just tryin' to earn my purple heart, sir."

Jarvis smiled. Plank seemed fairly chipper. A good sign. Motor machinist Mike Watley lay prone on a table beside Turner, a bandage around his head as well. Hoffman caught the torpedo officer's questioning glance and frowned.

Jarvis drew in a breath, "Do what you can for them, Hank. Anything or anyone you need, you got it."

"Might need some blood," Hoffman said.

Jarvis smiled thinly and clapped Clayton on the shoulder, "Got one-and-a-half delicious gallons right here, Doc."

That got a muted laugh in the compartment. Clayton grinned, "Glad to donate if you need it."

"Oh, you may both get your chance," Hoffman said. "Mr. Jarvis here is A-positive, and you're O-positive. Don't be surprised if I send a guy in a cape and tux after ya'."

The chuckles followed the two men aft. The forward engine room was empty except for two men monitoring the dormant engines. The after engine room was a little more crowded, with a gaggle of men standing by the hatchway to maneuvering looking lost.

"Let's lock this room down and get the pressure up," Jarvis said. "We need about three-thirty PSI in here and in maneuvering."

"The salvage system won't do that, sir," Fred Swooping Hawk stated glumly. Too glumly. The man seemed almost drowsy to Jarvis.

"Control will pump some six hundred or even three thousand into the system," Jarvis said. "Let's go."

The wheel on the after bulkhead that controlled the stored air supply for pressurizing compartments was turned to the right, pushing the pressure needle on the gauge up. At three hundred thirty PSI, the pressure at seven hundred, and sixty feet of depth, the wheel was turned the other way. As it turned, the system hissed briefly and then seemed to lose pressure.

"Maneuvering, what's your pressure?" Jarvis asked into his phone.

"*Two hundred PSI,*" came Harry Brannigan's thankfully calm voice.

"And you, after room?" Jarvis asked the phone.

"*We're at three-thirty, sir,*" came Andy Post's voice.

"Control, we need more gas in the salvage lines," Jarvis said. "Maneuvering is still low."

"*We're blowing the safety and negative tanks,*" came Begley's terse reply. "*We need the pressure right now.*"

That could mean only one thing. Even with the bow buoyancy tank blown long ago by the captain, the boat was still sinking. She was negatively buoyant.

"How fast?" Jarvis asked tensely.

"*Frank estimates ten feet per hour,*" Pendergast cut in.

Jarvis didn't react, but he felt his belly twitch. The boat was already at seven-fifty. Without propulsion, the only way she could move up through the water was to blow air from inside her various ballast tanks. However, she couldn't simply blow them all. The Japanese were still up there. The best thing would be to creep away at slow speeds beneath the salt layer until they could get far enough away to surface. Without being detected. Or at least far enough away to prepare.

Without propulsion, however, it was now impossible for the ship to plane up. They needed to get the water *out* in order to exercise any of their options.

"How about that damned pump?" Jarvis almost growled.

"*Working on it,*" was all the response he got.

"*The motor room is flooded, sirs,*" Brannigan reported. "*Not completely, but enough that I had to throw the breakers. We can't reactivate until we get most of that water out. If we suffered a major short...*"

None of the officers needed him to finish. They all knew what a catastrophic short-circuit could mean. It would mean at best that they would have to spend many hours drying and repairing gear... and, at worst, that they'd be stranded for days or even weeks.

"Tom, we need to get that room pressurized and stop any further flooding, or we drop like a stone," Jarvis said again.

There was a long pause and then, "*All right, dammit... go ahead, control, give them the air they need from the 3K.*"

A moment or two later, another hiss could be heard on the other side of the bulkhead. After a few seconds, the hatch to maneuvering opened, and Jarvis rushed inside.

The source of the flooding was immediately obvious. Thankfully, a now fairly light trickle still fell from the overhead. Although pressure had been equalized, for the moment, gravity still forced some water in. A pair of men were finishing a clamped fitting over the blown pipe, and two more were moving around the room and drying things off.

"How goes it, Chief?" Jarvis inquired. "What can we do?"

"Open the bilgeways and activate the trim pump as you said, sir," Brannigan said evenly. "There's a few feet of water down in the motor room, and I had to take the electrics offline."

Jarvis frowned, "Yeah... and we're still settling down. We're in a bit of a pickle here, Chief. The Japs are still on top of us, so we can't blow everything and surface. But right now, we're still negatively buoyant."

"We gotta stop that leak, too, sir," Brannigan stated.

As if on cue, Andy Post stepped into the room with a pair of mattresses. He was followed by Walter Murphy carrying a pair of extendable boat hooks.

"What if we brace these up against the overhead, Chief?" Post asked. "Use the boat hooks to keep them in place."

"Long as the pressure holds in here, that should work, sir," Brannigan said with a grin. "Finally gonna get to do some real sailoring, huh, Murph?"

Murph grinned, "Bout time I earned my keep, Chief."

Jarvis nodded, "If you've got things in hand here, Andy, Chief... we need to go forward and see to other problems."

"We're good, sir," Brannigan said.

Jarvis led the way forward and decided that it would simply be best to pressurize the whole boat. If men could move between compartments, they could get this done faster. As he moved to the forward bulkhead in the after engine room, he turned the salvage air wheel and pressurized the next compartment forward. He did this compartment by compartment. By the time he got to the control room, the crew there looked either grim or pissed.

"We're at seven-seventy," Pendergast snapped out. "Are you gonna use up all of our air, Jarvis?"

"Not now, Burt," Jarvis stated wearily. "What's the pump sitch, engineer?"

"Drain pump inoperative," Frank said. "Trim pump is okay, though. Tank's working on it. Maybe ten minutes."

Begley slid down the ladder from the conning tower and approached, "Status?"

"Pressure is up to three-thirty except in the forward two compartments," Jarvis stated. "Which I'll do now. The leak seems under control in maneuvering, and I'm going to have Tank go below and work the pumps and bilge valves to get that water out."

"You keep pressurizing the ship and we'll have nothing left for the MBTs," Begley said tightly.

"We need the men to be able to move around," Jarvis said. "I'll get forward battery and torpedo opened and then recommend we blow main ballast. It ought to give us enough rise to stop us and get us headed up. We can always flood the internal tanks to stay at one depth...

but this creaking and groaning is going to drive everyone batty eventually."

Begley snorted, "Batty? For Christ's sake, Jarvis, we're pushing eight hundred feet here! I'm not sure *any* submarine has gone that deep... and come up again."

"Well, then we're gonna be the first," Jarvis said confidently. "Tank, get below. Buck, how about the air sitch?"

"We should be okay even after you pressurize the next two compartments," Rogers said. "There's enough air left in the three thousand to blow the tanks, and we've still got plenty in the two-twenty-five and ten-pound systems once we get higher."

"Okay, good," Jarvis said.

He certainly sounded as if he were in charge and nobody was questioning it, not even Begley or Pendergast. Either they were scared enough to trust in a man who had the confidence and wherewithal to do something, or they were biding their time.

"I'll go forward and salvage the compartments, sir," said Bob Jones, a torpedoman who'd been taking a trick at the planes on the bench next to Sherman "Tank" Broderick. "I'd like to check on the boys anyway."

"Okay, Jonesy," Jarvis said. "Go ahead. As soon as he opens up forward torpedo, Buck, blow the main ballast."

"Finally..." Pendergast muttered.

A few minutes later, Jones came back with Martin, Carlson, and Sparky in tow. The forward room's leading petty looked fit to be tied. The men were helping several others to stumble aft so that they could get a bit more attention from Hoffman.

"What the hell's goin' on, sir?" Sparky asked Jarvis but glared around at everyone in control.

"We're havin' a party, Sparky," Jarvis said. "Was wonderin' where you guys were."

"We gonna make it, sir?" Sparks asked.

"Course we are, Sparks," Begley said, a bit of his earlier pique coming back. "Old Jarvis here has got it all under control."

"Blowing MBTs," Buck said aloud, interrupting whatever might have been said.

A hissing filled the boat as air was bled from the three-thousand-pound high-pressure manifold into the six-hundred-pound manifold and then out into the main ballast tanks. At first, things seemed to be working. The depth gauge needle stopped at eight hundred and five feet and slowly began to move in the other direction. However, it only took a second before the men began to realize that the ship was taking on a slight up-bubble. An angle that was growing steadily higher as the ship began to rise.

"Sir..." Nichols reported. "It appears that MBT six-Charlie and six-dog, as well as number seven, aren't blowing... main ballast tank indicators show vents are open."

"Shut them, for Christ's sake, Frank!" Pendergast urged.

"Inoperative," Frank said. "Phone talker, alert after engine, maneuvering, and after torpedo to manually shut the vents."

The kid with the sound-powered telephone relayed the orders, and everyone waited. After a minute or so, his face blanched, "Sir... compartments report unable to shut vents. Possible blockage."

"The bomb..." Begley stated tersely.

"Shrapnel is blocking the vents," Jarvis muttered.

"Well, we're rising, though," Clayton tried to sound reassuring. "That's positive, right?"

Pendergast turned back to his plot in order to hide his expression, but the inarticulate sound of disgust he made wasn't concealed. Begley drew in a breath and tried to maintain some composure.

"Yes, we're rising," the XO said. "But we're also taking on an increasing up-angle. Eventually, if not stopped, the bow will rise so much higher than the stern that water will flood the ballast tanks through the openings on the undersides. We'll rapidly lose buoyancy, continuing to rise to a vertical position and then slide backward into the crushing depths until the pressure flattens this boat like a tin can. Eventually, we'll strike the seafloor twelve thousand feet below at about eighty miles an hour."

Jarvis nearly lost the battle against the urge to deck the man. This wasn't the time for such graphic descriptions. The men needed encouragement right then, not pessimism.

Instead, he drew in a breath and grinned, "But we're not gonna let that happen."

"Oh, no, Superman?" Pendergast snapped. 'You got some secret stash of air we don't know about? The fuckin' three-K is empty now, thanks to you."

"Buck, flood the bow buoyancy," Jarvis ordered, ignoring Pendergast. Like his pal Begley, the man seemed inordinately unnerved. "That'll keep us level, hopefully."

"And possibly start us back down again!" Pendergast erupted. "What the fuck are you trying to do, Jarvis? We're at eight hundred feet!"

"Go, Buck," Jarvis said flatly.

"Belay that, COB," Pendergast ordered.

"With all due respect, sir," Buck said, turning to face the man. "Shut the hell up."

"Who you fuckin' talkin' to, Chief?" Pendergast turned on the big man. "We need to get back on the surface, not let more water in! This fuckin' guy is gonna get us all killed!"

"You've done nothing but bitch and complain," Buck said, "this whole time. Why don't you shut up and let the real men resolve this? You solve one problem at a time, Pendergast. God all-mighty, whose dick did you suck to get posted to *this* ship?"

"As you were, Chief!" Begley snapped.

Pendergast, who was a big man himself, although not quite Rogers's size, lunged forward, his hands reaching for the COB's throat. Jarvis leapt forward as well, placing himself between the two men just as Begley grabbed Pendergast, and Sparky and Hotrod grabbed Rogers.

"That's *ENOUGH!*" Jarvis raged. Even as his voice thundered through the compartment, he knew this was a bad situation. Tensions were rising, and fear was finding expression as anger. Things needed to improve soon, or the men's overheated, overtired, and overstimulated attitudes would explode, and no good would come of it. "Goddammit! Set an *example!* We're gonna be fine. Now cool out, the bodayiz'. The next man on this boat who raises a fist to another is gonna get his ass whipped by *me*. You all got that? And the two of *you*, Tom and Burt, one more shitty comment or one more asinine snotty remark... and I'll *personally* handcuff you to your racks. If you won't help, then get the *hell* outta the way. Flood the fuckin' bow tank, Buck. *Now! Be conservative, though. A little at a time!*"

"Aye-aye, sir!" Buck Rogers said, grateful for Jarvis's forceful personality.

The threat was evidently taken seriously. There weren't many men aboard who would tangle with the tall and strongly built torpedo officer. Even Buck Rogers and Sparky Sparks, two of the biggest and strongest men aboard, would hesitate. Right now, a strong man was needed to rally the men and get the job done, and Jarvis had stepped up to take over. Although technically he was exceeding his authority and Begley could and probably *would* bring him up on insubordination charges, it didn't matter. All that mattered at that moment was that somebody was making decisions and working to save the ship.

"That's got it," Nichols was saying. "Up bubble holding at... ten degrees. Of course... we're not rising now... If we can get the water out of that motor room, we should be able to level off and drive ourselves up at worst."

"How you eat an elephant, sir," Buck dared to address Pendergast. "One bite at a time."

"We're not rising, though," Pendergast noted, sounding suddenly flat and logy.

"But we're not *sinking* either, Lieutenant," Clayton stated and gave Jarvis a wink. He placed a cigarette in his mouth and struck a match. It took three swipes, and the flame seemed to struggle to life.

CHAPTER 22

JUNE 2, 1942

750 MILES WEST, SOUTHWEST OF MIDWAY ATOLL

The sun was now well up in the eastern sky. A good handsbreadth over the horizon, the golden orb cast a glimmering finger of fire that traced a line from the edge of the world to the hulls of the two IJN vessels floating placidly on the gently heaving swells. The cruiser *Nikatoni* and the experimental submarine carrier *Ribaiasan* were hove-to only a hundred yards from one another.

On the light cruiser's navigation bridge, *Kaigun-Chusas* Kajimora and Pendo stood conferring with their first officers.

"We've heard nothing for nearly twelve hours," Pendo said, sipping tea from a china mug and lighting a cigarette. He offered the pack to Kajimora, who took one. Osaka and the cruiser's EXO refused. "It is our opinion that the American submarine was fatally damaged by your airplane and has sunk."

Kajimora smiled, "I agree, Commander. We, too, have had no sign of life. Is that not so, Yakuin?"

"Indeed," Osaka reported. "At last report, they were headed downward, and their electric motors shut down. We lost any sign of them at approximately two hundred and thirty meters."

"And nothing since," Kajimora stated confidently. "By now, their air would be getting quite thin if they had somehow survived a plunge to that depth."

"Concur, sir," the cruiser's XO, a reedy man in his mid-thirties, opined. "And their battery banks would be quite low as well."

"Still..." Osaka stated thoughtfully. "There was no breaking up noise."

"A salt layer," Kajimora put forward, waving his lit cigarette in a negligent expression of dismissal. "They probably folded right after we lost them. My considered opinion is that they're destroyed. I think we should proceed with our mission."

"Agreed," Pendo stated. "However, we are in something of a bind. One of our boiler compartments was breached. We can maneuver, but quite slowly. No more than eight knots."

"Perhaps we should proceed to Midway ahead of you," Kajimora stated. "You may maintain position here while you make further repairs and then come into the atoll after the invasion fleet has landed. No doubt there are sufficient dock facilities at Midway to offer your fine vessel any additional repairs she needs."

Osaka had to school his features. He knew that Kajimora was more than usually anxious for glory. He desired distinction over almost anything else. Even as the four men spoke, a sailor aboard the *Ribaiasan* was painting an American flag on the conning tower.

Pendo frowned, "Unfortunate... I do not like sitting idle out in the middle of nowhere."

Kajimora made a show of empathy, "I quite understand, my friend. However, there is little choice. You could accompany us, but at your speed limitation... there is no way we can reach the battle before it begins or most likely *ends*. Even at flank speed, it's likely we will barely make it. On the other hand, by staying here and tending to your ship, you both maintain a vital picket point along our invasion route's course... and you can be extra certain the American submarine is dead."

"True," Pendo admitted. "And logically, you are correct, Captain. I'm simply not pleased about things."

Kajimora smiled at the other commander, "You did batter an American fleet submarine into the depths, Captain. She can never again harass our merchant fleets. That's something to be proud of."

It was with a heavy heart then that the crew of the light cruiser *Nikatoni* watched as the massive and bizarre submarine known as *Leviathan* started its six diesels and headed on a sixty-five-degree course at fourteen knots. Perhaps it was the sound of the submarine's engines or the inattentiveness of the cruiser's crew... yet no one noticed that little more than a mile to the south and seven hundred twenty feet below, a large object was slowly rising to the surface.

———

The Japanese were correct. The air in the boat was getting quite thin. The temperature hadn't risen very high, thanks to the coolness of the ocean depths. Yet the carbon dioxide levels were so high that it was next to impossible for a man to strike a match in order to light up a smoke. Men were finding that they felt drained of energy and their heads ached.

Emergency oxygen flasks had been bled into compartments long before. That had helped, but even so, the work required to repair the damage, pump the bilges, and restart the motors had eaten a lot of good air. Not to mention battery life.

The air systems, except for the low-pressure system, were completely bled dry. The only reason the ship was rising that morning was because Tank had managed to coax enough life into the trim pump to get the water out of the motor room. However, there wasn't much juice left in the two massive Sargo batteries. What there was would be depleted by restarting and running the electric motors.

This was due to the fact that other leaks had sprung during the long and exhausting night. The damaged ballast tanks' air-lines had been damaged as well, and seawater had begun to pour into various compartments through over-stressed lines. The men had dealt with them, patching and pumping and bracing until the water had finally been stopped. But this had drained even more juice and air.

Now, *Bull Shark* was rising at a modest foot per second. That they were rising was blessing enough. In twelve minutes, hatches could be opened, and a suction created that would wind-tunnel fresh air through the entire ship. There was enough air left in the low-pressure systems to start the diesels, certainly the auxiliary generator, and get the boat back to full life within a couple of hours.

On top of all of that, the men were famished. Because the refrigeration and air conditioning had been shut down, neither the cold room nor fridge room had been opened to prevent spoilage. There had been some pastries to go around and coffee, but what the men of the *Bull Shark* really needed was a few thousand calories to get their own batteries back up to full charge.

Watley and Turner were still unconscious. Turner had stirred slightly during the middle watch but hadn't come to. Hoffman said it was most likely due to the low oxygen in the boat. Mike Watley definitely had a depressed skull fracture. He'd need surgery, more than what Hoffman could do out at sea aboard an ill-equipped submarine. He'd cleaned the wound and debrided as much as he could. Watley was stable but certainly not out of the woods.

It was a weary and irritable crew, therefore, that received the news of the Japanese light cruiser still hovering about over their heads.

Joe Dutch sat at the sonar set, using his highly trained ears to listen and to give the other technicians a break. Thanks to the submarine's quiet state and the movements and activities of the Japanese, he detected the ship when they were about six hundred feet from the surface.

"Contact," Dutch said tiredly. "Surface contact bearing one-niner-zero. Range... maybe twenty-two hundred yards. Assess the cruiser with only auxiliary systems running. No screw noises. No movement."

Begley was on watch in the control room with Burt Pendergast stationed at fire control. It had been a long night, and Begley and Jarvis had managed to work out a schedule that gave all the officers and men some rest and eased the tension between the ranking officers some. At that moment, the torpedo officer was snoozing away in his rack.

Begley was glad of that. With Burt at the TDC, he wouldn't have to argue his decisions. And his decision would be to blow the cruiser straight to the moon.

"We're gonna take him out," Begley announced. "Keep a careful ear on him, Dutch. Below there, Mr. Post, I want periscope depth."

"Sir... we're positively buoyant and without propulsion..." Post said dubiously. "I don't think I'll be able to stop her."

"Use the blowers to get rid of some of this air," Begley suggested.

"Sir... that'll simply put more air in the MBTs," Post replied.

Begley's head ached and his temper was frayed, "Then bleed some of this pressure off through the exterior ventilation valves, for Chrissakes, Post!"

A pause, "Yes, sir... we'll have to be careful about that, though. I'm still doubtful that'll stop us in time."

"Then flood the safety and negative tanks," Begley informed him, annoyed that he didn't have Frank Nichols as diving officer at that moment. Post was a good engineer and knew how to trim a boat during combat, but an actual dive wasn't his usual forte. Oh, well... "Once we're at sixty-five, we can open main induction through the snorkel and get the engines and motors back online."

Post's voice still sounded uncertain, "Aye, sir."

"Burt, tell forward torpedo to make sure depths are set at six feet, and speed is high," Begley said. "And to open the damned doors if they ever closed them last night... shit, I can't even remember..."

The men in both rooms had, in fact, closed the outer doors using the manual system. Once again, Sparky and Perkins stood by their tubes, Y wrenches in hand, ready to go. The room phone talker relayed the order from the conning tower.

"Oh, holy sheep shit... here we go again..." Sparky grumbled as he fitted the big door wrench to the stud for tube number one and began to crank. The stud turned a long worm gear that connected it to the outer torpedo door shutter.

"Least we get a chance to give a little back," Perkins huffed as he cranked his own wrench around.

Behind the two men, Perry Wilkes and Pete Griggs were slowly turning the JK sound heads beneath the keel. It was necessary, as was manually opening the doors because hydraulic power had long since been shut down. Wilkes, as the third man in charge of the forward room, was taking his turn, and Griggs had been given the back-breaking monotonous task as an unofficial punishment detail.

Griggs had crashed early in the evening watch and seemed snappish and irritable to the point of insubordination. Sparky had decided to let it go, wondering if Grigsy was one of the dopers he, Murph, and the COB had talked about the other day. He'd heard from Murph during that same long night that both Smitty and Wexler, two usually reliable guys, had fallen into the same funk. Branigan and Duncan reported that Ingram, Swooping Hawk, and a few other men had, too.

The senior enlisted decided to let things lay overnight. They let the gold-brickers sleep it off and then gave them some shit work early in the morning watch.

"Now passing eighty feet," Post announced. "Flooding safety tank... still ascending, about a foot per minute now. Pressure in the boat is still over two hundred."

"Good," Begley stated. "Standby to open main induction... phone talker, alert after engine room to standby to kick the auxiliary. Also, let maneuvering know I want the motors online as soon as there's juice."

"Sixty-five feet!" Wendell Freeman announced from his place at the wheel, beating Post to the punch.

"Okay, open main induction, fire up the genset," Begley ordered. "Burt, sound general quarters. Sound battle stations torpedo."

The battle alarm gonged throughout the ship, waking any men who were lucky enough to be getting some rack time. Unfortunately, the gonging also drowned out Andy Post's warning about the air pressure. It wasn't heard in time to prevent what happened next.

The snorkel pierced the surface. The main induction valve, which was built into the snorkel, was opened to emit fresh air into the boat. However, as the internal pressure of the submarine was almost six times that of the surface air, a roaring vortex blasted through the boat, sending loose objects whirling into the air and knocking several men off their feet in the engine spaces. Thankfully the hurricane didn't last long, and no great damage was done.

However, the rapid depressurization did mean that now the open ventilation ducts, meant to be used on the surface only, began to act as inlets for seawater. It took another few minutes to wrangle these closed and pump the excess water overboard.

Once internal and surface pressure was equalized, the snorkel's air inlet began to do its job. The inrush of air went first to the engines, and once the auxiliary generator was started, some was bled off into the boat. It didn't make the air any fresher, but within a few seconds, the O2 levels rose, and men began to feel better.

"Jesus Christ!" somebody in the control room griped.

"Status?" Begley asked, a bit unnerved.

"Boatload of stained skivvies, Captain, sir," Dutch grumbled.

"We've got motors!" Post called from the control room.

"Helm, ahead slow," Begley ordered. "Post, keep me at periscope depth. Up attack scope."

Electrician's mate Paul Baxter was taking a turn as radar operator and periscope assistant and pushed the appropriate button to raise the slim attack periscope. Begley snapped the handles down and turned the scope toward his port beam.

"There she is!" he said triumphantly. "Japanese light cruiser, and she's just sitting there! How about the main engines, Andy?"

"Coming online now," Post said as the ship began to truly vibrate as the big powerful GM diesels roared to life, belching acrid smoke out through their alternate exhausts and up the snorkel's outflow pipe.

"Let's put one and two on charge," Begley said. "Three and four on propulsion. Helm, all ahead one-third, put your helm left full and steady up on... three-four-zero. I want to fire from his quarter."

Orders were acknowledged, and the submarine was once again a living, breathing thing. Her powerful diesels and generators driving the four GE motors at four knots, even on two engines. The other two motors were pouring their combined two and a half million watts of power across the battery busses and re-energizing the ship's massive storage cells.

"Switch to hydraulic power throughout the ship," Begley said. "Okay, Burt, here's your first set of data..."

———

Pat Jarvis was awakened by a sense that something had changed long before he was conscious enough to register what it was. It wasn't "an alarm" exactly, just an innate sense that seasoned sailors tuned into after years at sea. And Pat Jarvis had been at sea most of his life, man and boy, in one form or another. He even knew when diesels started in deep sleep.

He rolled out of his rack, slid a T-shirt over his bare chest and threw on his shorts and sandals. He'd had a vague dream about being in a storm and was surprised to see loose paper and other small objects lying on the deck of his stateroom. He stepped out of the tiny cabin he shared with Begley and Andy Post and nearly slammed into Paul "Buck" Rogers coming out of the chief's stateroom. The two men grinned stupidly at each other for a second, both knowing why the other was in such a hurry.

"Sounds like we're on top and running under growlers," Rogers said.

"Bet you a bottle of fine Irish that the XO is gunnin' for that Jap cruiser," Jarvis stated, waving for Rogers to go ahead of them and toward the control room.

Rogers chuffed, "No bet here, sir... what the hell happened? Why's there so much stuff all over the place?"

Jarvis blinked away the last of the heavy sleep, "I dreamed we were in a storm... guess it wasn't a dream?"

"Buck... Pat...?" Came a muffled and somewhat disjointed voice from behind the next baize curtain.

Rogers and Jarvis stared at one another with wide eyes before they both piled into the small captain's cabin to see Turner struggling to sit up in his bunk. Above him, Webster Clayton was leaning over his to look down in surprise.

"Skipper!" Buck exclaimed.

"You're awake!" Jarvis added.

Turner groaned, "Yeah... but I'm not happy about it... what the *hell's* going on around here, anyway? Was that the battle alarm I just heard?"

Jarvis blinked. Maybe that was what had roused him. The alarm must have been turned off by the time he came out of his exhausted sleep.

"Yes, sir," the COB said, sounding far more with it than the gunnery officer. "We think Mr. Begley, who's on watch, might be going after one of the Jap ships."

Turner looked at him stupidly, "Ships? Are they both still up there? How long...?"

Buck looked pained. As the COB, he wanted to man his post. Needed to man his post. Jarvis knew exactly how he felt but knew he could wait his turn since Pendergast was at the TDC already.

"Go, Buck, I'll update the skipper," Jarvis said.

Rogers smiled thinly and vanished through the curtain. Clayton jumped nimbly down from his bunk and began to collect articles of clothing that were scattered over the small compartment.

"Did somebody turn on an industrial fan or what?" Clayton asked dazedly as he pulled on his borrowed khaki trousers and blouse.

"Boat wasn't properly depressurized," Jarvis realized. "Christ..."

"Give me a report, Lieutenant," Turner asked.

"Long story, sir," Jarvis said. "We took some hard knocks. A Jap floater laid an egg on us, and we went down to eight hundred."

"Jesus!" Turner said and smiled. "And we're still in one piece? Goddamn, the Bureau of Ships got their money's worth on this girl."

"The boat took a casualty as did some of the men," Jarvis explained. "Including you. Doc thinks concussion and fractured ankle. It's daybreak, I think, and we're obviously on top now. It was touch and go there for a while."

"Good god..." Turner said. "And Begley is OOD with who as AOOD?"

"Pendergast," Jarvis said tightly. "Another long story, sir..."

"Get up there, Pat," Turner said with a scowl. "Backstop them. If the XO is taking us into combat..."

Clayton scoffed, "There's some problems to work out, Art..."

"Then fill me in while you help me get dressed and at least to my control room," Turner grumped. "Go, Pat!"

"Aye-aye, sir!"

———

"Helm, right standard rudder," Begley said and peered through his scope. "Okay, Burt, constant bearing... mark!"

"Zero-two-five," Baxter said.

"Angle on the bow is one-five-zero starboard..." Begley reported. "Range?"

"Looks like fifteen hundred yards. That's one-five double-oh yards, sir," Baxter reported.

Jarvis's head appeared in the open conning tower hatch. He didn't come all the way up, just paused to watch and listen.

"Welcome to the party, gunner," Begley said, not taking his face away from the eyepiece. "You're just in time to see me wipe this Nip from the face of the Earth! How about it, Burt?"

"Working on it..." Pendergast said. For some strange reason, he found himself shivering. But he didn't feel anxious... yet he couldn't control it. His hands quivered and made it difficult to operate the complex computer.

"Down scope, sir?" Baxter prodded gently.

"Negative," Begley said. "I want to watch him *burn!*"

"XO..." Jarvis began, eyeing Pendergast suspiciously. What was taking so long?

The men all over the submarine heard it even before Begley's exclamation confirmed it.

"They've spotted us!" Begley said. "Six-inch guns going off, and their Ack-acks too! Shit, hurry it up, Burt!"

"Drop the scope and evade!" Jarvis hissed. "For Christ's sake, Tom!"

"No, I've got em' in my fucking sights!" Begley said.

"Shoot!" Burt finally announced.

"Okay, give me a three-degree spread, Burt!" Begley exclaimed.

"Ready!" Pendergast almost shouted.

"Fire one... fire two..." Begley stated, giving the standard seven second interval. Pendergast pushed the plungers down, and the ship juddered as each ton-and-a-half torpedo was blasted free of the boat by a fist of compressed air. Thankfully there had been enough time to recharge the three-thousand-pound system, at least partially.

Yet something had been forgotten. With so many officers still in bed or getting out of bed, there hadn't been time to run compensation calculations for the firing of the torpedoes. Even as Begley was about to order the next shot, he felt the bow rising slightly.

"Oh, shit!" Jarvis croaked. "We're gonna breach!"

"Fuck it, fire three!" Begley ordered.

Again, the ship juddered and again, there was a slight breeze created as the number three torpedo tube's poppet valve drew back the air that had been used to fire the fish. The open snorkel then sucked the additional pressure out into the morning air.

"Tube three fired electrically!" Pendergast exclaimed, caught up in the thrill of the kill.

Jarvis landed in the control room and turned to Buck, "Rig ship for surface! We're about to go topside... I sure hope those fish don't miss! Get us on four-engine speed, Andy! Quick! When we do, Buck, activate the blower and blow safety and negative."

The up angle increased, and everyone felt the ship begin to rise. Just as Jarvis was giving his orders, Web Clayton entered the control room with Art Turner's arm slung over his shoulder. He helped the captain over to the master gyro table so he could support himself.

"Can't fire tube four!" Pendergast shouted from over their heads. "Sparky reports impulse charging system empty!"

"What in the Christ..." Turner muttered. "Helm, hard left rudder, now! All ahead full!"

"Captain?" Begley's voice drifted down through the open hatch. "Sir, I've got the cruiser pegged! She's dead in the water!"

The boom of naval guns close at hand reverberated through the ship. Jarvis bit his lip, and Turner clenched his fists, "So will we be in a few seconds! How about those fish, sonar?"

"Hot, straight, and normal, sir!" Joe Dutch reported. "Thirty seconds..."

"Get me on my fucking bridge!" Turner said to Jarvis.

Jarvis moved over to his captain who promptly jumped on his back, piggy-style. Having little choice in the matter, the *Bull Shark's* torpedo officer climbed the ladder into the conning tower and up to the bridge hatch, which Baxter was opening even as he slid around the ladder and out of the way.

A blast of cool and quite refreshing Pacific water doused the two men. Turner helped to hoist himself up, and Jarvis got him to the small bridge just in time to see that the first torpedo missed, going wide astern of the cruiser, now shockingly close and off their starboard beam. However, the next fish struck near the stern, blasting open the hull in a spectacular burst of seawater, fire, and smoke. Several seconds later, the second torpedo hit, nearly tearing the ship in half.

"Yeah!" came a triumphant cry from below.

Immediately, the light cruiser rolled to starboard, her tortured hull greedily gulping in thousands of tons of the Pacific. Even as she rolled and began to sink, her boilers ignited and, in turn, ignited a magazine and the ship disintegrated in a world-shattering *ka-boom* that seemed to echo forever across the vast and endless swell.

"God help them..." Turner muttered.

"No possibility of survivors from that," Jarvis breathed.

"We'll look all the same," Turner said, suddenly feeling tired and suddenly feeling the throbbing in his ankle. "And I think it's time we had a meeting aboard this ship, Pat. After we get the mess picked up and the men are fed."

"Yes, sir," Jarvis agreed, unable to take his eyes from the roiling sea and burning fuel oil that heaved upon it.

"Oh, and Pat?"

"Yes, sir?"

Turner looked at him sternly for a moment before he allowed a crooked smile to cross his lips, "Let's open the torpedo room hatches and take a suction through the boat, huh? You guys *stink*."

CHAPTER 23

JUNE 2, 1942

STATION HYPO – 1645 LOCAL TIME

It was going to be a long night. Had Joan Turner really known what she was getting into, she might not have taken this job. It was one thing for Joe Rochefort to practically live in the dungeon... but she had two young kids that needed her.

Thankfully, Joe Finnegan's wife was used to the long hours and occasional overnighters. She was happy to keep the Turner kids for the duration of the Midway operation. Joan had been told she was certainly free to leave at a decent hour and be with her family... yet knowing what was at stake for her country and that her husband was out there in the thick of it made her stay. She was as much a patriot as anyone.

There was plenty of work to do, although when it came to the actual Japanese fleet movements, there had been nothing for days. Yamamoto had called for radio silence, and radio silence is what they got.

However, other fleet broadcasts and orders did hint at what might be happening. In fact, Wally had intercepted a message that morning, and the code-crackers were nearly through deciphering it. Thanks to her work on the date cypher, messages now came with a fairly accurate time-stamp. She looked up from a particular piece she was working on to see

Joe Finnegan strolling over to her desk with a message flimsy in his hand.

"How you doing, Joan?" he asked.

Joan cocked an eyebrow at him, "I know that look, Joseph... what's the story? Is something wrong?"

Finnegan drew in a breath, "We're not sure... but I thought you ought to see this."

Joan swallowed hard and took the paper. She read it twice.

```
To: IJN fleet command
From: Kaiju
Kaiju and Sentry intercepted American fleet
submarine at encrypted.X
Sentry forced American down and proceeded to
depth charge for over two hours until we
arrived.X
American boat rose to periscope depth, fired
three torpedoes, two misses and one near
premature detonation.X
Detonation produced minor damage to Sentry
at encrypted.X
Aircraft from Kaiju dropped two-five-zero-
kilogram bomb on American position, forcing
submarine to hard dive.X
Lost contact at two hundred and thirty
meters and did not regain by mid-morning.X
Presume American sunk.X
Left Sentry to complete minor repair and
wait for Kondo.XX
```

Joan scowled, "Doesn't sound good, does it? Do we know these code names for the ships?"

Finnegan nodded, "We believe *Kaiju* is the submarine carrier, and

Sentry is referring to a destroyer or light cruiser they sent to escort. We haven't done the times yet, as you can see."

"And you think the boat they're talking about is *Bull Shark?*" Joan asked.

Finnegan sighed, "We've checked the coordinates. The report was made about seven hundred and fifty miles from Midway, right on the track between there and Saipan. Right where Art is supposed to be stationed."

"Hey, Joe, I've got another one," somebody called from over by the radio set. Finnegan grimaced, excused himself and rushed over to get the next message.

Joan simply sat behind her desk, staring at the flimsy in her hands. Part of her didn't believe what was written on the message. They lost contact with the American, but no confirmation on a sinking... so that could mean *Bull Shark* just got away. Another part of her couldn't help but be afraid, of course. Part of her knew that this was a war, and in war, young men died. Especially young men doing dangerous work... and there was little more dangerous than serving in a submarine.

She looked up again when she heard Finnegan's shoes tapping on the floor as they hurried toward her. The smile he wore eased her tension considerably.

"Well, I should've known," Finnegan said, shaking his head. "Sorry to alarm you, Joanie... but I think the Japs jumped the gun."

"How so?"

Finnegan chuckled, "To IJN fleet command, blah, blah, blah... have not received update from *Sentry*. Attempted direct communication with no response. Assess comm damage, blah, blah, blah. Yeah, com damage my foot."

Joan grinned, "You think they got eaten by a shark, Joe?"

He chuckled again, "I think they underestimated ole Anvil Art Turner and paid the price."

As if to underscore this, the heavy door opened, and Ed Layton rushed in, waving at the Marine guard with one hand and waving another message flimsy in the other.

"Ha!" he said and rushed over to Joan's desk. Rochefort noticed and moved to join the little group. "Got some great news, Joanie. Your husband bagged himself a light cruiser this morning."

"Details, Ed?" Rochefort prodded as he strolled up.

"Nice robe, Joe," Layton teased. "What's next, you install hammocks in here?"

"If it helps my people get the job done, I'll put in massage tables," Rochefort said. "Now, what are you on about?"

Layton held the sheet of paper so he could read it, "I'll summarize for you. An after-action report from USS *Bull Shark.* June one through June two... spotted by scout planes and dove to periscope depth. Met light cruiser and was depth charged... fired three torpedoes, two misses and one close premature that damaged cruiser. Bombed by floatplanes and dove to... Christ... eight *hundred* and five feet! Think that's a world record... okay... boat suffered casualties, etc...."

"What do you mean, *etcetera?*" Rochefort cranked. "For Christ's sake, Ed, Captain Turner's *wife* is sitting right here."

Layton flushed and looked embarrassed, "Sorry, Joan... I'm just breezing through the high points. A few injuries, including Art. Just a bonk on the bean and sprained or fractured ankle... ouch... but the boat took on some water. They got her up to the surface, and then the XO fired another three fish and sank the light cruiser. The report says they're addressing some minor damage to the upper deck and are proceeding Midway in pursuit of *Leviathan.* Not bad, huh?"

"A relief," Finnegan said. "We've got the IJN side of things, and they think they've sunk another of our boats."

"Good," Joan said. "That means that Art's driving right up that other sub's rear end even as we speak."

"Got a hell of a husband there, Joan," Layton said. "The Old Man is pleased... although a bit distracted considering that Fletcher's and Spruance's task forces will be tangling with the Kido Butai tomorrow or the next morning at the latest. They're already on station now, waiting."

"What happened to Admiral Halsey?" Rochefort asked. "I thought he was in charge."

"Jesus, you really *have* been down here too long," Layton commented with a shake of the head, "Bill Halsey is laid up in sickbay. Soon as *Yorktown* came in, he was admitted with a severe case of dermatitis... shingles. Nimitz assigned Frank Jack Fletcher to take his place."

"God be with them..." Joan said, wrapping the men on Midway and the men in the carriers up in her wishes for her husband's and his crew's safety as well.

CHAPTER 24

600 MILES WEST, SOUTHWEST OF MIDWAY ATOLL

B *ull Shark* was drifting on a nearly glass-flat sea. After having run at two-engine speed most of the day and making certain that the batteries were topped off, it was represented to the captain that something needed to be done about the damaged ballast tanks.

The last Japanese bomb had done a lot of minor but spectacular damage aft. A full fifty feet of the decking above the after torpedo room and maneuvering rooms had been blasted away, leaving only bent and twisted support framing. Shrapnel from the explosion had entered the open vents of number seven as well as number six-Charlie and six-dog main ballast tanks, thus jamming them open. Half a dozen men were now crawling over the exposed hull, tied to it by safety lines, and using a variety of tools to pull the jagged metal pieces from the vents.

"I think number seven is okay, sir," Mike Duncan was saying as he stood near the engine room access hatch with Turner and Pendergast, the second engineer.

Turner held a makeshift crutch made from a pair of boat hooks, towels, and some of Hoffman's duck cloth medical tape. He gazed at the unsightly wreck near the stern of his submarine and sighed.

"It could've been worse," he stated. "How about the crack at frame one-oh-four?"

"Harry says he can weld that," Duncan reported, "from inside, and we can do a patch job up here. The dockyard really ought to do it properly, but it'll do until we put in. Our little portable welder isn't made for bit work... but we can swing something."

"That your assessment, Mr. Pendergast?" Turner asked.

"Yes, sir," Pendergast said stiffly. "I don't like the looks of those number six vents, though, Captain."

Turner agreed. The shrapnel hadn't just inserted itself into the open vents, it'd bent them, and several of the risers were misshapen, "Recommendations?"

"I say we weld 'em shut," Duncan said. "Uncouple them from the vent controls and weld any shut that are bent up. Worst case scenario, those two MBTs remain full of air. Best case, the intact vents can be used, and they'll just take longer to flood."

"What's faster?" Turner asked.

"Welding," Pendergast said, again stiffly.

"Then let's do it fast and dirty, gentlemen," Turner decided. "We don't have time to make it pretty. Patch her up and let's get on with the job. Thank you."

He turned and hobbled forward to mount the cigarette deck where Begley was posted for his watch. Turner stood far aft of the bridge, near the 20mm AA gun and looked around him. He didn't like what he saw. No, that was probably not accurate... he didn't like what he *felt*.

The mood of the boat had been strained before they'd met the cruiser. But now, after he came to, Art Turner sensed that the general emotional state of the ship had sunk to right around dismal. There were half a dozen men on the defaulter's list; the officers were tense and quiet and only spoke to one another when they had to. No... that wasn't correct, and he knew it. Begley and Pendergast only spoke to the *rest* of the officers when they had to.

Web Clayton had given Turner the details after they'd done a thorough search for Japanese survivors... and found none. Clayton's account of the battle between Jarvis and Begley soured the captain's mood even further.

Outwardly, he had to deal with the situation officially and do so fairly and justly. He was still trying to determine what he *should* do. There were many factors, not the least of which was that within one or two days at the most, a huge naval battle would be fought near Midway. A battle that might literally alter the course of the war. He needed a functioning ship with men that worked well together so that they could all face whatever lie ahead.

Inwardly, Turner seethed because he knew that wasn't what he had. He didn't blame Pat Jarvis one bit. The man probably saved the ship. He definitely had leadership qualities..., and Turner's current XO most certainly did not. That included Burt Pendergast, who was simply Tom Begley's tag along, and thought and felt whatever Tom thought and felt.

Again, Turner missed Elmer Williams. While Williams had still been finding his inner confidence on their last patrol, he had a good command style. It was very much like Turner's own... walk softly and carry a big stick. Kindness and understanding first and then an ass-chewing later if absolutely necessary.

Pat Jarvis was a bit gruffer, but he was still a thoughtful and conscientious leader. His big personality and stature, combined with a quick smile and a mild but firm approach to correction made him popular among the crew. Pat was a big, rough, New England fisherman who preferred a pat on the back and to share a smoke or a beer with you. If, and when, it came time to drop the hammer, Jarvis would do so in a way that let a man know there was a problem, but that it was the problem and not the man that needed addressing.

Yet he'd still stepped over the lines of the regulations and brow-beat Begley. Jarvis had superseded him and did what he thought was right... and by the strict rules of the book, he'd done wrong. Of course, Turner applauded his actions, and he knew the men did, too. Probably earned Jarvis even more respect in their eyes.

But Begley would no doubt push the issue. Jarvis had embarrassed him and shone him up in front of the crew. That wouldn't sit well with a man like Tom Begley. Even if the XO let it go, something told Turner that Burt Pendergast wouldn't. Especially when it came to Paul Rogers. Those two had almost come to blows, and that would've been bad for the chief.

"God *dammit*," Turner growled under his breath. "Why the *hell* did they have to take Elmer away?"

That was only one of his problems. There were, he was now certain, some dopers in his crew. Sailors were always prone to excess. That was nothing new and even understandable. Men subjected to enormous stresses and enormous dangers had a tendency to kick up their heels on shore. Who could blame them?

But the continuous use of sedatives and stimulants aboard a submarine eroded a man's performance. He suspected that every man on the defaulter's list was one of those using. The problem was that Turner couldn't prove it, nor did he know the source. If he could find that, he'd eject the son of a bitch off his ship with prejudice, and the man would be damned lucky if it happened anywhere in sight of land.

As he looked forward, Turner saw a group of men near the bow having cigarettes. One was Plank, the boatswain. The others, Turner suddenly realized, were the men on the disciplinary list. There was Johnny Wexler and Jack Smith from after torpedo, Doug Ingram and Fred Swooping Hawk, as well as Pete Griggs and a new fireman who'd come aboard at Pearl.

Were they all grouped together because they were all in hock? Plank wasn't, though... maybe the boatswain was using his authority and position to have a talk with the men and try and straighten them out. Turner hoped so. All of those men had proven to be good sailors. A few were new, but Wexler, Smitty, and Griggs were good solid torpedomen. The Navajo Indian had proven himself to be a fine submariner already. The kid was just about ready to qualify for his dolphins, picking up on everything very quickly. Turner hated to see him get roped into such a dirty business.

Turner noticed that several others had taken note of the little cabal on the bow. Tank Broderick, who was headed aft with an electric welding set, stopped, and took a long gander forward before continuing on his way. That seemed odd... but then again, maybe not. The COB, who was inspecting the AA guns, also took note. Turner could tell that not only had Buck noted the gathering, he'd also noted Tank's reaction to it.

Turner thought about inquiring of Buck, but he decided against it. Let the chief of the boat do his thing first. The shit flows uphill on *Bull Shark*, Turner had said at the very beginning, and he had to stick to it. He'd let Buck handle the men, insofar as he could up to the point of the inevitable Captain's Mast. Before that, though, Buck would make recommendations. Turner would keep his thoughts on what to do about the officers to himself.

When it came to morale, the shit flowed *downhill* from the officers to the men. If there was a problem, he knew it mostly lay there.

————

"It's been rough, guys," Griggs was saying. "I feel like I'm all jittery all the time. Guess that shit yesterday really shook me up."

Wexler scoffed, "How's that any different than any other shit we been through, Pete?"

"I dunno," Griggs snapped angrily. "The fuck *difference* does it make, Johnny?"

Wexler chuckled with little humor, "You just want another little pill, right, Pete? That how we deal with our shit now? Poppin' little blue pills?"

"Maybe you oughta try it, John," Smitty grumped. "You been a fuckin' rain cloud since we left Pearl."

"What the hell do you know about it, Jack?" Wexler asked acidly.

"I don't know nothin' about it," Smitty shot back. "You ain't said two damned words. Just walk around with a hangdog face all the time. Can't talk to ya'; can't hardly work with ya'."

"This sub shit is tough," Ingram admitted. "Easy to get wound up, huh, Fred?"

Swooping Hawk nodded and frowned. He felt the same way, although he couldn't quite understand why. It hadn't been like this before.

"Why not take a relaxer or a shot of hooch now and then?" Plank asked. "It's not the end of the world. Helps you get through things. Hell, I do it. Shit... the fuckin' second engineer can't get enough."

Wexler laughed bitterly, "That sour bastard? Christ, I guess he *can't* get enough. How do you know so much about it, anyway, Plank?"

Plank puffed on his smoke, "I know Pendergast and Begley a few years now. And who do you think's the one provides the fringe bennies... ha! That's a good one... on this boat?"

Freddy looked at Ingram, "I thought it was just you."

"Me and Steve," Ingram admitted. "He's got a guy who gets us some stuff."

"Okay, so where is it then?" the new fireman asked. "I ain't seen anythin' today at all... and after yesterday..."

"Yeah, well... that's a problem," Plank admitted, casting a glance aft.

"What do you mean, a problem?" Griggs asked. "Shit man... we're already on the skipper's shit list, thanks to your buddy, Begley. A little kiss from Amy wouldn't hurt right now."

Ingram flushed and exchanged a glance with Plank, "My stash was wrecked last night."

"What?" Smitty asked incredulously. "Don't tell me you hid it in the fuckin' motor room, Doug? What're you simple 'er somethin'?"

"Take it easy," Plank said, smiling slightly. "It ain't Dougie's fault. Where the hell *else* was he gonna keep it? In the fuckin' head?"

"But Jesus, Doug!" the new fireman cranked. "You know this is a *submarine*, right? Sometimes we take on water and shit?"

Ingram cast his eyes down and shifted uncomfortably. Fred Swooping Hawk laid a hand on his shoulder and squeezed, "That's enough, Horris. You ain't exactly a brain surgeon. And you're new here too, so watch your mouth."

Horris Eckhart glared at Swooping Hawk but didn't retort. The

Navajo was a strapping young man and Eckhart was a reedy kid still showing a few pimples.

"Hey, it's no big deal," Plank reassured them. "I've got a few goodies stashed away. You'll all be good until we get back to Pearl. Which I figure won't be more'n a couple of days, week at the outside on account of the damage. Now you guys all let that head of steam bleed off. You come see me at the turn of the watch and I'll fix you up. That includes you, too, Wex. I know somethin's stuck in your craw, and believe me, a little relaxer at bedtime won't hurt any."

Wexler grumbled something and walked away, pitching his butt over the side. The rest of the men broke up, leaving only Ingram and Plank to stand alone near the bullnose.

"I really am sorry, Steve," Ingram said sheepishly.

Plank shook his head, "Nah, it ain't your fault, Doug. That was a good spot you had. Who'd have thought it'd flood like that. That's not our problem, really. Your stash was the little one... it's mine that really chaps my ass."

"What do you mean?"

Plank lit another Pal-Mal and sighed, "I went down into the storage locker in the pump room, and *somebody* went into my seabag and took what was in it. My bet is that this same shitbird got into the boatswain's locker and found my working stash."

"So, we're out?" Ingram asked, slightly alarmed for a variety of reasons.

"No... I got a little put away besides," Plank said with a sigh. "But like I said, it's not much. Enough for a couple days if all them guys want something... after that... well, we'd better put in."

"But what about the thief?"

"Yeah... that worries me," Plank admitted. "Somebody knows about us. I don't think it's one of our customers, either."

"Then who?"

Plank looked aft again, "I got a feelin' it's that fuckin' bruiser, Broderick."

"Tank? You really think so?"

"He was in the pump room while we was down," Plank explained. "For a while. He's got access to it on account he's a first-class electrician. Christ, he'll probably make petty after this jaunt. I don't know, but you see the way he eyeballed us a few minutes back?"

Doug frowned. He had noticed that. Broderick had come on deck with the welding gear and stared at their little group for a long time. Ingram couldn't be sure, but he thought he'd seen a smile on the big man's face, too.

"What're we gonna do about it?" Ingram asked.

Plank shook his head, "I dunno... need to be careful. Tank is in good with a lot of the officers and the chiefs."

"So are you," Ingram noted. "Me, I'm on report."

Plank grinned and slipped something blue into Ingram's palm, "Don't you worry about that, son. You and me are in good with the XO and ole Pendergast. It'll work out."

CHAPTER 25

JUNE 3, 1942

400 MILES W, SW OF MIDWAY ATOLL

It was fortunate that *Bull Shark* had so much non-commissioned officer experience. Between Buck Rogers, Mike Duncan, and Harry Brannigan, Turner could set a fourth watch if, and when, he needed to. At the sound of eight bells signifying the end of the morning watch and the beginning of the forenoon, Turner posted the COB as OOD and Clancy Weiss, the ship's yeoman, as AOOD. The other two chiefs had enough going on in the maneuvering and engine rooms.

All of the officers and Web Clayton, therefore, were assembled in the wardroom. Turner had the forward torpedo room cleared, and the hatch from forward battery to the control room dogged. There was no steward, so Ensign Andy Post elected to serve out the coffee Eddie Carlson had left them. The tension could've been sliced with a combat knife.

"All right, gentlemen," Turner began, lighting up a Lucky Strike and taking a long pull from his coffee. "We've got a problem on this boat, and it's high time we nipped it in the bud."

The men shifted uncomfortably and cast quick glances at each other. There was a hardness in the captain's tone. A no-shit sound of command that made them all uncomfortable.

"First," Turner began, "let me say that I at least partially blame myself for the quagmire the boat is now in. I suppose that I got complacent after our last patrol and thought that some of the changes made at New London would work themselves out. That has not been the case, nor has it been the case that the issues that cropped up after leaving Pearl have been resolved, either."

Again, no one said anything. It wouldn't do to interrupt the skipper now.

Turner drew in a breath, "To begin... we have a minor drug use problem aboard this boat. I've kept my mouth shut, hoping that the COB would be able to handle it, but thus far the men who are acting as suppliers have not been found... although I suspect they're known by some of the crew. I believe, though, that it's possible that one or more of *you* has either indulged or turned a blind eye."

Turner was surprised when no one protested. That was smart if his suspicion was correct. The officers who weren't involved wouldn't speak up, and those that were wouldn't for fear of incriminating themselves through the protest.

"Well, I'm not here to find out who," Turner said flatly and then leaned in, and his eyes flashed. "But I'm telling you men in no uncertain terms. This *shit* ends... *right here* and *right now*. If you know anything, you deal with it. If you know what men may be involved, you get with the COB, and he'll handle it. I want this quashed ASAP, gents. I won't have it on my goddamned boat. You hear me? I *won't* fucking *have it!* This ship is the most sophisticated weapons system ever built. It requires every component to work perfectly. And the most valuable and vital components are these seventy men under our commands. They must be focused and disciplined. Why the hell do you think we get two weeks of R and R at the best hotel in Hawaii? It's because we *earn* it by spending up to three months crammed into this damned drainpipe. Any deviation from the norm can disrupt the crew's morale and performance... we've seen that since the Panama Canal. Am I making myself clear?"

A round of yessirs floated around the table.

Jarvis and Begley looked particularly uncomfortable. Nichols, Dutch, and Post appeared stoic, but Turner knew they had little to do with either the drug issue or the next he was going to bring up. Pendergast, for his part, looked placid. That struck Turner as strange.

"Now, we come to a situation that's been brewing since Panama as well," Turner stated, drawing heavily on his cigarette. "I like to give all of my officers a lot of rope. We're all professionals here. Every man at this table, even Frank, who comes to us from the reserves, has been through sub school. All of us are college educated, and all of us have naval experience. However, two of you have been a negative influence since you came aboard my damned boat, and I have had enough."

Begley and Pendergast now both looked uncomfortable. That was fine by Turner because they *should* be uncomfortable.

"Tom and Burt," Turner said with a sigh. "I'm sorry to have to air this dirty laundry like this, but it affects all of us. You're both holding the reins far too tight. You have an attitude as if you think this boat is a damned battleship and that every old naval custom should be observed. You seem to believe that your positions as officers sets you far and away above the lowly enlisted men on this boat. Well, let me straighten you out on that once and for all. You're not. You're in charge, but you are not more valuable than any of these men. More than any ship, a submarine is a *team*, gentlemen. I'd prefer officers that take time to shoot the shit with the crew, or have a smoke on watch on the bridge, than officers who seem to expect to be treated like royalty. You hound the men for the smallest infractions rather than addressing your concerns to the chief of the boat. I've noticed, the other officers have noticed, and the *men* have noticed that you single out anyone on this ship who isn't White. Every one of our Black sailors, Hispanic sailors, and even our Navajo sailor has been put on report by you two for the pettiest *shit* I've ever heard of. Things that Buck should have, and would have, dealt with... or that shouldn't have been an issue *at all*. Well, Tom and Burt, while you're technically within your rights... this crap stops today, too. Maybe you think

Whitey is God's greatest invention. Maybe you think Eddie and Henrie and Leroy ought to be picking cotton rather than wearing silver dolphins. I don't know, and I don't care. Whatever racism you have, you leave it in your rack when you come on duty in my goddamned boat. Is that clear?"

"Aye-aye, sir," Begley said stiffly.

"Yes, sir, but—" Pendergast had the balls to say.

"But *nothing!*" Turner snapped and glowered the man into silence. After a very long and uncomfortable pause, he went on, "This was a superb boat before you two came aboard. Now it's a *shit* show. I'm not necessarily blaming you two for all of it; that's not fair. However, you deal with your part and right now. Because if things persist, and we actually *make it* back to Pearl, I'll have you both transferred right off my boat *with* prejudice. I know you're both capable men, and I'm hoping that this private little ass-chewing will get you, and all of us, back on the straight and narrow. As I said, I bear some of the responsibility here."

Pat Jarvis opened his mouth to say something, but a look from Turner stopped him. Everyone shifted and sipped coffee and smoked and waited.

"All right, one last bitch," Turner said. "Tom, I'm fully aware that you intend to prefer charges of insubordination against Pat. You feel he strong-armed you during that battle and overstepped his bounds as your XO, correct?"

Begley nodded gravely, "Insubordinate and disrespectful, sir."

Nichols scoffed, "Oh, please..."

Begley shot him a look. Nichols met it head-on.

"Mr. Jarvis saved the ship, Captain," Post protested. "I'm sorry, but if he hadn't acted..."

"I was on watch at the sound gear," Dutch said. "I agree with Frank and Andy. We needed decisive action, and Pat only took over because Tom wouldn't make a decision. Hell, Burt here nearly got into it with the COB at the time. And then there's the attack on the cruiser."

Turner held up a hand, "I didn't ask for opinions, gentlemen, not yet. Yes, Tom, Pat may have gone beyond the bounds... but from what I hear and what I *saw*... it's a dammed good thing he did. You were in command and entirely mismanaged that whole affair."

"Sir!" Begley protested.

Turner's gaze bore into him, and Begley fell silent, "And if you want to talk about offenses that merit a general court, let's discuss what happened yesterday morning when you surfaced. You didn't properly de-pressurize the boat. You didn't set a proper diving watch and make compensations for either the pressure or the fish you fired. You allowed the ship to breach during an attack, subjecting the boat to enemy gunfire... a very sloppy job, XO. Yes, you sank the ship, but had she not been stationary... we might not be having this very pleasant discussion right now."

"Sir, I have to protest on behalf of Mr. Begley," Pendergast put forward tentatively. "There was a lot going on, and he dealt with it as it came. Maybe it wasn't textbook... but it worked out."

Turner nodded, "So, you're saying that I should go easy on him for flying by the seat of his pants and dealing with the situation the ship faced without making it official?"

"Yes, sir!" Pendergast enthused.

Turner looked back to Begley, "What do you say, Tom?"

While Pendergast had entirely missed the hidden meaning behind Turner's question, Begley hadn't. He drew in a breath, cast a quick withering glance at Jarvis and then nodded, "I agree, sir... I'm willing to let the matter drop if that's your wish."

"Oh, come on!" Pendergast unwisely went on. "This fuckin' guy all but shoved Tom out of the way, went against orders, and did whatever he damned well wanted. This is total bullshit, Captain."

"AS YOU WERE!" Turner roared, the thunder in his voice rattling the coffee mugs stacked in the pantry. "Son, you ever speak to me like that again while aboard this ship and not only will I relieve you of duty, I'll have you clapped in irons! Who the *hell* do you think you are, sir!?"

A very tense and gloomy silence fell over the wardroom. Turner was not pleased. He hoped that his command authority would straighten things out, but he suspected nothing had really been solved.

"Look," he finally said with more calm than he felt, "maybe by tonight, but certainly by tomorrow morning, we're likely to enter the biggest damned naval battle since Jutland. I need everyone on this boat at tip-top efficiency. I need all of you, all of the men, and myself at his best. This little pow-wow here is to clear the air and start with a fresh slate. Since I feel that maybe I dropped the ball a bit, I'm willing to let all of this go. Everything that's happened up until now is in the past, gents. As of this watch, we start fresh, and we go forward with purpose. We're out here to fight the Jap, not each other. So, let's take a deep breath, shake it off, say our sorries and go forward like gentlemen. All right? No charges, no defaulter's list... everybody gets a clean sheet. If there's any hard feelings, let's take them out on Tojo, huh?"

That got relieved smiles and a few chuckles. Web Clayton grinned. Tom Begley nodded and even managed a small smile. Pendergast only nodded but did look relieved. He knew he'd crossed a line and misjudged his captain. He thought that Turner's easy-going manner was all there was to the man, in spite of warnings to the contrary.

––––––––

"What do you suppose they're talking about in the wardroom?" Ralph "Hotrod" Hernandez asked Paul Rogers as they stood together on the bridge.

Rogers looked away from the horizon and the foaming bow wave that nearly rolled over the deck and cocked an eyebrow at Hernandez, "Ain't none of our business, Hotrod."

The quartermaster of the watch returned the look, "Ain't it? Lotta shit been goin' down on this boat past few weeks, Buck. My money's on that the skipper is lowerin' the boom."

"Your money, Hotrod?" the COB teased. "Would that be pesos or the three or four nickels you got left after that non-regulation craps game night fore we left Pearl?"

Hernandez chuffed, "Hey, those Marines took advantage of me,

Chief! I am but a simple peasant, after all... not used to the ways of duplicity practiced by you White folk."

Rogers shook his head, "Jesus Christ, Hotrod... don't you ever worry that your smart mouth is gonna get you into trouble someday?"

"*No, señor* ... I don't speaka the English too goodly..."

Both men laughed. It felt good to do so after the past couple of days. Rogers drew in a breath of clean sea air.

"I think the skipper is cleaning house," Rogers said. "Getting shit straightened out with Begley and Pendergast. I hope the drug thing, too."

Hotrod laughed, "You know that Ingram kid is part of it, right, Buck?"

Rogers grinned, "You think I don't know what goes on in my boat, Chico?"

Hernandez chuckled, "Okay then... do you know about Plank?"

"Plank?" Rogers asked. "You sayin' he's involved?"

Hernandez looked at his friend, "You screwin' with me, Paul?"

Rogers laughed, "Yeah... and I believe you're right. I also think there's somebody else aboard who's maybe... taken care of it for us."

"What do you mean?"

Just then, a voice called up from the open bridge hatch, "Permission to come up to the bridge?"

"Come on up, Tank," Rogers said and grinned at Hernandez.

Sherman "Tank" Broderick, acting radioman, mounted the ladder and came to stand near the two men. He held a message flimsy in his hand and held it out to Rogers.

"Morning Fox," Tank said. "There's some... news."

Rogers took the report. The gobbledygook nonsense that usually proceeded and followed the actual message had been stripped away, and he read. After a moment, his face went a little pale, and he looked at the other two men.

"It's started," he said. "The Japs just bombed Dutch Harbor in Alaska... so far, there's been little damage, but the base there suspects no less than two light carriers offshore. Christ..."

"Does that mean Midway is under attack now?" Hotrod asked, staring forward as if he could see their destination four hundred miles over the horizon.

Rogers shrugged, "Nothing in here about it. Hey, Tank... let me ask you somethin'..."

"Sure, Chief."

Rogers exchanged a glance with Hernandez, "Sherm... yesterday I saw you scoping the guys and their little bull session up forward. Call it a hunch, but... do you know somethin' about this little dope ring we got aboard?"

Tank frowned, "I ain't no fink, Chief."

Rogers nodded, "I'm not asking you to name any names, Tank... and I'm not accusing you of being a cokie or anything... just if you know somethin'."

Tank drew in a breath and cast a quick glance over his shoulder and up at the lookouts. Among them were Fred Swooping Hawk, Doug Ingram, and Perry Wilkes from forward torpedo. He drew in a breath and met the COB's eyes.

"Yeah, I do," Tank stated. "I found a stash while I was in the pump room the other night. I tossed it overboard. I also... also figured out where more might be and tossed that, too."

"Christ..." Hotrod intoned.

Rogers frowned and nodded, "Okay, so whoever it is doesn't have the junk to hand out anymore. That's something anyway."

"Probably not," Tank said. "They might have a little left, but as far as I know, the boat's almost entirely clean."

"And you don't wanna tell us who's involved?" Hotrod asked.

Tank shook his head, "You know I can't, Ralphy. Least not now."

Rogers shrugged, "Well, when those guys start getting a case of the French Fits or whatever cuz they can't get their fix, you'd better hope they don't know it was you tossed their goodies into the drink."

Tank grinned, "I ain't worried, Buck. While I can't say nothin'... that situation you're talkin' about may give you some clues, though."

Any further discussion was interrupted when Fred Swooping Hawk called out excitedly, "Bridge! Plane bearing two-four-zero far... looks like he's heading toward us, but not exactly!"

"*Bridge, conning,*" came the voice of Clancy Weiss over the speaker. "*SD reports contact at range one-six-zero-zero yards. Range diminishing.*"

"Very well," Buck said. "Freddy spotted it, too, Clancy."

"*Should we dive, Buck?*" Weiss asked.

Rogers held up a pair of seven by fifty binoculars to his eyes, searching the horizon for the bird. "Not quite yet, Clance... give me a high look from the periscope. Your search sector is two-six-zero to two-two-zero. How about you, Fred?"

Up in the lookout perch, Fred Swooping Hawk trained his own binocs and tried to get a clearer picture of the aircraft that was still almost eight miles distant, "I believe it's a flying boat, bridge! Still hard to tell... but I see two engines mounted to the wings."

Rogers saw that as well, "Looks like a PBY. Tank, get down to the radio shack and give them a call on the aviation band. Let them know who we are and ask what they're up to."

Tank nodded and dropped down the hatch.

"*Bridge, conning,*" came Weiss's report. "*High look confirms. Assess PBY headed on a zero-eight-zero track.*"

"We should probably dive," Hotrod opined. "They can be on top of us in three or four minutes, Buck."

It was the conservative thing to do. Until Begley had come aboard, nobody would've ever been criticized for diving the boat upon sighting a strange aircraft. And just because it was probably an American plane didn't mean they were safe. From ten thousand feet and at a hundred twenty knots, a submarine was a submarine.

Buck held his glasses to his eyes and looked at the dark shape low on the horizon again. It definitely *looked* like a big Consolidated PBY...

"*Bridge, control,*" Captain Turner's voice said from the speaker. "*Belay diving. We've got the PBY on the box.*"

"Thank Christ..." Hotrod muttered.

"Bridge has the word," Rogers said into the speaker and then stuck his tongue out at Hotrod. "See, Ralph? Oh, and what do you mean thank Christ? Don't you mean *gracias, Cristo?*"

"*Si.*"

———

Ensign Jack Reed was startled at first when he saw the long slim shape of the submarine headed on a dead-nuts track for Midway. His first instinct was to bring his PBY flying boat down low and attack the lone boat. The blue-tipped shells he'd had loaded into his guns were supposed to tear the hell out of the Jap bombers from Wake, and they'd no doubt ruin an IJN sub's day.

However, when his co-pilot Ensign Gerald Hardeman saw the boat, he said he thought it was one of the big American fleet subs. He'd been right, too.

"*PBY, PBY, this is SS-333, do you read?*" a strong voice asked and then repeated the hail.

"Ha!" Hardeman shouted triumphantly. "You owe me twenty fat ones, Bob!"

"I'll take it off the *fifty* you owe me, Jerry," Ensign Robert Swan, the navigator, retorted.

"SS-333, this is PBY WPB-44, Ensign Jack Reed commanding," Reed replied with a grin. "How do I know you boys are really Americans and not just clever Japs?"

"*Betty Grable... Joe DiMaggio... John Wayne, A-number one,*" came a horrible Japanese accent and then a belly laugh.

Reed's crew joined in before a new voice broke in over the channel.

"*Ensign Reed, this is Captain Art Turner speaking... I assume you fellas are out trying to locate the IJN task force?*"

Hardeman, who was taking his turn at the controls, banked the flying boat into a wide circle that would orbit the submarine far below. Reed unconsciously sat a little straighter in his seat before replying.

"Yes, sir... and we found the bastards, too," the pilot reported. "Just a couple of hours back. Maybe three hundred nautical behind you and a bit to the north. A whole damned armada, too... transports, cruisers, tin cans, couple of battle wagons—"

"Tell him about the flat tops!" Swan needled from behind Reed.

"I am, Bob..." Reed hissed and then said, "Saw a couple of flat tops, too... but been told by Fleet that those aren't the main ships. So, we still ain't scoped the Jap carrier fleet yet."

A pause and then, "*Glad to confirm they're really out there. We're tempted to go back and send a few dozen pickles their way, but we've got orders, too... say, Reed... you haven't seen a big submarine ahead of our track, have you? A monster with two tubes on her back?*"

Reed looked over at Hardeman and raised his eyebrows, "Uhm... no, sir... nothin' like that. Sure we'd have noticed something like that."

———

In *Bull Shark's* radio shack, Turner leaned heavily on his crutch and sighed, "Figures. We think they're only a hundred miles ahead of us. Maybe less. Bending on all diesels to make the big show. On your way back, if you spot them, let us know or relay it to Midway and ask them to notify us, okay?"

A crackle of static and then, "*That's a Rog, sir. Good hunting.*"

"You too, Mr. Reed," Turner said and handed the mic back to Tank. He turned to Web Clayton, who was standing in the hatch. "Well, that's it, Web. A few hours ago, the Japs hit Dutch Harbor, and now one of our scouts has spotted the invasion fleet. Means the Kido Butai can't be far off... my bet would be north, northwest of Midway."

"The fuse has been lit," Clayton agreed. "The question is can we get back before the firecracker goes off?"

"My engines will get us there," Frank Nichols said from just beyond Clayton.

"The *real* question, though," Turner said as he hobbled out into the control room, "is with us running on all four as if we've got front row seats to see Bob Hope and the USO show at Midway... will we hear that Jap bastard before he sends a salvo of fish our way?"

CHAPTER 26

JUNE 3, 1942

MIDWAY ATOLL - 1700 LOCAL TIME

The mood on both Sand and East Island was tense, to say the least. The Marines had been working practically around the clock to fortify Midway. Strings of barbed wire encircled the islands on the beaches, and in the shallows, anti-landing ordnance had been laid. There were anti-tank mines and gun emplacements behind the wire, and the men were still working to dig trenches.

The airfield, now overcrowded with the Marine Corps air group, the new Navy Avenger torpedo bombers, and the Army Air Corps' B-17s and B-26s, was a constant source of activity. In order to prevent the air group from being bombed while on the ground, all of the Army aircraft and most of the scouts and fighters were sent up just after 0400. In this way, it was hoped, the Japanese couldn't wipe them out on an early-morning bomb run. Thus far, this hadn't happened, but it would eventually, and everyone knew it.

In Captain Simard's office, three men huddled around a large table that had been set up with a series of charts pinned down to it. One chart was the atoll itself; others showed the areas west, northwest, and north out to about five hundred miles. On the charts were very few notes, which was not in any way comforting.

"The group that Ensign Reed spotted has just been attacked right about here," Captain Logan Ramsey, the base's operations officer, reported, marking the chart. "B-17 flight reports some hits... but the reports are conflicting."

"Yeah, but we already know those aren't the main ships," Colonel Harold Shannon, USMC, stated. "Admiral Nimitz has already laid that out. His Ultra folks indicate that this is an auxiliary fleet. Probably the invasion force."

"True enough, Harry," Simard said. "But it doesn't hurt to knock them about if we can."

"Certainly not," Shannon stated. "Yet what we should be worried about is the Kido Butai. That carrier force is gonna hammer us, and more likely than not, it'll be at dawn. Probably would've been today, except for that bad weather our scouts keep reporting to the northwest."

"You're saying that's where they'll come from?" Simard asked.

"Has to be," Shannon opined. "It's the only place we can't look. We know Fletcher is to the northeast, so that's out... areas to the south would've taken too long for the carriers to end around to and be here today or tomorrow..."

"I agree with Harry," Ramsey stated. "We've got good scout coverage out to about four-hundred miles... except that northwest corner... this area here... *that's* where the Japs must be."

Simard drew in a breath and let it out slowly, "I can't disagree, gentlemen. Question is... what can we *do* about it?"

"Same as always," Ramsey said. "We launch our birds early in the morning and head them that way. I'm also sending out a squadron of PBYs with torpedoes to hit that westerly force tonight."

"You know..." Shannon said, tapping the southern edge of the Midway chart. "I'm concerned about here... we don't have any coverage to the south."

"Well, we've got the nineteen subs Bob English sent out," Simard stated. "Positioned as indicated at the one-fifty and two hundred circles."

"Yeah, from two-forty to due north," Shannon stated ominously.

The three men looked at the chart and the decidedly insignificant pips that indicated the probable location of the boats. Ramsey sighed and nodded slowly.

"If I were a Jap," Shannon went on, "and wanted to slip in, past the defensive line... I'd send something in from the south."

"Sort of come in the back door, you mean, Harry?" Simard asked.

"Right," Shannon said. "Not to mention that this is where the reef passage is. My Marines have the islands pretty well covered... or as covered as they're likely to get. But what about out to sea? Is there anything we can do to at least hedge our bets?"

Simard frowned, "Well... in truth, there may be. I'm about to let you gents in on a bit of a hush-hush asset. I don't know if you remember a few nights ago a sub put in here. She was here a few hours, took on fuel, and departed."

Ramsey nodded, "Sure, the *Bull Shark*. Lieutenant Commander Art Turner the CO... but he's not on the list of boats Bob English sent us."

"Right," Simard stated. "SS-333 is on a detached assignment. A seek and destroy."

Shannon looked interested, "To seek and destroy what, Cyrill?"

"This," Simard said, pulling a large glossy photograph from the top drawer of his desk. "Brought to us by an OSS man who rode out on the last batch of Fortresses. Take a look."

The two men gazed at the fuzzy picture of what looked like an odd ship. After a moment, Shannon looked at Simard with raised eyebrows. Ramsey frowned and then drew in a shocked breath.

"Is this a submarine?" Shannon asked.

"It is," Simard said, lighting a cigarette. "Nine thousand tons, five hundred feet long, and capable of sending eight Aichi floatplanes and their ordnance into the air."

"Sweet Jesus..." Ramsey breathed. "This is real? I mean, this isn't a mistake or some kind of propaganda from Tojo or something?"

Simard sighed, "Mr. Clayton, that's the Office of Strategic Services man, said his agent is reliable... and we've got proof of her existence. It's believed that this ship, named *Leviathan*, was the one that performed that raid on Attu two weeks back. We've also intercepted *Bull Shark's* last after-action report stating that they engaged the boat but failed to sink her. Captain Turner believes she's headed our way."

"Yamamoto's ace in the hole?" Shannon asked. "As if he needs one, if Ultra's data is good."

"Maybe, Harry," Simard stated, "and maybe the very thing you're concerned about."

"Yes, but eight planes aren't really a big threat to us," Ramsey stated confidently. "Christ, we've got task forces sixteen and seventeen hanging out there ready to jump on the Kido Butai."

"And not defend us, Logan," Simard pointed out. "Directly, that is."

"And we've got a hundred and twenty-one aircraft of our own," Ramsey insisted.

"Who will be busy flying to the northwest to find the Jap fleet," Shannon put in. "Leaving our southern flank exposed for a night attack maybe... or a mop-up. Either way, it'd be nice if we could put something out there."

Simard frowned, "Our PT boats and private vessels are all assigned to the lagoon... and I wouldn't send them after that monster in any case... but maybe we can get Turner in position. Jack Reed reported he spoke with *Bull Shark* earlier, and they were a little less than four hundred miles at about a two-fifty and running on top. Either we send him a code right now or do it with the evening Fox. But what if we stationed *Bull Shark* to the south, Harry. Say... two hundred miles? Those Aichis have a range of about six hundred... and they probably won't launch anywhere closer than two..."

"If he pours on the coal, no day diving," Shannon offered, "he could be in position by what, Logan?"

"Oh-five-hundred... maybe oh-six at the latest, if we radio him a course right now," Ramsey said, tapping the chart and drawing an imaginary line with his forefinger.

"Then let's see it done," Simard ordered. "I've met Captain Turner. Anvil Art they're calling him after he sunk four Kraut ships in less than a month. He won't be happy about missing the big show."

"Hell, he couldn't get up north in time anyway," Shannon said. "But if he gets where we need him, and he's good... he may just save us some trouble. Imagine what eight floaters could do coming in with all of our air cover gone or distracted... or come in low at night and blast the airfield, fuel dump, or even saturate the beachheads and open a hole for the amphibs? It could be ugly."

"True enough, Logan," Simard said. "Give Turner his marching orders."

300 MILES SOUTHWEST OF MIDWAY ATOLL

The *I-X Ribaiasan* had not run at flank speed on a direct course for Midway. Kajimora had planned to do this until his executive officer explained why it would be a terrible idea.

"Sir, should we continue on our present course," Osaka had said an hour into their journey after breaking off from the light cruiser. "We will either sail directly into scouting flights or possibly a submarine picket or even a surface vessel. We know that Admiral Yamamoto's forces are approaching Midway from the northwest. The Kido Butai should be in position soon. The invasion fleet is headed on the course we are now."

"But the Americans have no idea we're coming," Kajimora had stated with arrogant confidence.

"Don't they?" Omata Hideki had put in, adding his experience to the impromptu council of war. "Then why was that submarine out there? *Exactly* on the path between Saipan and Midway?"

Kajimora exhaled cigarette smoke brusquely and sipped from his mug of tea, "Dumb luck."

"Perhaps that's partially true, sir," Osaka insisted. "Yet as the great Sun Tzu said, we must prepare for what the enemy is *capable* of doing, not what we believe he *will* do."

"You're quoting Chinks now, Osaka?" Kajimora said icily.

"Wisdom is wisdom," Osaka pointed out. "Regardless of the source. This is why our Navy uses the Mahan doctrine to guide us. However, my point is simply that if we alter course due east, we gain two important benefits."

Hideki frowned for a moment, looked down at the chart that Osaka had brought with him into the wardroom and then nodded and smiled thinly. Kajimora, who was too stupid or too obstinate... probably both... to see it, only waited expectantly.

Osaka went on placidly, "No matter what is known, or not known, by the Americans... once the battle begins in earnest, they'll know it. Since *we* know the air assaults on Midway will come from the northwest, we can also assume that the Americans will concentrate whatever forces they have in that direction. There will be an opening to the south or southeast. Perhaps light air cover and shore batteries, perhaps men on the beaches... but far less opposition from that angle."

Kajimora was beginning to see it now and nodded, "So, we can sortie our planes from that direction and surprise them when their backs are turned. Is that what you're saying?"

"Indeed," Osaka said. "Is that not so, Omata?"

Hideki nodded, "Hai, Osaka san. Our pilots are very skilled at night flying. We can have them skim the waves until they're right over the reef, ascend high enough to drop their bombs at low levels for accuracy, and then zoom over the atoll before the Yankees can get any anti-aircraft batteries organized."

Kajimora nodded again, "Intriguing. Hardly a war-winner, however. Even with heavy three-hundred- and fifty-kilogram bombs, the total ordnance dropped is still under three thousand kilos."

"Yes, sir," Hideki said with enthusiasm, warming to the subject. "Yet with the element of surprise, our pilots can fly lower and slower. They'll have time to pick their targets carefully. Avoiding the airstrip, of course. We know that the Admiral wants that intact for *our* aircraft later on... yet fuel and munitions storage, barracks, AA positions are all vulnerable and being knocked out will only aid Admiral Kondo's invasion force."

"Not to mention demoralize the Ame-cohs," Kajimora said with a wolfish grin. "Then they can circle off to the east or west and rejoin us for re-arming and another sortie."

Osaka frowned but nodded, "Yes... although that second attack will not be so easy. The Americans will certainly be on guard then."

"Yes... but our pilots will also have first-hand knowledge of the base's layout," Hideki added. "They can come in from the clouds on the second run. This should offer them some level of safety."

"War is not a safe business," Kajimora pronounced haughtily. His manner was that of all men who found it easy to send others into danger knowing that they themselves would be safe.

Hideki frowned but nodded slowly.

"What is the second benefit you mentioned, Yakuin?" Kajimora inquired.

"We leave the beaten path and should be safe to run on the surface," Osaka said. "If we change course now, we can be within striking range of Midway by zero-four-hundred local time. That gives us enough time to launch our aircraft and have them reach the atoll in a body by..."

"Zero-six-hundred or shortly thereafter," Hideki finished. "We may even catch some of their planes on the ground."

Kajimora leaned back in his chair and puffed languidly on his Golden Bat. He didn't like that these two men had come up with this battle plan without him. He didn't like being pushed into action, gently coerced into following another man's ideas. Especially if that man was Yamamoto's pet.

However, all things considered, the plan was sound and perhaps the only way in which his ship and her airplanes would get to take part in the epic battle ahead. And after all... he *was* the captain. Whatever glory they won would first shower onto him and only onto his subordinates by default. It was easy enough to craft a report that would enhance Kajimora's own reputation and, while not directly damaging the other two men's... diminishing it.

Kajimora smiled and lit another smoke, "Concur, Osaka san. Give the necessary orders. Let us do all we can to position ourselves for glory.

Make sure that the men and pilots are well-rested. Tomorrow promises to be quite taxing."

And so it had gone. Now, hours later, Osaka stood on the bridge watching the relatively placid Pacific meet the broad bow of the submarine and erupt into froth that flowed rapidly along her sides. Tomorrow will be taxing, the captain had said. If there was ever a greater understatement, the first officer couldn't think of it.

One way or another for himself, for the ship and perhaps even for the Empire, tomorrow would certainly be a day that would not be forgotten.

300 MILES WEST SOUTHWEST OF MIDWAY ATOLL

Tom Begley was not pleased. Not pleased at all. Not only had that bastard Jarvis gotten away with insubordination... hell, practically mutiny... the damned skipper had brought up everything in public. At least as far as the officers were concerned. Chastising him and Burt in front of the others and intentionally embarrassing them.

As if that weren't enough, Begley and Pendergast had to grin and bear it. To make nice and act like they weren't treated like shit.

Goddamn Turner...

Everything he'd planned for, everything he'd hoped for, was now, more likely than not, dashed. Would Turner make an issue of the things he talked about? The unfortunate circumstances around the battle with the cruiser and that monster sub? As if that were Begley's fault. He'd taken over when Turner was injured.

The ship had been saved, and Begley had even sunk the light cruiser that had attacked them! And did he get any thanks? No, sir. Just criticism and held up to ridicule in front of the officers.

Then there was Steve Plank's little black market. It had worked well before. Begley enjoyed the extra income and had no problem running interference. Somehow, though, the Captain and the COB had sniffed it out. Of course, Burt wasn't any help. The man was one of the users, dropping sedatives to calm his nerves and then taking speed or even sniffing that junk up his nose to kick himself back into gear.

And now, apparently, one of the assholes in the crew had found the stashes and tossed them overboard. Burt was acting strange... manic almost. More than one of the regular customers was having withdrawals, Begley guessed.

He'd *had* to put them on report, for Christ's sake! How would it have looked if a couple of gold-brickers were allowed to keep playing at that game? He was damned if he did and damned if he didn't.

But now what? The junk was gone, or mostly... but one of the men *knew* about it and who was involved. Did he know about Burt? Jesus... did he know about Begley's involvement? Could this unknown man use it against him?

Begley had to do something. He needed a way to distinguish himself in the eyes of the higher-ups. Even more than that, he needed a way to do so that would make Turner and his pet Jarvis look bad. At least that would soften any blows that came from that direction. Both sides would have something to complain about, and maybe everybody would keep their mouths shut.

Begley was in the radio room with Doug Ingram, who was practicing on the gear as part of his ongoing submarine qualification education. Joe Dutch, another of Turner's brown-nosers, was on the bridge as AOOD. The door to the shack was closed, leaving little room for both men inside, but it did leave enough room for Begley to seize an unexpected opportunity.

"Sir, incoming coded message," Ingram announced. The electrician felt a bit uncomfortable with the XO hanging over his shoulder. The mood in the boat lately had been sour, and Ingram knew that Begley knew it was partly his fault.

"Let's have it," Begley said, holding a pencil over his notebook.

Ingram read off the code blocks as they came in. When they were all jotted down, Ingram repeated the message as it was repeated so that Begley could double-check.

"Should we put it through the decoder, sir?" Ingram asked, indicating the machine that was used to assign the coded letters to their actual meaning.

"No," Begley suddenly said, getting an idea. "I'll do it by hand."

Ingram looked at him and blinked, "Well... should I enter it into the transmission log, then?"

"No," Begley said flatly.

Ingram shifted uncomfortably in his chair, "But sir... it's SOP..."

Begley looked at him for a long moment, "Lotta things are SOP, Doug. And a lot aren't, too. Like sneaking dope aboard a submarine, right? Or being so foolish as to leave it lying around where anybody can find it? Or where it gets soaked when the boat floods?"

Ingram's face flushed beet red. He knew that Begley and Pendergast were in on the black market scheme... but that didn't mean that Begley couldn't lower the boom on him.

"Relax, Doug," Begley said in a friendly manner that was not reassuring. "I'm just pointing out that sometimes we bend a rule or two. This is one of those times. Now let me have the decoder strips and I'll see what this is all about."

It only took a few minutes to manually decode the message. It was short and to the point. *Bull Shark* was to alter course due east and proceed to a set of coordinates at flank speed. She was then to institute a search for the submarine carrier expected to be headed for a station *south* of Midway.

Begley smiled. Here perhaps was a way to kill two birds with one stone. He handed the notepaper to Ingram.

"Send an acknowledgement to Midway," Begley stated. "You'll need these first code groups... then I'll burn this message, and we pretend this never happened, understand me?"

"Sir?"

"You forget you heard a message and that I decoded it," Begley stated. "You keep my little secret, Doug, and I'll keep yours and Steve's. Deal?"

Doug smiled, "Aye-aye, sir."

"Okay, let me see you send that and then we'll burn that paper," Begley said.

Ingram did as he was told. He stared at the code groups for a long moment or two and then sent the coded response. Begley then used his cigarette lighter to incinerate the notepaper and let the ashes flutter into the small wastebasket near the radio gear.

"Okay, you keep up the practice, Doug," Begley said, stepping out into the control room. "Good work."

For a long, few moments, Doug Ingram sat in the radio shack and stewed. He didn't like the situation. He'd never liked Begley or Pendergast, for that matter. The men were slimy, arrogant, and abusive. Even when they tried to be gregarious, they only came off as a pair of grifters.

They both, Pendergast especially, had always treated Doug as if he were sort of simple. Constantly underestimating him and pushing him around because they knew they had something on him. Not always overt, but when Ingram had transferred away from their duty station a while back, he'd been pleased.

He was tired of people pushing him around. Even Steve, with his big toothy smile and friendly ways, was only using Doug and Doug knew it. Good old Dougie. Such a nice kid. So easy-going. Not particularly bright but obliging.

Well, maybe they didn't know everything. Maybe Doug Ingram wasn't such a softy after all. What no one knew, not even Ingram in any technical sense, was that he had an eidetic memory. He could see wiring diagrams or parts' lists and be able to recall them in exact detail hours and even days later. It was a talent that had helped him become such a good electrician.

So, it was mere child's play for Doug Ingram to pull out a small bit of scrap paper and write down the code groups from the last message exactly as he'd heard them and seen them on Begley's notepad. It took him only a few moments to run the decryption and decode the message and read it for himself.

Ingram didn't know *why* Begley had elected to keep the message a secret... or at least out of the official log. Yet, he suspected that the XO was up to something, and it would either be to his benefit or the captain's detriment. Doug wasn't sure what to do with the knowledge, but he at least felt better knowing that now *he* had something on Begley for once.

CHAPTER 27

"You know..." Turner pondered as he stood at the master gyrocompass table and looked over the chart of Midway Atoll and the surrounding waters. "I wonder where this sub carrier will go..."

"Probably not straight at Midway," Jarvis opined.

"I agree with Pat," Nichols said. "It wouldn't make much sense. I mean, we're already within three hundred miles. Do we know about fleet deployments at all, skipper?"

Turner bit his lip, "Not much. I know Task Force 17, consisting of *Enterprise* and *Hornet* and their escorts, have probably already met with Task Force 16. TF16 is Admiral Frank Jack Fletcher's group. He's in overall command because Admiral Halsey's in sickbay at Pearl... Fletcher's using *Yorktown* as his flag. Not exactly sure where they are, but my guess would be here someplace."

Turner indicated an area of ocean to the north, northeast of Midway. Andy Post leaned in and nodded.

"That makes sense," Clayton said. "And jives with what I last heard. Unfortunately, I left Pearl before exact plans were finalized... I also know that Nimitz has sent a bunch of submarines to act as pickets."

"Probably from southwest to north," Post said. "To cover the likely Japanese approaches. We already know that there's a fleet headed in from just south of west. And if the skipper is right about our carrier groups, then the main Jap carrier force is probably coming in from the northeast. In a direct line from northern Japan."

"So, the atoll's eastern and southern flanks are wide open," Turner stated, tapping the eraser of a pencil against his chin, "at least as far as naval assets are concerned. What are your thoughts, XO?"

Turner was making an attempt to live up to his word. To put the mistakes of the past behind them all and move forward the way that a good submarine crew ought. Unfortunately, Tom Begley and his friend Burt Pendergast were not the kind of men who could put aside their perceived injuries so easily. They didn't have the introspection to see their own faults for what they were and to take steps to correct them.

Oh, Begley could act the part, certainly. And he'd had the discussion with Burt about it as well. Play the game. Most commanders who felt as Turner did would've simply relieved the two officers of duty and been done with it. But Turner's willingness to try and move past the issues at hand was considered a weakness by the two new officers. Just another example of why Turner didn't deserve the boat, and why Begley did.

And now, fate had stage-managed a true opportunity. Without the directive from Midway, Turner would continue to follow his course. Now, though, thanks to a bit of luck, Begley was in a position to set himself up for success.

Begley could recommend that the *Bull Shark* go exactly where she'd been ordered to. If they were successful, then he'd get the credit. If they failed, or if the *Leviathan* wasn't where Midway thought she'd be, then the only blame would be on command. Perhaps even on Turner, as command felt that once they'd given a captain a directive, it was the captain's job to make it work. At worst, there'd be no blame and at best... Turner's shiny armor would be tarnished in the eyes of his superiors.

"Well, sir..." Begley began thoughtfully. "As you say, from the sea, the southern end of the atoll is unprotected. If I were the sub carrier captain, I'd want to end-around and hit the island there. Sort of... come in the back door, you might say."

"Makes sense," Jarvis admitted. Begley thought Jarvis made the admission grudgingly and was inwardly pleased.

"Yeah, it does," Turner said. "I was thinking something along those lines, too... figure he'll sortie his birds from two hundred miles at a minimum. He's ahead of us, but probably doesn't have our turn of speed... Tom, plot me a course so that we end up right about here by 0400. Frank?"

Nichols did some rough calculations in his head. "We'll have to overload. We'll be making smoke... but I can get twenty-one, maybe twenty-two knots out of her... that is if you don't mind exceeding MEPs and risking blowing a cylinder."

Turner nodded, "That's fine. We've got much bigger considerations than that, Enj. Andy, go grab my night book, will you? OOD, make a note in the log. We're altering course on my authority to intercept suspected Japanese carrier submarine. Make sure you give yourself credit after working up our heading, Tom."

Jarvis's face remained passive, but Begley thought he caught just a hint of something. He was right, too. Jarvis wanted to snort with derision at the idea that Begley would *ever* forget to give himself credit, but he refrained.

Post brought the night book and Turner made a few notes, "Just noting to keep lookouts sharp, activate the Sugar Dog every ten minutes and do a complete Sugar Jig sweep every fifteen. Let's keep the conning tower, control room, and both battery compartments rigged for red after dark... and shorten the watches to three hours for the men. Want everybody as rested as possible. Tomorrow's gonna be a helluva day, I think. All right, gents... I'm getting off this damned foot for a while. I smell frying steaks for supper."

———

Several hours later, Doug Ingram came off watch, grabbed himself some warmed-over supper, and made his way to his rack to catch some much-needed shut-eye. He was down to his last half-dozen Amies... well, in truth Plank was in charge of them and had only given Ingram two. After what had happened earlier, Ingram knew that he'd need something to help quiet his mind down enough to sleep.

He'd overheard Begley making his "suggestion" to the skipper. And now the boat was on course for the point where Midway had ordered her. Yet nobody knew about that but Begley and Ingram. What to do about it, though...?

"Hey, Freddy, you home?" Ingram asked softly, wrapping his knuckles on the frame of Swooping Hawk's bunk. The curtain was pulled, and no light peeked out, so his friend was likely already asleep.

Then a muffled groan came from within. A mumbled something, and rustling as if somebody were shifting and trying to get comfortable.

"You need a little help getting some sleep?" Doug inquired, putting his face close to the curtain. "I know I do... here."

Ingram pushed his hand under the hem of the curtain. In it was one of his last two Amies. Fred had been a good friend to him, and he deserved to share in what was left.

That's when the curtain was yanked aside, the reading light snicked on, and the stern face of Paul "Buck" Rogers stared back at Doug. Ingram drew in a breath and froze, his fist still resting on the mattress next to the COB.

"Naw, kid, I'm wide awake," Rogers said softly.

The curtain on the bunk below slid aside, and Tank Broderick rolled out and got to his feet, standing close to Ingram so that the young man wouldn't try to run, "Me too."

"What...?" Ingram tried to ask but couldn't quite get the words out.

"Think we should be askin' you that, kid," Rogers said. "What's in the hand?"

Ingram's fist opened, seeming to do so almost against his will. Inside lay the blue bullet-shaped sedative. Tank nodded at Buck.

"That all you got?" Rogers asked.

"No... I... I've got one more, Chief."

"Probably the last of it, I'd guess," Tank stated.

Ingram blinked at him, "It *was* you, wasn't it? One that found the stash in the pump room and in the boatswain's locker?"

Tank nodded.

"Why didn't you report it to anybody?' Ingram asked, glancing at the COB.

"Didn't want to fink on anybody," Tank said. "I got no real problem with somebody bending the rules now and then... except when it comes to the safety of our ship and all of us. And you and Plank's little business has already upset the apple cart enough."

"So, you found the stuff and tossed it?" Ingram asked.

"Best solution I could think of," Tank said with a shrug. "Until Buck here come to me and lain out his suspicions... about you and about Begley and Pendergast."

Ingram swallowed, "What about them?"

"Come off it, kid," Rogers said. "I know that Pendergast is using too. And I know that Begley and Pendergast are, and have, covered for Plank. Nice little side business. But those two assholes are gonna fuck up this ship and get us all killed. Probably would've already if it weren't for Mr. Jarvis and the skipper."

"This is a good time to come clean, Doug," Tank said. "Lay it all out for us, and we'll keep your part quiet. We already talked with your customers. They fingered you and even Steve. But I know you know a lot more about the officers."

"Help us prove their hands are dirty, and we'll see yours are kept clean," Rogers added.

"Don't be a hero, kid," Tank pushed. "You think those two shitbags would hesitate for a *second* to toss you to the wolves if they thought it would save their skins? Coming clean now is better than later when it's too late."

Ingram knew that Broderick's words were true. He had no illusions about how much loyalty either Begley or Pendergast would show a lowly electrician first-class if they were pressed by anyone. They could simply claim that it was Ingram and Plank all along.

"What about Steve?" Ingram asked.

"We'll deal with him," the COB stated, "but we need your help. Know anything that's useful or provable?"

Ingram drew in a deep breath and let it out slowly. As a matter of fact, he did. He slowly reached into the pocket of his jeans and pulled out the folded bit of scrap paper on which he'd decoded the message from Midway.

"How far in Dutch am I?" Ingram asked.

"Depends on how much you help," Rogers said.

"Okay, Chief... here," Ingram handed the paper over, feeling an unexpected wash of relief.

"What's this?" Rogers asked.

"A message from Midway," Ingram explained. "Came in while I was on watch. Just before we changed course. Mr. Begley was in the radio shack with me. He decoded it and then burned the note. Said I should keep it to myself."

"And you copied it from memory?" Tank asked in admiration.

"Yeah... I've always had a good head for words and numbers and stuff," Ingram said with a shrug. "Can recall most things like that for a long time."

"I'll be damned..." COB said, glancing at the message. "And the son of a bitch was gonna keep it to himself and had the *balls* to suggest this course to the Old Man."

"Fuckin' prick..." Tank muttered.

Rogers rolled out of the bunk and patted Ingram on the shoulder, "Good work, kid. Hand over the dope, though. I've got to show it to the captain."

"Okay, but..." Ingram hesitated and then handed the two pills over. "I just take them to help me sleep."

Rogers and Tank nodded. The chief pocketed the Amies, "Yeah, that's what Freddy and Pete and Smitty and a few others say. And they take the Bennies just to help them wake up... as if Navy coffee wouldn't do the trick."

"It's how it starts, Doug," Tank said kindly. "I know. I used to be hooked on some junk too, a few years back. It might be a little rough for a while, but after a few days, you'll be all right and much better for leaving the shit alone."

Ingram was dubious about that. He'd been taking product off and on for over a year. Even as he climbed into his rack, Ingram was doubtful that he'd get any sleep that night. Ironically, though, he was wrong. He didn't realize that the weight he'd been carrying about the whole business had been weighing on him so heavily that when it was finally removed, the tremendous sense of relief was just as effective at lulling him into sleep. A far more peaceful and guilt-free sleep than he'd known in a long time.

The soft rap of knuckles on the frame of his stateroom didn't surprise Turner. He'd left orders to be awakened thirty minutes before the change of the watch. He'd have been up in any case, yet it was nice to have a little help. Especially with any pertinent information he'd require before going on watch himself.

When Buck Rogers stuck his head through the curtain, however, Turner was a bit taken aback. Buck was supposed to be on watch with him, and should they actually make contact with an enemy, he'd be at his station in any case.

"Buck?" Turner asked as he slipped into his sandals. "How'd you get elected to wake me up?"

Rogers didn't smile. Instead, he cleared his throat and, in an oddly formal manner, asked, "Permission to enter and address the captain."

Turner cocked an eyebrow at him, "Of course, COB. Come in and take a load off. What's with the stiff neck all of a sudden?"

Rogers entered and held out a full mug of coffee for Turner and settled into Turner's desk chair with his own. He took a long pull and seemed to be trying to come to a point but didn't quite seem to know how to get there. Turner gave him time and sipped from his own mug.

Finally, Rogers cleared his throat, "Sir... how long we known each other?"

"Hell... got to be nine years now," Turner said thoughtfully. "I was a wet behind the ears ensign and you a newly rated torpedoman... S boat out of Norfolk. Met in that hash house on the base."

Rogers grinned, "Sure enough. Couple of LTs with shiny new bars thought they could give you a hard time. Said bubble heads ought to get their start on destroyers so you at least knew what the *real* Navy was like."

Turner chuckled, "Damn near got tossed in the brig that morning."

"Oh, nothing happened, though, sir."

"Yeah, but it was about to... until you and a couple of the boys from the torpedo gang came along and told me the skipper wanted to see me pronto."

Rogers chuckled, "Said he was royally pissed off on account of how you tuned up a couple of Marines the night before. Said the Provost Marshal was thinking of charging you with brutality on account of how bad you hurt them jarheads."

Turner chuckled now, "The look on those two idiots' faces was priceless."

Rogers grinned, "Then a couple years later at Coco Solo, you really *did* wipe the deck with a couple of Army pukes. Damnedest thing I ever seen. Glad you and me never had to tangle."

"I know I can be a hard ass sometimes, Buck, but nothing to fight over," Turner said with a smile and then more seriously, "Paul... something on your mind?"

Rogers drew in a breath and grimaced, "Sir... you know we're about as close friends as any enlisted and officer can be, right?"

Turner nodded, "Far as I'm concerned, Paul, that doesn't matter unless we're on duty and we have to maintain the forms."

"And you know I'm a straight shooter," Rogers said. "I respect the Navy and the chain of command and all that."

"Paul... if you've got something to say, just come out and say it," Turner said, spreading his hands. "No barriers, huh?"

The COB sighed and pulled a folded sheet of paper from his khaki uniform pocket and handed it over to his captain, "I need you to take a look at this, and then I've got some... news."

Turner read the dispatch and looked up at Rogers, "Makes sense. What Begley suggested earlier. When did this come in?"

"1700 while Mr. Begley had the watch," Rogers said. The news fell flat, and a heavy silence followed.

"It's almost midnight," Turner stated.

"Yes, sir."

Turner drew in a long breath, "Why wasn't I informed, Buck?"

"That's the news, sir," Rogers said, shifting uncomfortably in his seat. "This came in while Doug Ingram was training in the radio shack. The XO was standing by, sir."

Turner thought he got the picture. He swallowed a healthy gulp from his coffee, wishing he could lace it with some of Hoffman's depth charge medicine, "So, let me see if I have this straight... a dispatch comes in from Captain Simard suggesting we deploy south of the atoll in order to snag *Leviathan*. Begley decodes it and then neglects to tell anybody. He must have sworn Ingram to silence... so a few minutes later, he just happens to *suggest* this course of action while we're all in control."

"About the long and short of it, sir."

"I doubt that," Turner said and more darkly. "Son of a bitch... what's your read on it, COB?"

Rogers snorted, "I think he's settin' himself up for the spotlight, sir. I know I shouldn't be talkin' like this..."

"Go ahead, Buck... I did ask."

"I think he figures that if we nail this bastard Jap, then it's his idea and he gets the medal," Rogers blurted. "And if we fail, one way or another, maybe it makes you look bad and takes the sting out of anything you put in his or Mr. Pendergast's FITREPs."

Turner shook his head and then held the paper out in front of him, "How'd you get Ingram to show you this? I assume he copied it at the time of reception?"

Rogers grinned, "Kid's got a photographic memory, I guess. But oh... this is the flip side. He's involved with the drug ring aboard. Him and Steve Plank, who's the main source. I guess Begley and Pendergast have served with them before and have run interference."

"Jesus Christ..." Turner muttered. "What the hell's happened to this boat...? So, you know who the users are?"

Rogers looked pained, "Yessir... but if it's all the same to you, and it's not too bad, I'd prefer to handle it... in-house, if you see what I mean."

"Okay, Buck," Turner said after a moment's contemplation, "I trust you... but that doesn't include Plank. Somebody's got to go down for this shit, and I need at least the big fish. Not to mention those two so-called officers."

"Thanks, sir," Rogers said. "The handful of guys who were Plank's customers are good guys. They'll fall back in line, no problem."

Turner had a pretty good idea of who they were, "As for the rest, Buck... we'll leave it alone for now. Let's get through this Midway operation, and then we'll handle it. I appreciate you bringing me this."

Rogers shifted uncomfortably, "Way I figger it, sir... I owe you. I should've discovered this sooner... nipped it in the bud way earlier on. Kinda feel like some of the crap that's gone on is my fault."

Turner laughed sardonically, "You're a damned good chief of the boat, Paul. However, at the end of the day, and when it's all said and done... the captain is responsible for the conduct of the men under his command. I tried to make that clear earlier. Tried to give everybody some slack... but maybe that was a mistake. Maybe the powers that be jumped the gun when they gave me this boat."

Rogers's indignation flared, "With all due respect, Art... that's a load of horse-shit. We *had* a great boat and crew before Mr. Williams got yanked. You weren't the one who assigned those two... officers... to this ship. Just because you don't run the boat like Captain Bly don't mean your command style isn't any good. Bullshit... sir."

Turner grinned, "Thanks, Buck. Okay, let's go refill these mugs, grab a sweet roll or two, and hit the deck."

CHAPTER 28

JUNE 4, 1942

0300 MIDWAY TIME

The general alarm bells were ringing, and all over the submarine, men were rousing from their bunks, gulping down last mouthfuls of food, and rushing to their battle stations. From the bridge to the conning tower to the control room, the men on watch remained vigilant.

They studied their charts. The sonarmen, two of them, listened intently on their passive equipment. In the radio room, the two operators listened on the boat's two independent systems for uncoded broadcast traffic and prepared to manage the many transmissions that would soon come their way. The steersman in the conning tower kept his eyes glued to his rudder angle indicator and gyrocompass repeater.

Men in the torpedo room stood by for orders. Other men were stationed in the battery compartments, constantly checking the specific gravity of each of the massive storage units' pilot cells. In the engine rooms, the motor machinists tended to their massive growling diesels. In the maneuvering and motor rooms, the machinists and electricians oversaw the operation of the great vessel's electrical systems and the huge motors that drove her propeller shafts. In the big ordnance lockers, men carefully passed up belts of ammunition for the many 20mm cannons above as well as used chain hoists to carefully lift large bombs up through the watertight hatches and into the waiting hangars.

The pilots assembled on the main deck and watched as the flight crews readied their planes and placed them on the catapults for launching. In the periscope sheers, lookouts scanned the horizon with the naked eye as well as powerful binoculars. And on the bridge, four men observed it all.

"Wind is light from the east northeast," Hideki said. "Quartermaster, make your course due east, ahead flank."

The enlisted man repeated the orders into the bridge transmitter, and the ship turned ponderously to port.

"We are not yet on station," Osaka said. "But I believe by the time our planes return, we shall be in an even better position."

"Make sure to tell your pilots that this is mostly a reconnaissance flight," Kajimora reminded Hideki unnecessarily. "And that they should only attack Midway if our main carrier attack force arrives. I want to be able to spring a surprise later on if need be."

"Yes, sir," Hideki said. He'd already briefed his pilots on that very point. To him, it only illustrated the captain's ineptitude. He wished Ryu were in command.

Ryu Osaka wished the same thing. He found it wearisome to constantly have to endure Kajimora's arrogance and condescension, all the while having to surreptitiously compensate for the man's incompetence.

"Omata, at this distance, how long until the planes reach the atoll?" Osaka asked.

"It will be another thirty minutes or so until they're in the air," Hideki said. "Maintaining a conservative speed... they should reach Midway just after dawn. If I'm not mistaken, this should coincide with the initial bombing wave from the Kido Butai."

"Unless it's already happened," Kajimora said.

"I believe we'd have heard of it," Osaka opined. "In either victory or defeat, Admiral Yamamoto's radio silence order would be lifted."

"Let us hope you're right, Yakuin," Kajimora stated with a wolf-like smile playing on his lips. "And that we're not simply sending our valuable planes into a well-prepared American fortress."

"Our pilots know their business," Hideki put in. "Not to worry."

The men watched as the flight crews entered their aircraft. The flight deck officer waved his flag, and first one and then the other Aichi floatplane was catapulted into the pre-dawn night. Without any of them realizing it, the first offensive Japanese attack on Midway had been launched.

50 MILES TO THE NORTHEAST OF *RIBAIASAN* – 0400

The gonging of the general alarm was silenced shortly after it'd been sounded. For some reason that Art Turner couldn't quite put his finger on, the alert bells sounded like those of a church. At least they weren't mournful.

As the men, enlisted and officers alike, got settled into their battle stations, the command staff held an impromptu council of war in the control room around the master gyro table. Webster Clayton was there as well.

"All right, gents," Turner said. "We're in position. Just about exactly two hundred miles due south of Midway. My thinking is to commit us to a box search pattern. Make it... thirty miles on a side. We run at three-engine speed for two hours on each leg, and we should end up back here by noon. Thoughts?"

"Running on top muddles our sound gear," Joe Dutch stated. "We just can't listen and run the rock crushers... and I think we'll need to listen."

"Agreed," Begley stated. "That ship is still a submarine, and we won't pick her up visually or on radar until we're right on top of her. Far closer than the sound heads could."

Jarvis hated to do it, but he had to agree with the XO, "And they have the advantage of airplanes. They can spot us from much further away."

Nichols frowned, "We could run all engines on a fifty, sixty split. Get the same fifteen knots but quieter."

"Maybe even a little less if we get the auxiliary online at full power. She makes a lot less noise, and we can get a little more juice out of that generator."

Turner nodded in approval, "Okay... that's you engineers' marching order. Make those tigers purr like kittens. I'd prefer to run on batteries, but I think we need the speed to cover a large enough area quickly enough to have a chance of finding this guy."

"What about your snorkel?" Clayton asked.

"Same problem for us," Turner said. "Yeah, we can run at radar depth, but we'll actually need more power to get the same speed because completely submerged, the drag coefficient is greater. And our problem is sound. If we're forty feet deep, our diesels still mask our passive sonar. We're also then limited to no lookouts and a radar range of only a few miles. That double-secret spy-gadget snorkel is a great invention, but it's hardly a superweapon. It has its place... but not in an operation like this."

Andy Post was frowning at the chart, where Turner had drawn four circles to indicate the four waypoints of the search pattern. Turner noticed his expression and asked what was on the junior officer's mind.

"Well, sir..." Post said, running a finger along the chart. "We need to both cover this area and rely heavily on our sound gear... but maybe we're thinking about this in the wrong way..."

"How do you mean, Mr. Post?" Begley asked, just managing to keep from sounding snide.

Post drew in a breath. He was hesitant to put forward a suggestion. Not because he didn't believe in it, but because of the way things had been on the boat over the past month.

When they'd first started on their last patrol, Post had screwed up the trim compensations and caused the boat to breach while attacking a German U-boat. The skipper had been magnanimous about it, and the XO... the first XO... had helped Andy see that anybody could make a mistake and it was okay, so long as you learned from it. On that same patrol, he and Murph had dealt with a possible ship-killing flood casualty in the after room. That had further strengthened Post's confidence in himself.

Yet recently, he'd been shunted to the background with Begley and Pendergast around. It seemed that if an idea didn't come from the two of them, it wasn't worth talking about. However, now, the captain and Mr. Jarvis were there, and Andy knew they'd listen.

"Well, sirs..." Post cleared his throat, "we're thinking to cover the area at a constant speed. But that's not *really* necessary. Since we can't both run hard and listen... why can't we take turns at each?"

Turner's eyes glittered, and he grinned, "Go on, Andy."

"If we were dead quiet in the water," Post asked Dutch, "with the engines shut down, what's the furthest you think you could hear another ship from?"

"With the gain cranked all the way up and the JK head trained right on the target's bearing," Dutch was pondering. "Assuming a ship, or let's say a submarine, was running on top at full speed... probably fifty thousand yards. If she was submerged, probably twenty at best. But again, that's pointing the receivers *right* at her."

"Okay..." Post was tapping his chin and doing some calculations as well. "So, you need to do a thorough sweep through a complete three-sixty... maybe a minute, right?"

"I'd prefer two sweeps in two minutes," Dutch said. "Just to double check."

"Okay... and suppose the boat is running on top but at one-third?" Andy asked.

"Is there a *point* to all of this?" Pendergast asked and frowned.

Begley held up a hand.

"In that case, I'd give us thirty thousand yards," Dutch stated, beginning to smile himself.

"So, what if we dash ahead for say... twenty minutes at full power," Post proposed. "Then shut the diesels down completely and drift for a few minutes, sweeping the whole time with sound *and* radar. Then repeat that process all along our search pattern."

"A dash and listen," Jarvis said appreciatively. "That's a great idea, Andy."

"So, we leapfrog six or seven miles," Turner said, "then kill the engines and drift another few hundred yards while we sweep. Then we get to listen for as far ahead as our next stop *and* as far *back* as our last stop. Double... no *triple*-checking ourselves each time."

"It does lengthen our time on each leg," Begley stated neutrally.

"Only by about twenty minutes, sir," Post defended.

"I like it," Dutch said. "Rivers and I can both get on the gear and backstop each other."

"What about an active ping?" Pendergast asked. "Wouldn't that detect something out to fifty grand even if it were stopped?"

Dutch frowned, "Yes... but that works both ways, Burt."

"We'll keep that in reserve," Turner stated. "If we *do* detect something, we can ping it because we can always high tail it to that bearing once we do. You and your Black gang think you can handle all this choking and blowing, Frank, Burt?"

Nichols grinned, "They'll handle it, or I'll know the reason why, sir."

"Very well," Turner said formally and then smiled. "Let's go hunt us a sub carrier."

CHAPTER 29

MIDWAY ATOLL – 0500

"John, I know you're here to document this thing," Captain Simard was saying as he shared a cup of coffee with his officers in his office. "But I've got a favor to ask."

Director John Ford had come out to Midway at the behest of Admiral Nimitz. The admiral wanted something for posterity and wanted it in full sound and picture. Ford, although he'd been in pictures all of his adult life, and then some, still found it a nutty notion that a major war could now be *filmed* for the viewers at home.

Yes, there had certainly been motion pictures back during the Great War. The idea of stringing images together and projecting them onto a screen had come about nearly as soon as Thomas Edison had lit up Orange Park, New Jersey. Ford was still haunted by the films of *Titanic* leaving her birth in Southampton on her one and only cross-Atlantic voyage.

Yet those had been in the black and white days of silent films. Now, in this modern era, it was possible to film a war in living color and vibrant sound... although black and white cameras were still widely used for simplicity's sake. And now, here he was, the guy who'd directed

Stagecoach, out in the middle of the Pacific and about to come under attack by a huge force of enemy aircraft... and he was supposed to stand there and get it all on camera.

"You mean other than standing out in the open with my gear and my Marine and hoping the Japs aren't harsh critics, Skipper?" Ford asked wryly.

Shannon grinned, and Simard chuckled, "Exactly, John. Well, in addition to shooting your masterpiece, I need a guy who can document the Japanese units as well. Keep track of what kind of planes and how many. My request is that you and your little team head to the top of the powerhouse. You'll have a great view of both islands and the whole shooting match from that vantage."

Ford nodded. It made sense and would be a stellar filming location, "Well, sir... it sounds good... but not to sound like a sissy or anything... won't the power station be one of the Japs' primary targets?"

Shannon laughed, "Not much gets by you, eh, John? It *might* be... but honestly, as the Japs intend to occupy this base, our thinking is that certain targets will be left alone. The runways and the power station among them. Since they're attacking during the day, knocking out power doesn't *really* matter all that much."

"And it's one less thing to repair once they get here," Ramsey stated.

"Okay, you're the bosses," Ford said. "I'm just a fearless patriot here to make a historical life-changing film that will enrich Americans for decades to come."

"I love a man who's humble," Shannon said and laughed.

250 MILES NORTHWEST OF MIDWAY ATOLL

Lieutenant Joichi Tomonaga didn't care for taking off from a carrier deck into darkness. Of course, he cared even less for trying to *land* on one in the dark. Thankfully, this was rarely, if ever, done.

However, as his Nakajima B5N torpedo plane, colloquially referred to by the Americans as a "Kate," rose laboriously into the pre-dawn air, he found that he was clenching his teeth. The plane was loaded down by two two-hundred -fifty-kilo bombs, and as she left the end of the flight deck, the aircraft seemed to dip uncomfortably low before her wings began to lift her and her payload into the sky.

Tomonaga grinned to himself, knowing that his rear gunner, a young seaman new to airplanes, would be close to wetting his pants. The bombardier behind Tomonaga laughed knowingly as the swift and powerful plane rose toward the darkness above.

Tomonaga climbed to ten thousand feet and began a lazy orbit that would carry him in a great circle around the four carriers below. He was in command of the first bombing raid on the American Midway station, and he must ensure that his other thirty-five B5Ns, the thirty-six dive bombers, and the highly important thirty-six escorting Zeroes were formed up properly on him before they headed for their objective.

By the time the hundred planes were organized, dawn would have begun, and there would be enough light for each airplane to clearly see the others and maintain a strict formation. In the two hours it would take to reach the atoll, the sun would rise, and there would be plenty of light to clearly identify targets, both ground-based and airborne.

"*Emperor's Wrath flight leader,*" came a voice from the radio. Tomonaga recognized it instantly as that of their task force leader, Admiral Chuichi Nagumo, aboard the *Akagi*.

"This is Tomonaga, Admiral," the flight leader said. "You honor me."

A slight chuckle, "*Indeed, young man... no, I think it is* you *who honors us all. Your bravery and loyalty to the emperor, and this great endeavor, is a symbol both to the courage of the Japanese heart and to the Japanese people. I want to wish you good luck and good hunting. I know you will bring glory to us all.*"

Laying it on a bit thick was Tomonaga's first impression. The sentiment was appreciated, but in the pilot's mind, he was doing nothing more than his duty. Perhaps, if he were to be honest with himself, he wouldn't even elevate it that high.

The fact of the matter, as far as any Japanese knew, the Kido Butai and her tremendous power were sneaking out of the darkness and attacking an enemy without warning... again. It felt less dishonorable than the first time, the day of Pearl Harbor, as there was now an official declaration of war.

Yet war was, as some American had once stated, hell. Someone else had once stated that all was fair in love *and* war... was that an American as well? If so, then they would have to eat their words, as everyone must sooner or later.

"Thank you, Admiral," Tomonaga replied. "You do us all too much honor. We are nearly ready to proceed. On your orders, sir."

There was a pause. A rather long one, Tomonaga thought. Had the Old Man gone to the head or something? Finally, Nagumo came back over the channel, "*You may proceed, Lieutenant. Yamamoto will be proud of you.*"

600 MILES WEST OF THE KIDO BUTAI, ABOARD BATTLESHIP *YAMATO*

The admiral whose name had just been invoked stood before his operations table and frowned down at the almost ridiculous number of toy ships that sailed across its glossy painted sea. On it, the Kido Butai and its escorts occupied a position only a few flying hours from the little brown splotches that represented midway. To the west of the atoll, just slightly south of west, Admiral Kondo's invasion task force was only a bit further away. The battleships, cruisers, destroyers, and light carriers escorting the large fleet of cargo and transport Marus. Far to the north, too far to be placed on this map, the fourth task force would even now be readying to attack Dutch Harbor once again. Yamamoto's own powerful surface fleet was clustered far away from the battle that must even now be ready to begin.

Not for the first time, he questioned the wisdom of his choice to keep his powerful surface ships far away from the carrier action. The logic was sound, of course. Even the mighty *Yamato*, the world's largest and most powerful battleship, was shockingly vulnerable to air attacks, as all big surface ships were. Even with a screen of destroyers and her own anti-aircraft emplacements, the massive battleship could be sunk by a mere handful of dive bombers and torpedo planes. Even the woefully outdated crates the Americans were still flying.

"You look pensive, sir," Matome Ugaki said as he approached with a mess steward in tow.

Yamamoto looked up and smiled grimly at his chief of staff, "You move like a cat, Matome. I didn't even hear you come in."

The steward set the tea service down on a sideboard and began to pour.

"I think it is more that your mind is taken up entirely by tactical and strategic thoughts, sir," Ugaki said with just a hint of playfulness in his tone. "Thank you, young man. Leave us, please."

The steward bowed and went out. Ugaki held out a steaming mug to his superior, "You need something, sir. There is also a little food so that you might maintain your strength."

"*My* strength," Yamamoto said ironically. He sipped the tea. It was hot and strong, just the way he liked it. "It is not *my* strength which is needed, or which will be tested today, Matome... not mine, nor yours nor even that of our mighty lady here. No, it will be the strength of those thousands of young men out there. And the strength of their leader, Nagumo... I hope his is up to it."

Matome only nodded. He knew when his friend was ruminating and when to remain silent. Yamamoto smiled at him knowingly.

"There are several things on my mind, Matome... do you know what they are?"

Ugaki almost laughed. The man never ceased to teach. Even to teach Ugaki, who was as close to Yamamoto's rank as one could get, "I believe you are concerned about *this*... and *this*..."

Ugaki reached out and touched a single pewter submarine sitting all alone to the south of Midway. He then pointed to the cluster of American ships set ambiguously to the east, northeast of the atoll.

Yamamoto smiled, "True enough. We do not know where the

American fleet is. I guess they will be somewhere northeast of the islands, perhaps five hundred kilometers away. And our special asset... I don't know her position either. I hope, especially after receiving the report about the loss, or potential loss, of the *Nikatoni*, that Kajimora will have the wisdom to see that placing his ship on the theoretically unprotected flank of Midway will be most useful to me at this time."

Ugaki actually scoffed. He didn't know Kajimora well, having only met the man once. Yet the impression he'd gotten then and all that he'd heard since was not reassuring, "I don't believe that wisdom and Kajimora go well together."

Yamamoto chuckled, "I agree... yet our young friend Osaka and his CAG Hideki are both intelligent and wise. I would be willing to wager that they will impress upon their captain the tactical advantage of this position. Let us hope that once there, the man uses it properly. You have earned two points, my friend. Care to try for four?"

Although his tone was casual, Ugaki knew that Yamamoto was serious. The chief of staff didn't hesitate, "You're concerned about Nagumo's ability to see this through successfully."

Yamamoto nodded gravely, "He's had too many easy successes in the Indian Ocean of late. Yet we both know that had the man attacked Midway after leaving Pearl Harbor... this entire mission might not be necessary."

"He is capable," Ugaki offered.

Yamamoto inhaled and sighed, "Yes... under the right conditions, Nagumo can be relied upon. However, in my opinion, he does not adapt well. Suppose things *do not* go to plan? What if, for example, the Americans are more aware of our plans than we think?"

Ugaki frowned, "Sir, our code is one of the best kept secrets and best constructed in the world. Perhaps only second to the Nazi's Enigma. And as you know, we're already adapting a new alteration. I cannot believe that the Americans have broken it."

"I agree... but we must remember that the Americans are neither cowards nor are they stupid," Yama moto stated. "Right now, we have the advantage. We have a larger fleet, better-trained pilots, and more advanced equipment... with one glaring exception."

"The radar," Ugaki admitted. "At least... the Kido Butai isn't equipped with it."

Yamamoto nodded, "Yet if we don't act swiftly and decisively, the great size and industrial might of the United States will simply crush Japan under its heel. This is why this operation and the one I have planned for *Ribaiasan* must work. Yet my concern is that we don't *know* where the American carriers are. We *think* there are two, but what if there are three? What if Midway has more aircraft than we suspect? Under those conditions, the odds are far more even."

Ugaki shuddered and looked down at the board, "And you're worried that if this is the case that Nagumo won't be decisive enough to adapt and overcome the odds."

Yamamoto nodded slowly, "Which ties into my final concern."

Ugaki swallowed and shifted from one foot to the other. He suddenly felt like a first-year cadet being reviewed by a senior officer. He had a fairly good notion of what the Admiral wanted.

Yamamoto smiled indulgently, "Say what is in your heart, Matome. There is no need to handle me with kid gloves. You should know by now that I am not swayed by my own publicity. Your honesty is one of the things that makes you so valuable to me... both as my chief of staff and as my friend."

Ugaki sighed, "Very well, sir... you are questioning the wisdom of keeping our task force so far from the site of the battle. That if things *do* alter, that we cannot come in to support the Kido Butai in time?"

Yamamoto nodded, "Precisely. We're a thousand kilometers away. This entire campaign may be decided in the next twelve hours, and even at flank speed, we could only halve the distance in that timeframe. What do *you* think, Admiral?"

Ugaki decided to take Yamamoto at his word, "I believe hanging back this far is... too cautious. I think that we should move in as quickly as we can to support the action, whichever way it goes."

Yamamoto said nothing for a long moment. At first, Ugaki thought that he might have gone too far, in spite of what Yamamoto had said. Finally, though, the venerable admiral nodded and even smiled thinly, "You have earned your four points... I agree, Matome. Please go to the CIC, update the captain, and make signals to the rest of the fleet. All possible speed for the Kido Butai."

CHAPTER 30

"All stop!" Turner ordered.

"Helm, bridge, all stop," Hotrod Hernandez, quarter-master of the watch, said into the bridge speaker.

"*Maneuvering answering all stop,*" Dick "Mug" Vigliano, the boat's best helmsman, replied.

"Go Sugar Dog," Turner ordered. "Lookouts, complete sector scan."

Above them, in the lookout perch built into the periscope sheers, Turner had four lookouts rather than the usual three. In this way, there were two after lookouts each concerned with a ninety-degree sector. Above their heads, at its maximum height, the SD air search radar hummed, sending out radio waves and receiving them. This needed only be done for a few seconds and would be terminated before the SJ surface sweeps so as not to confuse the two readings.

"*Negative on the Sugar Dog,*" Begley reported from his position in the conning tower.

"Go Sugar Jig on PPI," Turner ordered.

The SD mast was lowered and the SJ elevated, and it also began to hum as it turned in two complete three-hundred-sixty-degree revolutions. Down below, Balkley would have several radar displays at his command. One would be the simple reflection return scope that showed any contacts as spikes above a line of green that represented the horizon. Additionally, the returns could be displayed as pips or blurps on the planned position indicator. This simple but effective device was a cathode ray tube on which could be superimposed a chart image. Then over this, the radar returns could be displayed, giving the radar operator and deck officer a top-down picture of the area out to the radar's visual horizon.

Everyone on the bridge waited in silence, just as their ship did with her diesel engines shut down. It seemed to Turner to be the longest two minutes of his life.

"*Negative contact on Sugar Jig,*" Begley reported a bit glumly.

"No surprise there, we just started," Turner muttered. "One more sprint to go before we turn south."

"Wait!" came an excited voice. Not from the speaker, however, but from the open bridge hatch.

"Something, conning?" Turner prompted.

A pause and then Begley replied, "*Balkley thinks he hit something at extreme range, sir... right on the line... faint but noticeable. Range twenty-four thousand yards, bearing three-four-five.*"

"A ship?" Turner asked, mildly annoyed at having to prompt vital information from his XO. Probably couldn't be helped if the contact was too faint. "Anything on sonar?"

"*Balkley doesn't think it's a ship, sir,*" Begley finally said. "*Seems far too faint. Rivers and Joe report nothing on sound.*"

"*Mierda...*" Hotrod cranked under his breath.

"Yeah..." Turner grumped in commiseration. "*Something's* out there... conning, tower, fire up the diesels."

Behind them, the underwater exhausts belched, and the ship began to rumble as the four sixteen-cylinder GM engines roared to life.

"Helm, all ahead flank," Hotrod ordered. He looked at Turner as if to ask a question.

Turner knew what he was asking. He grinned, nodded, and pointed just to the right of the boat's bullnose.

"Helm, right rudder, steady up on course two-eight-five," Hotrod stated.

Turner's initial thought when they'd arrived at their starting point was to conduct the box search in a clockwise fashion. At the last moment, however, he had changed his mind and decided to go the other way, running due west on their first leg.

"*Bridge, maneuvering answering all ahead flank,*" Mug reported. "*Steadying up on course two-eight-five... Bendix log indicates twenty-one knots.*"

"*Muy rápido,*" Hotrod said and grinned as the wind began to howl in his face.

Turner smiled, feeling good for the first time in days, it seemed. He adjusted his crutch and leaned more heavily on the teak railing, "*Muy rápido,* huh?"

"This is how we say very fast in my home village," Hotrod replied in a thick Latino accent.

"You mean Long Beach, California?" Turner jibed.

"For sure, dude," Hotrod replied in a heavy surfer drawl. Both men laughed.

It was just after 0500 when the diesels were cut, and the ship coasted along as she rapidly shed speed. Once again, the radar drill was observed. Once again, the SD detected nothing, but something did appear on the SJ.

"*Just as before, sir,*" Begley reported. "*Very distant, very faint contact on the horizon, twenty-four thousand yards, bearing zero-eight-zero.*"

In just over twenty minutes, *Bull Shark* had gone nearly seven nautical miles, but the odd contact had gone nearly sixty. It had also crossed more than a hundred degrees of azimuth. It could only be one thing and only mean one thing.

"An aircraft," Turner stated. "Or a group of them. Based on that data, they're headed straight for Midway, wouldn't you say, Hotrod?"

The quartermaster was nodding and looking at a small notebook he kept with him while on duty, "Yes, sir... moving at over a hundred and forty knots."

"Can you project a baseline and possible origin, Hotrod?" Turner asked.

Hernandez frowned, "I'll need some help on that, sir. Permission to go below and consult with the plotting party?"

"Go ahead, I'll con," Turner said and grinned. "I think we've got her, or at least a place to look."

It was a few minutes later, while the eastern sky was just beginning to lighten, when Hotrod reappeared with Burt Pendergast and a chart and maneuvering board. The men arranged themselves and their gear around Turner. The captain helped to hold the fluttering paper chart steady.

"Based on the information," Pendergast said. "I believe we can determine a course of zero-three-five true for the contact. I estimate the track line would lie approximately eleven miles off our bow. If we proceed to that point and then head two-twenty, we'll eventually reach their origin point."

Hotrod frowned slightly when Pendergast said, "in my estimation," but he said nothing. Turner tapped his chin for a moment.

"Their origin, but we have no way of determining where the mother ship would go after launching... that's a major guess."

"I say we follow the plane's track," Pendergast stated. "The carrier may simply sit right where they launched. Figure a few hours to Midway and a few hours back... no more than three hundred miles off, I'd say."

Hotrod shifted but said nothing. Turner sensed he had a different viewpoint. Turner had also noticed the subtle slight from Pendergast. Had it not been for Hotrod's notes, Pendergast might not have been able to make his assessment. The petty officer deserved to be heard.

"What are your thoughts, Hernandez?" Turner asked a bit more formally than usual.

Hotrod cleared his throat, "Winds are nor'easterly, sir, so he'd probably have run into them to get his birds aloft. Also, it wouldn't be a good idea for his planes to return along the same track they came on, just in case Midway sent out chasers. My guess is that our foe either continued east to put himself more southerly or perhaps north... but that seems unlikely."

Turner nodded, "Concur. A few hours at fourteen knots or so, and he's more southerly. And we know there's nobody out here but us chickens. Burt, as acting navigator, I want you to plot me a direct course to the southwestern corner of our search area. I'll bet that if we head there and stop, we'll be a lot closer to our enemy. We can ping and see if we tag anything. Worst case scenario, we hunker down and wait to see if we can track the returning planes."

"That doesn't help our boys at Midway, sir," Pendergast almost, but not quite, managed to hide the disapproval in his voice.

"That ship has sailed now, Burt," Turner stated. "The planes are already on their way."

MIDWAY ATOLL – 0545

Ford, his cameras, and his Marine escort were set up on top of the powerhouse. They weren't alone. A couple of Marine squads were posted there with them, including snipers and two crews to work a pair of light .30 caliber machine guns on tripods. Ford was dubious about that... how were they going to shoot down Jap fighters and bombers with a light machine gun?

The view was pretty good. From this vantage, Ford could see the entire base well, including both Sand Island and East Island. He had a very clear view of the airfield where he'd watched the B-17s take off after the PBY scouts had over an hour earlier. Now the Marine fighters and light bombers were lining up and lifting off as well.

Ford's Marine watchdog had a telephone set slung around his neck and had tapped into the phone lines that were hooked into the system on top of the power station. The young man's eyes suddenly went wide, and he looked at Ford.

"Sir! We've just received a radio message from a PBY... many planes headed Midway, range one-fifty bearing three-twenty! Holy cow, sir! This is really happening, isn't it?"

Ford treated the young man to a reassuring smile that he hoped was visible in the early dawn light, "Seems that way, Treadway... and quit calling me sir."

"Yes, sir!"

Ford laughed. He took a few moments to get some B-roll of the Marines on the roof with him and do a panorama of the base. He then spoke with several of the men, especially one team serving one of the LMGs.

"What's your name, Marine?" he asked the man in charge.

"Lance Corporal Dave Brevert, sir," the young man said confidently.

"How are you feeling about all this, Lance Corporal?" Ford asked.

"Excited, sir," Brevert replied and then smiled. "I think we're all scared, sir. Only natural, right? But this is what we been training for. If the Jap tries to set one boot on this base, he's gonna wish he'd stayed in Tokyo, sir."

That produced a cheer from his men. The rest took it up as well and Ford smiled, turning his camera, and taking it all in. He had to admire the grit of these young men. Like them, he was scared, too... yet like them, Ford was aware of a definite, if ludicrous, feeling of excitement.

"Sir! Sir!" Treadway almost bleated. "Another message from the PBY... two carriers and the main body of ships sighted, carriers in front! Heading one-three-five, speed twenty-five... bearing is three-twenty, about a hundred and eighty miles away... the B-17s have just been ordered to intercept and sink the bastards, sir!"

"Let's pray they're successful," Ford said earnestly. "And quit calling me sir."

"Yes, sir."

Several tense minutes went by as the Marine aircraft left the runway. Dawn had come in earnest by then, and an eerie sort of loud silence had fallen over the base. It wasn't silence in the true sense, of course. The hum of dozens of aircraft engines overhead and the strangely clear sound of angry and protesting gooney birds seemed to come from everywhere. Yet the men themselves were quiet. Standing at their AA batteries, huddled in their dugouts and manning their machine guns, all seemed to be holding their breath.

At around quarter after six, something changed. Ford swung his camera into the sky and watched as the fighters above the islands seemed to all turn to the northwest in a body and zoom out to sea. He swore that he could see tracer fire far out, almost to the horizon... and it was getting closer.

"Oh, Jesus, sir... here they come!" Treadway breathed in fearful awe.

The hum of aircraft had almost vanished as the fighters turned to intercept the Japanese. Now, however, as they all returned, the hum grew and grew until it was no longer the comforting drone of friendly air cover but the enraged roar of almost a hundred fifty airplanes buzzing around one another like angry hornets.

Ford tried to count them. Tried to distinguish friend from foe. The Japanese were coming in in V-formations. The Zekes seemed lower than the bombers, and far less organized as they swooped and soared, as they tangled with the Marine Buffalos and Wildcats. Above them, the Aichi bombers were harder to tell apart. Ford thought there were both Kate torpedo bombers and Val dive bombers, but he couldn't really tell them apart... only that they were coming and beginning to dive out of the clouds and toward him.

"Gotta be over a hundred Japs!" Ford shouted to his Marine escort. "I'd guess about equal parts Kates, Vals, and Zekes! Phone that in, private!"

It was 0630 and hell had finally come to Midway. Overhead, both Zeroes and American fighters were being hit, trailing smoke, and bursting into flame. Ford noted that when a Zeke was struck, it seemed to bloom into a fireball almost instantly. Although they seemed more maneuverable than the Wildcats and certainly more than the squatty Buffalos, they couldn't seem to take a hit well, especially in their wings. The fat and sluggish Brewster Buffalos might be slower and less maneuverable than the Zero, but they could take several hits and keep flying at least.

The level bombers roared overhead, beginning to drop their ordnance as the Vals plunged down from the clouds, seeming to head straight for the ground, their engines whining and their bombs whistling as they were released.

Fireballs erupted and roared, filling what had moments before been a tense quiet with an audible fury that brought with it waves of searing heat and wind.

"Christ, look at 'em go!" a man shouted, pointing at the nearest AA battery.

Ford admired how all the men manning defensive guns, both Marines and blue jackets alike, seemed to be operating under careful discipline. There was no sporadic firing or just opening up and dumping ammo belts into the sky. Every man, from the light machines to the big AA cannons, was firing at specific targets. And they were scoring hits, too.

Planes were now falling out of the sky. Some Americans and, it seemed to Ford, more Japs. Although ordnance was falling, much of it was missing the targets... but not all.

"Jesus, that Zeke is headed for the hangar and—"

A lone Zero, and not a bomber, flew in low over the aircraft hangar and dropped a small bomb. The effect, though, was not small. The hangar erupted into a ball of flame and smoke, sending debris high into the air. One piece even flew toward the men on the powerhouse. In Ford's camera, it appeared as if the piece were coming right at them. In the next instant, the shockwave blew him off his feet, and he was knocked to his back, hitting his head. Just before the blackness claimed him, he saw Treadway's face appear...

"Sir, sir!" the kid was shaking the director. "You all right, sir?"

Ford blinked and allowed the Marine to help him back to his feet, "I... I'm not sure. I'm not dead?"

Treadway grinned, "No, sir, just bonked your noggin. Looked like you went out for a few seconds there, sir."

"Christ..." Ford said, picking up his camera and examining it for damage. The heavy-duty unit still seemed to be functioning. "Thanks, Treadway... and quit calling me sir."

"Yes, sir! Wow... look at that... they're going for the dummy! Ha! Stupid Nips!"

The Marine was right. On the center of the airfield the Marines had left a dummy plane. Thus far, although many buildings had been hit, including the gasoline storage facility, which was burning like some gargantuan torch, the Japanese had indeed been sparing the airfield. However, several planes were making a go for the decoy... and paying the price for their impudence. At least three enemy planes were shot down trying for the dummy.

Ford and his camera watched one incident that particularly amused him. Odd to be amused in the middle of such a conflagration... A Zero had been shot down and crashed, pretty well intact, only about a hundred feet from his position. In their seemingly indomitable way, a bunch of sailors and some Marines ran out and crowded around the plane. To Ford's astonishment, they began to drag the pilot out, w/.ho was certainly dead... and began picking through his clothes and through the cockpit.

"What the hell...?" Ford asked no one in particular, not really expecting an answer.

Treadway had one, though. He laughed, "They're trying to get them a souvenir, sir! Oh look, here comes an officer... ha-ha-HA!"

A Navy officer ran out to the group, waving his arms and shouting at the men to get the hell away from there and get back to their posts. There were a lot of smiles and laughter, even from the officer. Ford was amazed.

Not for the first time that day, and certainly not for the last, he was amazed at the bravery and *calmness* of the men around him. If they were scared, they didn't show it. They all seemed to be having the time of their lives, which in a very real sense, they were. Even when one of the Jap pilots finally succeeded in tagging the powerhouse... they'd tried eighteen times, and, so far, nothing had hit them... the men around Ford were cool and collected.

A two-hundred-pound bomb struck near the corner of the build-ing, shaking it to its foundations but not destroying it. Ford was once again flung down, striking something that opened up gashes in his forearm and calf. Before he could struggle back to his feet, several Marines were picking him up, and one of them, a corpsman, was already beginning to bandage his cuts and the back of his head.

"You're all right, sir," Treadway stated. "Just a few cuts and bruises. Jones here will patch you up real good. Don't you worry about that Navy Doc, sir."

"That's right, sir," another young Marine reassured Ford. "Jones here is a swell doctor, you'll see."

Ford grinned, "Thanks much, Jones... And Treadway, for the last goddamned time... stop calling me sir!"

"Yes, sir!"

Ford only shook his head ruefully and looked around him. Already, the Japanese were beginning to veer off. His watch, which somehow hadn't been broken, said it was a little after seven in the morning. Only a half hour or so... then he noticed something else, off to the south.

"Hey, are those... our floatplanes?" he asked in confusion. To his knowledge, the only seaplanes at Midway were the big Catalinas.

"I don't think we got any of them little floaters," a Marine offered doubtfully.

Ford stood and turned to the south. He saw eight airplanes with pontoons slung beneath, skimming the water. Apparently, a couple of the PT boats that had been racing around the lagoon and firing up at the Japanese noticed too. Several of them turned and began firing at the floaters.

"What the hell?" Ford asked, making a grab at his camera. He was pleased to see that once again it had survived... but displeased to find that the film had run out. "Damn! Somebody grab me a new reel from the case, quick!"

As he watched, the eight floatplanes suddenly rose from a hundred feet or so up to nearly a thousand. They were right over the beach, and they all released their bombs seemingly as one unit. Even as the explosives began whistling, heralding their destructive intent as they fell, the floaters banked away, climbing high and heading back out to sea.

The beachhead was hit by eight large bombs, blasting up columns of smoke, flame, and sand high into the morning sky. Ford was shocked and horrified to see that at least one bomb had miraculously landed dead center in one of the large defender's dugouts. Turning it into a crater of black smoke, angry red flame, and horrific death.

"Here, sir!" Treadway said, handing a new reel of film to the stunned director.

Ford hurried to insert the new reel and get the camera going. However, by the time he did, the floatplanes were far out of sight, and the battle, at least for the moment, was over. Although the men around him could stop and take a breath, Ford knew that his work was far from over. He needed to document the aftermath and the preparations for what would doubtless come next.

CHAPTER 31

ABOARD IJN CARRIER AKAGI

225 MILES NORTHWEST OF MIDWAY ATOLL – 0705 MIDWAY TIME

The bridge of the Kido Butai flagship was a cramped and crowded place. Admiral Chuichi Nagumo stood amid the seeming chaos and watched his men work. By now, radio reports were beginning to cycle in regarding the initial attack on Midway, and although losses had been heavier than expected, the news was generally positive.

"Admiral, we are receiving a transmission from flight leader Tomonaga," *Akagi's* captain said, bowing slightly. "He wishes to speak to you."

"Indeed?" Nagumo stated. "Very well, Captain."

The two officers left the navigation bridge and moved aft to the radio shack. There, an impossibly young radio operator handed his admiral a telephone handset, "Lt. Tomonaga for you, sir."

Nagumo nodded his appreciation and spoke into the handset, "This is Nagumo, please proceed, Lieutenant. You were successful?"

A burst of radio static and then Tomonaga's voice oddly distorted by the sound of his engine in the background, *"Hai, Kaigun-chujo. I believe we did moderately well... however, we did lose approximately one-third of our aircraft. American resistance, both in the air and on the ground, was heavier than expected."*

Nagumo drew in a breath, "I see... and your assessment of the atoll's vulnerability at this time?"

"*I would estimate it as softened but not weakened by any great extent,*" Tomonaga admitted. "*We struck many targets. Most of the buildings on base were destroyed or burning. However, ground forces, air cover, and lagoon vessels remain steadfast. I strongly recommend we re-arm and head back for an additional bombing run. I believe this will complete the task and allow our invasion force to come ashore with a large advantage.*"

Nagumo drew in a breath and heaved it out slowly. It was by no means a disaster... and yet... and yet if the attack flight leader was calling for another attack, it meant that their *success* was certainly not complete. It meant that action must be taken quickly. Action that went against Yamamoto's orders.

"I will take your suggestion under advisement, Lieutenant," Nagumo stated. "However, such an operation will take time to coordinate. Be advised that you and your fellow aircraft may not be able to land once you reach us."

A pause and then, "*I understand, sir... but believe this is vital.*"

Nagumo acknowledged this and handed the phone back to the radioman. He turned to the ship's captain, "Find Admiral Kusaka."

"I am here, sir," Rear-admiral Kusaka stated, coming into the navigation bridge from the observation deck outside. "How may I be of service?"

Nagumo almost laughed. How indeed? How can you alter the course of the battle? How can you see into the future so that you can properly advise me?

"Lt. Tomonaga requests we send another bombing raid to Midway," Nagumo said unhappily. "What are your thoughts on the matter?"

Kusaka frowned and then shrugged, "Tomonaga is a good pilot, an intelligent man. I know it's not part of the plan... yet in truth, another attack can only improve our situation, yes?"

Nagumo frowned as well, "Perhaps... but it is somewhat vaguely concerning. This and our remaining bombers are all armed with torpe-does. That will slow things down."

"Yes... but when all is said and done, we may be glad we took this additional step," Kusaka advised.

Nagumo managed a small smile, "What must be done, must be done, eh? What is that old Royal Navy expression the Brits have...?"

Kusaka smiled more broadly, "Groan you may, but go you must."

Nagumo nodded and looked about him, "Where is the flight officer?"

"Here, sir," a middle-aged man said, rushing forward from where he was consulting with the captain. "How may I serve?"

"We need to launch another sortie to Midway. We must re-arm our torpedo bombers for a land attack. Level bombing and dive bombing, as before. We must coordinate with the other carriers and be ready as quickly as possible."

The man frowned, "Sir... we have returning aircraft that must be recovered. They are low on fuel, and some are damaged."

Nagumo felt a flicker of his earlier annoyance and worry, but it passed quickly, "I am aware of this, Commander. I did not *ask* for a recommendation. What I want is an accurate estimation of how long to prepare another bombing group?"

"I ask forgiveness, Kaigun-chujo," the man said, lowering his eyes. "I only... ahem... I would say an hour, perhaps a bit more. Re-arming will take much of the time."

Nagumo drew in a breath and shrugged, "Then it takes time. Please proceed."

It was only a quarter after seven in the morning. Nagumo already felt drained of life, and the sun had only been up for a matter of minutes. His worries were compounded a few minutes later when he was handed a radio report.

"What is this?" Nagumo snapped at the messenger. "Is the pilot still on the radio?"

"He... no, sir, but I... that is, we can get him back," the youngster gulped.

Nagumo restrained himself and nodded at the young man, "Thank you for this."

Much earlier in the morning, Nagumo had done what the Americans had done. He'd sent out a variety of scouting flights from all four carriers. Following every other point on the compass, his sixteen scouting planes were covering a wide and thoroughly planned area in an attempt to locate the American carriers Yamamoto determined must be out there someplace. One of them, the one who'd followed the northeasterly track, was the one who'd radioed in the report that Nagumo now held in his hand.

"Get him back!" he snapped at the radio operator.

"I have him already, sir," the man said, earning a point of admiration from his supreme commander.

Nagumo took the handset, "Pilot! What do you mean there are ten ships! Clarify this report, damn you! I must have better information."

The pilot acknowledged and asked for *Akagi* to wait. In the meantime, Nagumo ordered the flight officer to delay the re-arming of the torpedo planes until he learned more. After all, the reason that the second half of his bomber assets were loaded with torpedoes and dive bombs was so that Nagumo could smash the American carriers.

It was Yamamoto's feeling that once Midway was attacked, Nimitz's fleet would come crawling from wherever it was hiding to confront the Japanese. *This* was the ultimate trap Yamamoto had planned. The carriers would appear, and the Kido Butai would crush them and send them to a watery grave.

Ten minutes later, the scout pilot came back on the line, "Akagi, Akagi... *ships appear to be five destroyers and five cruisers.*"

Nagumo frowned and then nodded. He thanked the radioman and moved back to the main bridge. There he found the flight officer speaking with the ship's captain.

"Commander, it would appear that we have time enough," Nagumo stated. "Let us and the other carriers retrieve our returning heroes. We can then refuel them, re-arm the torpedo planes with level bombs, and launch a refreshed CAP."

"*Hai*," the officer said, seeming relieved and hurrying off the bridge and down to his hangar where he could supervise the operations personally.

"Perhaps we will have our cake and eat it as well, as the Yankees say," Kusaka said, appearing magically at his superior's side.

"Perhaps, Kusaka san," Nagumo said. "Or perhaps all of Japan will curse my name for my indecisiveness."

The two admirals stepped back out onto the observation deck to look down at the flight deck below them. Already, the new Zeroes were being brought on deck and spotted for takeoff. The eight of them, and another ten from the huge *Kaga* and half a dozen each from *Hiryu* and *Soryu* would constitute a refreshed, refueled, and fully armed combat air patrol. This gave Nagumo some comfort, as his carriers would be protected while they recovered the first bombing aircraft and readied the next sortie.

Once the incoming planes were recovered, the hangar could immediately begin refueling and re-arming them for ship-to-ship combat. At least the time spent readying the next Midway bombing mission wouldn't leave the carriers sitting idle... or as idle as they might have seemed minutes before.

"Admiral..." the same messenger who'd been rebuked by Nagumo ten minutes earlier approached the two lofty flag officers. Nagumo turned at the sound of hesitation in the youngster's voice and treated him to a smile.

"What is it, young man?" the vice-admiral asked gently.

The lad cleared his throat, "The scout has just radioed in and amended his report, sir..."

"And?" Kusaka urged.

"He now says the ten ships he saw before... they are escorting an *Enterprise*-class carrier."

Kusaka's eyes lit up and he grinned broadly, "Does he! We *have* them, sir! It must be *Enterprise* or *Hornet!*"

Nagumo felt himself pale ever so slightly, "We have them... or do they have us, Kusaka? We are not ready for a carrier strike."

"Shall we call down and change the arming orders again?" Kusaka asked.

Nagumo considered this for a long moment and then shook his head, "No. No... I do not like doing things by halves, Kusaka. We shall continue as directed."

Before Kusaka could reply, one of the lookouts out on the bridge wings shouted a warning. He'd spotted something in the clouds above. He'd spotted aircraft, and they were not those of Tomonaga's flight.

Nagumo cursed his ship's and his fleet's lack of the ingenious and tremendously useful invention of the radar. Oh, some ships in the Imperial Navy had it. Ironically, he knew that *Yamato* did. How unhelpful that was now. And how short-sighted that his mighty Kido Butai had nothing like it. Not one of the big carriers had a radar system. They still relied on the fallible eyes of men to locate aircraft. How useful it must be, having instantaneous range and bearing on airplanes dozens of miles away. How ludicrous that only the battleships in Nagumo's fleet had radar and had no true understanding of how it could be deployed in such an operation.

Yet the Americans had it. To his knowledge, the majority of their ships had radar. Even some of their damned submarines had the equipment. So, why didn't he?

Kusaka turned and exited the bridge again, Nagumo hot on his heels. The flag officers approached the young sailor and demanded a report.

Admirably, the young man, not yet twenty, didn't even look in their direction. Somehow though, he managed a slight bow at the waist while keeping his binoculars trained on the sky to the southeast.

"Many planes, sir..." the sailor reported. "I believe... torpedo bombers, B-26 Liberators so far..."

Nagumo spun on his chief of staff, "Send out a general broadcast to the fleet! Order them to—"

All around them on the sea, every ship, from the carriers to the humblest destroyer, opened up with an impressive fusillade of anti-aircraft fire. Far above their heads, the CAP of Zeroes wheeled to the attack, homing in on the enemy aircraft and soaring into battle.

For the next half hour or so, American, and Japanese aircraft flittered around one another. The Americans attempting to avoid the flak from the surface ships as they dove down to launch torpedoes at the carriers. The Japanese went after them, shooting down torpedo planes and bombers seemingly with impunity at first. However, after the initial confrontation, it became clear that the aerial battle wasn't entirely one-sided. The Japanese took losses as well, but nothing compared to the slower American aircraft.

The Americans were at a distinct disadvantage. They had to home in on slow-moving targets. Slow by airplane speeds, at any rate. They must hit their objectives, and their enemies knew it. The Zeroes, on the other hand, knew exactly what the Americans were doing and could easily predict their movements and intercept them.

Two of the B-26 bombers were shot down almost immediately. Several more were damaged and had to turn away. The new but too few Avenger torpedo planes managed to drop their weapons, except for one or two that were shot down before they could descend to a good firing position. However, with speeds of thirty knots and quick reactions, *Kaga, Akagi, Hiryu,* and *Soryu* all managed to dodge the torpedoes and the bombs aimed at them.

Well into the eight o'clock hour, a flight of larger B-17 flying fortresses appeared through the clouds and began attacking *Kaga* and *Akagi.* The attacks were courageous, and although they came close, no real damage was done. There were two bad moments for Nagumo. The first came when one of the Fortresses, badly shot up and smoking, plunged out of the sky and headed straight for the forward flight deck of *Akagi.* Nagumo watched in fascinated horror as the big bomber angled toward his ship. At the last moment, however, the pilot must have regained some control because the steep descent levelled off. It almost worked... yet the bomber still struck the flight deck and, almost unbelievably, bounced up and over the side!

Moments later, another stricken B-17 angled toward them. Nagumo thought wryly that he was going to begin to take things personally when he saw that the B-17 was aiming right for the carrier's tall island. There was no time to run, however. If the big plane struck the navigation bridge, which it certainly seemed intent on doing, the end would come quickly.

However, the end did not come, and the burning Fortress swooped only meters from the bridge before smashing into the ocean.

"Victory!" the carrier's captain roared, raising his fists into the air in a most undignified but understandable fashion.

Nagumo's worry of earlier seemed to evaporate, and he couldn't help but be infected with the enthusiasm of the younger men around him. He even deigned to smile at his chief of staff, "Extraordinary, Kusaka! Not a single hit, except for that one unfortunate aircraft. Perhaps we are indeed blessed."

Kusaka smiled back, "Yes, sir. Not only have we struck Midway, but we've managed to destroy a good portion of *their* own assault forces. Many planes were lost. We lost some, sadly, but nothing as compared to the Americans. What planes of theirs remain are even now scurrying away."

Nagumo allowed himself to be pulled along by the tide of elation and fellowship that seemed to linger all across the crowded bridge. His misgivings about sending more bombers to Midway now forgotten. Perhaps fortune was indeed smiling upon them once again.

"Excellent," Nagumo said. "Order our smaller ships to begin retrieving any downed survivors, both ours and theirs. Who knows, we may learn something useful."

240 MILES SOUTH, SOUTHWEST OF MIDWAY

"*Bridge, control,*" the tinny voice of Burt Pendergast crackled over the speaker. "*We have arrived at the southwestern corner, sir.*"

"Very well," Turner said. "All stop, Hotrod. Conning tower, bridge... activate the Sugar Dog and then the Sugar Jig. Kill the rock crushers."

Orders were acknowledged, and the *Bull Shark* once again laid to, gently swaying in the mild sea. Turner frowned for a long moment. He didn't like this. He felt as if he were playing cat and mouse, and in spite of all evidence to the contrary, was, in fact, the mouse rather than the cat.

"Control, bridge... Pat... sound battle stations gun action. Get me crews up here for the Pom-Pom and the Oerlikon," Turner finally ordered. "And a couple of guys with Ma Deuces. If we're right and the Jap planes do show up, I don't want to be caught with our britches down."

Jarvis acknowledged with what sounded like eagerness. After a moment, Tom Begley asked permission to mount to the bridge.

"Skipper..." Begley began, not quite sure how to proceed or what was the best course of action. "Won't we be in the opposite boat if they show up? I mean, we'll need to dive pretty quick and with all of these weapons manned..."

Turner thought momentarily about asking if command had sent him secret orders not to man the AA weapons. He decided against it, though. Whatever scheme Begley was trying to hatch would play itself out, and Turner felt that paying out a little more rope would only allow Begley to fail more quickly. Instead, he only shrugged, "Small risk, XO. Worst case, we lose a couple of fifties. So what. They can be replaced. But if those birds *are* returning from Midway, then they probably dropped all of their ordnance. They may, or may not, strafe us... but if they do, then I want to give them something to think about. We'll leave off the deck guns, though."

Men began to pour up through the bridge hatch and the mess access hatch. Among them were Tank Broderick with his beefy arms full of ammo belts and a fifty-caliber machine gun. Next came Steve Plank, the boatswain's mate with an armload of his own. Behind them, Buck Rogers, Eddie Carlson, and Fred Swooping Hawk. Plank and Broderick mounted their weapons into special stanchions on the cigarette deck and slapped in belts of ammunition. Buck Rogers went forward and began readying the quad-barrel Bofors 40mm Pom-Pom with Eddie

Carlson assisting. Near the after end of the cigarette deck, the young Navajo Indian readied the twin-barreled 20mm cannon.

Begley frowned and dropped back into the conning tower. Turner lit a cigarette and offered the pack to Hernandez.

"I've got a funny feeling, Hotrod," Turner said as he watched his men efficiently preparing *Bull Shark's* not inconsiderable Ack-ack compliment.

Hernandez smiled and lit a smoke. He was about to say something when the bridge speaker crackled to life.

"*Bridge, conning!*" Begley said excitedly. "*We have contacts on the Sugar Jig! Low to the horizon, bearing one-three-zero... range twenty-four thousand... speed one-two-five. Assess returning floatplanes.*"

"Concur," Turner said. "Standby to answer bells on batteries. Give me slow ahead and bring us around on that bearing. Want a minimum profile. Oh... and have sonar send a max power active ping. Let's see if their friends are close by as well."

There was a long pause before the XO said, "*Sir... shouldn't we dive? And should we give ourselves away like that?*"

Turner's patience was not infinite, especially when it came to Begley, "Conning tower... if you're unable to follow my orders, then you may retire to your stateroom and Mr. Jarvis will fill your place."

Another pause as the bow slowly began to turn around to come to the northerly course that would head the boat straight for the aircraft. It would also present the smallest possible profile while allowing the Pom-Pom and the Ma Deuces to fire.

"*I'm capable of following your orders, Captain,*" came Begley's stiff reply.

"Then do so," Turner said coldly.

After a moment, the sound of a high-pitched sonic blast reverberated through the ship, even reaching the men in the lookout perch thanks to the sound conductivity of the hull. A sonic boom was racing outward from the WCA super-sonic sound gear mounted below the forward torpedo room on the ship's keel.

Because sound traveled more than four times as quickly through water as through air, the wavefront of the pulse would reach a fifty-thousand-yard radius in less than thirty seconds. This was the maximum range at which a return might be expected to be detectible by the passive sound equipment. The ship would know, therefore, if there was an object within twenty-five nautical miles in less than a minute.

"*Bridge, conning tower,*" Begley reported finally. "*Negative contact on echolocation. We do have a track on those birds, though, sir. They appear to be headed two-one-zero.*"

"Very well," Turner said and while still holding the transmit button down. "Then that's where the bastard is. And that's where we're headed. Get us back on diesels, quartermaster. Gunners, standby to open fire! You may do so when you think they're in range. Don't give em' an inch!"

A round of cheers rose up from the AA gun crews. Hotrod gave his orders, and once again, the diesel exhausts rumbled with expelled fumes as the big engines cranked to life. The ship was just beginning to reverse her turn, her broadside on to the oncoming planes when the lookouts began to shout and point.

From high up, eight tiny black objects swooped down toward them, growing rapidly into the distinct shape of airplanes.

"Lookouts below!" Turner ordered.

"Pick your targets carefully, boys!" Pat Jarvis whooped. At battle stations surface, Jarvis's role moved from torpedo officer to gunnery officer, and he was on deck supervising. "Walk your tracers right into 'em!"

All around the cigarette deck, cannons and machine guns began to chatter and pop, sending hundreds of rounds of lead into the sky, every few rounds being a bright red tracer that could easily be seen even in the bright morning sunshine.

It quickly became clear that the floatplane pilots weren't up for a major battle with the submarine. For although they opened fire with their wing cannons, most of the rounds falling harmlessly into the sea, they were surprised by the vehemence of the fleet submarine's aggressive defense.

A few rounds came aboard, chewing up wooden decking but otherwise doing no noticeable damage. However, the aircraft quickly broke formation and veered off, encircling the submarine's kill zone and reforming on their continued course to the south, southwest. Had any of them looked back, they might have been surprised to see that the lone dogged submarine had turned onto their course and was collecting an impressive frothy bow wave as her speed climbed up to and even exceeded twenty-two knots. Her hull hammered through the sea, a cloud of smoke beginning to trail her as her overloaded diesels chugged their hearts out, pushing the thousands of tons of steel and men toward her target.

One of the eight planes did not stay with its brethren, however. It began to lose speed and altitude, oily black smoke pouring from its starboard engine manifold. Turner ordered the men to cease firing, as the other planes were out of range by then and he wanted to see what would happen to the one that must have hit.

It didn't take long for the floatplane to descend and level off above the waves, barely managing to bounce down and skid to a halt just as flames began to pour from the cowling around the radial engine.

"Lookouts to the bridge!" Turner ordered into the speaker. "Boatswain, time to earn your keep. Get below and grab some rescue gear. We're about to have guests."

Turner rubbed his hands together. They'd rescue the enemy pilots from the drink. Who knows? Perhaps they might learn something useful...

CHAPTER 32

USS HORNET'S VT-8 TORPEDO SQUADRON

0915 APPROACHING KIDO BUTAI BATTLE FORCE

Lieutenant Commander John Waldron was beginning to doubt himself. The previous evening, he'd had a conference with the skipper and the CAG. They both believed that the Japanese fleet would be further north, and Waldron, having calculated their position independently, had come to the conclusion that they were, in fact, to the southwest of Point Luck, where their own fleet was stationed. Waldron had tried to argue the point, showing Micher and Ring his data and how he'd used what Station Hypo had sent to come to his conclusions.

He'd been overruled, however, and was forced to go along with Stanhope Ring's plan to fly west. Waldron had agreed... at least until all the Devastators, Wildcats, and Dauntlesses were in the air. Yet even as they'd formed up and headed west, Waldron's gut told him that they were headed in the wrong direction... he *knew* it... deep down in his bones, he knew it.

He'd tried, in vain and probably foolishly, to convince the flights to go the way he'd calculated. Ring had quickly overruled him, even going so far as to threaten a general court if Waldron didn't shut his damned mouth. Well, that had done it.

Waldron might not be able to gain control of the entire attack force, but he *could* at least order his group of fifteen torpedo bombers to do what he felt was right.

"Okay guys, listen up," Waldron had said when his slow and cumbersome TBDs had begun to lag behind the dive bombers and fighters. "I know what our op orders say... but I also know they're wrong. Ring is gonna lead us nowhere, and we just can't afford that."

There had been a long pause on the channel before Ensign George Gay finally spoke up, "*Skipper... what're you saying? That we should ditch Ring and his birds?*"

Waldron had known that the next words out of his mouth would dramatically change things. It would certainly open himself and his men up to possible disciplinary action. They *could* make the difference between finding the Japs or not. To really go out on a limb, his next words could very possibly alter the course of the battle. He dismissed that thought immediately as being far too arrogant. He was just one man, and even his fifteen planes were a mere nuisance as compared to four powerful Japanese carriers, their heralded Zeke fighters, and their support ships. To Waldron, it was simply a matter of doing what was right.

What he could not know, and would never know, was that his fanciful notion about changing the course of the battle was not only correct but understated. Waldron and his fellow airmen would indeed alter not just the Battle of Midway but the entire course of the war. However, it was Waldron's decision and not the fifteen torpedoes he and the twenty-nine other men in his squadron carried that would be the decisive element.

So, he'd ordered VT-8 to follow him as he banked onto a course of two-two-zero. That had seemed like hours ago. Now, here it was a quarter after nine and all they could see was blue ocean below them.

"Christ, Skipper," Waldron's radioman and rear gunner stated glumly. "How much longer we gonna do this?"

Waldron glanced over his shoulder and grinned, "You got a date or somethin', Sully?"

Aviation gunner's mate third class, Hugh Sullivan, chuckled, "Yeah, me and Rita Hayworth got ourselves a nice room at the Royal Hawaiian. Hate to let her down."

Waldron laughed, "Wow... that the dream you were havin' before we rolled out for this party?"

Sully grinned, "Yeah, and I'd like to get back to it ASAP if it's all the same."

Waldron shook his head, "Okay, then find me some Japs; we send all these fish straight into their four carriers and go home. Easy-peasy-Japanesey."

Both men's laughter was choked off when Waldron spotted something far ahead through a break in the intermittent cloud cover. He leaned forward in his cockpit as if another few inches closer would make all the difference, "Jesus... you see that, Sully?"

Sullivan also cranked forward and up, straining against his straps, "No, I don't... wait... holy cow, Skipper! That a Jap fleet down there!?"

Waldron laughed, "Unless we been going in circles... Put me on the open freq."

"Go."

"All aircraft, all aircraft," Waldron said into his mic. "Have spotted Japanese battle fleet. Repeat, have spotted the buggers and we're going in!"

A crackle and Gay said, "*Are you shittin' us, John?*"

"That's a negative, George," Waldron all but whooped. "You boys know the drill. Three lines. We each attack a different flattop. No less than five fish per ship. Sully, get on the medium band and tell *Hornet* what we got and where we are! Tallyho!"

Even as the aircraft formed into three lines ahead and began their long descent, Waldron began to pray. While he was elated that they'd found their objective and that he'd been proven right... he was also scared shitless.

Yeah, they'd found the Japs... but they were alone. They had absolutely no cover. The Devastator, while a sturdy aircraft, was not a high-performance bird. To top that off, the torpedoes were a bit wonky, too.

The airplane was slow and maneuvered like a cow. Further, in order to properly deploy their weapon, the Devastators had to drop to less than a hundred feet off the deck so that when dropped, the torpedo would run straight and true. Drop it too high, and the fish would simply plunge straight down, go too deep, or turn way off course.

This also meant that at a hundred knots or so, the low-flying and slow torpedo bombers would be easy pickings for the spritely Zeroes. Deep down, Waldron knew that the chances that any of them would survive without a miracle... like Ring pulling his head out of his ass and altering course and showing up just in the nick of time... was next to nil.

As the plane dropped out of some low-slung clouds, one of the Jap carriers seemed to magically appear directly ahead. They were all visible, all four of them, headed straight across his path in two lines of two, not counting the dozens of DDs and cruisers and battleships that swarmed the area. Even as Waldron spotted his objectives, they spotted him, and the sky seemed to light up like Christmas Eve with thousands of tracers from the AA guns of the carriers and their screening ships.

And then there were the Zekes...

"Jesus Christ!" Sully gulped from behind Waldron as he spun in his seat to man the rear machine guns. "What the hell have you gotten me into, Chief?"

"VT-8, VT-8," Waldron shouted into his mic. "To hell with doctrine! Everybody go for that nearest flattop! We only get one shot at this, boys!"

Waldron shoved the throttle to the stops, racing his engine and pushing the stick forward into an angle of attack that bordered on deadly. If he could just get down to the deck... get low fast enough, he could drop his weapon and veer off... maybe even bail out in time...

But it was not to be. Even as he levelled off at seventy-five feet, a pair of Zeroes homed in on him and opened up with their wing cannons. Waldron's Devastator was hammered as rounds tore into the plane, shattered the glass of the canopy, and brutalized the fragile flesh of the men inside. Torpedo Squadron Eight's commander's last earthly act was to depress the trigger that released his Mark thirteen torpedo. Both it and the burning aircraft splashed into the sea a moment later.

Such was the fate of all of the Devastators. One by one, the aircraft were torn to shreds by machine gun fire and exploded or somersaulted into the concrete-hard water to break apart. Several weapons were deployed, though. However, including Waldron's own, none of them found a target, as was so often the case with airplane launched torpedoes. Only one fish actually struck the carrier, and it failed to explode. Another was targeted by one of *Soryu's* anti-aircraft batteries and exploded when hit by machine gun fire.

One plane managed to ditch with its pilot still intact and breathing. Somehow, Ensign George Gay survived and was able to get out of his plane before it sunk from under him. He quickly inflated his Mae West lifejacket and rose to the surface. From the dubious cover of his seat cushion, which he placed on top of his flight helmet and peeked from under, Gay watched in awe and fear as the battle waged around him. He would be a spectator to what happened next, observing the fight from the front row of the theater, his ticket paid for by the blood of his fellow pilots and crew.

ENTERPRISE DIVE BOMBER GROUP – 0935

Wade McClusky was fit to be tied. He and his thirty-one dive bombers had arrived at the coordinates of where the Jap fleet was supposed to be and found nothing but empty ocean. Because of the order for radio silence, he and his group couldn't call back to the Big-E or to any other groups that might be out over the big blue and ask for information. They were on their own and were wasting gas.

"What do we do now, Skipper?" McClusky's rear seater asked. "Where the hell are the damned slants?"

McClusky chuffed, "Do I look like I got a friggin' crystal ball up here? Hell... they're out here. Might have altered course. Maybe got wind of where our flattops are steaming and headed that way. We're gonna institute a box search. A quick two hundred mile square and see what we can see. Otherwise... I'm damned."

That information radioed to the other planes, McClusky turned due west, following a fifty-mile-long course that would give him and his dispersed aircraft a good hundred-mile radius of ocean to view. They *had* to find something out here...

It was another of his pilots who first spotted the surface disturbance and reported it in only five minutes later. McClusky was as much surprised as elated and slid his aircraft southerly to take a look for himself.

Sure enough, fifteen thousand feet below, a hair-thin line of white seemed to cut across the endless blue. The bow wave and wake of something gray that didn't quite match the surrounding water.

"Jackson, glass that som'bitch down there and tell me what you think," McClusky ordered, slowing his plane to just above a stall and beginning a leisurely circle around what was obviously a ship.

Jackson leaned out and used the pair of small binocs they carried to get a better look. After a moment, he chuckled, "I'd say it's a lone tin can, Skipper. She's definitely got a big bone in her teeth, though... in a hurry to go someplace fast. If she ain't makin' thirty knots, I'll eat my boots."

McClusky chuckled, "I concur, kid... I say she's steaming to rejoin her fleet. Headed damn near due north... all aircraft, all aircraft... believe we've spotted Jap destroyer rushing to get back to her nest. We're gonna form up and follow that course. Now let's get moving before some wise guy down there gets it in his noodle that it might be fun to start plinking at some dive bombers."

A crackle and another pilot asked, "*We ain't gonna take him out, Wade?*"

"These thousand pounders we're carryin' are ear-marked for a couple of Jap flattops, Bob, and that's just where they're goin'. Fall in, and let's head out."

Twenty minutes later, McClusky's guess was proven right. Below *Enterprise's* dive bombers, a very large fleet could be seen through the cloud breaks. It was a glorious sight, and even more so because off to the right of McClusky's squadron was another group of dive bombers that had to be from *Yorktown*.

"*Where the hell are the Zekes?*" Lieutenant Richard Best asked over the radio.

"Dunno, Dicky," McClusky said excitedly. "Hell... I think they're all down near the deck... looks like Devastators down there... Jesus... don't look a gift horse in the mouth! That big som'bitch must be *Kaga!* God, she's a beast... that's target one! Here we go, boys!"

McClusky pulled his bomber over and began his nearly vertical dive. All around him the sounds of wind rushing past his canopy and the ever-increasing scream of his twelve hundred horsepower Cyclone seemed to thrum straight into him. Even as he engaged his dive brakes to slow the descent down enough so that the bomb would drop faster than the plane, McClusky and Jackson both screamed. A primal sound of exhilaration, terror and rage... an utterly unconscious human sound that carried with it so much emotion that no words could adequately do it justice.

All thirty-one SBDs were headed for the mighty *Kaga*. It wasn't how they were supposed to do things, but the men in the dive bombers were beyond logic and planning. Near the middle of his dive, however, one pilot retained enough sense to realize what he was doing.

Lt. Richard Best called out over the radio, ordering the planes nearest him to shift targets to the carrier *behind Kaga*. Two others had time to alter their trajectory, and even as Wade McClusky's thousand-pound bomb smashed through *Kaga's* flight deck and exploded in a hangar full of readying aircraft, stacked ordnance, and fuel lines, Best homed in on the Kido Butai flagship.

KIDO BUTAI FLAGSHIP AKAGI – 1015

Everyone on the overcrowded bridge was roaring and cheering like mad. Discipline had completely gone by the board at that point. Even

Nagumo, the great leader and consummate stoic's face was split in a broad smile.

Wave after wave of American attack planes had come. B-26 Liberators, B-17 Flying Fortresses, Avenger torpedo bombers, and more from Midway had attacked and been destroyed or driven off. Multiple squadrons of torpedo bombers had harried from the northeast, and not a single one had survived or damaged one of the invincible Kido Butai beyond the superficial. There was a thin column of smoke rising from *Soryu,* but the carrier's captain had confidently reported that this was only a minor fire from a glancing blow caused by one of the Midway bombers nearly an hour before and was nearly contained. The ship was by no means incapable of fighting.

It was clear by now that the American carriers were out here with them. The Wildcat fighters that had orbited and danced with the Zeroes for some time had already left, flying northeast to no doubt land and refuel. The torpedo planes had come from that general direction as well, certainly confirming the scout's earlier reports.

Of course, Nagumo and Kusaka both agreed that there must be more than one carrier out there. They'd finally recovered both the earlier Zero CAP as well as the first Midway strike force and had already launched the refreshed Zeroes. A good thing, too. As they watched, the thirty fighters had decimated the incoming torpedo bombers and chased away the Wildcats. Not without some losses, however.

"We must get the attack planes airborne and headed for Midway once more," Nagumo said to Kusaka as they stood on the observation deck. "Then we can refresh the first strike group we recovered and put more in the air. No doubt the Americans will be sending more aircraft."

"Sir..." Kusaka began, hesitated, and began again. "Should we not cancel the Midway mission? After all, we have *achieved* Admiral Yamamoto's goal. We have drawn the American carriers to us. Would it not be better to re-arm our bombers for a surface-ship action?"

Nagumo was suddenly overcome by a wave of depression. In an instant, his good humor seemed to vanish like smoke. It wasn't simply Kusaka's suggestion... he himself had been pondering the very question for nearly an hour now. It was the constant need to re-evaluate and second-guess himself that was most wearisome.

The vice-admiral shook it off, smiling in order to regain some of his good humor. He shook his head, "No, Kusaka. We have chosen this course and will follow."

Kusaka dared to push further, "Sir, I've spoken with Admiral Yamaguchi aboard *Hiryu*. He states that as much as half of his bombers are still armed with dive bombs and torpedoes. He requests permission to launch an attack immediately on the American carrier."

Nagumo turned to his aid and raised his eyebrows, "Attack? Send several dozen planes straight into the jaws of the American sharks without even a single Zero as protection, Kusaka? No! No, this is madness! You saw what happened to the American torpedo planes. They come out of the clouds with no escort... or little to speak of... and even with the small number of fighters they sent ahead, the torpedo planes were obliterated. Ours are not so robust, even. They wouldn't survive five minutes."

"Perhaps not..." Kusaka had to admit to the wisdom of this. "Yet might not the distraction be enough to *delay* the American's next attack? Might that not give us more time to refuel our aircraft and re-arm for a larger scale assault?"

Nagumo struggled to maintain his good humor against the proper but annoying questions and suggestions of his aide. Little did he know that in the next few moments, his sense of well-being would vanish permanently and be replaced with abject horror.

"Contact!" one of the young lookouts shouted from forward, aiming his binoculars nearly straight into the sky. "American aircraft coming out of the clouds... dive bombers!"

Akagi's captain seemed to materialize beside the two admirals and looked skyward with his jaw agape, "No... no!"

"What is it, Captain?" Nagumo said, waving an arm at the two-dozen Zeroes circling less than five hundred meters over their heads. "Surely our CAP will banish this latest annoyance?"

"Sir... you don't understand," the captain said glumly. "The Zeroes are too low... so busy have they been targeting the low-flying torpedo planes... we didn't prepare for a high-altitude attack!"

"Then send them up!" Nagumo almost shouted. "The American dive bombers are as slow and cumbersome as ours. Alert the Zeroes to climb and destroy them!"

Even as he said this, Nagumo could see that was exactly what was happening. However, what he couldn't realize, never having flown an airplane, was that even the mighty Zero could only climb at less than a tenth of the speed that a dive bomber could descend. The ascending aircraft had to fight against the pull of gravity and the resistance of the air. The descending aircraft *used* the pull of gravity and exceeded terminal velocity through the power of its engine. It would be great luck indeed if even a single dive bomber could be eliminated before releasing its payload.

Once that was done, of course, the bomber was once again forced to level off and climb away, making it extremely vulnerable. For although the Dauntless was a robust and fairly nimble craft for a dive bomber, it was no match for the swift and deadly Zero. Of course... at that point, whatever damage was going to be done would have been done. It would be little consolation to destroy an entire *flight* of dive bombers when their bombs eliminated even one carrier.

The true implications of these facts struck Nagumo like an onrushing locomotive as he watched. His own mouth descended in disbelief as the black specks raced downward toward the mighty *Kaga*... felt his belly churn as he *saw* the tiny black specks separate from the now discernable shapes of airplanes and streak downward toward the carrier in front of him...

Yet this horror was nothing as compared to the heart-stopping sight of a huge column of fire and smoke blasting from the center of *Kaga's* flight deck. Then it was joined by another... and another... and *another*...

How could this be? They had been so victorious just a moment before! Every attack by the Americans driven off. Their poor tactics and combat strategies shattered into nothing against the impenetrable wall of superior Japanese numbers, technology, and combat experience. And now... now the mighty *Kaga* was a pillar of flame!

"Incoming! Incoming!" the lookout shrieked. "Dive bombers... headed for us! And *Soryu!*"

Nagumo simply stared straight up, unable to move, unable to protect himself from the death that raced toward him from the clouds. Three... only *three* airplanes? Could not the Zeroes stop even *three* of them?

"Sir! Sir!" Kusaka shouted, grabbing his admiral by the sleeve of his crisp white jacket and hauling him into what small protection the navigation bridge could offer.

Nagumo would later try and recall the events of the next few moments, yet they always seemed to be a jumble of sights, sounds, and smells that were blurred by their nightmarish quality. He and Kusaka were nearly knocked from their feet as the entire ship, a huge and mighty aircraft carrier, was shaken as if by the hand of the Gods. Men screamed, sirens wailed, and a roar like that of a rushing waterfall drowned out the sound... yes, a good analogy... drowning... that was exactly how Nagumo felt.

His eyes were drowning in the overwhelming sight of the *Kaga* in flames, the *Soryu* smoking and listing, and his own ship's flight deck burning out of control. Too much imagery to process... the wooden deck blackening and peeling as the voracious flames devoured the wood. A Zero, spotted on the flight deck and ready to launch, *burning* at its chocks. Burning... a metal airplane *burning*...

His ears drowned in the sound of the mournful cry of the ship's alarms, the rumbling all about, and the cacophonous shouts of men. The sound of panic, mostly. A few voices calling for order, but mostly panic.

And the *smell*... no, not smell... let us be poetic about this... the *stench*. The stench of things burning that should not be burning. Wood, aluminum... and flesh. A reek so heavy and so vile that it could be tasted in one's mouth... How could such things be?

In just a space of minutes, everything in Nagumo's existence had changed. His world, his universe, had altered forever. It was simply too much for a single man to manage in so short a space of time. In five minutes, the mighty Kido Butai... the carrier force that had struck Pearl Harbor... the unstoppable juggernaut that had won Japan the Indian Ocean and the Pacific all around them in only a matter of *months* had been decimated. No, not decimated... Nagumo thought absently that people threw that word about far too casually. Decimation meant destroying one out of ten. No, this was far greater in scope. Three of his four carriers, half of the total Kido Butai... had been smashed in five minutes!

Nagumo saw Kusaka's sweating and pale face before him. It seemed to swim up out of his nightmare only to act as a reflection of his own horror.

"What have I done, Kusaka?" Nagumo all but whispered.

"Sir... we must go," Kusaka managed.

"Go?" Nagumo said, casting an arm about him. "Go where? Where is there left for me to go? Where... for *any* of us, now, my friend..."

CHAPTER 33

USS BULL SHARK

400 MILES SOUTH. SOUTHEAST OF THE KIDO BUTAI

The floatplane bobbed in the light swell, looking as peaceful and unthreatening as any aircraft that wasn't flying. The two men who were climbing out of the cockpit and standing on the pontoons to watch the approaching submarine tried to look unthreatening as well.

On *Bull Shark's* bridge, Pat Jarvis stood behind Turner and Hotrod Hernandez, absently fingering the holstered .45 clipped to his belt. He also watched as Steve Plank and several men stood by on the long foredeck of the submarine with boat hooks, coiled lines, and throwable liferings. He didn't trust the man, now that it'd been revealed that he was the leader of the drug black-market aboard.

He didn't trust the friendly waves of the Japanese, either. That had proven to be a common ruse. Draw a ship in with pleas for help and then suddenly a weapon would appear, and a handful of sailors would die before the rescue ship eliminated the threat.

"All stop," Hernandez ordered.

The sound of the diesels quieted some as the ship came from down off a one-third enunciator setting to no turns. It took another hundred yards for the vessel to come to a complete stop, putting the airplane just fifteen or so yards off her starboard bow.

"Do you men speak English?" Turner asked.

"*Hai*," the taller of the two men said. "I do, but my co-pilot does not. I am Lieutenant Kenji Gato."

The other man snapped something out in harsh and not very friendly sounding Japanese. Gato said something soothing to the man and he quieted, but only just.

"You speak very well, Lieutenant," Turner said. "Do you wish to be rescued? How about your man, there?"

"He fears that you will interrogate us," Gato said, a wry smile playing on his lips. "That you will torture him to learn all of his valuable knowledge."

Turner actually chuckled, "And does he have any?"

Gato laughed, "If you wish to know the best geishas in Tokyo or which of the whores in Borneo delivers the best value... then certainly he is your man."

That got a chuckle from the men on deck. Turner nodded to Plank, "Lieutenant, my men will throw you a line and life ring. Please secure yourselves and prepare to be hauled over. We will not harm you, but I advise you to leave any weapons you may be carrying behind."

"I understand, sir," Gato said. "I have already instructed Ensign Kabashi to drop his. We will cause no trouble."

"Not like you'd be introducing anything new to this boat," Jarvis grumbled under his breath.

The two IJN flyers were quickly brought over, each man being helped to climb up the slippery side of the pressure hull and to get settled on deck. They were then patted down quite thoroughly by Rogers and led aft to be addressed by the captain.

"Welcome aboard USS *Bull Shark*," Turner said. "I'm Captain Arthur Turner. My men will see you below and get you some dry clothes. Your own will be laundered and returned to you. There is hot coffee and some pastries in the wardroom. I'll be down momentarily to speak with you."

"Thank you, sir," Gato bowed. "If it's permitted, I would like to remain for a moment."

"The captain said— "Plank began.

"That's all right, boatswain," Turner said. "Take Mr. Kubashi down below; I'll speak to the Lieutenant."

Plank and Rogers led Kubashi down through the now open forward torpedo loading hatch. Turner was just about to inquire as to what the pilot wanted when Webster Clayton appeared in the bridge hatch.

"Permission to come to the bridge?" he asked.

"Sure, Web," Turner replied.

Clayton came up and moved forward, and his mouth dropped open. Even more astonishing was the huge smile that appeared on Gato's face.

"Web!" the Japanese pilot said, any trace of accent now gone. "You old spymaster! What the *hell* are you doing out here in a submarine?"

"George!" Clayton asked and then laughed. "I'll be god *damned!* I should've known."

"What the *Christ*...?" Jarvis muttered, involuntarily reaching for his sidearm.

"Will somebody please explain this to me?" Turner asked, looking from one man to the other.

"I'm Captain George Gato, sir," the Japanese pilot replied, still smiling. "United States Army Air Corps. Temporarily... yeah, seems like years... seconded to the OSS."

"Fuckin' *what!?*" Hernandez blurted in bemused surprise. He then looked around and blushed slightly. "Uhm... sorry, sir."

Turner had to chuckle and patted the quartermaster on his shoulder, "Never mind, Hotrod. Can't say I blame ya'... Web?"

"He's telling the truth, Art," Clayton said. "Maybe we'd better go below and discuss this in private."

"Yes... maybe we *should*, Web... but I'm trying to track a damned enemy ship here," Turner cranked.

"I can help you there, sir," Gato said, looking to either side of him where Tank Broderick and Bill Borshowski, the assistant cook, held weapons on him. "You're only about thirty miles away. Just keep following this course."

Turner blew out his breath, "You heard the man, Hotrod... get us back on track. Ring up a flank bell and let's get underway. Resume the normal watch. Secure the guns. Pat, you wanna give me a hand down?"

Tom Begley smirked as he watched Pat Jarvis descend the ladder from the bridge with Turner riding on his shoulders. They repeated the act going down the ladder into the control room as well. Just before his head disappeared below the hatch combing, Turner looked at his XO.

"Mr. Begley, please take the bridge. I'll be in the wardroom."

The captain's tone had been neutral, but Begley could sense the strain in Turner's voice. As if he had to make an effort to be civil. All at once, the alarming thought that the captain might *know* about his little deception swam into his consciousness.

Could that be? Did Turner know?

Begley tried to dismiss the notion out of hand. Surely a man like Turner would confront him... but then again, maybe not... Turner was the type to give you some leeway until you either proved yourself worthy of it or that you needed to be managed.

Yes, but this was different...

Begley frowned as he went up the ladder. Turner and Jarvis were going to the wardroom to talk to their new prisoners... along with that shady Web Clayton. Shouldn't Begley be invited as well? After all, he *was* the XO...

No... something had changed since their little chat in the wardroom yesterday. A subtle shift in Turner's attitude toward him. And now that Begley thought about it hadn't the COB been a bit stand-offish too? Begley swore he'd seen more than one wry look from Rogers aimed in his direction.

Ingram couldn't have said anything, could he?

Begley decided that for the moment, there was little he could do. They needed to find that Jap sub carrier and sink her. And if that happened while he was on the bridge, so much the better.

Forward in the wardroom, Eddie Carlson set out coffee and a plate of donuts. Turner then asked Eddie to seal the compartment. The hatches to the control room and forward torpedo were dogged. Eddie was allowed to stay, however.

"So, you're Shadow?" Clayton asked. "I'll be damned..."

"I don't get this," Jarvis said. "I didn't think any Japanese Americans were serving right now."

Gato smiled thinly, "I couldn't tell you, Lieutenant. I've been out of the country for over a year now."

"They aren't," Clayton said. "Any Japanese Americans in the service have either been discharged or put on sabbatical. Many Japanese Americans are even being placed in... protective custody."

Gato scoffed, "Concentration camps, you mean? Well, I guess all's fair in love and war... and it's nothing compared to what's going on in the Empire."

"How do you mean?" Turner asked.

Gato drew in a breath, "Take me, for example. My parents and grandparents still live in Japan. I went over last spring to visit, before the troubles... well, before any *official* trouble. I wasn't there a week when a man from the ministry of the Navy showed up at my parent's home. I was informed that they knew I was an American and knew that I was a flyer in the American Army."

"Uh-oh," Jarvis muttered.

"What they did not know was that I was also involved with the OSS," Gato said. "However, it was represented to me that in spite of the fact that I had been born in the United States and educated there, I was still Japanese. There was a need for naval aviators, and I was offered a commission."

"Just like that?" Turner asked. "Weren't they worried that you'd become a spy or something?"

Gato shrugged, "At the time, as far as anyone knew, there was no hostility. Of course, the Emperor and the Prime Minister were planning to attack America for some time... and I think it gave them pleasure to waylay Japanese Americans who were in Japan into their service."

"Tokyo Rose..." Jarvis muttered.

Clayton nodded, "Except we think she might actually *be* a turncoat... go on, George."

"I don't suppose there are any cigarettes?" Gato asked.

Turner grinned and pulled a pack of Lucky Strikes from his breast pocket and handed them across with his lighter. Gato smiled and lit one, drawing deeply on the smoke and sighing contentedly.

"Oh, that's good..." Gato enthused. "All I've had for over a year are Golden Bats or those horrible Peacocks... now, back to the question... I was quite handsomely recruited. I was offered money, a good rank, and a posting that put me in close proximity to some of the more famous admirals. Yamamoto, Nagumo, and so on... I was offered other inducements as well."

"Broads?" Jarvis asked.

Gato grinned, "And how! But there was an underlying threat, too. That if I didn't cooperate, my family living in Japan would pay the price for my treachery... *treachery*... as if they should talk."

"You resisted, of course," Clayton stated.

Gato chuffed, "Oh, I laid it on thick enough to be convincing. Of course, as you know, Web, my being there wasn't a coincidence. Several of us were sent over to become sleeper agents. Anyway, I turned my back on my western upbringing and embraced my traditional imperial heritage... and here I am."

"Has it been hard?" Clayton asked.

"Yeah... have you had to attack Americans?" Jarvis asked with just a hint of suspicion.

Gato eyed him for a long moment and nodded slowly, "In other words, did the geisha girls and the good pay *really* turn me? No, Lieutenant, they did not. The IJN drafted me and threatened my family. I had to do this for them and for *my* country... *our* country. So far, I've been pretty lucky in that my duties have involved scouting missions. On the few attack sorties I've flown, I've been able to miss without drawing suspicion... and that included this morning. So, no, Mr. Jarvis, I'm not a goddamned Benedict Arnold."

Turner's mouth was drawn into a thin line, "But you can understand how the question would come up, Captain?"

Gato exhaled a stream of smoke and nodded. He even went so far as to look a bit abashed and smiled at Jarvis, "Sorry, Lieutenant... this hasn't always been easy for me."

"Yeah... I get that," Jarvis said. "No hard feelings?"

Gato's smile broadened, "You from New York?"

"Rhode Island," Jarvis said.

"Oh, yeah... I can hear that... no hard feelings," Gato said.

"What can you tell us about the *Leviathan?*" Turner asked. "And the plans for Midway?"

"Plenty," Gato said. "At least about the former. As for Midway, the Captain and XO might know more. Except that I was told that the mission this morning was mostly recon. The captain wants to hit Midway later this evening after the noise has died down and before the landing force arrives. I guess Yamamoto expects everything but the shouting to be over by dark."

"Christ, I wish we knew what was going on up there," Jarvis observed.

"We will sooner or later," Clayton stated.

"As for the ship," Gato continued, "she's a beast. Imagine a boat like this half-again as long, twice as wide, and three or four times as heavy."

"We've seen a photo," Clayton said.

Gato grinned, "Good... but I bet it doesn't do her justice. What a Frankenstein's monster this thing... but damned ingenious. Yamamoto himself was involved with her development. He's got this idea about using sub carriers to attack the U.S. mainland. He's got some smaller and more cost-effective versions of our ship on the drawing boards but built this thing way ahead of schedule as a secret weapon."

"To do what?" Turner asked. "I mean, okay... a sub that can launch eight planes is pretty interesting... but not a war-winner, I should think. The ship's probably slow and handles like a pig."

"Every weapon has its purpose, sir," Gato said. "She's got legs. Can go around the world almost two times without refueling. I don't know all the details, but the Old Man has some plan for South America."

Turner looked at Jarvis and then at Clayton, "We've seen something of that. Happened across a couple of Fubukis off the Galapagos last month."

Gato frowned, "Christ... I was afraid of that. This Midway operation is only a stop for *Leviathan*. From what I've heard coming from the wardroom, our real target after this mission is to hit the Panama Canal. To bomb a section and take it out of commission at least temporarily."

"Good God..." Turner breathed.

"Makes sense," Clayton said with a nod. "And we've suspected Yamamoto has had Panama in his sights for a while now."

"Yeah, it would be a big break for the Japanese," Jarvis stated. "Even if the canal was knocked out for a few months while it was repaired, it would mean a huge slow down for us getting ships into the Pacific. Most of our ship-building efforts are on the east coast."

"I think Yamamoto understands that," Gato said. "He must know how powerful our industrial capability is. That's why they hit Pearl the way they did... but in truth, it didn't accomplish what they hoped. So now the IJN is here at Midway, which is Yamamoto's way of mopping up our carriers. Take them out, and we've got nothing that can really stop the IJN in the Pacific... other than subs, of course. But subs aren't enough."

Clayton nodded, "He stems the tide of our shipbuilding and replenishment capabilities long enough to fortify his positions in the western Pacific. Crafty old bastard."

"Hmm..." Jarvis mused. "Maybe that's what was going on down there..."

Turner looked at him, "Off the coast of Chile, Pat?"

"Yeah," Jarvis continued thoughtfully. "If we can't get ships through the canal, then they have to go around Cape Horn or the Cape of Good Hope."

Clayton nodded grimly, "So, the Japanese could station submarines off the tip of South America to pound anything we try to send through..."

"The Straits of Magellan and Drake's Passage would be prime locations for submarine ambushes," Turner stated.

"And they'd need someplace close enough to re-supply and re-fuel," Clayton muttered. "Like Valparaiso in Chile... holy Christ..."

"So, what's your ship doing now, Gato?" Turner asked.

"Sitting out there recovering those seven birds," Gato said. "Should take about an hour."

"Then what?" Jarvis asked.

Gato shrugged, "Probably sit tight or maybe even come in a little closer for the evening attack."

"So, we need to get them while they're sitting out there," Jarvis opined. "About thirty miles away, you say?"

Carlson moved silently over and refilled Gato's coffee. He smiled up at the steward, "Thanks... yes, I'd say so... although we've been talking here for a while, so maybe twenty miles ahead."

"Better to creep up on them or come in aggressively, you think?" Turner asked.

"Hell, I'm no sub driver," Gato shrugged. "But I'd think it'd be easier for you if they were on top. Also, if you want to get a closer look at the boat... then torpedoes might not be a good idea. Personally... I'd rather see the crew taken prisoner than killed if possible."

Turner nodded, "I understand."

Gato sighed, "Technically, they're my enemy... but I've spent some time with them. Most of the enlisted are just kids drawn into the Navy to serve. The officers... well, they have a better understanding of the political situation. The skipper's a grade-A prick... but the XO and the CAG are good guys. I think if push came to shove and they had no choice, Commander Osaka, that's the XO, would agree to capitulate to save his boys."

"And the skipper?" Turner asked.

Gato smiled and looked at Jarvis, "Not a chance. He hates you round-eyed Whities."

Carlson guffawed.

"Maybe you wanna transfer over, Eddie?" Jarvis jibed.

"Me, sir? Oh, no, sir," Carlson stated earnestly. He waited just a beat more and said, "I *love* you round-eyed Whities."

Gato roared with laughter, and Clayton joined in along with Jarvis.

Turner feigned tolerance as he rolled his eyes and then grinned, "Yeah, welcome aboard *Bull Shark*, Captain... it's a regular goddamned Bob Hope comedy cruise."

Gato smiled, "I can see that."

The phone next to Turner buzzed and he plucked it from its place on the wall, "Wardroom."

"Skipper, Nichols here... I'd like to ask if we can slow up a bit. This overloading is getting me worried. We're smoking a lot, and I really would like to take a closer look at numbers three and four."

"Very well, Enj.," Turner replied. "I think we're gonna dive anyway. I'll inform the XO."

Turner then called up to the bridge. He informed Begley that he wanted to dive and proceed at radar depth. When Begley inquired as to why, Turner only said that he felt they were getting close and didn't want to be overheard and that once dunked, to ring up a two-thirds bell.

It was perhaps thirty minutes later, moving at a modest five knots, that *Bull Shark* got the first faint scent of her prey. Joe Dutch was in the conning tower sitting beside Chet Rivers. Both men were putting their highly trained and sensitive ears to the task at hand. When the first transient was detected, neither one knew who heard it first. They both simply looked at one another and smiled.

"Very faint contact," Dutch let Rivers report to Begley. "Some kind of mechanical transient, sir... barely detectible... but appears to be bearing... zero-zero-niner... range maybe twenty-four thousand yards."

Begley turned from the periscope, "Are you certain of that, Rivers?"

"It's hardly distinguishable from the background," Dutch added. "Yet it seems to be growing stronger."

"What is it?" Begley asked.

"Unknown," Rivers said. "But definitely artificial."

Begley grinned wolfishly, "Then we've *got* the son of a bitch! Stay on him. Helm, come right to zero-zero-niner. Dutch, can we increase speed?"

Dutch frowned, "I wouldn't recommend it, sir... we'll lose him in our own increased screw noise. At least this far out. Maybe when we're a few miles closer."

"Damn..." Begley stated. "That means we've got at least two and a half hours to catch him up at this rate..."

"I don't think it's screw noise," Rivers offered. "Sounds more like... industrial activity. Maybe some generators running... just too faint to tell this far away."

Begley scowled, "Very well. Phone talker, alert the captain that we may have detected an enemy contact at twelve miles and are proceeding on course to intercept."

CHAPTER 34

USS YORKTOWN

1440 MIDWAY TIME

Lieutenant Tomonaga knew that his was a one-way mission. He knew that when he had lifted off *Hiryu*. After witnessing the destruction of no less than three of the mighty carriers in the Kido Butai in a span of minutes that could be counted on a single hand, Tomonaga's heart had broken.

He knew, or thought he knew, that even if he had the fuel to make the return trip to his carrier, that she wouldn't be there for him. If the Americans could find and sink three carriers so easily, then why not the fourth? It seemed inevitable, just as the Japanese victory had seemed inevitable just ten hours before.

Tomonaga had practically begged. First Admiral Yamaguchi, and then on the radio to Admiral Nagumo. He'd pleaded for an additional strike on Midway. Yet, for some reason, command had dithered and changed its mind and then changed it again! Perhaps it was this that had given the Americans time to find them and send in that utterly destructive dive-bombing sortie. How could it be otherwise?

And when someone finally... *finally* made a decision, it was to re-arm the original aircraft that had attacked Midway to attack the American carrier that had been sighted to the northeast. So, here was Tomonaga, flying toward the big carrier in a plane with bullet holes, low on fuel and not enough ammunition in his machine guns to make more than a demonstration of resistance. And that was to say nothing of his and his fellow pilots' exhaustion. He'd seen how the American torpedo bombers had faired against his own fleet. He had no illusions about how he'd fair.

What did raise his spirits ever so slightly was that when he came within visual range of the American carrier, it was trailing several pillars of smoke. He'd heard the reports that the Vals had scored several hits but that the ship hadn't sunk. In fact, to Tomonaga's eye, she looked to be under power and moving again! How could that be? The mighty *Kaga* had been turned into a floating torch after one attack, and here was this American carrier, not quite as large, moving under her own power after three bomb strikes!

Yes, it was true that the American planes carried heavier loads... but even so... well, it was no matter. Chuji Tomonaga's torpedo would *not* miss, and he would exact his pound of flesh here and now. He would, with his last act of defiance, strike a devastating blow for the emperor!

At least he wasn't alone. At least he wasn't flying into the slathering jaws of the beast without company. Several other torpedo bombers were with him. Even as the carrier grew larger, Tomonaga could see the American fighters homing in on him. He grinned to himself. He and his fellow bombers were still flying at high speed and a thousand feet above the sea. The idea was that the Americans wouldn't realize how fast the two enemies were closing the distance until it was too late. They would overshoot and have to turn around. By then, Tomonaga could dive down to the deck and slow enough to release his weapon.

It was working! The dots that were the Wildcat fighters suddenly expanded and became the menacing shapes of enemy aircraft. The Americans must have realized their mistake, for as the two groups of aircraft passed each other at something like four hundred and fifty knots, bright tracers glittered in the afternoon sky, flashing past Tomonaga's canopy like fireflies. One or two rounds struck his plane, but it was of no consequence. He laughed out loud as his oil pressure alarm began to blare, as if that mattered any longer.

The flight leader dove toward the sea, pulling back on his throttle, which temporarily quieted the angry engine alarm. Once at thirty meters, he levelled off and aimed for the carrier's bow, now growing huge in his forward windscreen. Just a bit closer...

Tomonaga risked a quick glance over his shoulder in time to see a pair of Wildcats arcing in and angling toward him. He knew it was only a matter of seconds before they opened fire and peppered his vulnerable bomber with leaden death. But as he turned back and judged the distance to the carrier, he laughed again. The fighters were too late.

Tomonaga said a quick prayer and punched the torpedo release button. His aircraft bucked upward slightly as its heavy burden was suddenly released. He shoved the throttle to the stops and began a laborious climb up and away from the carrier.

He wasn't evading to try and save his life. His oil alarm, blaring once again, told him that his engine was only moments from seizing. The Wildcats, far more maneuverable than his own plane, would see to his destruction long before he lost power. No, he wanted to live long enough to see his victory.

As he gained altitude, Tomonaga threw his plane over into a reverse of his turn, barely avoiding a stream of machine gun fire from the nearest F4A4 and headed back toward the carrier. He saw that several other of his brethren had released their weapons as well, and that two of them were boiling just past the carrier's bow. The big ship had turned sharply to port to avoid them, but Tomonaga knew it was in vain.

His own fish, and one more, slammed into the carrier's flank, sending up two huge pillars of foam that were quickly joined by debris, flame, and smoke.

"Banzai!" Tomonaga screamed as his engine died and dozens of American slugs tore into his plane. "Banzai, Ame-cohs!"

Tomonaga's crippled bird began to spin and break up even before it struck the water and disintegrated. The pilot died knowing that he had succeeded but not knowing his act of sacrifice wasn't enough to spare the day.

270 MILES SOUTH OF MIDWAY ATOLL

"One out of seven is a very light price to pay for what our pilots have reported," Kajimora was saying.

He, Osaka, and Hideki were sitting around the table in the large wardroom reviewing the notes that the pilots and the flight operations team had made. Recovery of the aircraft was complete, and the submarine was lying to, running four of her six diesels in order to top off the charge in her three giant batteries.

"I wonder how Lieutenant Gato would see it," Hideki said glumly. "It's a shame to have lost one of our best pilots."

Kajimora lit a cigarette and shrugged, "These things happen in war. What is more to the point is that we've lost one of our eight airplanes. Being so far out, I wonder if it would be possible to acquire a replacement before we're sent on to our primary mission."

Osaka wanted to reach across and backhand the bastard right across his foul mouth. Two men possibly died within the past several hours and all the man could think of was the airplane. Of his own glory.

Kajimora, although not overly bright, was quite intuitive. He sensed his first officer's mood and smiled thinly at him.

"Oh, you disapprove, Yakuin?" Kajimora asked.

"While it's true the loss of the plane is regrettable," Osaka stated. "The loss of human life is more so."

Kajimora shrugged, "Of course. But we have other pilots. We don't have another aircraft. This cuts down on our initial effectiveness when we attack the canal. Like it or not, Osaka, the logistics of war exist. You'll be a better officer... a better *captain* when you realize that."

Osaka did not rise to the bait. He only bowed ever so slightly at the shoulders, "As you say, sir."

"Now, gentlemen," Kajimora began more formally, signifying that the meeting should move on. What must occupy our minds now is our next move. Do we, as I've planned, wait until this evening to launch another sortie to Midway? Do we wait until what will have no doubt transpired to the north is complete and for radio silence to be broken? That would no doubt allow our revered admiral to direct us... or do we begin now for our destination? It's ten thousand kilometers away, after all."

"I'm commander of the air group," Hideki obfuscated. "I operate my assets at your pleasure, Captain."

"But what is your opinion, Hideki?" Kajimora asked. "After all, you are one of the ship's senior officers. What does your tactical mind suggest?"

Hideki drew in a breath, "If it is a matter of... the logistics of war, then we must consider our primary objective. To launch another sortie to Midway at dusk will at best prove useless if the Kido Butai has been successful. At worst, should the operation still be underway, we could lose more aircraft, further dulling our blade, so to speak."

Kajimora nodded sagely, "Well put, Commander. And you, first officer? What is your opinion?"

So, you can steal the glory for yourself if we win, or blame me if we lose? Osaka thought.

He considered for a long moment. Part of him wished to advise Kajimora to do something foolish and therefore prove himself the fool Osaka knew him to be. To him, attacking Midway again was foolish. Virtually pointless, as Hideki had stated.

If Nagumo had not yet subdued the island, then it was possible that the seven remaining floatplanes in *Ribaiasan's* air group would fly into danger alone. Seven aircraft against what their pilots have already reported being a sturdily fortified position wouldn't be enough and would most likely result in the loss of most, if not all, of the planes.

A disgrace for Kajimora... but Osaka was not cold enough or calculating enough to commit fourteen men to their deaths just to embarrass his captain. That was something Kajimora would do, and Osaka would not stoop to that level.

The prudent thing to do was to wait. To wait until after the battle that must still be raging to the north. Once Yamamoto broke radio silence, the submarine would know exactly what was happening and what the admiral wished of them.

On the other hand, continuing to their primary objective would demonstrate initiative. The submarine, even at flank speed, couldn't get more than a hundred fifty kilometers away before they must receive some radio traffic. Worst case scenario, they could turn around and arrive at Midway atoll within a day.

"I believe we should proceed with our primary mission," Osaka stated. "By now the Midway campaign will be nearly decided. The Aleutian campaign as well. I think it would be well for us to continue on to what our admiral wishes for us to do... no matter what the outcome... even should the Americans somehow have driven our forces off—"

"Inconceivable!" Kajimora laughed.

"—Yes... but should that have happened, then Admiral Yamamoto will want us to attack Panama all the sooner," Osaka finished. "If we have prevailed, as we all think is the case, then he will have no need of this one ship at Midway."

Kajimora fell silent for a time. It was the right answer, and the idiot should have recognized that immediately. Osaka and Hideki exchanged furtive glances while the captain made up his mind.

"Quite correct," he finally said. "I'm glad we agree. Perhaps all is not lost in terms of our aircraft. Our South American operation may have already taken root."

Osaka blinked at him, "Sir?"

Kajimora smiled in a way that was neither pleasing nor comforting, "Oh? You haven't heard then... how interesting. Then perhaps the great Yamamoto doesn't know of it either. Well, Yakuin, we can discuss it further en route. Since it is your watch, would you please report to the conning tower and do the honors of getting us underway? I think cruising speed will be sufficient for now."

Osaka frowned as he rose and bowed, "Hai. It shall be done."

As he made his way aft and into the expansive control room and then up the ladder into the conning tower, Osaka wondered exactly what the captain was talking about. To his knowledge, neither the Imperial Navy nor the Imperial Army had any interest in South America... or did they? Certainly, many of the countries there had already expressed support for the Axis. Yet verbal support was a long way from joining the fight against their enemies, especially with the United States being so close to them.

"Helmsman, please come to a course of one-three-zero degrees. All ahead two-thirds. Inform the maneuvering room I wish them to make turns for ten knots."

The helmsman acknowledged, and the maneuvering room enunciator indicated the speed had been dialed in. He was just about to go topside when the sonarman behind him called his name.

"What is it?" Osaka asked.

"Sir..." the young, enlisted man said, frowning and holding a hand to his headphones. "I thought... I thought I heard something to the north... very faint, but definitely a mechanical noise of some kind."

Osaka grimaced. As superb as the ship was, it had proven to have two unfortunate flaws. First, she lacked a radar set. This was enormously foolish to Osaka, and the assurances of Yamamoto himself that one was scheduled to be installed made little difference.

The second flaw was that the sound gear had proven to be somewhat inadequate. Perhaps due to the ship's extra engines and motors as well as the unusual shape. The sound profile of the wide-bodied hull moving through the water could possibly limit their effective passive range.

In any event, Osaka was pragmatic enough to simply accept what was rather than worry over what was not. He sighed and shook his head.

"How far?" he finally asked.

"Indeterminate," the man said. "The increased power on the diesels has masked the sound."

"All stop," Osaka said, rubbing his chin. "Rig ship for dive. Helm, tell maneuvering to stand by to answer bells on batteries. Assistant deck officer, have the diesels shut down. So note in the ship's log."

The submarine, which had already gathered way now, began to

slow. The lookouts came down the bridge hatch along with the quartermaster, and the hatch was closed and dogged down.

"Hatch secure!" the quartermaster reported.

"Main induction closed," came the engineer's voice from below. "Diesels shut down."

The sudden lack of vibration was in itself almost deafening.

"Bow planes rigged out," came a voice from the control room. Then another, "Pressure in the boat. Diving board is green."

"Very well," Osaka said. "We will belay the dive for a moment more. Your report, Dikata?"

The sonarman was listening intently and frowning, "Yes... yes... I'm getting it now. Much clearer... contact! Light slow screws, bearing three-zero-five... range four thousand meters! Assess submarine running on battery power only."

Osaka felt his stomach lurch. The contact was only two miles away, and he didn't have to make any leap of faith to believe that it was *not* a Japanese submarine.

"Heading?" Osaka asked.

"Constant bearing, sir," Dikata reported and turned, his face pale.

Osaka nodded, "What would you say that noise you heard was earlier? His motors?"

The young man shook his head, "I don't think so... it was more of a mechanical sound... like..."

"Like his torpedo doors being opened," Osaka stated. "I don't suppose you can identify whether it's American or one of ours? We do have boats in the area."

Dikata listened and frowned again, "I'm not entirely certain, but the machinery noise sounds very much like that fleet boat we engaged a few days ago."

Osaka actually chuckled sardonically, "Of course it is. Diving officer, make your depth one hundred meters, smartly! Helm, all ahead two-thirds. Open main ballast tank vents. Flood negative tanks and the safety tank. Flood bow buoyancy. We have a guest."

"So, Osaka san," Kajimora's voice said as his head appeared in the open control room hatch, "our vanquished enemy has returned from the afterlife, eh?"

"So it would seem, sir," Osaka said grimly.

"Well," Kajimora said confidently, "let them come. He cannot fire on us submerged any better than we can."

"No," Osaka admitted, biting his lip. "But he can call in his friends."

————

"Contact is headed down, XO!" Rivers reported. "His turns are increasing, and I hear flooding noises."

"Confirmed," Ted Balkley reported from the radar station. "SJ returns are growing fainter."

Begley was looking through the periscope and could clearly see the oddball Jap submarine beginning to dive. At only two miles off and with a periscope height of over twenty feet, his view was good. He scowled, "No time for a shot, I'm afraid. We're not near close enough... damn... stay on him, sound."

Pendergast's head popped up through the hatch, "Should I continue the plot?"

Begley cocked an eyebrow at him, "Of course... why not?"

Pendergast shrugged, "He's submerging. We can't shoot at him."

"But we can hound him," Andy Post's voice drifted up from below.

"Who asked you?" Pendergast snapped.

"As you were, Burt," Begley said. "Yeah, keep the plot going. We can't shoot, but we've got a full battery, and we can dog the prick. Inform the skipper that we've made definite contact."

Behind him, at the chart desk, Hotrod Hernandez had a maneuvering board and was making his own notes, occasionally checking the DRI and the magic eye display on River's sonar set. Joe Dutch, who was in the conning tower as well, smiled at Hernandez and went over to assist.

Begley continued to watch through the periscope lens as the huge submarine slowly vanished from the surface, "Taking her sweet time about going down..."

"Sir... recommend we dive as well," Dutch offered.

Begley shot him a withering look, "Thank you, *engineer*. Diving officer, make your depth three hundred feet. Shallow bubble. Let's see where this guy goes. Helm, slow to all ahead one-third."

"XO, assess turn rate on target as... four knots," Rivers reported.

Begley rubbed his hands together, "This is where we earn our submarine pay, boys."

CHAPTER 35

As Turner and the other men who'd been in the wardroom entered the control room, he was pleased to see everyone at their posts doing their jobs efficiently. Pendergast and Post working at the master gyro table, Buck Rogers at the high-pressure manifold and overseeing the others, men at the bow and stern planes, Wendell Freeman as backup steersman, and more.

"Captain Gato, what can you tell us about the target's characteristics?" Turner asked his guest. "Speed, maneuverability, armament, and diving capabilities?"

Gato frowned, "I wasn't part of the regular crew, just the flight crew, however... I know their test depth is about a hundred meters... uhm... three hundred feet. Top speed surfaced is fourteen and submerged about seven. Things enormous, which makes it sluggish from what I heard. Six diesels, six electric motors, and three batteries... and six torpedo tubes forward. Couple of AA guns on deck and a four-inch."

"So, although she's humungous," Nichols opined, "she's not a giant."

Gato nodded at him, "Yes. Her biggest advantage lies in her air wing."

Pendergast looked down at his chart in order to hide a sneer.

"Fat lotta good that does 'em down here," Rogers said and chuckled.

"Captain, would you please assist my plotting party?" Turner indicated Pendergast and Post along with their assistants. "Any other useful information you have would be greatly appreciated."

"We're taking advice from the *Japs* now!?" Pendergast blurted. "Captain, I really—"

"That'll do, *Lieutenant*," Turner snapped. "This man happens to be a captain in the Army Air Corps."

Pendergast seemed to be losing control of himself. Almost against his will, he laughed sardonically, "Oh, how convenient! Sir, a Jap is a Jap. We shouldn't trust a word he says."

"You're relieved," Turner managed to say calmly, although it took a mighty big effort.

Pendergast blinked in surprise, "Sir?"

"You heard me," Turner said. "You're relieved of duty. You can sit the rest of the battle out in your stateroom. I won't have this crap on my ship, mister. *Dismissed!*"

Pendergast scoffed, threw his pencil and dividers down on the table, and stalked out. Turner swore he heard the man mutter something mutinous as he did so, but at the moment he had other things on his mind. Web Clayton only shook his head, and Pat Jarvis looked like he was ready to chew through a steel plate.

"Let him go, Pat," Turner said softly. "Take your post, please. Captain... I sincerely apologize for my officer. There was no call for that."

Gato took it in stride, "I guess that's gonna be the reaction I get from a lot of people now."

"Doesn't make it right," Jarvis said and patted the man on the shoulder before going up the ladder.

Turner suddenly felt very tired. As if the act of trying to hold together what was once a happy and effective crew was eroding him. His submarine hadn't been the same since they'd left New London, and although now was not the time to deal with it, Turner told himself that when they put in after this, some major changes would occur.

———

Burt Pendergast was enraged. He slid the curtain closed and flopped onto his bunk, seething. Did nobody but him or Tom object to *anything* that went on aboard this fucking boat? Turner brings some goddamned Nip pilot aboard and assigns him to the plotting party pretty as you please... Jesus Christ!

Burt didn't feel quite right. For over a week now, he'd been out of sorts and not quite able to level off. It wasn't as if he'd never served on submarines before... although this experience had been vastly different than the S-boats he'd served on during peacetime.

Those had been leisure cruises by comparison. Now he was out in the Pacific, and this was the real deal. High-speed runs, depth charges, shooting down airplanes, violent storms... and nearly drowning at almost eight hundred feet!

My God... that had been the worst. It hadn't even been two full days! Burt didn't want to admit that if it hadn't been for that prick, Jarvis, he probably wouldn't be able to reflect on it now.

Jarvis... of all the goddamned boats in this man's Navy, he had to get posted with that son of a bitch. Fucking skipper's *pet* is what he was. Guy practically mutinies and gets away with it Scot-free! What kind of shit was that?

Pendergast found himself shaking now. He told himself it was with anger, but he was only deluding himself. Even as he reached inside his pillowcase, deep down he knew what was really wrong.

Yet when he pulled out the small foil packet and unwrapped it, exposing a handful of pills and several paper packets, he found himself calming just at the sight.

He picked up a blue Amy and popped it into his mouth, swallowing it down with a gulp of coffee he'd snitched from the wardroom. He looked down at the small collection in his hand, thinking about how long this underwater chase might last.

"Fuck it," he said, and popped another sedative.

———

There really was no reason for Turner to go up into the conning tower while the ship was submerged, so he stood by the ladder and clung to it for support. His ankle throbbed after having been on his feet all morning, but the captain bore the discomfort. Soon he might have to order hydraulic power shut down, and the men at the sound heads, planes, and helm would have to manhandle their gear in an ever hotter and more humid submarine. The least he could do was put up with a little pain in his foot.

"How we doing up there, XO?" Turner asked.

"Sound has a good lock on them," Begley said. "We're a thousand yards off their tail, headed down as they are, but at a steeper angle."

"Wonder if there's a salt layer down here someplace?" Post said to no one in particular, looking at the bathythermograph over the gyro table.

"A salt layer?" Gato asked. "As opposed to what?"

Post grinned at the pilot, "The ocean isn't isothermal... all the same temperature. Sometimes the salt density changes at certain depths. Well, when there's more or less salt, it changes the density and temperature of the water. This change reflects sound waves. So, going under one can hide you from an enemy's sonar."

"No kidding?" Gato asked. "Damn... wish the sky had that!"

"Well, you guys got clouds to hide in, sir," Rogers opined with a grin.

"Now passing two-zero-zero feet," Nichols called out. He turned to the captain. "Sir... I am a bit worried about that damage we took yesterday. We welded the seam over the maneuvering room... but I'm not sure it's one hundred percent."

Turner frowned, "You saying we can't go deep, Enj?"

Nichols shrugged, "I'm saying that if we go *too* deep, it could pop the weld. It's just a quickie patch."

"How deep is too deep?" Clayton asked, remembering the harrowing experience of less than forty-eight hours before.

Nichols frowned, "Hard to say... but I doubt we could do eight hundred again. What do you think, Tank?"

Tank Broderick was taking a turn at the bow planes. He turned halfway around on his bench and said, "I think I did a good job on that weld, sir... but it is still a patch job. I'd lay money that the welds I put in to seal MBTs six Charlie and dog will hold better, on account those tanks aren't exposed to the kind of pressure the hull is."

Turner nodded, "Okay, gents, I'll keep that under advisement. But based on what George here says, that boat can't go near as deep as we can. And that reminds me... everyone, this is Captain George Gato, USAC."

Introductions were made, and the men went back to their jobs. More than one probably had some concerns about the fact that Gato was Japanese, but unlike the second engineer, they wisely kept it to themselves. Whatever misgivings they might have about Gato, they had none about their skipper. Besides, it wasn't the first time *Bull Shark* had a guest aboard who wasn't entirely American or who hadn't started out that way. All the original sailors fondly remembered Fritz Schwimmer and how he'd come to their side.

"Sir! Dem sty-lus a'twichin'... I tink we done found how you call... one o' dem salt layer!" Henrie Martin, ship's cook, said excitedly. Having nothing to do in the galley for the time being, he was working on his charting skills and assisting with the plotting party.

Turner had to smile at the man's heavy Cajun accent. It was more pronounced during casual situations when he laid it on thick, but in truly stressful situations, it sometimes came out all on its own. He grinned at the man, "That's for true, Henrie."

The light chuckle that floated around the control room was good to hear. It had relieved some of the heaviness that followed after Pendergast had been sent forward. Turner looked over to Frank Nichols.

"Two-seven-zero feet," Nichols reported. "Kind of shallow for a halocline way out here in two-thousand-fathom water."

"My God..." Andy Post breathed. "Twelve *thousand* feet... two miles down..."

"Hard to imagine, isn't it?" Turner said conversationally. "Makes you wonder what's down there... what incredible secrets lie beneath our keel right now..."

"Or monsters," Clayton said with a wry grin.

"We've got our own monster to worry about," Turner said. "*Leviathan*... how apropos. What's the story, Joe?"

"We've lost him!" Rivers blurted from above.

That was bound to happen. Turner watched the stylus tracing an erratic path on the smoked card over his head, "Let's keep going down until we find the bottom of this layer. See if he comes out of it."

A few minutes passed, and the stylus once again began to run smoothly. Nichols reported they were at three hundred seventy feet. Turner ordered all ahead one-third and that Nichols should hold their depth at four hundred.

"Did your ship have one of these, George?" Turner asked, pointing to the simple but effective bathythermograph.

Gato shook his head, "Not that I recall. Hell, they don't even have radar for cryin' out loud. So, what do we do now, Skipper? If we can't hear them?"

Turner smiled thinly, "We play the waiting game. See if they descend through the layer. If not, we go back up and ping for them. The frustrating part about this kind of job is that we don't have any way to attack another submarine at depth."

"You can't fire a torpedo?" Gato asked.

"We can, although it's better not to from this deep," Turner explained. "Problem is we have no way to *aim* the damned thing. We have to set the depth manually. It's harder to determine depth underwater when you're close to the same depth. It's far easier to calculate depth from above, so there's some degree of inaccuracy. Even if the enemy ship was sitting still at X feet, your fish could miss. Or they could move up or down in the water column and cause it to miss. No... what we're doing now is simply waiting them out. This is a contest of endurance. Which ship can hold its breath the longest... which of us has a bigger battery capacity?"

Gato frowned, "With all due respect, sir... they have three batteries to your two. The ship's internal volume is several times yours."

"Yeah, but they got more gear to run and more guys," Post stated. "So it might be close."

"Let's hope so..." Turner muttered.

Bull Shark waited.

"Where are they?" Kajimora asked, exhaling smoke with his question.

Osaka stood beside him at the periscopes and looked back to the sound operator. The young man fiddled with his equipment and touched his headphones.

"American vessel is one thousand meters astern," the operator finally reported. "Appears to be making turns for four knots."

"To our three," Kajimora grumped. "Helm, increase speed to match."

"Aye, sir," the helmsman said, adjusting his enunciators. "Maneuvering answers. Depth now eighty meters."

"Perhaps we will find a salt layer," Kajimora opined.

Osaka frowned, "Perhaps... although with the ocean being so deep, it is unlikely. What is more likely is that we will simply outlast the American. Our battery capacity and air supply are greater."

Kajimora cast a glance at his first officer, "Indeed, Yakuin? And you know that for certain?"

Osaka bristled but maintained his composure, "It is a mathematical certainty. Although we have at least twice as many men aboard, our internal volume is much greater than even the big American boats. We have three batteries instead of the usual two, and are using no more power down here than they... at least to no appreciable degree. I believe it's simply a matter of time. Even if they find a salt layer and lose us... which is not their goal, we can simply stay above the point where we lose their sound signature and wait. Sooner or later the American, like a whale, must rise to the surface to breathe. Then we have him."

"Or he has us," Kajimora pointed out. "I would feel better with another option. I would prefer that we had planes above waiting to drop bombs on them... or even depth charges."

Osaka nodded, "Yes... but that is not possible now."

Kajimora turned to Hideki, who was also in the crowded conning tower, "What say you, air group commander?"

Hideki straightened his crisp white uniform, "What Commander Osaka says is true, sir. We have recovered our planes, but they are now stored in the hangars."

Kajimora seemed to be getting impatient, "I'm *aware* of that, Hideki. However... we do have the ordnance loading hatches. Can we not prepare them for flight while we're sitting down here doing *nothing?*"

Hideki exchanged a look with Osaka and then shrugged, "I do not know... it's never been done."

"Neither has launching two squadrons of floatplanes from a submarine,' Kajimora pointed out, feeling smug now that he'd thought of something creative that his juniors had not. "But it's *possible,* is it not? Men can access the hangars from the pressure hull... so could we not prepare at least a few planes so that we could launch quickly once on the surface?"

Hideki actually smiled, "I can't say for certain, Captain... but I will look into the feasibility immediately."

"Good, do that," Kajimora stated, lighting another Golden Bat off the dying ember of the one he'd been smoking.

"Sir... I'm losing contact," the sonar operator stated. "It appeared that the American was diving more quickly than us... and now his machinery sounds are becoming distorted... I can barely... he's gone, sir!"

"What is our depth?" Kajimora blurted.

"Ninety meters," the helmsman replied.

Kajimora grinned, "So... I believe we've found a salt layer indeed, Yakuin."

"I stand corrected, sir," Osaka said flatly.

"Helmsman, all stop. Diving officer, hold depth," Kajimora ordered. He picked up the telephone hanging from the overhead near him and activated the general alert circuit. "All hands, this is the captain. Our enemy has cloaked himself in a sound layer, deafening us both. Now we will deafen him as well... rig for silent running."

"This will make loading more difficult, sir," Hideki said as he crept down the ladder.

Kajimora smiled, "Just tell your men to be as quiet as possible, Commander. If the American is indeed hiding in a halocline, then he won't be able to hear you anyway."

Osaka wanted to correct his captain. Wanted to explain that the salt layers did a good job of reflecting high-frequency noises, but some low-frequency sounds could still pass through. However, that could do no good, and Hideki himself knew enough to exercise caution in any case.

Ribaiasan waited.

CHAPTER 36

STATION HYPO

1830 LOCAL TIME

Joan Turner paced the central aisle that led from the security door to the rear of the basement office space known as the dungeon. The tension in the facility was thick and cloying and seemed to hang over everyone like a dense New England fog. Of course, she had to admit, it might be at least partly due to the fact that she was pacing like a caged lioness.

Reports of the battle at, and around, Midway had been pouring in all day, both coded and uncoded fleet reports. Very little had come in from the Japanese, though. At least nothing that seemed directly related. Every so often, a messenger from Admiral Nimitz's office, or even Commander Edwin Layton himself, would come down and update the Ultra team on what was going on.

Just before noon, in fact, the commander had burst in, practically bowling over the Marine sentry, and had been smiling and laughing and slapping backs like a madman. He'd actually wrapped Joe Rochefort up in a bear hug, lifted him off his feet, and spun him around. He'd even come over and hugged Joan Turner, although more reserved.

"What the hell's gotten into you?" Rochefort asked, a bit flustered but appearing pleased.

Holmes, Finnegan, Joan, and just about everyone else had gathered around Layton. The commander laughed and shook his head, "We've just received a report from Fletcher. Three... *three* for Chrissakes, Jap carriers are burning and dead in the water!"

"My God..." Jasper Holmes breathed in disbelief.

"Damndest thing I ever heard of," Layton said, shaking his head. "They attacked Midway, Midway attacked them... and nothing. Japs must've thought they had won the day. Then a bunch of torpedo planes from *Hornet, Enterprise,* and even *Yorktown* come swooping in... no hits. We lost most of them, poor fellows."

"Jesus, Ed, that's horrible news," Rochefort opined.

Layton nodded, his elation damped for a moment, but it returned almost instantly, "Yeah... but then, around ten their time, *Enterprise* and *Yorktown* dive bombers show up and start *hammering* the Japs! Way the report read, the Japanese air cover was orbiting really low in response to the torpedo planes and never saw the dive bombers coming until the last minute! *Kaga, Akagi,* and we think maybe *Soryu,* but we're not sure if it might not have been *Hiryu,* are wrecked. In five goddamned minutes!"

That had certainly lifted everyone's spirits. A major victory that justified all the late nights and early mornings. Yet only a few hours later, Layton had returned looking ashen. This time, the news was bad.

He explained that the remaining Japanese carrier had sent a combined strike and located *Yorktown.* She was hit with several dive bombs and torpedoes. At last report, Fletcher had moved his flag, and the ship was listing, and Captain Buckmaster had called for an evacuation. That had killed the good mood and sent Joan herself spiraling into worry for her own husband, about whom she'd heard nothing in quite some time.

Now it was nearly six-thirty, and she was tired. Tired of the dungeon... tired of the strong coffee and the smell of men who hadn't bathed in a day or more... tired of how worried she was about Art. He'd gone off before and she'd had no word. That was normal in the submarine service... but somehow, this was different.

Before, she'd simply been the dutiful Navy wife. Staying back and taking care of the homestead while her man went off to war. She had the mundane to keep her occupied. Cooking, cleaning, playing with the kids, and talking to teachers, chatting with her girlfriends... a sort of normality. But this, this was different. Now she was Lieutenant Joan Turner, Navy officer, even if she thought it was a bit silly and somewhat honorific. She was now *inside* the circle. So far inside and in a way that gave her access to things she wouldn't otherwise have known about. In a strange and twisted way, her current situation was both better and worse than it had been before.

"What's the lesser of two evils?" Joan muttered to herself. "Not knowing and accepting that... or knowing too much and yet still lacking information?"

"Joanie."

Joan stopped and turned to see Joe Rochefort standing right behind her with a knowing smile. Next to him was Joe Finnegan and even Jasper Holmes.

"Oh... I'm sorry, am I driving you fellas bonkers?" Joan asked sheepishly. She realized that her pacing must be at the very least distracting.

Rochefort shook his head and actually reached out to take her hand, "No, but I can see it's driving you nuts. You've done enough on this one, Joan. Why don't you go home? Take it easy."

"Go see your kids and chat with Gladys," Finnegan added. "You don't need to hang out in here with all of us."

"Oh, I couldn't..." Joan began to protest, if a bit weakly.

"You can and you will, Lieutenant," Rochefort said with a smile. "You're dismissed; that's an order."

"Wow... better mark this day down, Joan," Holmes added. "Not every day old Joe here gives one of them out."

Before Joan could answer, the heavy door burst open and once again, Ed Layton rushed in, waving a sheet of paper in the air.

"Jesus Christ, Commander!" the Marine sergeant exclaimed.

"Sorry, Sarge, sorry!" Layton said, not sounding the least bit sorry. "We got another one, boys...! And lady! The fourth Jap carrier is going up like a torch! That's four for four, ha-ha-HAAA!"

The entire room broke out in applause. Layton grinned all the way across his face, "Hey, that's for you folks, too. Couldn't have done it without you. Absolutely first-rate work! Top-*notch!*"

After the hullaballoo had died down somewhat, Joan asked Layton if he'd heard anything about *Bull Shark*.

Layton's mood softened a bit, "No, Joanie, I'm sorry... but look, you know as well as anyone that we call it the silent service for a reason. No need to worry."

Joan sighed, "But we've heard from just about every other boat around Midway today... why not Art?"

"He's on special assignment, you know that," Layton said. "Come on, let me walk you out. I think Joe is right, and you should knock off for the day... hell, for the week. You know as well as I do that Art's chasing down a phantom and that he probably won't report until it's all said and done. We did have contact with him early this morning. I don't know old Anvil Art as well as some of the rest of you, but from what I do know and what I hear, your husband is gonna be fine. Hell, he'll probably come in and get himself another damned medal!"

Joan allowed herself to be bolstered by his infectious enthusiasm. It wasn't hard to do. All the work Ultra had done over the past few weeks, and the stunning announcement that the entire Kido Butai, or at least that of it that was engaged at Midway, had been destroyed was glorious news indeed. She had to believe that her own husband would also prevail.

280 MILES SOUTH OF MIDWAY ATOLL

The waiting was becoming intolerable.

For hours now, *Bull Shark* and her crew had sat idle, hanging four hundred feet below the ocean's surface, remaining both quiet and vigilant. With nothing to do but watch the temperature and humidity gauges rise, the crew was becoming restless and bored, as well as anxious.

Burt Pendergast was chief among these. Although like the others aboard who'd partaken of Plank's little supply of helpers, the anxiety was somewhat artificial due to the withdrawal from the chemicals that their bodies had begun to crave. Unlike those other men... Ingram, Swooping Hawk, Griggs, Smitty, and a few others... Pendergast's supply hadn't been cut off days before. The enlisted men were having a bit of trouble, but by now their bodies were detoxifying, and they hadn't been exposed to enough of the sedatives, uppers, or even the cocaine to become dangerously addicted.

Their second engineer, however, was a different story. Although his use had increased since coming aboard *Bull Shark*, it hadn't started there. He'd used all of the substances off and on for the better part of a year. And his assignment to the submarine had pushed him into a level of dependence that had crossed the line from recreational use to abuse.

Fortunately, at least, he was confined to his cabin and, with the two Amies still affecting his system, now considerably mellower than anyone else on board.

Why not? What the hell else was he gonna do?

"What's our position?" Turner asked after a long period of silence.

"Dead reckoning indicator says we've drifted maybe a hundred yards or so," Hotrod Hernandez called back softly. "Doesn't seem to be a lot of current around here, sir."

Near Hernandez's position at the chart desk in the conning tower, Joe Dutch sat on his stool next to Chet Rivers and half-listened with one ear cup pushed back so that he could both hear the returns on the sound gear and any orders directed his or Rivers's way. He looked at his partner, who squeezed his eyes shut and shook his head no.

Dutch turned around and looked at Begley, who was waiting for an answer to a whispered question. He shook his head no as well. Begley clenched a fist and yanked a pack of cigarettes from his blouse pocket and lit one.

"Do you think he got away?" Web Clayton asked Turner almost in his ear. The captain was hunched over the gyro table with the rest of the plotting party. Gato leaned in as well to hear the answer.

"I don't think so," Turner said.

"But we're in that salt layer doodad, right?" Gato pressed. "Would we even hear them leaving?"

"No way to know," Turner said. "If they were quiet enough about it, we might. High-frequency sound is easier to block than low."

Gato frowned and wiped the long sleeve of his Japanese uniform across his forehead and eyes. He looked at the thermometer mounted near the bathythermograph. It read eighty-six degrees. The humidity monitor read seventy-five percent.

"Like a sauna in here," Clayton muttered, voicing Gato's thoughts. He placed a cigarette in his mouth and struck a match. The flame sputtered and sparked and seemed to take an inordinately long time to flare.

"I don't know how you people do this every day," Gato cranked as he reached out for one of Clayton's Winston's. "I thought you had AC on these boats."

"Shut down for quiet," Andy Post stated wryly.

"Hell, be thankful we're at four bills," Frank Nichols said, joining the clutch. "Water temperature is only fifty-seven. If we were at periscope depth, it'd be over ninety in here already."

The senior submariners, officers and enlisted alike, grinned wickedly at one another.

"Dis nuttin', Mr. Gato, sir," Martin said. "Give it four or tree more hour, and every pipe in dis here control room be dripping like a broken faucet... that's for true."

Post snickered and elbowed the man, "No respect for officers around here... seriously though, Lieutenant. We were down so long once you couldn't even light a butt. Just not enough oxygen left in the boat."

"Oh, well... I feel much better now," Gato grumped but smiled good-naturedly.

The control room fell silent again. Turner marveled at how quiet a submerged submarine could be, especially with all major machinery deactivated. No engines ran, no motors turned, no refrigeration equipment chugged and clanked. In each compartment, men had taken their shoes off to walk around if necessary. Every so often, the hull would emit a tiny creak or a little pop as temperature variations from within and without expanded or contracted her steel shell ever so slightly.

That's why when the faint but distinct sound entered the boat like a ghostly wisp of a passing breeze, it was all the more startling. The sound had been long and low and almost mournful, but it had also been unnatural in origin. It was the sound of a distant object impacting with the metal of another distant object.

Begley's eyes all but bugged out of his head as he stared the question at his two sonar operators. Dutch and Rivers's eyes met, and they were both wide with surprise.

"What the hell was that?" Begley hissed. "Sounded like metallic thunder... but really far off."

The description was apt. However, with the enhancement of the JP sound head, the two men at the sonar gear had a clearer and better description. Dutch nudged Rivers.

"Sir..." Rivers turned halfway around. "I'd say that somebody within two thousand yards or less dropped something awfully heavy on a metal deck. That sound was due to the distortion of the initial sound wave through the distance of water and being bent by the halocline."

"The other boat?" Begley asked hopefully.

"Undoubtedly," Dutch said. "That or somebody's running a dump truck fifty miles away."

Begley slid down the ladder into the control room to report quietly. For although everyone was being discreet, and a submarine's inner hull was coated in cork insulation for both sound and heat retention... Turner had heard Rivers's report.

"Sir, did you hear that?" Begley asked.

"Yeah... and I heard Joe and Chet's report," Turner said.

"Assess the Japanese submarine, sir," Begley said.

"Concur," Turner replied.

"Shall I engage the drive and put on an up bubble to go up and locate them?" Begley asked.

Turner shook his head, 'No... no, let's play it a little cooler, XO. We're at about a hundred and sixty PSI at this depth. Let's use the two-twenty-five air supply to slowly... I mean *slowly*, Buck... pump the negative tank to sea. Then we blow MBT seven and the bow buoyancy. That ought to give us positive lift and we can slowly rise, nice and quiet like. We'll peek over the lip of the salt layer and have ourselves a good listen."

Begley was obviously not pleased with this conservative approach. He felt, and rightly so, that by ringing up a one-third bell and using the planes they could drive the submarine up and still not be heard by the enemy. However, he couldn't really argue, so he nodded and went back up the ladder.

There was a very low hiss as Buck Rogers himself worked the two-hundred-twenty-five-pound air manifold and carefully and slowly bled air into the various ballast tank systems. After this, the negative tank was pumped dry. Above the control room helm pedestal, the depth gauge needle began to quiver but didn't move appreciably.

Next, Rogers pumped the air from the safety tank. Now the needle began to rise, slowly at first but with a steady increase. The boat took on a slight rise by the bow, and she began to rise toward the evening light.

"What was that!?" Kajimora raged, barely able to control his voice.

A moment before, a resounding *boom* had echoed through the ship as somewhere aft and below, something heavy was dropped. The realization that he hadn't been blown to bits was short-lived, replaced almost immediately by the implications of what the accident might mean for his ship.

Osaka couldn't answer the question, but he had a fairly good idea, "Phone talker, from aft forward... all compartments report."

"If the Americans have failed to find us by now, they must certainly know our location after *that!*" Kajimora seethed. "Damn incompetence!"

The young phone talker's face suddenly blanched as he turned to make his report, "Captain... ordnance loading bay two reports... reports that a depth charge slipped from the hoist and fell to the deck."

Kajimora felt his stomach churn. Obviously, the hydrostatic pistol initiator hadn't been set or installed, or there would certainly have been an explosion followed by other sympathetic explosions.

"Sir," Osaka said calmly. "I shall go and investigate. Recommend we engage the drives and surface. At last report, three aircraft are ready to launch with bombs and depth charges."

"We're not ready," Kajimora protested, sounding almost plaintive.

"Ready or not," Osaka said. "That low-frequency sound has no doubt alerted our adversary. We must seize our chance and surface to get as many planes aloft as possible before they find us."

Kajimora let fly a string of vituperative that would've impressed the most seasoned sailor, "Very well! Go, Yakuin. Tell Hideki I want no less than four aircraft armed with bombs and the other three at least fully loaded with ammunition for their guns! Now *go!*"

"*Hai*!" Osaka said and vanished down the hatchway.

"Helm, all ahead full!" Kajimora ordered. "Diving officer, prepare to surface the ship. Blow all main ballast tanks, fifteen-degree rise on bow planes, ten-degree down angle on the stern!"

Osaka ran through the huge ship. Past the first battery compartment and into the third, where the ordnance storage areas were located. He nearly collided with his friend.

"Ryu!" Hideki said, eyes wide. "It's all right! The depth charge wasn't armed."

"I know," Osaka said. "We'd be dropping into the depths if it had. We're headed to the surface now. We must get every aircraft we have launched as soon as we get topside. What can we fly?"

Hideki shrugged, "The guns are all loaded. We're still working on the next bomb load. As you know, this is very difficult to do while the planes are in the hangars. At least two bombs or charges can only be attached once the plane leaves the hangar."

"All right," Osaka said. "Then what we must do is catapult aircraft and lift others into the sea. They can take off on their own. Otherwise, we'll have to launch as they're ready and hope we have the time. How about fuel?"

"This is done and has been for some time," Hideki said. "What is going on?"

"I believe the American submarine has been hiding *below* a salt layer," Osaka explained.

He followed Hideki into one of the side bays where men were very carefully attaching the hoist to a new depth charge. Above them, through the water-tight loading hatch that opened into the port hangar, were the sounds of men at work in the confined space.

"And you think that since we made that racket that they heard and will pursue us?" Hideki asked.

"Exactly."

"But they cannot fire underwater at us any more than we can," Hideki protested. "So, what of it?"

"How do we know there isn't an American destroyer up there?" Osaka insisted. "Or that the American submarine cannot outlast us? No, Omata... our stalemate has been broken. Now it is time to *act* and to act *decisively*. Definitive action is how great victories are won. If I learned nothing else from Admiral Yamamoto, it is that. The American will follow us to the surface and try to get a firing solution on us. If we get there ahead of him and run on our diesels into the wind, we can gain enough distance so that by the time he tries to fire, we will have a surprise of our own."

"And can we not fire on him?" Hideki asked.

Osaka grinned at his friend, "Yes, we can... and we will. We will strike him from the sea and from above! First, we swat this pest out of our way, Hideki... and then we head for Panama and put the cork in the bottle of the American war machine!"

CHAPTER 37

"Getting anything, fellas?" Turner asked as he hauled himself up the ladder and into the conning tower.

"Just some distorted machinery noise," Dutch cranked. "We're in the salt layer now?"

Turner nodded, "Yeah, rising at about ten feet per minute. Figure we'll be out of it in five or so."

"Sir..." Begley began. "Shouldn't we get underway? If that Jap sub began moving the minute they made that noise... they might be a couple thousand yards away from us now. And they'll get to the surface first."

Turner looked at him for a long moment. There were times when he was convinced that it was Begley's inexperience that made him do the things he did. Then there were other times, such as when Turner found out that Begley hadn't reported that coded directive when he felt that the man was intentionally challenging or conspiring against him.

At that moment, the captain had had enough. Yes, it was the XO's job to make suggestions or offer another point of view... but not after the captain had made a decision and certainly not in front of the men. Turner met his eyes, and Begley was surprised by the cold fury in them.

"Are you questioning my orders, mister?" Turner asked in a low and dangerous tone.

Begley blinked in surprise, "No... sir... I'm just pointing out that—"

"That with all of your *vast* experience in the combat trainer and in peacetime war games that you know better than I do, right?" Turner asked. "Such as when to and when not to report a coded directive from Midway, for example?"

Begley's mouth opened and closed, but nothing came out. His pallor was all the confirmation Turner needed, "I think you can best help me by assisting the plotting party below, XO."

Begley croaked out a yessir and all but jumped down the ladder. Turner wiped his face and cursed under his breath. He caught Pat Jarvis's eye and sighed heavily, "Remember what they said at sub school?"

"Watch out for those overly friendly strippers, they don't *really* think you're special?" Jarvis asked and grinned.

Turner laughed and was grateful to Jarvis for that, "Okay, that too... but no, I mean one of my instructors... hell, it might've been Mush Morton now that I think of it... told us that we should all pray we get a happy ship... that used to be us..."

"My abuela used to have a saying, sir," Hotrod Hernandez said kindly and with a straight face. "*Si el pollo está caliente, el día es bueno...* words to live by, Skipper."

"Wow, that sounds nice, Hotrod," Ted Balkley noted from his seat at the radar station. He didn't seem to notice the barely contained snickers from Mug Vigliano at the helm. "What's that mean?"

Hotrod smiled warmly and said, "Oh... it means that if things are bad, they can always get better."

Vigliano guffawed. Although he spoke Italian, it was close enough to Spanish that he could pick up most of it. Balkley looked confused.

"Jesus Christ, Hotrod!" Turner said as he laughed. "What have I told you about that shit? Balkley, he's putting you on. It means if the chicken is hot, the day is good."

"And that's what you use to guide your life, Hotrod?" Vigliano asked.

Hernandez shrugged and bowed his head modestly, "Well sure. Always listen to your granny... you're pretty good with the Spanish, Captain... do you speak it?"

"*Sí,*" Turner deadpanned, and that broke up the conning tower and all of the tension and gloominess that had been hanging over it for some time.

"Contact!" Rivers blurted out, instantly bringing everyone to attention. "Submerged contact, bearing zero-four-zero... range three thousand yards. Running on electric motors, sir... making four knots, I'd say."

"How deep?" Turner asked.

Rivers and Dutch both frowned. Dutch shook his head, "Without an active ping, we can't tell, sir... but I guess higher in the water column than us. They seem to be headed southeast."

"How much you want to bet that's the direction from which the wind is blowing," Turner said. "All right, we've got him. Helm, all ahead two-thirds. Steady up on the sound bearing."

"That'd be one-three-zero true," Rivers stated.

"You heard the man, Mug," Turner said. "Sound the general alarm! Battle stations torpedo!"

The gonging rang through the ship. It was mostly unnecessary, as most of the men were already at their posts or waiting for the word. But now that the captain had made it official, the excitement, fear, and expectation began to ramp up throughout the boat.

In his cabin, Burt Pendergast was jerked from a restive sleep filled with bizarre dreams and unpleasant imagery. It took his addled and over-groggy mind many long seconds to comprehend what he was hearing. When it finally did, he sat up in his bunk and tried to force himself back to full awareness but found that it was like swimming in pudding.

He leaned over and began to fumble inside his pillowcase. His hand finally found the bit of foil and pulled it out. He clumsily unwrapped the packet and the contents spilled across his lap. He selected two of the little headache powder packets, opened them and then tipped his head back. The white powder went down into his nostrils, where he snorted it in deeply and then coughed.

Immediately the cocaine began to work on him, but not fast enough. In Pendergast's muddle-headed state, he was terrified that someone would burst through the curtain to tell him that he was needed in the engine spaces or maybe even to go topside and man a gun.

"I'm in no shape for that shit..." he muttered aloud, his own voice sounding oddly garbled in his ears.

He picked up the two remaining Bennies and blinked at them. What did these do again? God, why am I so jittery and stupid?

He suddenly remembered that the Benzedrine was meant to pep you up. Good... he needed pepping. Pendergast popped the two pills in his mouth and chased them down with the dregs of the cold coffee that still sat on the little table near the bunks. He lay back and waited for the speed to kick in, not knowing that he now had narcotics and barbiturates fighting for control in his bloodstream.

"Depth now one-five-zero feet," Frank Nichols said from his position behind the men at the diving station.

"Switch to hydraulics," Turner said from above. "I think the time for stealth is over. Get the AC going too. Pat, get ahold of the torpedo rooms. Set depth on all weapons to four feet. Speed fast."

"I think they've surfaced... yes, I can hear diesels coming online," Rivers said. "Range to target three-seven-zero-zero yards."

"All ahead full," Turner said. "We don't want them to get *too* far ahead. Gato, get up here!"

The pilot's head appeared in the hatch, "Sir?"

"How long does it take that boat to launch her birds?" Turner asked.

"They can get all eight in the air in about a half-hour if they push it," Gato replied. "They have to drag two out of the hangars, unfold the wings and vertical stabilizer, and then attach the sponsons. Then the cranes lift them onto the catapults, and they launch in succession."

"Christ, and they're already almost two miles ahead and will no doubt start running into the wind at flank speed," Turner mused. "Which is?"

Gato frowned, "I think fourteen knots."

"Frank, get me to periscope depth, smartly," Turner shouted down the hatch. "Standby to switch to diesels on snorkel."

"Periscope depth, aye," Nichols said. "Full rise on the bow planes, twenty-degree down angle on the stern... flooding safety... depth now one-two-zero feet..."

The submarine had two sets of horizontal planes. Two on the bow and two near the rudder. In order to move the ship up and down in the water column, the submarine was kept as close to a neutral or even slightly positive buoyancy when submerged as possible. In this way, the boat could be moved vertically through the water column not by the noisy venting and blowing of ballast tanks but by adjusting the planes and flying the boat through the water, not unlike an aircraft.

The bow planes were angled in such a way as to use the water pressure flowing over them to lift the bow by angling the planes upward or pushing the bow down by angling the planes downward.

In contrast, the stern planes worked in the opposite way. If you wanted to go deeper, you angled the stern planes upward, which lifted the stern of the boat in relation to the bow. This allowed the screws to point upward, thus pushing the submarine deeper. The opposite was true to go shallower.

"Assess target is accelerating," Dutch stated.

"Making turns for nine knots and increasing," Rivers confirmed. "Range is opening... now four-two-five-zero yards."

"Oh, no you don't..." Turner muttered. "Confirm range to target, sonar. Give me an active ping. Pat, start your solution. Buck, you down there?"

"Yes, sir," Rogers called out from the control room where Turner knew he'd be.

"Start getting a gunnery team together," Turner said. "I have a feeling we're gonna need to do some topside work."

There were chuckles in the control room and in the conning tower. From below, somebody muttered, "You don't say…"

"Enough men to work both deck guns, the AAs and a couple of Ma Deuces, Buck," Turner said. "We're gonna have to fight off some aircraft while we set up on this bastard, I think."

"Yes, sir!" Rogers enthused. Like most of the men aboard, he loved gunnery.

Generally speaking, a submarine's job was not to actively engage targets on the surface. That is to say, airborne targets or offensive ships. A submarine was most effective when it remained undetected and could deploy its limited supply of torpedoes effectively against enemy shipping.

However, like all the fleet boats, *Bull Shark's* surface armament was significant for a ship of her size. Now with two five-inch deck guns, a 40mm four-barreled Pom-Pom and a 20mm two-barreled Oerlikon, the ship could not only defend herself aggressively but mount a respectable offense as well. This was further augmented by attaching .50 caliber machine guns to special stanchions on the cigarette deck.

The difficulty for the men manning this impressive armament was that the submarine's upper surfaces offered little protection against incoming fire. This was especially true when dealing with marauding aircraft.

When it came to airplanes, unless the guns were already manned and ready, a submarine's best option was to simply submerge and remove herself from the plane's ability to damage her. Under normal circumstances, this is just what most submarines did.

However, Turner had a dilemma. First, he needed the enemy submarine to be on the surface in order to have any hope of hitting her. That also meant that *Bull Shark* must be on or near the surface herself. While the submarine could fire torpedoes from periscope depth or even deeper, she couldn't keep up with a ship running on diesels while she ran on electric motors only.

Certainly, in *Bull Shark's* case, things were different. The unique snorkel feature allowed the submarine to run on diesels while at periscope depth. However, this also kept her shallow enough to be vulnerable to either a torpedo attack or a bombing run from enemy airplanes. So, it was either stay deep or fall behind, stay at periscope depth and hope for a firing solution before the boat was bombed or depth-charged into shrapnel… or surface and be able to fight back with everything she had. This was what Turner intended to do, for even if the boat survived the aerial attacks at periscope depth, she might not be able to effectively deploy her weapons under those circumstances.

————

A powerful whine began to grow, its wavelength stretched out by the Doppler Effect and seeming to take a long time to increase to full volume before gonging against *Ribaiasan's* outer hull. The sonar operator had time to lift the headphones off his ears before the powerful active ping deafened him. He turned to his commanding officer and quite unnecessarily announced that they'd just been subjected to an active sonar blast.

Kajimora nodded, "Range?"

"American submarine appears to be directly behind us at four-five-eight-zero meters," the young man said. "Unable to determine their speed on passive sonar due to engine noise interference."

Kajimora knew that too. Under other circumstances, he'd chastise the fool for telling him what he already knew. At that time, however, his mind was too absorbed in combat. He turned his periscope to face aft and pressed his face to the eyepiece. He saw nothing. On the surface, he had a periscope height of sixty feet and should be able to see a surface object for nearly a dozen miles, especially with the sun still hanging above the horizon.

The enemy was still submerged or at periscope depth with their scope down. That meant that the American would be falling well behind. Even the best submarine speed on battery power alone was hardly more than ten knots.

Above him, he heard the distinct sound of a steam catapult being fired off. The elongated scream of hissing steam as the catapult car was rocketed forward, dragging the airplane along with it and accelerating to over ninety knots in a matter of seconds, and then the *clack, clack, clack* as the car was braked at the end of the hundred-foot run filled Kajimora with excitement and a sense of triumph. That was the second aircraft, and it would only be minutes before the next two were launched.

Kajimora knew he had plenty of time. Even should the American submarine come to the surface and run at flank speed, he had time to get all of his airplanes off the deck. It was rumored that the newer fleet boats could run at over twenty-two knots on the surface. Even if that were so, at an overtake speed of eight knots, it would take the American nearly twenty minutes to come within effective torpedo range.

Plenty of time to launch his birds and harass the submarine while she tried to close with his own. It might even be enough time for Kajimora to get a firing solution of his own. At high speed, the sonar would be useless, but with the American directly behind him, it should be possible to get good range bearings from the periscope and then turn to port or starboard enough to send his torpedoes astern. One way or another, the foolish American was driving right into *Leviathan's* hungry jaws.

Up on the bridge, Ryu Osaka and Omata Hideki were not as arrogantly optimistic. Optimistic, yes, but not so much that they would underestimate their adversary. This was the same submarine that had evaded them several days before, diving to more than seven hundred feet and then surfacing to more likely than not sink the light cruiser that had been *Ribaiasan's* escort. And now here they were again, appearing out of nowhere as if by sorcery.

While the Japanese ship had her advantages, most of which lie with her air group, Osaka knew the American had them as well. They were faster, more maneuverable, and better armed. Also, there was perhaps an hour of daylight left. Once that was gone, the aircraft would not be nearly as effective, while the American, probably equipped with radar, would not be in any way hindered.

"We must strike hard and fast, my friend," Osaka told Hideki. "If they get close enough to fire a full spread of torpedoes..."

"I understand," Hideki said, smiling reassuringly as he watched the flight crews quickly fastening the pontoons to the next two aircraft. "I've loaded three planes with two two-hundred-kilo bombs and three with two depth charges each. These can be set at a variety of depths from the airplane cockpits. All seven are fully loaded with rounds for their machine guns. The American is only rushing to his own death."

Osaka nodded, "I hope so, my friend. But let us not underestimate them."

"I've ordered our pilots to search astern," Hideki said, holding up a heavy-duty two-way radio. "They should be able to see them even at one hundred feet or more in these clean waters."

As if to prove the point, the radio crackled, *"Eagle's Nest, Eagle's Nest... Eagle One. Have spotted submerged submarine running astern. Estimate four kilometers astern. They appear to be at periscope depth, as something is drawing a feather line on the surface."*

"Acknowledged, Eagle One," Hideki said into his radio.

"Eagle's Nest, shall we attack?"

"Negative, Eagle Flight," Hideki said. "Standby for reinforcement. Your ordnance supply is limited. We must choose our time wisely."

"Acknowledged, Eagle's Nest... will observe and advise."

"They *could* hit them, Ryu," Hideki said. "The submarine is on a steady course and making herself obvious. Eagle Flight One has bombs, and Two has depth charges."

Osaka smiled at his eager friend, "Not yet, Omata... not yet. I want to hit them with a *coup de gras*. At best, we sink them... at worst, we force them to surface and then our aircraft can hammer them with machine gun fire while *we* set up for the torpedo kill shot."

Hideki smiled, and the two men watched as the next two aircraft were lifted onto the catapults. Even if these were the last two, both men felt that it would be more than enough to rid themselves of the hound now nipping at their heels.

———

"They've got two birds aloft," Turner called as he gazed through his search periscope. Even reinforced to function at high speeds, its image still shivered considerably at their current speed. "Dammit, I wish we were closer! I'd send a few pickles their way and at least give them something else to think about..."

"What do you think his height is?" Hotrod Hernandez, now acting as periscope assistant, asked.

"Hard to say..." Turner said, pointing at the open ONI-208-J vessel recognition book lying open on the chart desk. Hotrod had flipped through until he found the page with the I-class submarine silhouette. "Probably no higher than that guy. Maybe add ten percent. He's got these two cranes rigged out to either side of the conning tower... but they don't matter. Use his known radio mast height and add ten feet, I'd say."

Hernandez glanced at the book, "I'd say forty feet then."

Turner nodded and adjusted the stadimeter knob on the periscope barrel just under the right handle, "Range... mark."

"Two-nine-zero-zero," Hernandez reported, reading the stadimeter range scale on the front of the periscope.

"Still too far," Turner grumbled. "What's our speed?"

"Bendix log indicates twenty-two knots," Vigliano stated.

Turner did the math in his head, "If we fire at a thousand yards, which is the earliest I'd do so... we've got nineteen hundred to cover at a closure of eight knots... just under eight minutes. Dammit! There go two more planes!"

"What if we surface and hit them with the deck gun?" Jarvis asked. "If she's right ahead of us, it should be child's play to send a few rounds up their ass."

"Yeah, and get bombed into razor blades before we can load and fire," Turner said unhappily. "I'll bet you a twelve-year-old bottle of single-malt that as soon as they've got all their birds up, or at least most of them, they're coming after us and dropping a henhouse full of eggs. Two of them are already circling up there."

"Confirmed," Balkley said, studying both the SD and SJ radar displays. "SD indicates multiple airborne contacts maintaining a range of a thousand yards or less."

"Orbiting us," Jarvis grumped. "Dammit, if we only had the AAs manned already..."

"Guns we can deal with," Turner said. "But I'm not gonna risk going topside and opening us up to bombs while we get our shit together... Not just yet... uh-oh..."

"Skipper?" Dutch asked, voicing everyone's concern.

"I think they're forming up!" Turner said. "Frank, be ready. If we need to dive, you're gonna need to shut the induction and kill the rock crushers in a hurry!"

"Standing by!" Nichols said with an odd calm.

Turner watched as the four tiny black airplane silhouettes joined together far forward and began to circle to his left as a single formation. He spun the scope around and watched as the airplanes banked counter-clockwise and then suddenly angled straight for his lens, which was pointed off the port quarter. He gritted his teeth, "Attack run! Shit! They're lined up abeam... won't be able to evade! Hard dive! Hard dive! Down scope!"

Ah-ooga! Ah-ooga!

The diving alarm blatted, and the deep rumble and vibration of the diesels suddenly quit. After another moment, a man called out from below that main induction was closed, and the bow suddenly dipped forward at a steep angle, nearly throwing Turner off his feet. The only thing that kept him from sliding into Vigliano's chair was the death grip he held on the periscope handle and Hotrod's own death grip on his sleeve. Turner flipped the handles up and braced himself as the scope slid down into its well.

Chapter 38

"Eagle's Nest, Eagle Flight One," the flight leader called over his radio as he examined the dark shape beneath the ocean, topped by a line of foam. "There appears to be something... strange about the target."

A pause, and then the CAG came on, *"Eagle Flight One, Eagle's Nest... specify."*

"Well, sir..." the pilot puzzled. "It appears as if... engine smoke is coming out of their periscope... and that appears quite larger than usual... no, wait... I see *two* periscopes now. One forward and thin, with another behind that is very large and emitting the smoke. I... I can't explain it, sir."

Hideki looked to Osaka in hopes that he'd offer some explanation. The first officer's greater submarine experience might give him and his pilots a clue.

Osaka frowned, "Ask how fast the target is going."

Hideki did so.

"Unknown... however, target appears to be closing on Eagle's Nest," the bewildered pilot said.

"Which means they're making greater than fourteen knots..." Osaka puzzled. "And there is no way they can do that on battery power alone... and if they're making smoke, this indicates that they're running at flank and overloading their engines..."

"At periscope depth?" Hideki asked in disbelief.

Osaka drummed his fingers on the teak bridge railing for a long moment, and then a slow smile began to grow, "Evidently, our side is not the only side that can innovate, Omata. Have you ever heard of a snorkel?"

Hideki frowned, "Something divers can use to breathe beneath but close to the surface of the water..."

Osaka nodded, "During the Great War, a Scot began fooling around with such a device for a submarine. As you know, the diesels, like the men who run them, must breathe. This is why we have the main induction valve that we open when running on the surface. It allows the diesels to draw in air that is then compressed and super-heated in the pistons. Now, suppose that you attach a telescoping pipe to the main induction. A pipe, perhaps... three or four feet in diameter. Like the periscope, it can be raised and lowered. Now you can remain at periscope depth and still run your engines, both providing speed and electrical power."

"Ingenious..." Hideki had to admit. "But I have never heard of such a thing being tried."

Osaka shrugged, "Intelligence reports have it that Norway is developing something like it. No doubt our Nazi allies would literally *kill* for such an advantage. Perhaps the Americans have made such a thing work. At any rate, this means that the submarine chasing us is catching up while staying below the surface. I believe it's time we did attack, my friend."

Hideki grinned a predatory grin and raised his radio, "Eagle Flight, Eagle Flight... permission to attack the target. Bombers first and depth chargers second. Depth charges set to thirty meters. Drop one only and reserve the second."

The pilot of Eagle's Flight One banked his aircraft and looped around to approach the target from its starboard quarter, from directly out of the sun. He was one of the planes armed with two two-hundred-kilo bombs. Dive bombs. He circled around from one thousand meters and then angled down, lining up the painted reticule on his windscreen with a point just forward of the submarine's dark shape below the water. Even as he roared in, he couldn't help but feel as if he were approaching a giant shark. A predator whose lust for blood was solely focused on *his* ship.

"Steady..." he told his observer and bombardier. "Steady..."

"They are diving!" the co-pilot exclaimed, pointing ahead.

The pilot laughed, "Too late for them! Banzai! Drop, drop, drop!"

The plane jolted as its two bombs were released and the pilot yanked back on the yoke, pulling the floatplane out of its steep descent only one hundred meters above the sea.

———

Even after the engines were shut down, *Bull Shark* had enough way on her that she plunged down at an impressive rate, not needing to vent her ballast tanks. This was good because Turner would be headed back up after the assault was over, assuming they survived it.

"Now passing one hundred feet!" Frank shouted from below.

"Mug, all ahead full!" Turner shouted. "Right standard rudder!"

"Splashes!" Rivers shouted as, in unison, he and Dutch yanked their headphones off.

"Rig ship for—"

Turner never finished. Four explosions, occurring five seconds apart, turned the ocean around the submarine into a roaring, boiling maelstrom. Eight hundred kilograms of high explosive, more than seventeen hundred pounds of TNT, blasted the ocean and threw up thousands of tons of seawater into the air and shoved even more outward in all directions.

The dive bombs had plunged into the sea and detonated at about sixty feet. Although the blast was powerful, water's incompressibility directed most of the destructive force toward the path of least resistance.

Upward. While water was shoved aside in all directions, only to smash back into the vacuum with incredible force, setting off pulsing compression waves in all directions, most of the energy was sent up. However, enough remained to slam into the plunging submarine, rocking and shaking her hard enough to smash light bulbs and send loose objects... and men... tumbling to the decks.

"—for depth charge!" Turner shouted over the din.

"Splashes!" Rivers reported, daring to set the headphones on his head but not exactly over his ears again. "Assess depth charges, sir!"

"Left full rudder!" Turner snapped.

"Sir, my rudder is left full!" Mug replied.

Bull Shark drove downward, her speed now reduced to a mere eight knots but still fast enough to make the depth gauge needle swing visibly.

"Now passing one-six-zero feet!" Nichols called out.

How deep had the depth charges been set? Periscope depth? No... maybe a little deeper to get beneath them?

"Now passing two-zero-zero—"

Nichols stopped when the sound of two audible clicks seemed somehow to cut through the sound of his voice, and then the explosions of two three-hundred-pound ashcan warheads boomed in the darkness. They'd been fairly close but not close enough to do any more than rattle the men inside the boat. Although more bulbs and gauge glasses shattered, and more cork insulation fluttered about the compartments, no one was very badly knocked about.

"Maybe a hundred feet!" Rivers said, gasping as he reset his headphones.

Dutch nodded, "Concur."

"Sir!" the control room phone talker shouted up. "Maneuvering, con... flooding from overhead. Chief Brannigan says the weld has cracked."

"How bad?" Turner asked.

A pause and then, "Annoying but not dangerous yet, he says, sir."

"Well, it won't be a problem long," Turner said. "Frank, put us on the roof! Get the drain pump online! Sound battle stations gun action! Get your guys ready, Buck!"

————

"Report!" Hideki shouted, looking back, and wishing he could see more. The periscope sheers and other masts blocked the view astern, as did the three and a half meter cylinders that were the submarine's airplane hangars.

"Ordnance deployed," Eagle's Flight One stated. *"Four bombs detonated, two depth charges deployed... no debris or oil slick, however. The submarine was diving hard, and we can no longer see them."*

"They went deep," Osaka said. He thumbed the bridge speaker. "Conning tower, bridge. Assess target has gone deep and is falling behind. Recommend throttling back and doing an active sonar search."

"And give up our advantage?" Kajimora asked. *"Nonsense! How much longer on the aircraft?"*

The crews were just getting the next two planes rigged. Hideki held up five fingers.

"Five minutes, Captain," Osaka said. "Recommend slowing for an active ping. We can speed up again afterward. But this will assist our planes on knowing where to drop their depth charges."

Kajimora swore and made a dismissive sound, *"Negative!"*

Osaka wanted nothing more than to drop down through the hatch and ram his fist into the arrogant fool's mouth. He clenched his fists hard, counted backward from ten and then said in a tone that sounded extraordinarily calm to his ears, "Then recommend an active ping anyway. We may get a contact."

"Negative, Yakuin. That would allow our enemy to home in on us."

"We're already running at high speed, sir," Osaka stated. "They know *exactly* where *we* are. It would be advantageous if *we* could say the same."

Hideki grinned but held his tongue.

"Were you promoted during the last watch?" Kajimora scolded.

Osaka nearly lost control. He actually reached down and squeezed the grip of his sidearm. The warring emotions played in him for a long moment. The urge to go below and put a bullet in the bastard's brain very nearly won out. It was only the technical order that Hideki gave his pilots next that saved Kajimora's life.

"Eagle's Flight!" Hideki said into his radio. "Did you mark the position of your weapons drop?"

An affirmative.

"Good, now listen," Hideki said, glancing at Osaka for confirmation. "We shall assume the target is still chasing us, but now at a reduced speed of..."

"Nine knots," Osaka said almost absently.

"Nine knots," Hideki continued. "Set the depth on your weapons to seventy meters and calculate time and distance of where the submarine is. Drop your weapons... fifty meters ahead of your calculated plot. Understand?"

A long pause, and then the pilot of Eagle's Flight Two and Four acknowledged.

"Tell them to watch for the surface wake," Osaka informed his friend. "It will not be large and will lag behind the submarine's course, but it will act as a marker."

"Start your run," Osaka said. He then repeated Osaka's advice and went on, "Eagle's Flights One and Three, since your ordnance is expended, orbit far back and stand by for a strafing run in the event the submarine comes to the surface."

———

Bull Shark now altered her angle and drove upward at a steep twenty degrees. Turner ordered up a flank bell to compensate for the speed loss. Men crowded the conning tower and, in the wardroom, where the gun service hatch was located. Other men waited near the mess room hatch so they could access the stern deck gun faster as well. Already each of these teams, in addition to the two gun servers, had four men ready with shells clutched in their arms and ready to pass up more in train.

In the conning tower, Buck Rogers, Clancy Weiss, the two cooks, and four more men waited to act as ammo servers for the two cannons. Martin and Borshowski each held a big .50 cal in their arms. The other four men, which included Fred Swooping Hawk, Doug Ingram, Horris Eckhart, and Steve Plank, all held armloads of ammo.

"Now passing one-six-zero feet!" Frank called out.

"Splashes!" Dutch and Rivers said in unison. "Ahead of us, sir!"

"Christ!" Turner exclaimed, wrapping himself around the bridge ladder. "Everybody *hang on!*"

His shout was rather anti-climactic. The ashcans descended at a rate of seven feet per second, and if they were set at the same depth as before, the submarine would have to wait a good fourteen seconds for the explosions. Yet they didn't come. More than one man was counting, and they were all surprised to reach twenty... then twenty-five...

"Now passing nine-zero feet," Frank reported.

"Blow all main ballast, safety and negative tanks, Frank, now!" Turner snapped, suddenly realizing that the Japs had set their weapons to try and get the submarine while she was deep.

The hiss of the high-pressure air blowing water out the bottom of the open ballast tanks drowned out the two clicks below and occurred just to port and starboard of the ship's midsection. The concussive booms that shook her like a rag doll, however, left no question as to what happened. Although below the keel and more than sixty feet down, the explosive force did what it had done before... sent most of its energy upward.

Bull Shark was slammed upward and rocked side to side as the shockwaves struck her, toppling men from their posts, shattering more bulbs, loosening valve packings, and knocking the drain pump off its mountings.

Luckily the ship was already rising, so in a dramatic display of physics, the three-hundred -eleven foot, sixteen-hundred-ton submarine... minus the water that allowed her to dive... burst from the sea like a porpoising orca. A full hundred feet of her bow came clear out of the water, trailing foam down her sides and from her limber holes between the deck and the hull. The bow crashed down, sending up sheets of spray in all directions nearly as high in the air as she was long.

Turner found himself lying at Vigliano's feet and felt a deep and repetitive throbbing in his ankle. As he sat up and tried to pull himself to his feet, a pair of strong hands grasped him under the arms and hauled him upright. Pat Jarvis's face swam into Turner's vision.

"You all right, sir?" Jarvis asked. The concern Turner saw on Jarvis's face was touching, yet it seemed bizarre when contrasted with the blood that ran down the left side from a small gash over his left temple.

"I'm alive... but I'm not sure I'm pleased about it... the ship?"

"Rigged for surface, sir," Jarvis said. "Gun crews are already headed upstairs."

"Good... help me up there," Turner said. "Get the XO in here to take the periscope, Pat..."

"You want me on deck to oversee the firing party?" Jarvis asked.

"No... want you on the TDC, at least until we lock into that son of a bitch," Turner said, starting up the ladder using his two hands and one foot.

"XO to the conning tower!" Jarvis said. He then ducked and got one of his broad shoulders under Turner's ass and propelled the skipper up and through the hatch. Even before his shoulders were up, Paul Rogers had his hands under the captain's armpits and was heaving him up on deck.

"Jesus, sir!" Rogers said and grinned. "You drive like a maniac."

"Not my fault, occifer... I'm drunk," Turner said and grinned crookedly. "Now shoot those fuckers down, Buck!"

Even as he gave the order, anti-aircraft weapons began to clatter all around him. The din was chaotic and wonderful to Turner's ears. He was finally getting to fight back. He'd never been one to take being shot at or bombed while being unable to respond with very great aplomb.

It didn't take long to man and ready the AA cannons. It took even less time for the two machine guns to be set up. One simply inserted the stud of the weapon into the stanchion mount, opened the feed tray, slapped in a belt or drum of ammo and charged the weapon. Then you started knocking down Jap cocksuckers.

Which, evidently, was exactly what was in progress on either side of the cigarette deck, with boatswain's mate Steve Plank screaming out that very thing as he opened fire with his Browning M2 "Ma Deuce" fifty cal.

"Pursuit course!" Turner barked at Hotrod, who'd come up to the bridge to act as quartermaster. "All ahead flank! Somebody get me a pair of damned binoculars."

Hernandez handed him the big and powerful 7x50 models that served the Navy so well. Turner brought the rugged Bausch and Lomb glasses to his eyes and scoped the fleeing *Leviathan*.

"God *damn* that's a girl!" he exclaimed, scanning the huge submarine as it desperately tried to leave *Bull Shark* behind.

On the foredeck below him, Turner saw that Eddie Carlson and Tank Broderick were at their customary positions on the five-inch. Fred Swooping Hawk was just feeding a fifty-two-pound, five-inch shell into the breech, even as Tank spun the azimuth wheel and Eddie adjusted his elevation.

Behind them, on his raised blister forward of the bridge railing, the COB was swinging his four-barrel Pom-Pom to track one of the floatplanes that was swooping in on a strafing run. Buck leaned back, pressed his rear end hard into the butt-strap, and raised the barrels of the impressive Devil's Piano and opened fire. The throaty rattle of the big cannon made Turner's blood run swiftly. Even more so as he watched with admiration and pride as Buck walked the tracer rounds across the sky and right into the oncoming Aichi's path.

The big shells smashed into the plane, ripping into it, and tearing through its fragile aluminum hull as if it were little more than crepe paper. The pilots were hit multiple times, their bodies hideously mangled by the big slugs. Their pain, if any, didn't last long as the aviation fuel in the wing tanks ignited and the plane became an incandescent ball of fire and smoke that tumbled into the sea.

"Scratch one floater!" Buck roared triumphantly.

"Down! Down!" screamed Doug Ingram from beside Steve Plank, where he was acting as ammo server and lookout. "Two coming in!"

"*FUCK YOU, Tojo!*" Bill Borshowski, mess attendant second class and Henrie Martin's assistant cook, screamed in almost mindless rage and defiance as he swung the twin barrels of his 20mm cannon straight at the onrushing aircraft and squeezed the firing handle. His battle cry matched the staccato beat of his weapon as he sent dozens of rounds into the starboard of the two planes.

Once again, another aircraft erupted into flames and burning debris. Borshowski didn't get the chance to fire again, as his assistant, fireman Horris Eckhart, tackled him and drove both of them to the deck. As the two men hit the deck along with both fifty caliber teams, the Japanese plane opened fire, sending its own 20mm rounds skittering across the ocean, stitching a straight line up to and over the submarine's deck right in line with the after five-inch gun. Several rounds tore into torpedoman Johnny Wexler, cutting him in half at the abdomen and killing him instantly. At least one round either ricocheted or hit Jack Smitty and plowed a furrow in his right thigh. It was almost impossible to tell whose blood soaked his jeans, as a great deal of Wexler's was already covering him.

Even as Smitty began to scream, mostly from horror rather than pain as yet, Doug Ingram leapt to his feet, managing to dodge the hand that Plank shot out to hold him down. He grabbed ahold of the M2, swung it to his left, lined up as best he could on the Aichi floatplane, only a hundred feet above the sea and began firing. He'd only ever fired the weapon a few times at drills. Yet, he remembered very clearly the advice he was given. When firing at a fast-moving object like a plane, you didn't aim *for* the object; you aimed *ahead* of where it was going. Let the plane come to your bullets and simply watch the tracers. Watch where they went and walk them right into your target.

Ingram held down the trigger as he too screamed out with adrenaline-fueled fury. So keyed up was he that he didn't even hear the weapon dry firing. All he could do was watch in astonishment as the red lines of his tracers suddenly met the airplane, and the airplane's left wing become a bright smoking pillar of flame.

Ingram felt the hand of Plank on his arm, "You got him, kid!"

"Radar, bridge... range to target?" Turner shouted into the bridge transmitter over the howling wind of the ship's twenty-two knots of speed.

"*Bridge, radar... two-one-zero-zero yards, sir!*" Balkley's voice said from the speaker.

"Hotrod, give me a little right rudder," Turner said. "I don't want to come straight up his six; I want to shoot from his four or four-thirty. Hear that up there, boys? We're gonna angle out to his starboard quarter!"

Carlson and Tank didn't even look back as they acknowledged. On the heels of Turner's declaration, Carlson depressed the firing pedal and the big gun boomed out, throwing its shell straight at the other submarine but just missing her masts by feet.

"Incoming aircraft!" somebody shouted from behind the bridge.

They'd gotten three, Turner knew. The sun was nearly gone below the horizon now, and they still had three left. One in the air and two on the carrier about to be launched. The oncoming darkness would only help the submarine, but Turner knew this battle would be decided long before then. Either *Bull Shark* or the carrier would be dead long before the thirty minutes or so until full dark would pass.

CHAPTER 39

"Sparky! Mr. Jarvis says order of tubes is two, four, six. Depth six feet, speed high," the compartment phone talker shouted a bit too loudly.

"Take it easy, Parker," Sparks said nonchalantly as if there wasn't a desperate anti-aircraft battle and deck gun action going on above and abaft all their heads. "Jump to it, Grigsy, Jonesy."

Sparks was letting his men handle the torpedo procedures. As he watched, with Perkins and Wilkes standing by as well, the two junior torpedomen went to work. After the COB and Sparky had sat him down, Griggs had straightened himself out nicely. He shook off the dope he was starting to get used to and, as if to make up for his earlier slackness, dove into his duties and his studies with admirable tenacity.

Griggs was adjusting the depth spindle on the three portside tubes. As he finished with number two, Bob Jones came in and adjusted the speed selection. Once Jones moved down from tube two, Wilkes came in and quickly tested the impulse air flask and set the ready fire lever.

"Phone talker, report tubes two, four, and six ready to fire," Sparky called back to Parker as he himself stepped forward and flipped up the safety guards on the manual firing triggers.

"Forward torpedo reports ready to fire," Jarvis announced as he fiddled with his machine. "Just need some solution data."

Begley was staring into the search periscope, turning it back and forth. Jarvis wondered what the hell he was looking at. The Jap planes?

"XO?" he prodded.

"Captain's on the TBT," Begley snapped.

"He sounds a little busy up there," Jarvis said. "I could use a periscope observation in the meantime!"

Begley ignored him. Jarvis stared at the man's backside only feet away and had to clamp down on the desire to plant his foot in the seat of the XO's pants, "Radar, give me a fix. Joe, Chet, give me an active ping. I need some course, speed, and range settings."

"*Conning tower, bridge! Incoming strafing run! Duck!*"

Nobody questioned the captain's urgent shout, both over the speaker and down the hatch. Everyone toppled from their chairs and flattened themselves on whatever piece of deck they could manage. Begley, however, either didn't hear the warning or didn't heed it because he still stood behind the search scope, spinning to face just aft of the starboard beam.

"Get down, ya' damned fool!" Jarvis snapped, reaching out for Begley's leg.

Every man in the conning tower heard it. The scream of a radial engine as an airplane came in low. Even over the sounds of the roaring diesels, the distinct airplane engine was audible, as were its 20mm cannons opening up on the submarine's topsides. The sound was joined by the far louder and deeper rhythmic tattoo of *Bull Shark's* own machine guns and cannons.

The pilot walked his rounds across the water and then up and over the conning tower, chewing up the deck, the men and punching several thumb-sized holes in the pressure hull of the conning tower and the ship herself. The rounds that entered the tower smashed the SJ radar screen, gyrocompass repeater at the helm, chewed into the chart desk, and severed several of the cables that led into the sonar set. By some miracle, none struck the XO, who was actually watching the plane fly overhead and saw it explode when the COB nailed it with the Pom-Pom.

Pat Jarvis had had enough of this fool. He and the other men leapt to their feet, each looking at what damage had been done. Jarvis himself grabbed Begley by the back of his shirt and yanked him away from the scope. He grabbed the handles and spun around until he had the looming shape of the Japanese submarine in his sights.

"Constant bearing, mark!" Jarvis exclaimed.

Ted Balkley, now acting as periscope assistant since his surface search radar screen was shot to hell, read the bearing off the ring. "Three-three-five!"

"Mug, rudder amidships!" Jarvis barked as he adjusted the stadimeter knob, placing the crosshairs on the submarine's mast. "Range... mark!"

"One-one-five-five!" Balkley exclaimed.

Jarvis ran back and slid into the seat at the TDC, where he began cranking in the values, "Ted, poke your head up and see what the hell's going on up there!"

Balkley scrambled up the ladder. By then, Begley had recovered his wits and was headed back for the periscope, "Jarvis, what the hell—"

"Stow it!" Jarvis snapped.

The radarman popped up through the bridge hatch to see Turner and Hotrod at their positions. Turner was staring through the TBT, and Hotrod was continually clicking the switch on the bridge speaker.

"Teddy, why the hell isn't anybody answering?" Hernandez asked.

"Mr. Jarvis sent me up to find out, Hotrod," Balkley said.

Turner grunted, "Damned Japs must've taken out the speaker! Is Pat getting this TBT data?"

Balkley inquired below. Jarvis shouted up that he was.

"Sir, Mr. Jarvis and I just did a periscope observation, and he's cranking values into the TDC now," Balkley said.

"Okay, stay there, Ted," Turner ordered. "You relay when he's got a solution. Tell him I want to lead the fish, so put them out ahead of the target a little and give me a two-degree spread."

Balkley relayed that information. Jarvis acknowledged.

"Come on, Pat..." Turner muttered as he watched two more aircraft being placed on the submarine's catapults.

He tried not to think about the dead and wounded men behind him. Wexler and Eckhart had been killed. Smitty, Clancy Weiss, and Tank had been wounded in that last attack. Tank had removed his shirt and tied it around one of his big biceps and was still manning his post. Weiss had been hit in the shoulder by a ricochet and was sitting on the cigarette deck next to Smitty, with Leroy Pots pressing shirts to their wounds.

"Shoot, sir!" Balkley suddenly shouted, breaking Turner's reverie.

"Fire two... fire four... fire six!" Turner shouted, counting to seven between each order.

The ship shuddered with each launch, and the Captain and Hotrod watched as three boiling wakes lanced out from their boat and raced away, headed seemingly for a point ahead of their adversary.

Tank, Eddie, and Fred Swooping Hawk weren't watching. The Navajo slid another shell into the breech of the gun and secured it. Eddie took one last look through his sights, made a minor adjustment to the elevation wheel, and pressed the firing pedal. The big gun boomed, and everyone on *Bull Shark's* upper decks watched with amazed satisfaction as the shell flew straight and true and slammed into the target.

———

Kajimora had the American in his periscope sight and had already worked out a firing solution with his torpedo officer. As soon as the next two planes were airborne, he would make a sharp turn to starboard and open fire with his starboard tubes, and if he had time and if the first three didn't hit, he would continue the circle and fire the port tubes. The American would be his.

On the bridge of the *Ribaiasan,* Osaka and Omata watched as the cranes hoisted the next two aircraft onto the catapults. The flight officer at the tip of the bow raised his flag over his head, ready to launch. It was only a matter of seconds now...

Yet Osaka couldn't shake the feeling that seconds might be all they had. The American submarine's deck gun was homing in on them, and it would only be a few moments before the gunner had them bore-sighted. *Ribaiasan* had to maneuver, both to evade gunfire and torpedoes as well as so her own deck armament could be manned.

"Ready!" Hideki said, raising the radio to his mouth and a hand in the air to signal the flight officer to launch.

That's when it came. From astern, a thundering *boom* and then a heartbeat later, the ship was rocked with bone-jarring force as something smashed into the starboard hangar. The five-inch shell penetrated the metal skin, found a purchase within, and detonated.

Unfortunately for the Japanese ship, the shell had struck the next and final aircraft. The plane, loaded with aviation fuel and with a pair of bombs strapped to her underbelly, also detonated. Some of the force of the explosion found its way down the open loading hatch, killing half a dozen men before exploding several more bombs that were standing by there. Luckily for the submarine, most of the explosive force was contained in the compartment and above the platform deck. However, more men were killed, and a blaze began. Several welds below the water-line split and seawater began to pour into the munition's storage bays below the deck, most likely saving the ship from total destruction.

Most of the detonation inside the hangar, however, was directed forward through the two-hundred-foot tube. Like some monstrous cannon, the open end of the hangar belched a huge tongue of super-heated gas and flame and debris.

Osaka and Hideki were spared only by the force of the blast, knocking them both to the deck behind the bridge fairing. However, the airplanes forward of them were not. The tongue of flame engulfed the starboard aircraft as debris from inside the tube struck, shredding the vehicle, and igniting its own fuel. This explosion then consumed the other plane to port. This, in turn, sent a rolling ball of fire and death forward, incinerating the flight officer.

Below in the conning tower, men were sent tumbling in every direction. Only by wrapping his arms around the barrel of the periscope was Kajimora spared being flung across the compartment. The world around him seemed to roar in primal fury as bright orange flame lit up the open bridge hatch.

"Helm! Hard right rudder!" he half-yelled, half-coughed through the acrid smoke of electrical burnouts and the smoke from a fire that had started when the sonar station had been overloaded and began to burn.

There was no answer. The helmsman lay dazed against the bulkhead, blood flowing down the side of his face and staining his white uniform. Kajimora cursed and stumbled forward, taking hold of the wheel and yanking it hard to starboard, thinking that if he could get his bow around, he could fire his torpedoes.

For a moment, his bewildered mind believed that his action had somehow caused what happened next. Almost as soon as he turned the wheel, another ear-splitting explosion hammered the ship. The vessel's bow actually rose fifteen feet in the air, and she rolled twenty degrees to port. Kajimora's last conscious thought before he was thrown into the bulkhead and his head struck it, was to wonder what the hell he'd just done.

The captain hadn't caused the explosion, however. *Bull Shark's* torpedoes lanced across the other submarine's bow. The first two missed, but the third struck the hull right near the center of the forward torpedo room. The explosion ripped open the ballast tanks and the pressure hull and detonated several torpedoes sitting in their racks on that side. These then detonated those on the port side. The six that were in the tubes, ironically, never exploded. This was due in part to the fact that the sympathetic explosions blasted the entire forward end of the ship completely off, flooding the compartment and washing what was left of the torpedomen's bodies out into the sea.

This would have doomed the ship had the watertight door to the forward battery compartment not been sealed. Thus, although the ship's entire bow, nearly thirty feet of it, was gone, the ship's massive size and buoyancy kept her afloat.

The damage to men and equipment didn't stop there, however. The immense forces acting on the hull twisted it and bent it in strange ways that seemed to defy logic. Concussion waves flowed through the metal, deforming bulkheads and frames and finally twisting enough to cause the starboard propeller shaft to seize. As it ground to a halt, electrical surges from the three motors driving it flowed up through the circuits and across the buses, overloading the portside engines and starting electrical fires in the maneuvering room. Men in the engine rooms, maintaining enough of their wits to realize what was happening, killed all the engines and sealed fuel lines before the fires forward and aft grew hot enough to ignite the diesel in the lines and the subsequent half a million gallons in the tanks.

Although the ship was afloat, her wounds were mortal. She had no motive power, nearly a third of her crew had been killed and more wounded, and she was completely helpless and at the mercy of her enemy.

Ryu Osaka managed to pull himself to his feet, his body aching from cuts and bruises he couldn't even begin to identify. He reached down and assisted a dazed Hideki to his feet as well.

"Omata..." Osaka all but wheezed, "are you all right?"

"I..." the CAG had a cut over his left eye that was bleeding into it and down his face. His left arm seemed to be hanging limp at his side. "I'm alive. What... what happened?"

"We've been struck by a deck gun and a torpedo," Osaka coughed, the stink of the explosion still lingering in his nostrils. "We're dead in the water."

Hideki's face was pale with pain and horror, "What do we do?"

Osaka drew in a deep breath, coughed, and sighed, "We surrender, Omata. We get what men are still alive off the ship... and then scuttle her."

"Surrender?" Hideki said. "Become American prisoners of war? Be placed in one of their concentration camps and subjected to all manner of horrors? I would rather die here."

Osaka actually managed a smile at his friend, "Omata, you don't really believe that nonsense, do you? The Americans do not mistreat prisoners. Have no fear. Our men will be cared for. I cannot commit them to a watery death when they have a chance to live. They're young... all so young... can you come below with me? We must see how everyone faired and get you to the corpsman."

Hideki grimaced, "My left arm... I believe it's broken."

"I'll help you," Osaka said.

Before the men could go below, they saw the long slim shape of the American submarine pulling alongside them, only fifty meters away. Her impressive armament, more impressive now that Osaka could fully see it, was trained on them. A tall man with dark blonde hair stood on the submarine's bridge and raised a bull horn to his mouth.

"*Attention! Attention! Japanese submarine! This is Captain Arthur Turner, United States Navy, commanding the USS* Bull Shark. *Do you speak English?*"

Osaka momentarily thought about pretending that he did not. However, this would be foolish and only prolong the inevitable. When he saw a smaller man appear beside the captain and realized at first that he was Japanese, and then that he *knew* the man, Osaka knew it would do no good to feign ignorance of the American tongue.

"Is that... Gato?" Hideki asked.

"Apparently so," Osaka said. His voice held no anger, only defeat and resignation. He cleared his throat, "Captain Turner, I am Lieutenant Commander Ryu Osaka. I understand you perfectly."

"*Good,*" Turner said, not unkindly. "*Your ship is in a bad way, Commander Osaka. I'm happy to offer you any assistance I can in helping your crew to evacuate your vessel safely... however, I must know if you surrender first.*"

"Damn him..." Hideki said bitterly, more at the defeat than directly at the Americans. The Americans had won the fight, and that was that.

Osaka smiled slightly. He too had little choice but to take things in stride, "I am the executive officer, Captain Turner. However, I believe I can speak for my ship and crew... we do capitulate. And I thank you for your offer of assistance."

"*Glad to hear that, Commander,*" Turner continued. "*We have wounded here as well. However, I'm going to send a boarding party over in rafts. They will be armed, so please let your crew know that you have surrendered and not to resist. We're happy to help you, but I must warn you that we will tolerate no foolishness. Any attack on my boarding team will be met with immediate and deadly force. Is that clear?*"

Ryu met Omata's eyes, and the two friends actually smiled at one another. It's just what they would have said. Osaka looked back to his foe, "Agreed, Captain. I am going below now to see about my men. I will inform them."

"Can we really trust him, you think?" Hideki asked.

Osaka shrugged, "I do not know... but something tells me Arthur Turner is an honorable man. He could simply have torpedoed us again if he chose. Instead, he's sparing our men."

"Most likely to get a look at this ship," Hideki pointed out.

"I'm sure that's part of it... can you blame him?" Osaka asked wryly. "Come, let me help you below. It is time for you to rest now, my friend."

CHAPTER 40

"How many men on that ship, do you think, sir?" Paul Rogers asked Turner.

"Got to be twice our compliment at least," Turner said.

"Lot of damage," Pat Jarvis observed. "Probably killed a third of them."

All the officers except for Nichols, Dutch, and Post were on deck. The other three were moving through the boat, assessing damage and injuries. Henry Hoffman, the boat's pharmacist's mate, was doing what he could for the wounded men topside. The bodies of Wexler and Eckhart had already been put over the side. A sad but necessary action since the ship had no facilities to store the dead.

Begley shot the torpedo officer a withering glare but elected not to say anything. Instead, he addressed the captain, "Probably over a hundred men still alive. Sir, I'd like to volunteer to lead the boarding party. I can take Burt with me to give us an engineering assessment."

Turner frowned at that. He'd sent Pendergast to his quarters earlier and for a good reason. However, perhaps Begley had a point. Pendergast *was* an engineering officer, and maybe this would be a good exercise for him. Give him something to do and do it away from Turner.

"Very well," Turner said. "Take Buck and a couple of other men for security. Assess the situation and then report back. We can then figure out who to send over to offer assistance."

"Request permission to accompany Mr. Begley," Webster Clayton said.

Turner considered him, "Want to get a look inside that boat, huh?"

Clayton nodded, "Definitely. I didn't almost die forty-seven times out here to watch you gents have all the fun."

Turner smiled thinly, "Not me. I'm stuck here too... but okay, go ahead. Pat, you go with Clayton."

Begley's eyes flashed for a second at that. It seemed that no matter what he did, he couldn't get away from Jarvis. However, he quickly covered his reaction and turned aft, "COB, Ingram, Plank, you're with me. Let's rouse out the portable raft forward. Chief, break out small arms for the party. It'll be seven of us. Steve, please go below and inform Mr. Pendergast he's needed for a boarding action."

"Aye-aye sir," Plank said and met the XO's eyes.

Plank wasn't quite sure why Begley had asked for him and Doug as well as Pendergast. As he made his way down the ladders, he wondered if this had something to do with the black market operation that had been quashed. He still didn't know who'd found his stashes.

Rogers had intentionally neglected to confront the boatswain. He wanted to wait for a more appropriate time.

When Plank wrapped his knuckles on the number two officer's stateroom and slipped through the curtain, he found Burt Pendergast fumbling his sandals onto his feet.

"Steve!" Pendergast said excitedly. He seemed a little odd to Plank. Twitchy. "What's going on? Christ! It's like the end of the world up there."

"Yes, sir," Plank said, considering the second engineer and wondering if he'd gone off his rocker. "You all right, sir?"

Pendergast leapt to his feet and slapped his hands together, "I'm great, boatswain. Other than being sent to my room. What's on, anyway?"

Plank caught sight of the aluminum foil and the two or three pills that lay on Pendergast's blanket. He also saw that there were several empty headache powder packets there, too, and he understood. The man had probably mixed doses and was riding high for the moment.

Plank cleared his throat and moved to pick up the loose contraband, "We got the Jap sub, sir. Mr. Begley's leading a boarding team over to scope the situation. He specifically asked for you, me, and Doug."

Pendergast saw what Plank was doing and snatched up the drugs and trash. He quickly shoved them into the pocket of his khaki shorts, "He asked for me? And you? And Ingram...? Hmmm... maybe this is our chance, Steve."

"Sir?"

Pendergast's erratically shifting eyes locked onto Plank's for a moment, and he seemed more lucid, "Ingram ratted us out, Steve. Tank Broderick found your supply and tossed it overboard and then told the COB. They got Ingram to spill the beans."

"Son of a *bitch*..." Plank hissed in anger.

"You didn't know? Ingram didn't say?"

"No, sir... the little fink..."

Pendergast scoffed, "So, what do you think's gonna happen when we put in? I'll tell you what's gonna happen, Plank... that little bastard is gonna roll over on us. You, me, and Tom will probably get a general court while Ingram gets a damned medal. A stooley medal. Bunch of fuckin' bullshit..."

Plank drew in a breath, "We can't worry about that now, sir. We've got to go across with the XO."

Pendergast's crazy eyes glimmered as he reached out and took hold of Plank's shoulders, "Yeah... yeah... and it'd be a *shame* if something happened to the little fucker while we were over there, wouldn't it?"

"Sir?" Plank pretended to be ignorant.

"Oh, come on, Steve," Pendergast said, a cruel smile playing at his lips. "One of them *crazy* Japs might put a slug into him. Sad, when you think about it... but it sure would make that his COB's, the skipper's, or even that prick Jarvis's testimony hearsay, wouldn't it?"

Plank drew in a breath and nodded slowly, "That it would, sir. Then there's that big fucker, Tank. He's a problem too."

"Yeah, well, funny thing about problems, boatswain," Pendergast said quietly, "is that they can be dealt with... especially when they're perfectly *set up*. Let's go."

Back on deck, the last of the twilight illuminated the big, yellow inflatable raft that had been blown up and shoved over the side. Rogers and Ingram were already aboard, seated at the removable thwarts holding onto the oars. Begley, Clayton, and Jarvis stood on deck, holding Thompson sub-machine guns. As Pendergast led Plank down from the cigarette deck, he refused to meet Turner's eye. At the last minute, however, he turned back to the bridge.

"Sir, permission to take one more man," Pendergast asked Turner. "There's room in the boat, and we're a little top-heavy."

"Who'd you have in mind, Mr. Pendergast?" Turner asked neutrally.

Pendergast looked at the forward five-inch where Eddie Carlson and Broderick were still sitting. Hoffman, having tended to the wounds of Weiss and Smitty, was now wrapping a duck bandage around Tank's upper arm. A wooden splinter shaved from the deck by a 20mm round from the last Aichi had slashed a long but not very deep gash in Tank's arm.

"We could use a qualified electrician... I'd like Tank to come along," Pendergast stated.

"Tank's wounded," Turner said. "Why not take—"

"I'll go, sir," Tank offered cheerfully. "This is just a flesh wound, right, Hank?"

Hoffman frowned but shrugged, "Long as you don't get crazy, I guess it's okay."

"We've got other men," Turner pointed out.

"I'm up to it, sir," Tank protested.

"He's a crack shot, Skipper," Jarvis added.

Turner shrugged, "Okay, gents, it's your party. Good luck."

"Sir," Gato stepped forward, "I'd like to go also."

Turner shook his head at that, "No way, Captain. I'm not doubting you... but while the Japanese over there might tolerate us going over... they'll see you as a turncoat. It wouldn't surprise me if somebody over there would consider it a matter of honor to take you out... and maybe get a few others hurt or killed in the process."

Gato didn't like staying behind, but Turner did have a point, "Probably right, sir."

Weapons were passed out, and the men went down into the boat. Tank, holding a Tommy gun, sat in the stern while Plank, with his own SMG, sat in the bow. Rogers and Ingram rowed while the four officers sat on the sponsons between the others. Every man had a pistol, and aside from Tank and Plank, Rogers, Jarvis, and Pendergast had machine guns, as well.

Turner stood on the bridge and watched them go. He understood how Gato felt. He wasn't a man who liked sending others out to take risks. Not a man who felt comfortable staying behind while others went into harm's way. Yet he also knew that as Captain, that was more often than not his job.

He also couldn't shake an odd sense of dread. It was natural, yet it felt... ominous. He was, after all, sending eight men over to an enemy vessel, and they were heavily outnumbered. Was it a mistake? How many of them would be coming back...? How many wouldn't...?

———

It was clear that *Leviathan* was down by the head. So much so that Rogers and Ingram were able to row the raft right up onto the wooden foredeck, or what was left of it. Plank jumped out as soon as the bottom of the boat scraped against the planks and hauled in on the painter, pulling the rubber craft up far enough for Begley and Jarvis to get out without getting their feet wet. Rogers and Ingram came next, and they all hauled the boat well up onto the wood, and Plank secured the painter to part of the starboard catapult track.

"Jesus..." Pendergast said, looking around and fiddling with his .45. "This thing's a *beast*."

"Let's hope not a hungry one," Clayton commented.

"Let's split into teams," Begley suggested. "Any preferences?"

Begley cast a quick glance at Pendergast and Plank. Both men seemed to pick up on it. Although Begley had nothing planned, he felt that an opportunity might appear, and he wanted *his* men to be able to take advantage of it.

"I'll take Ingram and Tank," Pendergast said and met Begley's eye again.

"Very well," Begley said. "Boatswain, you come with me. COB, please accompany Mr. Clayton and Mr. Jarvis. Since, Mr. Clayton, I assume you want to get access to any of the ship's documents, why don't the three of you go forward and into officer's country? Plank and I will start in the conning tower and control room and work our way aft. I thought I saw a hatch open aft... probably venting... so Burt, you take your guys that way and work your way forward. The executive officer speaks English. Don't know about anybody else, so be on your toes. Anybody gives you any shit, burn 'em. This is completely fubar, so let's be on our toes."

After a round of agreements Pendergast and his team trotted aft, picking their way along the port side where the damage was minimal. Begley and Plank led the way up onto the empty cigarette deck and to the bridge. Jarvis held his team back on the main deck for a moment.

"Listen guys," Jarvis said quietly as he watched Begley and Plank inspecting. "I've got a funny feelin' about this. Everybody check your weapons and be ready for... something."

"Like what?" Clayton asked, clearing the .45 Colt 1911 he carried.

Rogers met Jarvis's eye and nodded, "I read you, sir. Mr. Clayton... Ingram and Plank were the ones running the drug ring. Ingram confessed to it all, but Plank doesn't know we know. More than that... Begley and Pendergast are involved to varying degrees."

Jarvis nodded, "Seems kind of fishy them coming over with Doug and Steve... but what about Tank? Pendergast asked for him specifically."

Rogers frowned, "Tank's the one that found the stash and pitched it."

"You're not suggesting... suggesting Begley is planning on *eliminating* the two enlisted men who can testify to his and Pendergast's culpability, are you, Chief?" Clayton asked.

Jarvis treated him to a crooked smile, "You're a spook, Web... what would you do?"

Clayton harrumphed, "Jesus Christ..."

"I'm just sayin'... let's look sharp," Jarvis stated. "We're probably not in danger... unless we witness something going on."

"Concur," Rogers said. "Okay, they're signaling all clear, let's move."

"You'd better watch your back, Pat," Clayton said, elbowing Jarvis. "Begley doesn't like you much."

"I can't imagine why," Jarvis said lightly as they mounted to the cigarette deck.

The conning tower was also empty when the five men went below. The air was warm and stale and stank of burnt plastics and rubber. Down in the strangely wide control room, a dozen Japanese men and officers stood around looking pensive. Several other men lay on deck, with a man who might be their version of a pharmacist's mate tending to their various wounds. One of the men on deck looked a bit older and had rank and insignia that might have indicated higher rank. He was unconscious, and the corpsman was wiping blood away from the side of his head.

Commander Osaka stepped forward, "I'm the XO, Commander Osaka."

"I'm the XO of *Bull Shark*, Lieutenant Thomas Begley. What's your situation, Commander?"

Osaka cocked an eyebrow at the man as if he'd just told a joke in very poor taste, "Our situation is that the ship is fatally damaged, and I estimate will founder within the hour. We have forty dead, thirty wounded, and one hundred and six men physically able. Many of them are aft attending to minor fires and other issues for the time being."

"And you still intend to honor your surrender?" Begley asked, brandishing his .45 but not pointing it directly at Osaka.

"I am a man of my word, sir," Osaka said coldly. "I have informed the crew not to resist your men."

"Good, because I have a team coming below aft," Begley stated. He pointed at the decorated man on the deck. "Is this your captain?"

"Hiro Kajimora," Osaka said. "It is fortunate that he's indisposed, Lieutenant... he might not be as reasonable about all of this."

"Do you have provisions for securing your men for abandoning ship, sir?" Rogers asked.

"We have life rafts and provisions being prepared now," Osaka said. "You are the chief of the boat?"

"Yes, sir," Rogers said.

Osaka nodded, "Very good. Our own is among the fallen. This may be helpful. We may be political enemies, but we are fellow sailors and submariners. Submariners everywhere respect the COB. Mr. Begley, I must now inform you that we did manage to get an uncoded distress signal out. I do not expect a response, but if there is a Japanese flying boat within range, it could be that they will arrive in the next few hours."

"And you expect us just to let your men go free?" Begley asked. "Or maybe wait around until a bombing squadron arrives to sink our boat?"

"I tell you this out of courtesy," Osaka said evenly. "What are your Captain Turner's intentions toward my men?"

"I don't know, sir," Begley said. "That depends on what we find here. He sent us over to do an inspection and see what you might need by way of food, water, support, and medical aid."

Osaka nodded, "Very well, then please conduct your inspection."

Begley turned to Jarvis, "Mr. Jarvis, you and your team go forward; I'll take Boatswain Plank aft."

Jarvis nodded, "Can one of your officers conduct us forward into your forward battery compartment, sir?"

Osaka nodded, "I will do so myself. Mr. Begley, please exercise caution. There is significant damage in the aftermost battery compartment."

"How many compartments are there in this monster?" Plank asked absently.

"Eleven," Osaka stated. "One more battery and one more engine room than is usual. There is an additional support compartment primarily dedicated to flight operations as well."

"Boy, would our folks like to get a good look at this ship," Clayton muttered as he followed Osaka through the forward hatch into the large and wide officer's country.

Osaka smiled at him after they all came through the hatch, "Sadly, sir, in an hour or so, this submarine will take her final dive... so deep no man will likely ever see her again. You do not wear insignia, sir... are you an officer?"

"No," Clayton said, extending a hand. "My name is Webster Clayton. I'm a civilian."

Osaka met his eyes and, after a long considering moment, drew in a breath and seemed to come to a decision, "Clayton... I have heard that name. You are with the American OSS, is that not so?"

Jarvis and Rogers exchanged a glance and both men's hands went instinctively to their sidearms in spite of the fact that they both held sub-machine guns at their left sides. Clayton looked a bit confused.

"You're wondering how I know that," Osaka said. "It is simple, sir... I am Shadow."

"Uh-oh..." Jarvis muttered, his guts beginning to churn.

Clayton's face blanched, "What... what did you say?"

Osaka, misinterpreting the OSS man's reaction, smiled warmly, "Surely your office has briefed you on me. I have been funneling them bits and pieces of intelligence whenever possible. I am code name Shadow... what is it?"

Clayton suddenly found his mouth to be very dry. He swallowed hard, licked his lips, and drew in a breath, "Sir... there must be some mistake..."

"Quite impossible, look," Osaka rolled up the sleeve of his grime and blood-encrusted uniform and displayed his forearm. On it was a stylized winged serpent. "Is this not the mark you're supposed to use to verify my identity?"

"So... you're a spy for *us?*" Rogers asked in bewilderment.

Osaka smiled, "Not precisely. I am a loyal Japanese citizen... but I do not agree with our emperor's or his prime minister's policies or this war. I do what I do to help to bring a swifter end to it and to the inevitable suffering of my people."

"Commander... you don't understand," Clayton said breathlessly. Certain that his veins ran with glacial runoff. "We have a man aboard who says *he's* Shadow..."

Osaka locked eyes with him, "Lieutenant Gato? He survived the crash?"

"What the hell..." Jarvis mumbled, again gripping the butt of his pistol.

"He landed and surrendered to us," Clayton explained, his words coming out ever faster and more frantic. "Said he's an American who got caught over there when the war started."

Osaka's eyes closed and he sighed, "No... Lieutenant Kenji Gato is most certainly *not* an American spy."

"Okay... so if you're our secret buddy," Rogers said, feeling a sharp stab of fear for Turner, "then who the hell is loose on our boat... and how does he know *your* code name!?"

CHAPTER 41

"I hate this, Hotrod," Turner said as he gazed across the hundred feet of water that separated his ship from the semi-submerged submarine off his port side. The shape was now just a silhouette against the clear night sky, illuminated only by the pale light of a rising quarter moon.

"At least it's quiet over there," Hernandez remarked.

"Yeah... too quiet. Why aren't they getting rafts over the side yet?"

"Sir," it was Captain Gato's voice drifting up through the bridge hatch, "Mr. Nichols asks if you could come down into control for a moment. He says he's got damage reports and repair estimates and he'd like to go over them with you."

Turner grumbled something dark. He had been waiting for those reports... but the thought of going down two ladders with his throbbing ankle gave him pause.

As if sensing the captain's reluctance on that score, Gato came up through the hatch until he was exposed up to his waist, "I'll give you a hand down and up, sir."

Turner sighed, "Oh, hell... I can make it. Just a pain in the foot. Okay, Captain, here I come. Keep your eyes peeled, Hotrod."

Turner laboriously made his way down into the conning tower. To his surprise, he found it entirely empty. Of course, there wasn't much need for any personnel to remain there. With the radar and sonar out of service, the compass on the helm smashed and the TDC not in use... there wasn't much of a need for anyone there at the moment. Besides which, half of his officers were off the ship.

He sighed and climbed down the ladder and into the now red-lit control room. Even as he did so, going slowly hand over hand and allowing his injured ankle to hang loosely below him, he wondered why the hell Frank hadn't just come *up* to the bridge... and why Turner hadn't thought of that himself before then.

Yet when he touched down on the deck and looked around, the reason for Nichols's uncharacteristic lack of zeal became readily and painfully apparent. All of the enlisted men were gone from their posts. Only Frank Nichols, Joe Dutch, and Andy Post were still in control. The three officers were lined up along the starboard side in front of the air manifolds. Standing next to Frank Nichols with a pistol aimed straight at his head was the *other* Japanese pilot, Lieutenant Kubashi.

When the cold steel of another pistol was pressed to his neck, Turner wasn't even surprised to see George Gato holding it. He did kick himself for his thoughtless comment just a few minutes earlier about how quiet things were, however.

———

There was a hatch into what would've been the after torpedo room. However, when Pendergast led his men down, he found that the compartment didn't contain any torpedoes or tubes. Just bunks and storage lockers. There were also nearly two dozen Japanese men standing around and waiting as if they'd fully expected guests.

"Do any of you speak English?" Pendergast asked, his eyes darting back and forth wildly.

Tank frowned and cast his own glance at Ingram. There was something truly off with Pendergast, and Tank was beginning to suspect that the man might be one of Plank's ex-customers.

Tank also began to wonder about how he'd been corralled into this group. Pendergast had asked for him specifically... and here he was with the officer who was behind the drug scheme... and Ingram *knew* that it had been Tank who'd thrown their junk overboard...

None of the men said anything, just looked confused. Based on their uniforms and their insignia, the American sailors thought that they might be enlisted men and part of the aircrew.

"Christ..." Pendergast muttered. "Why the hell don't they abandon ship? Why are they just sitting back here? Tank, secure that hatch, huh? I'm not sure I like this..."

The Japanese men didn't resist or even call out as Broderick closed and dogged the escape hatch built into the overhead. The men simply went and sat at their bunks or at a small table and lit up cigarettes. The Americans then noticed that three of the bunks were occupied by men who looked injured.

"We're not gonna get anywhere this way," Pendergast said. "We need to finish the inspection. I'll continue forward. Tank, Doug, you guys stay here and watch these Japs. I'll close the hatch behind me. Don't let anybody in who isn't from our boat. Got it?"

Ingram and Tank blinked in surprise and looked at each other. Tank frowned, "You don't want us to accompany you forward, sir?"

"No, I don't," Pendergast said angrily. "Otherwise, I wouldn't have ordered you to stay back here now, would I, *Tank?*"

Tank didn't like the tone Pendergast was using. Not just condescending... that was normal for him... there was something else in it. A quality the electrician hadn't heard before. Malice. When Tank looked over at Ingram, he could see that the younger man sensed it as well. However, there was nothing to be done but comply.

The lieutenant ducked out through the watertight door and into the big maneuvering room. The hatch was then swung shut and dogged down.

"Is it me... or was that strange?" Tank asked Ingram. "You known that guy for a while; what do you think, Doug?"

Ingram was about to answer when there came to his ears a faint hissing sound. He stopped and tried to find the source of the noise. None of the Japanese sailors seemed to notice, all of them making an effort to seem unthreatening in the face of Tank's Tommy gun, perhaps.

"Damn..." Tank said, reaching up to touch his ear and working his jaw. "Gotta clear my ears. What the..."

Ingram's eyes suddenly went wide, and he met Tank's gaze, "Pressure!"

"Calmly," Tank said, smiling. "We're outnumbered almost ten to one in here, Doug... calmly go over and look at the pressure gauge above the air salvage controls."

Ingram moved as if to stand against the bulkhead near the hatch and glanced sidelong at the pressure gauge. It read almost two hundred PSI.

Suddenly the face of Burt Pendergast appeared in the spyglass of the watertight hatch. He was grinning. There was a slight click and hiss as an internal intercom was activated.

"*Comfy in there, boys?*" Pendergast asked, his eyes dilated almost to their full aperture and his smile maniacal. "*I hope so because you and your Jap friends aren't leaving.*"

"What the *fuck!*" Tank growled.

"*This is what happens when you stick your nose into other people's business, Broderick,*" Pendergast taunted. "*And as for you, Doug... nobody likes a fink. You could really do us all some damage back in port... it's not personal, kid... just business.*"

"It's gonna be personal when I get my fuckin' hands around your throat," Tank growled, pointing the barrel of his Thompson at the door. Pendergast only laughed.

"*Go ahead, dumb ass... you blow out this window or try to open that overhead hatch and see what happens when over two hundred pounds of air per square inch tries to rush out a small hole. Hope you like strawberry jam! Oh, and if you think about trying to equalize... I've gone ahead and jammed the air controls from my side. Nice to know you, assholes.*"

"Well, isn't this a fine fix you've gotten us into, kid?" Tank said to Ingram and then grinned.

"Me? You're the one that threw Steve's stuff over the side," Ingram said, smiling thinly.

"You think Pendergast really *does* take it personally?" Tank asked.

"Doesn't get much more personal than this," Ingram said. "Now, how the hell do we get outta here?"

———

The Japanese XO was right; the central battery compartment was trashed. The place looked like it'd been burned to a crisp. Even the bulkheads were warped and blackened. What remained of an indeterminant number of bodies lay in heaps on the decks and near the starboard munitions and hangar access hatches. The stink of burnt paint, rubber, and flesh was making Begley sick.

The next compartment, the after battery compartment, was empty as well. That seemed strange, as this appeared to be the crew's mess and main quarters. Beyond that, a compartment with little more than a corridor and laundry then opened into the first of the three engine rooms.

The mystery of where most of the men were had been solved. Dozens of men were lined up along the bulkheads here, clutching bags and wearing life vests. A hatch in the overhead was opened and a ladder had been rigged. Men were going up one by one. An officer stood at the base of the ladder, and another stood on deck above with men assisting.

"You are American," the officer at the base said flatly.

"Yes," Begley said. "You're in charge of evacuation?"

"*Hai*," the man said. It was almost distressing how none of the Japanese seemed intent on attacking them.

Another group of men, nearly as many, began to pour through the watertight hatch to the next compartment. Like the others, these men held only small ditty bags and no weapons. What surprised Begley even further was to find that Burt Pendergast was the last man to emerge.

"Burt?" Begley asked. "What'd you find aft? Where are Tank and Doug? Why are your ankles wet?"

"There's flooding in the maneuvering room," Pendergast stated. His tone was strange. Only moments before, when they'd arrived, he seemed keyed up. Now, though, he looked haggard and sluggish. "Over the gratings. As for those two... they're not a problem, Tom."

The two men's eyes met, and Begley understood. He was shocked, but he thought he got it, "They... aren't?"

Pendergast shook his head and smiled, "I've stationed them in the after compartment, sir."

Begley *could* have acted. He could have ordered Burt to go and release Broderick and Ingram. He *could* have done the right thing. He didn't, though. In the end, Tom Begley did what he most often did... pursued his own best interests.

With Tank and Ingram gone, there was no one to testify that he or Burt had been involved with the black market aboard *Bull Shark*. Only Steve Plank could do that now, and he wouldn't talk any more than Burt would.

"Very well," Begley said. "Looks like things are in hand here, Burt. Let's go forward."

———

"So, you really are a loyal Japanese officer?" Turner asked Gato calmly, as if there wasn't a .45 pressed to his head. "Then who's the real Shadow?"

"Commander Osaka, sir," Gato said.

Turner chuckled, "Sir? You say that like you're *really* an officer and not an enemy soldier."

"I'm not..." Gato said softly, his voice trembling a little. "Everything I told you was true, sir. *Everything*. The only difference is that I'm not Shadow... but I am with the OSS. Mr. Clayton confirmed that."

"Okay, then you're a filthy turncoat," Joe Dutch snapped, his body tense.

"They've got my *family!*" Gato shouted, his voice breaking on the last word. Tears began to run down his face. "I'm sorry for this, Captain... but that lousy cocksucker over there is with Japanese intelligence. Right before I shipped out on the carrier, I was told and shown proof that my parents and grandparents were being held by *his* people... and that if I stepped out of line and didn't do *exactly* what he told me to do..."

"Which included getting on this submarine," Kubashi said in fairly good English. He grinned wolfishly at Turner.

"To what end, Kubashi?" Turner asked. "Do you really think you can hold an entire submarine crew at bay with a single .45?"

Kubashi laughed harshly, "I don't have to hold entire submarine, Ame-coh. Only *you*. Your crew will do nothing because they don't want to risk your life. Soon, one of our long-range flying boats will arrive to pick up our crew... and they will find that I have captured *great* prize."

"He's right, sir," Gato said miserably. "Commander Osaka said they got a message off. Admiral Kondo's invasion fleet should be nearly to Midway by now. They've got a seaplane tender with them. It wouldn't surprise me if one shows up in the next hour or so."

"And we aren't in a position to shoot them down," Turner stated unhappily. "Captain... George... are you really going to allow this?"

Gato's lower lip trembled, and Turner could feel the pistol against his head shaking as well. He hoped the man wouldn't get so distraught that he flinched and pulled the damned trigger.

"Sir... they'll kill my family," Gato said softly.

"Will they?" Turner asked. "How will they know, George? How do the Japanese even know the two of you are alive? For all anyone knows, your plane crashed hours ago."

"Do not listen to this Yankee's lies!" Kubashi spat. "I will report your treachery myself."

"Not if you're dead," Post added hotly.

Kubashi laughed, "Foolish young Gaijin. They'll be killed if I *do not* report."

"What do you mean?" Turner asked, knowing full well but wanting Gato to hear it.

Kubashi sneered at him, "It means that if I don't give order to spare them, Gato's family is executed."

Turner looked over and met Gato's eyes, "You understand what he's saying, George?"

Gato nodded ever so slightly.

"He's saying that whether you live or die, they're going to execute your family anyway," Turner said. "They may already be dead, George... I'm sorry."

"Quiet!" Kubashi hollered. "One more word and—"

It was then that one of the crew decided to act. Certainly, once the watertight door to the control room had been dogged, the crew aft had figured out what was going on. Either through direct observation through the observation port in the door or simply guessing. In either event, Chief Harry Brannigan had ordered all electrical power to the control room cut, plunging the compartment into both pitch darkness and chaos.

There were shouts, grunts, shuffling feet, and bodies moving. Turner himself dropped straight down to the deck, getting his good foot beneath him, and sliding sideways, ready to pounce. The two watertight doors banged open, and shouting men began to pour into the room just as the lights had come back on.

Kubashi and Andy Post were wrestling on the deck, each man with a hand on the .45. George Gato stood to one side and held his gun loosely at his side, looking confused and miserable. Sparky Sparks tackled him, grabbing for the gun and wrestling the pilot to the deck.

Turner was only feet away from Post and Kubashi and lunged forward, throwing his body on top of the two men and reaching out for the pistol. His hand clamped over the barrel, and he got a knee under himself, levering himself up and managing to get another hand around his first. He wrenched the barrel sideways, twisting the gun out of both men's sweating hands and rolling sideways and back onto his knees.

Kubashi wasn't one to give up easily. He had the slightly better position and got his hands around Post's throat and began to squeeze as he screamed Banzai over and over again. Turner didn't even try to warn him. He simply placed the .45's barrel against the man's head and pulled the trigger. The left side of Kubashi's exploded outward, spraying blood and brains all over the high-pressure manifold.

As quickly as the chaos had begun, it ceased. Men were picking themselves up off the deck and brushing themselves off. Sparky held Gato's arms behind his back, and Mike Duncan held the .45 at his own side. Harry Brannigan entered the control room wearing a big smile.

"Hope I didn't disrupt things too much up here with that electrical test, sir," Brannigan said with a crooked grin.

Turner was helped to his feet by Joe Dutch, "As a matter of fact, you screwed everything up, Chief... for that prick."

"What do we do with this guy, sir?" Sparky asked, seeming to take pleasure in cranking Gato's arms up painfully behind his back.

Turner looked at Gato. The pilot hung his head, and more tears began to flow, "I'm sorry, sir... I'm so *sorry*..."

Turner believed him. Felt empathy for the man whose family may or may not be executed if they hadn't been already. Still, he couldn't just let it go.

"Sparky, take him up to your room and handcuff him to a rack. We'll let Mr. Clayton decide what to do next. Harry... how did you know to kill the lights? And how'd this piece of shit get loose anyway?"

"We had him chained to a bunk in the crew's compartment," Duncan said. "Apparently, he had some way to pick the lock on the cuffs, I guess. Because when Jimmy Owens went to bring the guy some food, he was gone... or at least looked that way. We found Jimmy sprawled out on the deck with... with the back of his head beaten in with something and his .45 gone."

"Jesus..." Nichols said sadly.

"Where'd you get a gun?" Turner asked Gato just as he was being led to the hatchway.

"It's Clayton's," Gato said glumly.

Turner wiped his brow, "God almighty... let's get things in order here. Somebody get that man off my deck and put over the side. Quietly.

And form a detail to clean up the mess he left. Jesus... I wonder how things are going over on the other boat."

———

"Maneuvering's flooding!" Ingram said as he peered through the spyglass. "Water's up a foot or two over the grating already."

"Suffocate or drown, what a choice..." Tank grumped as he paced back and forth. He suddenly stopped and turned to Ingram. "What about the next hatch forward?"

"Closed," Ingram spat. "That bastard Pendergast dogged it on his way forward."

Tank snapped his fingers and smiled, "You know what happens to air when it's trapped in a confined space while water pours in?"

Ingram blinked and shook his head, unable to think clearly past his despair.

Tank chuckled, "It gets *compressed*, kid! Meaning that the pressure in that room is rising close to the pressure in here. Try the hatch!"

Ingram threw himself on the dogging wheel and heaved, but it wouldn't budge. The pressure differential was still too great, "Nothin' doin', Tank!"

"Shit... we're gonna get one shot at this," Tank said. "See if you can get a couple of these guys to help you with the overhead hatch."

"What're you gonna do?" Ingram asked worriedly.

"I'm gonna equalize the damned pressure," Tank said. "When that glass goes, kid, you try and muscle that overhead hatch open. Use a pipe or crowbar or something if you can. Try to get these guys to hang onto something."

Tank shouldered the Thompson and aimed for the glass. Although the difference in pressure wasn't as great as if the maneuvering room were dry, it might still create a wind tunnel effect in their compartment. The hope was that when the pressure dropped in the aftermost room, the overhead hatch would open and allow them to escape.

Ingram turned to the Japanese flight crew and began making wild hand gestures at the hatch and at Tank. They looked bewildered, and a few looked scared.

"Christ..." Ingram grumped as he pulled the collapsible ladder down from the overhead and climbed up and put his hands on the dogging wheel of the hatch. He then leaned out and mimed putting his hands on a bar in line with the wheel.

One man clapped his hands together and ran to a storage locker. He pulled out a four-foot oversized pry bar, climbed up next to Ingram, and slid the flat end through the wheel spokes. Then the American and the Japanese sailor grabbed the other end and waited.

"Goin' for broke..." Tank said and squeezed the trigger.

The three rounds shattered the thick glass, and instantly, the room became a hurricane. Loose objects flew about, papers fluttered, and the escaping pressurized air howled through the twelve-inch opening.

Tank actually felt the pull for a few seconds, "Go! Now, kid!"

The two sailors began to heave on the pry bar as they shouted a wordless cry of strain and defiance. With a resounding *boom* the big hatch cover flew upward, yanking the pry bar from the two sailor's hands, breaking Ingram's left arm and the force of the escaping air actually pushing the Japanese sailor halfway through the hatch before the pressure equalized.

"Goddamn!" Tank whooped. "Let's go! Come on, you guys, out, out, out!"

Ingram had already followed the other sailor up. The man who'd helped him miraculously being uninjured. He actually helped the American out of the hatch. Tank thought about going next, wanting nothing more than to run forward and go down another hatch and beat the piss out of Pendergast. However, he felt bad for these sailors who'd been trapped in the room with them. He helped them organize, line up, and go up the hatch. He and another man also gingerly fed the wounded men up as well.

Once done, the sailors went forward to where officers were obviously directing them to a set of rafts. Tank and Ingram ran along the port side upper deck toward the conning tower.

"You okay, kid?" Tank asked.

"Left arm's busted," Ingram said painfully, pointing to his left forearm with his pistol. "But I can still *shoot* with this one."

"Good," Tank said darkly. "Cuz somebody's got an ass-whoopin', and maybe a lead enema, comin' his way!"

———

"Do you want to come with us, Ryu?" Clayton asked as the four men stood in the captain's cabin.

After Osaka's revelation, he'd led the men into the cabin and unlocked the safe. There were documents and the captain's log along with his orders. He handed them over to Clayton.

"I'll drop a weighted bag over the side," Osaka said. "As is the duty when a ship goes down. Keep these safe, Mr. Clayton. You may find them useful. If they assist in shortening this war and saving more Japanese lives... then I feel I've *truly* done my duty."

"Shouldn't you come with us, sir?" Jarvis asked.

Osaka shook his head, "I can do more for my people this way."

"What about the Skipper, sirs?" Rogers asked nervously. "If the Commander here is the real spy... then there could be trouble on the *Bull Shark*."

Jarvis nodded, "That's true. Okay, let's head aft and meet up with the rest of the party. Is there anything you need, Commander?"

Osaka smiled thinly and shook his head, "It's already being attended to. We have life rafts and provisions. But I warn you, gentlemen... our invasion force is not far from Midway if they have not yet already arrived. It's possible that a seaplane is already en route. I'm sure your captain would like to take a hundred prisoners, but..."

Jarvis sighed, "But we don't have room for them, and we may have to run on top for a while... it's better if we just high-tail it out of here. You and your people will be all right, sir?"

Osaka regarded the big man with a warm smile, "Yes, thank you, Lieutenant. It's kind of you to worry about your enemy."

Jarvis shrugged, "Hey, we're all sailors."

They moved forward, and Osaka took up his station in the large control room. As the three Americans went through the watertight door, the *Leviathan's* executive officer went up on deck and tossed the bag overboard, where it promptly sank. He then went back down to the control room.

Jarvis's party found Begley, Pendergast, and Plank in the forward engine room. Jarvis looked around.

"Where's Tank and Ingram?" he asked in confusion.

"They... they got trapped aft," Pendergast said gloomily. "There were men there, and the maneuvering room was flooded. Tank closed the door and pressurized the after compartment... but once he did... I couldn't get the door open! By now, sir..."

"You mean... they're dead?" Clayton asked in disbelief.

"Have you gone aft to check on them?" Jarvis asked, anger rising now. "You just left them to die, Pendergast?"

"That's enough," Begley said sternly. "There was nothing Burt could've done."

"Oh? Did *you* go back and check on them, Tom?" Jarvis asked hotly. "Or how about you, Plank? Or maybe the three of you are just better off now that the two most damning witnesses to your little drug market are gone, huh?"

Begley's face drained of color, "I don't know what—"

"Save it, sir," the COB said. "We know. We know about you, about Pendergast, and this prick. Tank is the one who tossed the junk, and Doug is the one who finally laid it out for us, *sir*."

"You left those men to die to cover up your crimes," Clayton accused, bringing his pistol up.

Everyone followed suit. Six men held six weapons on each other in a stalemate that couldn't last, especially from the look on Pendergast's face. The man was pale, sweaty, and visibly twitching. The unhealthy concoction of uppers, downers, and the cocaine was playing havoc on his over-stressed system. If the shooting started, it'd be Pendergast that pulled the trigger first.

"Yeah, let's all relax," came a hard voice from the vicinity of the forward hatchway. "Pendergast, Begley, and Plank... drop your fuckin' weapons *right now!*"

Jarvis cast a quick glance over his shoulder and laughed out loud. Sherman "Tank" Broderick and Doug Ingram were standing just inside the hatchway. Tank held his Thompson aimed at Begley and his men, and Ingram held a 1911 aimed at them as well.

"It's over," Clayton said. "Drop your weapons."

"Fuck you!" Pendergast shouted. "No way I'm—"

Doug Ingram's .45 slugs smashed into the man's chest, blasting him off his feet and sending him sprawling to the deck. Tank's sub-machine gun clattered, and Steve Plank's own chest bloomed into a fountain of crimson gore as he pitched over backwards as well.

For a long moment, everyone simply stared. Tom Begley was the first to react. He didn't fire though, just let his own pistol clatter to the grating at his feet.

However, he wasn't still. Faced with the total ruin of his life, Begley did the only thing his horrified mind could think to do. He ran.

"Tom, stop!" Jarvis shouted.

Just then, as if scripted by a Hollywood director, the crippled ship groaned a long, loud, and mournful wail sung by tortured steel succumbing to stresses beyond the breaking point. The ship, heavy with water forward and aft, was being bent, and the forces were beginning to tear her apart.

Steel plates began to split, bolts snapped and shot across compartments, and frames began to twist and bend in a grotesque demonstration of uncompromising physics. The sound of rushing water could be heard seemingly from everywhere, and the lights began to flicker.

"To hell with him!" Clayton stated over the sound of the hatch to the next compartment being slammed and dogged shut. "Let's get the hell outta here!"

Jarvis cast a last glance at the end of the engine room and sighed. He led the way forward toward the control room and safety. When they arrived, Osaka and another man with a splint on his arm were the last ones there.

"The ship is sinking," Osaka said. "We must go now."

"Yeah, no shit," Rogers stated.

"Where are your other men?" Osaka asked.

"Dead," Jarvis said. "Long story, let's go!"

They went up the ladders and onto the bridge. Clayton helped Osaka's friend with the broken arm up. The man seemed surprised by the kindness but did not object. The XO was the last one up and slammed the bridge hatch shut in a last symbolic gesture.

Forward, the Japanese sailors were already in their rafts and floating away from the wreck. Two enlisted men stood by the last raft waiting for their officers.

"Good luck, Ryu," Clayton said as he and the other Americans jumped into their own raft, already knee-deep where it had been high and dry just an hour before. Jarvis cast off the line, and Rogers and Tank began to pull hard away from the huge submarine.

When they were nearly to the *Bull Shark*, the men stopped rowing. There was an enormous scream of metal, a booming as pockets of air exploded from somewhere inside the giant submarine and then a grinding, screeching, and heart-wrenching sound as the boat literally tore herself in two, the two halves coming apart just behind the conning tower. They stuck up into the night sky for a moment and then vanished below the sea, leaving only a roiling patch of eerily glowing foam, and sending three-foot-high waves out in all directions.

"My god..." Clayton breathed in horror.

"Yeah, it's not a nice sight," Jarvis stated. "No matter it's one of yours or an enemy's... watching a ship die is a terrible thing... maybe in this case more than others."

The men sat in hushed reverence for a long moment before it was broken by a voice from behind and above them.

"You fellas gonna just sit there all night, or can we get underway already?" Art Turner jibed.

"Oh, we're sorry, sir," Jarvis said. "Were you guys waiting on us?"

Epilogue

Aboard the IJN battleship Yamato

Admiral Isuroku Yamamoto stared down at his battle table in abject despair. Nagumo had finally broken radio silence near sunset and revealed to his superior the utter disaster that had been wrought. Four mighty carriers, two-thirds of the once invincible Kido Butai, were destroyed.

The confirmation that aircraft from *Hiryu* had destroyed one of the American carriers was hardly of any comfort to Yamamoto. One carrier to four? And the reports that scouting aircraft had spotted at least one other American carrier in the area as well.

Furthermore, the attack on Midway, while spectacular, was not definitive. The base had put up a solid defense and a single raid was not enough to subdue it. There were still American scouts and bombers patrolling. Admiral Kondo had confirmed this when he finally reported that his groups had been spotted and attacked more than once.

There were the successful attacks and ongoing invasions of Attu and Kiska in the Aleutians. However, rather than bolstering Yamamoto's mood, this had only dampened it further. Invading two almost barren rocks in comparison to losing most of the Kido Butai was hardly a victory. The entire Aleutian campaign had been mostly a ruse to begin with. The idea of occupying some islands that were connected to the contiguous United States had been some fool minister's idea of a brilliant tactic.

On the surface, the plan had *some* merit... but really, Dutch Harbor and the nearby bases hadn't been destroyed. Along with the failure at Midway, America still had its fighting forces intact and would simply make the lives of the men at Attu and Kiska miserable... more miserable than they would be in such a cold and Godforsaken place.

No, this failure was complete. While Yamamoto wanted to blame Nagumo... and did to a degree... he had to admit to his own failure as well. He knew that Nagumo was timid and wasn't creative enough to know when to change the plan. He could simply claim that he was following Yamamoto's directives and that he had no choice.

"Damn him..." Yamamoto grumbled, looking down at the dozens of tiny ships on the board.

With regret and even anger, he plucked the four carriers off the table and flung them across the room. Even as his battle group raced toward the last known position of the American task forces to exact some revenge, he knew it was futile. Even his impulsive order to *Riujo* and *Junio* to leave the Aleutians and steam south to join him was foolish.

No, he'd make a showing, but Yamamoto knew that by the same time the following day, he'd order all forces to return home. He'd already turned Kondo's back. His invasion force would be a tempting target for American submarines and bombers. Not to mention the forces on Midway and the other American carrier.

The door opened and Admiral Ugaki came in, holding a message flimsy in his hand. By the look on his face, Yamamoto knew that this, too, would be bad news.

"You have more troubles for me, Matome?"

Ugaki hesitated but finally handed the sheet of paper over, "We have had word of *Ribaiasan*, sir."

Yamamoto shut his eyes and drew in a steadying breath, "We've lost her."

"Yes, sir," Ugaki said sadly. "But she got off a distress signal. Kondo has dispatched several large seaplanes to the area to retrieve the crew before the Americans can get to them."

"That is... fortunate," Yamamoto said. "But in the big picture, my friend... another failure to add to an almost unbelievable pile. We've lost Midway... we have *not* crushed the American carrier fleet... we've lost our secret weapon that was intended for the Panama Canal... and we've lost the Kido Butai, or most of it. This is a truly terrible day."

"Nagumo should be drawn and quartered," Ugaki snarled, real anger in his voice. "He's a timid, foolish old man."

Yamamoto chuckled, "As am I, Matome... as am I."

"Don't say that, sir," Matome urged. "You cannot lay the blame for others' failures at your own feet."

Yamamoto actually laughed derisively, "That, my friend, is *exactly* what will happen. It is of no matter, however. We will go on. We must go on. There is no choice in the matter."

THE LOCATION OF THE SINKING OF LEVIATHAN

Even as he dogged the hatch to the forward engine space, Tom Begley began to regret his momentary act of desperation. Was it really worth this? Fleeing into a sinking submarine just to avoid a court-martial where the only evidence of his wrongdoings would be the testimony of others?

He actually decided to go back, turning to the closed hatch just as the ship began to break up. The screaming and rending noises were unnerving and seemed to come from everywhere. The bulkheads and pipes of the middle engine room began to bend and crack, and water sprayed everywhere. In a panic, Begley moved aft, away from the perceived epicenter of the destruction. The central engine compartment had no hatch, so he ran into the after compartment, where the destruction was seemingly even worse.

He'd never seen anything like it. It was as if the entire ship was made from taffy and was being twisted and stretched into impossibly horrific shapes. Behind him, a thunderous explosion told of a pocket of air that had been compressed and blown out of some storage locker or other. Begley saw the hatch in the overhead, only a few feet away just as the lights went out forever, plunging him into a darkness filled only by the horrifying sound of a dying ship. In the utter darkness, that sound became terrible... the sound of a thousand souls calling out in eternal damnation... calling out to him.

Water began to cover his shoes, then his ankles and then his calves with astonishing speed. In total fright that nearly robbed him of his ability to think clearly, he reached out, groping for the hatch wheel he'd seen only seconds before. Water was now to his waist...

Where was it...?

His hands found the cold steel, and he sobbed in relief. He threw his weight on the wheel and his sobs turned to laughter as it began to rotate. He shoved the hatch open even as the water reached his armpits and hauled himself up into the blessed fresh air of night.

He knew he only had a minute or two to get away. Soon the ship would break up or sink, and the suction of eight thousand tons would drag him down into the crushing darkness below. He ran toward the stern, running between the intact tubular hangar on his right and the blasted remains of the other on his left. More than once, he tripped over something and sprawled on the deck. At least once, he barked his shin and felt warmth trickling down his leg. He couldn't think about that now, just run and jump into the—

A tremendous roar, a shriek of abused steel and a lurch that tossed Tom Begley up and over the side of the ship. Suddenly, he was plunging downward into the warm waters of the Pacific, the death moan of the Japanese ship all around him.

Begley struck out in blind terror, trying to move, and not knowing which way was up. He was simply desperate to put some distance between himself and the sinking vessel.

Suddenly, a titanic force seemed to seize him, dragging him downward with unbelievable power. *Leviathan* reaching out from the grave to drag one more soul down into hell along with her. Begley flailed, kicked, and nearly cried out as he felt himself being pulled down with the sinking ship. Just as his lungs began to scream with an unbearable desire to breathe and just when he was certain his death was approaching, the sucking force was gone.

Begley opened his eyes and caught a faint glimmer of light and kicked for it, thrashing upward, using the last of his panic-fueled strength to reach salvation...

His head broke the surface and he gasped, drawing in huge gulps of air, his tears coming freely now. His fear being replaced by elation.

He'd survived! He'd beaten the odds!

After a few moments of catching his breath and letting his jangled nerves settle, Begley treaded water and turned a complete circle. Somewhere in the distance, he heard the sound of diesel engines. They sounded faint and grew fainter. His ship, *Bull Shark*... she was leaving him!

Turner was leaving him behind!

Then he heard the voices of men and turned in that direction. In the pale moonlight, he saw a cluster of yellow life rafts filled with dark figures, not more than a few hundred feet away.

Having no choice, Begley struck out, swimming slowly in their direction. It seemed to take hours, but finally, he seemed to get close and then someone shined a flashlight in his eyes.

A question was asked of him in Japanese. Begley tried to blink past the beam of the flashlight.

"Hello?" he called out. "I need help!"

The light clicked off, and a man who spoke good English addressed him, "Lieutenant Begley?"

Begley's heart soared, and he actually laughed, "Yeah... yeah... the XO of *Bull Shark*... is that you, Commander Osaka?"

"Yes... come closer; I'll help you into the raft, Lieutenant," Osaka said.

Again, having no choice, Begley swam the last few feet and reached up to take hold of the sponson. He paused for a moment, letting his aching limbs regain a bit of their strength, "Thank you, sir... thank you. You won't regret helping me... I have much to tell you."

"Indeed," Osaka said.

"Yes, sir... they left me... left me to die," Begley stated.

"So, you wish to help us by way of taking your revenge?" Osaka asked.

"Exactly!" Begley said, beginning to relish the idea.

"I see," came the oddly flat reply.

Begley looked up again and his heart seemed to stop. It was not a helping hand that he saw but the dark barrel of a pistol.

"No—"

The last thing Thomas Begley ever saw was a brilliant white flash as the pistol spat flame and lead bullets that penetrated his skull. Once again, he slipped below the water, his clothing and the water leaking into his body dragging him slowly down to join the dead submarine twelve thousand feet below.

"Why did you shoot that man, Yakuin?" Captain Kajimora said groggily from where he lay in the bottom of the raft, a bandage wrapped around his head.

Osaka gazed at him for a long moment and said, "He was of no consequence. We have lost enough today without helping the Americans... even a single American."

Kajimora chuckled softly, "There is hope for you yet, Ryu."

Osaka chuckled as well, "Let us hope so."

PEARL HARBOR SUBMARINE BASE – JUNE 8, 1942

After the lines were secure and the two brows snaked over and secured, Admiral Robert English practically bounded across to *Bull Shark's* deck, "Permission to come aboard, sir!?"

Art Turner stood on the main deck near the conning tower and saluted in return, "You're welcome, sir."

English vigorously shook Turner's hand, then Pat Jarvis's and the other officers in turn. Dutch, Nichols, and finally Post all received a warm welcome and a hearty pat on the shoulder.

"Damned fine work, Art!" English said enthusiastically. "Damned fine. Christ, you boys are in for another medal if Admiral Nimitz has anything to say about it."

"Thank you, sir," Turner said. "Though it certainly came with some cost."

English's ebullience flagged into respectful neutrality, and he nodded, "Yes... four enlisted and two officers. A heavy toll. It's a story I want to hear all about, Art. We've got the relief crew standing by. We'll have her shined up and good as new in no time. You and your crew are getting at least two weeks leave this time, no worries. The buses will arrive at noon to take your crew over to the Royal. But before that, I've got a few folks over on the pier who'd like to say hello."

Two men wearing working khaki began across the gangway. One was an admiral and was none other than Chester W. Nimitz himself. The other was a stocky lieutenant with close-cropped dark hair and wearing a huge smile on his boyishly handsome face.

"Elmer!" all of the submarine's officers seemed to call out in unison.

Nimitz grinned, "Met this young man on my way over. Says he just got off a flight from the mainland not a half-hour ago."

"Sir, welcome aboard *Bull Shark*," Turner said, saluting CincPac as good manners and duty demanded. He then warmly shook Elmer Williams's hand. "Damned glad to see you again, Elmer."

Nimitz and English beamed. The senior admiral spoke first, "Captain, I just wanted to come and welcome you in person. You've done a damned fine job. I also wanted to be the first to let you know that your lovely wife has been a real Godsend to us... but we'll talk about that later. I'd like to see you and your new XO in my office tomorrow at ten hundred. Oh, there's Buck Rogers; let me go over and say hello..."

"My new XO?" Turner asked English after Nimitz had walked down the deck to speak to the COB.

English chuckled, "Yeah, fresh from PXO School... Dick Edwards should've never let him leave your command, Art."

Williams grinned broadly, "I'll say... just what the hell did you fellas get yourselves into?"

"Oh, it's a tale, Elm Tree," Jarvis said with a broad grin.

Williams shook his head in mock disgust, "I leave you kids alone for six weeks and just *look* at the mess you made? See, this is why we can't have nice things!"

That got a big round of laughs from everyone in earshot. As the welcome back handshakes and hugs began, Turner caught sight of a shapely blonde wearing the uniform of the WAVEs. With her were two kids wearing giant smiles. He excused himself and hobbled across the gangway and into the waiting arms of his wife and children.

"Hi, Daddy!" Dotty Turner said excitedly.

"Hey, Pop... what'd you do to your foot?" Arty asked.

"Oh, it's a long story, gang," Turner said, clutching the three of them to him as if he never wanted to let them go. "But I bet somebody *else* has a story, too."

"I'll show you mine if you show me yours, sailor," Joan Turner whispered into his ear.

Art Turner laughed, and when the tears came, he didn't even try to stop them.

A Word From the Author

Here we are, safe and sound at the end of another exciting adventure. I want to thank you for reading this book and sincerely hope that you enjoyed this tale. I also want to thank you for indulging my occasional flights of fancy.

I think that sometimes with historical fiction, there is an expectation that the exact facts of history should be perfectly preserved. Perhaps that's true; I'm hardly one to say one way or another. However, as you've seen, I've taken some liberties in this book, as in the previous one. I've stretched and bent history a bit in order to hopefully create a compelling story for you. As stated in the preface, other authors better than I have penned many an engaging book on this period in history and can provide you with accurate facts. Yet I hope that I've provided you with some hours of enjoyment and escapism... because, to me, that's what a good story should do.

If you're interested in reading other books on this period and on the submarine war of WW2, then I suggest *Wahoo* and *Clear the Bridge*, both written by Rear-admiral Richard O'Kane. Although his works are a bit technical and sometimes a little dry, O'Kane does a great job of depicting the *real* submarine war. Also, read *Thunder Below*, written by Rear-admiral Eugene Flucky. Flucky's unique account of his command of USS *Barb* is also quite factual, but Flucky does a great job of bringing the real men of his command to life in a way that makes you forget it's *not* a work of fiction at all.

Further, for a recently published and quite historically accurate tale of the Battle of Midway, then I also suggest *The Eagle's Claw* by Jeff Shara. His fictional account of Midway is quite compelling.

Finally, I'd like to introduce you to my other series, **Investigator**. You can check it out on Amazon. Also, please visit my website and join my free crew roster email list. Not only will you get a free 45 page Jarvis novella, you'll also be privy to inside information, deals and other fun stuff.

www.scottwcook.com

You may also find me on that Facegram all the young'ns are jawin' about:

www.facebook.com/swcwriter

Thank you, and I hope to visit with you again soon.

Scott W. Cook

OTHER BOOKS BY THIS AUTHOR...

Scott Jarvis, Private Investigator Series

Choices - Book 1

The Ledger - Book 2

Play The Hand You're Dealt - Book 3

Isle of Bones - Book 4

Shadows of Limelight - Book 5

Sins of the Fatherland - Book 6

A Fortune in Blood - Book 7

That Way Lies Madness - Book 8

To Honor We Call You - Book 9

What Lies Beneath - Book 10

Suffer Not Evil - Book 11

He That Covets - Book 12

Whom Predators Fear - Book 13

A Florida Action Adventure Bundle - Books 1-3

USS *Bull Shark* – WWII Submarine Thriller Series

Operation Snare Drum - Book 1

Leviathan Rising - Book 2

The Cactus Navy - Book 3

Tokyo Express - Book 4

Behavior Reports - Book 5

Seas of Flame - Book 6

———

USS *Enterprise* - Naval Adventure Series

Wings of Destiny - Book 1

Wings of Vengeance - Book 2

———

Catherine Cook, an Age of Sail Adventure Series

A Heart of Oak

A Treacherous Wind Blows Foul

———

The Immortal Dracula Series

The Dead Travel Fast - Book 1

The Blood is the Life - Book 2

The Sword and the Spirit - Book 3

What a Hell We Would Make - Book 4

Decker's Marine Raiders Series

Pacific Blood - Book 1

Pacific Guts - Book 2

Pacific Grit - Book 3

Made in the USA
Las Vegas, NV
07 January 2025

15986150R00262